NAMASTE AND SLAY

NAMASTE AND SLAY

JENNIFER BRODY

All rights reserved. No part of this publication may be reproduced, stored in a retrieval system, or transmitted in any form or by any means electronic, mechanical, photocopying, recording, or otherwise without prior written permission from Podium Publishing.

This is a work of fiction. Names, characters, places, and incidents are either products of the author's imagination or used fictitiously. Any resemblance to actual events, locales, or persons, living, dead, or undead, is entirely coincidental.

Copyright © 2025 by Jennifer Brody

Cover design by Heather VenHuizen

ISBN: 978-1-0394-9727-6

Published in 2025 by Podium Publishing
www.podiumentertainment.com

TRIGGER WARNING

This is an adult-only title, so buckle up, slay queens—this book's got more red flags than a dating app swipe-fest. Expect animal disembowelment, rape, sexual assault, drugging, violence against women, narcissistic personality disorder, love bombing, gaslighting, kinks, breeder fantasies, a light orgy, oral sex, penetration, and physical violence (think fighting, killing, torture). If betrayal, gore, severed hands, or Namaste flipping into Nope-aste makes you clutch your pearls, stick to rom-coms. Can't handle heartbreak or "all sluts must die" haunting your nightmares? Tread lightly—or don't. Your funeral, girlie girl.

Read at your own risk—nobody's safe.

NAMASTE AND SLAY

CHAPTER ONE

AFTER

MORGAN

"Namaste, *bitches* . . . hold on!" Hannah says as we hit a patch of black ice. The car loses traction and slides toward the sheer cliffside, making my stomach flip. Just as I think we're going to plummet to our deaths, Hannah regains control of the car. I release my grip on the seat belt, my knuckles white.

I stare through the frosted window, my breath fogging it in patches. The road twists ahead like black licorice cutting through ice-crusted trees with steep drop-offs on either side. The Berkshire mountains loom over us like dark sentries.

My reflection is superimposed over the thick forest—messy brown hair twisted into a floppy top bun, hazel eyes that shift color with the light and look especially green layered over the pine trees, and freshly micro-bladed brows.

But the person staring back at me looks more like a ghost. Pale cheeks and pale lips and bloodshot eyes deadened from too much crying.

Hannah drives her white Audi sedan that's seen more than its fair share of dings, scrapes, and minor rear-ends, while Mia rides shotgun and paints her toenails soft pink with her feet propped up on the dashboard. The chemical stench of the polish doesn't help my carsickness from all these hairpin turns.

Hannah takes another perilous curve in the mountain road, throwing me against the window in the backseat. One thought circles through my head: *I don't want to be here.*

I keep checking my phone every two seconds. Even though he left me on read, and it hasn't chimed once since I got in Hannah's car back in Brooklyn Heights. Even though any minute we'll be off the grid and out of service range.

A bad habit, how I'm constantly checking my phone.

He'll never text again.

I reread my last words to him, typed into a text bubble. The ones where I broke up with him in a burst of humiliation chased by a sharp stab of heartbreak.

It's over.
I hate you.
You fucked my friend.
You destroyed everything.
Never speak to me again.

Okay, maybe *friend* is a little bit of an exaggeration. But she was in our friend group and went to the same boarding school as Hannah and Mia . . .

And Noah. My newly minted ex-boyfriend.

Mia catches me and snatches my phone away. "Quit pining for that major loser," she says, holding my phone hostage in the front seat. She exchanges a worried look with Hannah.

"Remember, this retreat is all about getting away from the boys in our lives," Hannah adds for good measure, catching my gaze through the rearview mirror before looking back at the road. "Oh, and that one toxic female slut-bag. She's been blocked. Permanently."

Hannah and Mia are my two best friends from college. We met as freshmen at Barnard, during our tumultuous first semester, filled with study cram sessions, too many parties, and, of course, boys. Now, we're roommates in a fifth-floor walk-up, cruising past our mid-twenties and trying to carve out a life in the city.

"Yeah, don't worry," Mia agrees. "We've already excommunicated her. The major loser can have her thirsty ass."

Both of their names have been banished from their vocabulary ever since my boyfriend *accidentally* on purpose screwed another woman.

"Morgan, listen, you're better than this," Mia goes on, pouting her glossy lips and layering on even more lip gloss from the endless supply stashed in her purse. "And you deserve better than him."

Her words make me deflate. I want to believe them, but I simply don't.

"Well, that's easy for you to say." I nod to the diamond engagement ring on her slim finger. It glints in a rare flash of winter sunlight. "Mrs. Soon-to-Marry-Your-College-School-Sweetheart."

I study my friends from the backseat. Hannah is all curls and hips and freckles, while Mia is dark hair, dark skin, dark eyes, all fiery smolder. They're trying to help me, but it's so infuriating. Without fail, if you go through a bad breakup, your girlfriends will make it their mission in life to get you back on the dating scene and suggest all the latest dating apps. This is especially true if they're already in serious relationships, like Hannah and Mia, and never had to date in the real world.

The world of awkward meat-market warehouse DJ parties, dick pics, Netflix and chill, one-night stands, and last but certainly not least, post-coital ghosting.

Mia met her fiancé, Grant, freshman year at a Columbia frat party, while Hannah retained her high school boyfriend, Tyler, who matriculated to NYU and remained a regular presence. It was hard feeling like the fifth wheel whenever we all hung out, through the revolving door of boys who came and went from my life, never staying long enough to become permanent fixtures.

But I thought Noah was different, and that I'd finally met the One.

I was wrong.

So, very, very wrong.

"Have you tried SugarFishing?" Hannah says in a hopeful voice, right on cue. "My client was talking about it. The app uses this new algorithm to pair you with eligible singles based on hobbies and shared interests."

"Seriously?" Mia says, frowning. Or rather, trying to frown as much as her fillers and Botox will allow. These days, you have to start fighting the aging process as early as possible. "You believe that works? Grant and I have like *nothing* in common. Opposites attract and all that."

"Well, you and Grant practically defy the laws of physics," Hannah says, shaking her head. "You make zero sense on paper, yet somehow you click."

"*Click* is an understatement," Mia says, flashing the rock on her finger. Then she glances my way. Guilt floods her face for rubbing it in.

"Anyway, maybe you should give SugarFishing a shot," Hannah picks up. "For real, what do you have to lose?"

They both look at me expectantly, Hannah through the rearview mirror.

"Only my dignity and self-respect?" I deadpan. "Plus, that's what you said about the One, remember? And, well, it turns out I had *everything* to lose."

The statement hangs in the air.

I said the quiet part out loud—the truth—breaking a sacred girlfriend rule.

Don't blame your friends. It's not their fault you fell hard for a cheating asshole, even if they're the ones who wrote that profile and pushed you onto the latest trendy dating app that promised you'd meet the One.

They lapse into silence, making me feel like a shitty friend. But I can't help it. Although it's been a few weeks since the *incident*—the one that ruined my life, my future, and all my hopes and dreams—my emotions are still raw.

My breakup flashes before my eyes like a grisly crime scene from those murder porn docs on Netflix. The ones that I used to love and now can't stomach because they remind me of him. We shared a love for those shows and used to watch them together. Only this time, I'm the victim in the armchair being interviewed about the aftermath of the crime with soft lighting and the camera slow-zooming in on my pain, exploiting it for the amusement of bored housewives seeking a thrill. The curated pictures of the good times flash over the screen as I recount how *perfect* everything was for the few months we dated.

How, in all that time, there were no warning signs. Zero red flags. All green flags and beige flags. How it could happen to anyone. How you could end up falling for the wrong guy and having your heart wrenched out, torn and bleeding for everyone's collective entertainment. All of them silently judging my choices.

Not to mention the backlash I would face if I decide to overlook his infidelity and take him back, like one of those sad, brainwashed politicians' wives we love to mock. Even though that's *exactly* what I want to do, with every painful thump of my shattered heart. That's the ugly truth. The quiet part I wish I could say out loud.

I know I did the right thing by breaking up with him. That "cheaters always cheat again." That's a direct quote from both Mia and Hannah, spoken in unison after they found me crumpled on our sofa, a tear-stained, heartbroken mess convulsing with sobs, the kind that rack your entire body. But if it's the right thing, then why does it feel so wrong?

We jerk around more woozy curves, snapping me out of my morbid thoughts and making my stomach churn with acid. The snowcapped mountains keep coming at us, each one taller than the last, and we continue cresting them, leaving civilization and the city and Noah and my breakup farther behind.

Finally, I break the silence.

"If I'm so great, then why aren't I still with him? Why do I feel like the loser? Not the other way around?" I hate how whiny and pathetic I sound.

"Look, I've been thinking," I go on quickly before they can respond "Noah said it was an accident, right? He was hammered after those work drinks. He doesn't remember anything—"

"Be serious," Hannah interrupts. "You don't *accidentally* put your dick in someone else. He was a privileged asshat of the highest order. Trust-fund loser. They're all over the city. I can spot them a mile away."

Because you are one, I want to tell her. *You went to the same boarding school.*

The elite kind with tuition that costs more than a liberal arts college. It's so different than my "humble" upbringing. They don't even have private schools where I'm from, unless you count homeschooling. New York may be one of the largest cities in the world, but it feels like a small town half the time, especially if you grew up in the Manhattan that Hannah, Mia, and Noah did, full of wealth and privilege and never-ending opportunities.

"Besides, this week is all about you," Hannah goes on, turning the wheel to the right around a hairpin turn, the car sliding over more black ice. "And recovering from that toxic relationship. Now, no more lame boy talk. Like the Bechdel test."

"Yeah, you're right—we're, like, totally failing it," Mia says. "We used to discuss it all the time in my gender studies classes. Two women have to talk about something *other* than a man."

"But wasn't that test developed for Hollywood movies?" I point out.

"It also applies to girlfriend yoga retreats," Hannah says, wrenching the wheel left this time and making my stomach lurch in the other direction. "Damn it, we're smart, educated, professional women who graduated from one of the best colleges in New York City. We've gotta have something to talk about other than boys."

There's a pregnant pause before we all burst out laughing. I take the moment to ask Mia if I can have my phone back.

"Nope." She drops my phone into her oversized boho purse on the console. "For safekeeping," she says, patting her purse. "Besides, there's no service up here. The center is totally off the grid. That's the beauty of this retreat. We're going cold turkey from tech. Like in that creepy *Black Mirror* episode."

I know it's stupid, but seeing my phone swallowed up by her oversized, Mary Poppins-like bag makes me feel nauseous. I lick my dry lips, feeling the low hum of panic building in my chest without that digital tether to the world.

When did this happen to me? When did I get so addicted to my phone? But the more important question rushes through my head in a wave of shame. When did I get so addicted to . . . *him*?

I want to do better. Maybe my friends are right. Maybe this retreat is just what I need to get over him. Do some serious healing and self-care and focus on myself. Prove that I really am better than him, like they keep telling me. That a boyfriend doesn't define my entire existence.

"Namaste, *bitches*," I say, toasting them with my pink Stanley cup.

They raise theirs—pale purple and soft turquoise—the steel clinking together.

"Don't you mean *Namaste and Slay*?" Mia says, pointing to the slogan on our pink crop top shirts—swag from a boutique athleisure wear brand that's one of my marketing and PR clients.

I snagged them from the samples closet as a little gift for our getaway. The front depicts a Buddha in lotus pose, clutching a knife in one hand. The trendy girlboss slogan curves into a rainbow over the outstretched hands.

Sure, it's probably cultural appropriation, maybe even borderline offensive, but the brand went viral on a short video platform last year thanks to my clever social media campaign, and now they can't keep them in stock.

We all laugh and chant together.

"*Namaste and slay!*"

Our voices fill the car, and we toast again. Hannah whoops and kicks on the radio, turning it all the way up.

We sing along at the top of our lungs to Taylor Swift's newest breakup anthem. Our shrill voices fill the car. It feels good. It feels like college again, only without calculus tests and syrupy jungle juice. It feels like being reborn.

It feels . . . *free.*

A discreet wooden sign marks the gravel driveway. The paint looks fresh. I don't know how Hannah spotted it in the snow that keeps falling faster and faster, transforming the landscape.

She slows the car, and we all squint at it through the frosted windshield.

The Namaste Women's Yoga and Rejuvenation Center.

"Is *rejuvenation* code for Botox?" Mia asks, poking at her forehead.

Hannah shakes her head and cranks up the heater to defrost the windshield. "No way. It's supposed to be a completely nontoxic retreat. Botox is basically poison for your face."

"Nontoxic is code for *non-fun.*" Mia pouts her plumped lips. "Guessing that means no booze either. Shoot me now. Glad I brought my Xanax."

I spot a slogan printed under the center's name:

Disconnect to reconnect.

"Look, it's official—no service bars." Mia holds up her phone as proof. "We're in a dead zone."

I swallow hard, glancing at her bag where my phone is. "You sure this is a good idea?"

I'm starting to get a little freaked out. The forest surrounding us suddenly looks denser, darker, more threatening.

"That's exactly *why* it's a good idea," Hannah reminds me, continuing down the gravel driveway. "We had to do something drastic to pry you off the sofa and kickstart your healing journey."

"Yeah, you've been binging true crime docs and downing carbs like it's your job," Mia adds. "And you have only one topic of conversation . . ."

They trail off, but we all know what they're referring to.

Noah.

The worst part is that I can't deny it. Even I can barely recognize myself anymore. What happened to the strong, independent woman I used to be?

I try to excavate her in my memory, but she's turned into a ghost. The last few weeks remain a total blur—a waking nightmare that I can't seem to shake. Somehow, I managed to trudge to work and back home, so I didn't let everything fall apart. Just most things.

I was pretty shocked when my roomies surprised me with this weeklong retreat. At first I protested, using my job as an excuse—but they'd already made arrangements with my boss. Apparently, even he had noticed my depressive, self-destructive, down bad behavior over the last few weeks (cue my total mortification).

Okay, right, my job was the only obligation that I really had, lacking any significant other now (*major ouch*) or any family (*something I don't talk about*). Yeah, I was a loser with no life.

I did try using my dentist as an excuse as I had a cleaning coming up. "We already called him," Hannah said, "and rescheduled your cleaning for after you get back."

"Even he thought the retreat was a good idea," Mia added. "I guess you were crying when you made the appointment and told him about your breakup?"

Ugh. The downside of having a dentist who also happens to be Hannah's.

I was out of excuses. I couldn't tell them the real reason I didn't want to go. What if he texted me, wanting to get back together?

Even I knew how pathetic it sounded. So, I had no choice but to keep my mouth shut and agree to the retreat, though I deeply regret it now.

"We lucked out even landing these reservations," Hannah says, snapping me out of my morbid thoughts.

"A client from the foundation tipped me off," she goes on. "They had a last-minute group cancellation. Even then, I had to pull some major strings." She lowers her voice like she's sharing a juicy secret. "Apparently, the guru who runs it is a spiritual advisor to major celebs."

Hannah would be the one able to pull strings for something like this. She works in nonprofit, which sounds really caring and giving on the surface, until you learn it's for her family's foundation. In reality, her job is to convince Daddy and Mommy's bougie friends to donate in the name of helping poor people, but really it's for—*wink, wink*—a hefty tax write-off and a golden ticket to their annual star-studded charity gala.

"Yeah, you said tons of celebs have gone to the Namaste Center?" Mia says, looking excited. "But I couldn't find anything about it. And trust me, I have Google stalking superpowers. I swear I scoured every inch of the internet."

Mia works in tech, so she's not kidding about her internet stalking abilities. She's also new money, banking a huge starting salary, which doesn't stack up against Hannah's old money. And in the social hierarchy of our little threesome, I'm the charity case. I come from nothing. Less than nothing. I'm just lucky they took pity and adopted me in college.

"That's because they don't advertise," Hannah goes on, shooting Mia a disdainful look. "It has to be secret, or they wouldn't come. Right?"

"Can't have the paparazzi lurking around. That would ruin the whole point."

"Exactly," Hannah says. "The more secret, the more exclusive. You're not even allowed to post anything to socials. Or you'll never get invited back."

"Not that you could post," Mia adds. "I mean, no reception. It's seriously off the grid. You weren't kidding, Hannah."

"Right, sounds more like a cult," I say darkly. "No social media. No advertising. Oh, and Hollywood clients."

"Wait, do you think the Kardashians have been here?" Mia says in a whisper. "That's so wild. I'll bet Kylie has."

Hannah raises her eyebrows. "My lips are sealed. I've been sworn to secrecy. But you never know . . ."

Mia squeals and bounces in her seat. "That's basically as good as *yes*."

That seals the deal.

"Ladies, hold on to your thongs," she says, aiming the car up the icy driveway. The poor sedan struggles to gain traction, not built for this weather. About a mile up, the road narrows even more and grows rougher. Snow continues to fall hard, quickly thickening to clumps.

Hannah cranks up the windshield wipers, flinging off gobs of clumpy snow. I catch sight of my reflection in the rearview mirror. I look like a haggard, gaunt version of myself.

Maybe I do need this retreat.

Noah did a major number on me. For the last few weeks, I've been struggling to understand what I did wrong, not the other way around. I thought that I'd finally figured it out. Cracked the code to a successful relationship. I stuck to my rules, played my cards carefully.

So, how did I screw it up?

That's how much he mind-fucked me, making me feel as though I'd done something wrong. While the woman he fucked was blocked and excommunicated from our group immediately, I haven't been able to block Noah yet.

Isn't that sad?

I'm still waiting for him to text me.

I miss u.

I love u.

I fucked up.

You're the love of my life.

Come back. Please forgive me.

[Insert selfie of his exaggerated, frowning, tear-stained face]

No dick pics, just pure remorse (though I did save those in case I ever need revenge porn one day . . .). It hasn't happened yet. Texting crickets. I used to be the one to wait to text him back, toying with him. Oh, how the power dynamics have shifted.

Flipped, reversed, left me reeling, spinning, and feeling out of control.

And now they confiscated my phone, and we're officially off the grid.

I cast my gaze toward the landscape, smudging the fog crystalizing on the window. The mountains look like something out of a postcard—an idyllic, winter panorama that people pay for. No wonder they hold retreats up here, even if it's the last place I want to be.

A flash of movement catches my eye. Something bolts in front of our car.

Screech. Slam.

BANG!

My seat belt jerks into my chest, whipping me back into my seat. My neck pops forward and back. The car slides to a stiff halt with a shudder.

Something large lies in the road in front of us. Twitching. Blood staining the snow and melting it like cotton candy.

"Oh no . . ." Hannah gasps when she sees it, too. I feel the urge to vomit.

It's a body.

CHAPTER TWO

BEFORE

MORGAN

Dating is like a high-speed car wreck, I think, watching the Manhattan traffic blur past in a rush of kinetic motion. The kind that could easily kill you in a split second. So, why do I keep subjecting myself to it, knowing I'll get hurt? And be left broken, maybe even maimed, for life?

At least, that's my checkered relationship history. I swore off dating after my last romantic mishap—two dates that ended with me sleeping with him, only to be ghosted the next day.

But here I am, on the cusp of another first date. And right now, I'd rather die.

Noah. That's his name, according to his profile on the app. Investment banker. Ivy League grad. Volunteers at a cancer ward at the local children's hospital on weekends.

He sounds perfect.

Too perfect.

That's why I'm second-guessing myself. The big catch? I met him on this new blind dating app called the One. The profile avatar is a black silhouette, like when you don't bother posting a picture. But in this case, that's the whole point. And everybody's talking about it. Hence why my roommates forced me onto it.

It's also . . . terrifying. I don't know why I let Hannah and Mia talk me into this—and now I deeply regret what *past me* decided. But the truth is, they can be pretty persuasive, if not downright pushy, especially when they team up. They had the sort of privileged upbringings where bad things didn't happen to them on a regular basis, so they don't get what the big deal is or why stepping outside my front door can summon so much dread and anxiety.

They don't understand how a simple jaunt to the store or running errands can result in an accident. But I do because I'm the kind of person where bad things did happen to me growing up, even though I've hidden that part of my life. Nobody knows the truth. And they never will.

I erased it—and I erased her. The girl I used to be.

I invented Morgan Steele.

She's everything I wasn't but aspired to become. And slowly but surely, I became her until the old me was gone, dead, and buried back home.

A car honks and jerks past me, swerving to avoid my foot. Warm wind wafts over my face, reminding me that it's late summer and fall has yet to descend over the city.

I catch a glance of myself in a storefront window—the kind of shop that I can't afford near the bougie wine bar where I'm supposed to meet my date, which I also can't afford—and almost don't recognize my reflection.

When I got to college, I traded in my brassy, dirty-blonde highlights for honey-brown hair that softly curls around my shoulders. My hazel eyes stare out unobstructed by thick glasses, thanks to LASIK, while a healthy dose of foundation conceals my freckled cheeks. My face is done up with tasteful touches of makeup and micro-bladed brows, thicker than anything natural. I've remade myself, polished down and whittled away my rough edges.

I still look like me, just a glow-up version that's had the money and time to invest in crafting a better model. Morgan 2.0. My designer clothes cost a fortune, but I bought them secondhand or pilfered them from the swag closet at TREND, the marketing and PR firm where I work. Unlike my roomies, who still have their parents' credit cards to pad their bank accounts. But nobody has to know I didn't purchase them at full price at an expensive boutique in the city.

I'm wearing a fuzzy, white, cropped sweater over dark straight-leg jeans and soft, brown leather boots. The look is casual yet tactile and sexy—and most importantly resembles what Zendaya wore on the cover of *Vogue* last month. I figured it was the right touch for . . .

Ugh, my date, I think, snapping back to reality. Dread pools in my stomach.

I tip my foot over the edge of the sidewalk, tempting fate. The yellow cabs don't even slow down. They seem to speed up, splashing spectacular puddles my way. "You're just unlucky," Mia said last week.

"Yeah, dating is just a numbers game," Hannah added. "The more you swipe, the more dates you go on—"

"You mean *survive*," I grumbled, remembering the recent ghosting.

We were piled on the overstuffed velvet sofa Hannah's dad bought for us when we moved into the flat. The dark green color complements the funky vibe of our first post-college apartment, a three-bedroom affair, though the third bedroom is more of a glorified closet that barely fits a dresser and a full-sized bed. That's my room. And I get a break in the rent for taking it.

"Fine. The more dates you *survive*," Hannah revised her statement, "the more likely you are to meet the One."

She said that completely devoid of irony, because it was true for her. She was the kind of girl who grew up believing in princesses and fairy tales and now got to live one out by marrying her high school sweetheart, Tyler, in a destination wedding next summer in Amalfi, Italy.

I groaned and facepalmed myself. "So, that's why you signed me up for this new dating app against my will?"

"The One!" Hannah said. "It's all anyone is talking about lately. A blind dating app for elite singles in the city."

"Yeah, like that Netflix show," Mia chimed in. "You know, you get to fall in love with their personality first."

"Yeah, well that sounds like my worst nightmare," I replied back. "It's hard enough randomly swiping, but now I don't even know what they look like?"

"I think it's progressive," Hannah said. "Plus, you need to change it up. Clearly, your picker is broken."

She was referring to the *ghoster-in-chief*. Or maybe it was the unhoused guy before him (he was always crashing with different friends before I put together that it was because he didn't have his own place). Or maybe the one before him who was into non-monogamy, only not the *ethical* kind, since he neglected to inform me that he had a girlfriend.

"Yeah, I know it's broken," I said back. "Which is why I've sworn off dating."

"Too late—I already signed you up," Hannah said, tossing my phone back. She must have snagged it while I was sucked into the new season of *Emily in Paris.*

It landed on the sofa with the app open. Shock rushed through me. My profile details had already been filled in. I frowned in confusion.

"You did this?" I gasped in horror, shooting them both death glares.

"Guilty as charged." Mia giggled. "Hannah got the ball rolling, but I finessed the fine print to make you seem extra desirable. You're welcome, by the way."

"It's official—you two are totally insufferable," I grumbled, snagging my phone. "I'm deleting it."

Later that night I plopped on my bed in my glorified closet bedroom to crash hard, but my sleep was disturbed. Nightmares came on suddenly, jerking me awake.

I sat up, panting. Images—memories I'd rather erase—rushed through my head, fragmented and jarring, while my heart thudded too fast. *My father's drunken slurring. The slap of his hands on skin. The shattering of a liquor bottle. Welts and crying and hiding in the closet.*

There was no way I could fall back asleep now.

Despite my earlier protests, I found myself bathed in the white glow of my phone, opening the app. "THE ONE" materialized on my screen with fancy animation, the letters untangling themselves and reforming into two hearts that merged into one. They beat together—*one, two, three*—then exploded on the screen. Before I knew it, I was swiping on autopilot, each blank avatar presenting a tantalizing possibility . . . or a ghost.

I had to admit this dating app did have some curiosity factors. It was possible that it was onto something.

Somehow, not having to analyze their pictures, scrutinizing and judging their appearances and clothing choices, made it easier to focus on the other aspects like their jobs, hobbies, and personalities. So, I kept on swiping.

And swiping. Until I passed out, forgetting all about it.

But the next day, while I was in the kitchen pouring myself a big cup of coffee, my phone chimed with "New Match."

I quickly clicked on it. The outline of a blank avatar stared back at me, reminding me of police outlines of murder victims at crime scenes, after the dead bodies had been hauled away. This was probably because I listen to too many murder podcasts and binge too many true crime docuseries, but I had a bad feeling.

Before I could un-match and delete the app, Hannah yanked the phone from my hand. Her fingers typed lightning fast. Within minutes, I had a date set with the mystery man for the next day.

And now here I am—contemplating stepping into oncoming traffic to put myself out of my misery. I figure a hospital trip would get me out of roommate jail for ditching my date.

The light turns green; the traffic races my way. I'm still halfway off the curb, tempting fate, when a cab going too fast hits an oil slick and slides toward me, aiming for the curb where I'm standing.

I freeze, bracing myself—

"Whoa, careful!"

Two firm hands grip me and pull me back onto solid ground.

The cab misses me by an inch. Maybe less. I'm breathless and shocked, watching as it speeds away from the scene as if it didn't almost just obliterate me.

I whip around and am greeted by ice-blue eyes. The rest of his face resolves in my vision, coming into focus. Wavy, dark hair grown out a bit too long. Dimples, more than one. Sharp, gray suit that cuts him in all the right ways. It all adds up to one thing.

He's hot. Like mega hot, but in a totally disarming, unassuming way.

"Uh, thanks," I stammer awkwardly.

"What were you thinking?" he asks in a concerned voice. "You're not a tourist, are you? The cabs here aren't known for stopping."

My cheeks burn hot.

"No, I live here."

I worry my accent has crept back out and given me away. He smiles warmly. Usually, my total mortification would send me quickly on my way.

But I can't look away from him.

"So what then? A secret death wish?" he teases, flashing that smile again.

"If you must know." I sigh. "I was trying to get out of a blind date. My roommates forced me into it, and they won't forgive me if I cancel. I figured a trip to the ER would be a solid excuse."

"A blind date, huh? Yeah, that does sound terrible."

"Tell me about it!" I say, relieved he gets it. "Like cue the major anxiety. Plus, I was forced into it against my will."

He cocks his eyebrow. "By the aforementioned roommates? So, this whole blind date wasn't your idea? Is that what you're saying?"

"Not even close," I admit. "I swore off dating after my last mishap. Truth be told, death seems preferable."

He smiles. "Really? Preferable to a date with this poor, unknown suitor?"

I don't know if it's the adrenaline still supercharging my bloodstream from almost getting hit, or the fact that he seems so empathetic and understanding, but I start spilling my guts to him before I can stop myself.

"I don't exactly have the best dating track record," I blurt out. "It's more like a crime scene. So, they're worried I'm gonna die sad and alone. Even though I'm only twenty-six. So, yeah, I think stepping into oncoming traffic is pretty much my only option."

"Why stop there?" he says. "Think bigger. Maybe you could get an insurance settlement out of it."

"Now you're talking. My marketing job sure isn't paying rent. Hence, the two roommates. The pushy ones."

His eyebrow quirks up. "Marketing job?"

"Don't remind me," I say with a groan. "I had all these big dreams coming out of college. I wanted to start my own lifestyle brand, but instead, I'm stuck hocking other people's ideas."

"Don't worry, I have a so-called fancy job. But I'm in a cubicle most of the time and barely see daylight. And I'm stuck making other people money."

"Wow, we have so much in common," I quip back. "The death of all our dreams and at such a young age."

He laughs. "Still gonna do it? Kamikaze rather than face that date?"

"I think it's my only valid choice."

I take a deep breath. The traffic makes me feel buzzed, wild and free, like anything could happen next.

And then it does.

"Well, maybe I should join you," he says in a casual voice. "It seems my blind date isn't going to show up, seeing as how she just tried to off herself in front of a cab."

The shock hits me first, then the complete and total humiliation. I'm not sure it's possible to die of embarrassment, but if it is, then I'm about to drop dead on the spot.

"Pretty sure you must be Morgan," he goes on, not letting me off the hook. "I had a hunch it was you, but then the marketing job and age sealed the deal."

"Well, now this is embarrassing," I stammer, my cheeks burning. "Noah, right? I'm sorry I ruined our date."

He shakes his head. "No way. Best first date I've had in forever. No expectations. High chance of injury."

That's the moment hope creeps back into my jaded, jilted heart. The witty banter. The way he seems so understanding. Those dimples. Well, really, the whole *freaking* package.

That's when he holds out his hand, and I let him whisk me away.

We ditch the wine bar, opting to cruise around the park instead. The rain turns from a drizzle to a downpour, but we don't care. I think we're both still buzzed from the near-death experience.

Everything turns liquid and blurry but also scintillating and exhilarating. Skipping in the rain. Jumping in puddles. Laughing, so much laughter. Soaked to the bone shivering, and that's when he does it. He leans in . . . closer . . . and kisses me. And doesn't stop.

His lips are softer than I imagined, juicy and molded to mine, tasting of rainwater and something sweet and pheromonal that makes me want to drink him down deeper.

And that's when I know. He crashed into me and smashed me to pieces. I'm a goner. He's got me—and I don't want him to ever let me go.

CHAPTER THREE

AFTER

MORGAN

"What the hell was that?" Hannah gasps, her face white as the snowy scenery. The windshield is frosted and fogged so we all climb out of the car to survey the damage and see how bad it is.

I feel sick when I see it.

The body on the side of the road looks twisted and broken. Tawny fur slashed with red. We circle around the vehicle, carefully avoiding the carnage. The front of her car is dented more than it already was. One headlight droops out like a detached eyeball.

A voice cuts through the frigid air, pelted with snow.

"Girlie girl, such a shame. They're endangered, you know."

I jerk my head toward the man's voice. He emerges from the woods wearing hunting garb. Camo snowsuit. Hunting rifle slung over his shoulder. Snowshoes strapped to his boots with thick leather straps. They look handmade. Ski poles held in his hands, sharpened to points.

I try to make out his face, but he has a neck gaiter covering the lower half.

"Wh-what is it?" Hannah says, still shaken from the wreck.

The poor animal keeps twitching in the snow. Spasming. Not quite dead, but not alive either. Hot bile rises in my throat. I turn away from the gruesome sight. What is wrong with me? I grew up in the wilderness, hunting and fishing, unlike my friends with their posh city upbringings. But they don't know about that—and I need to keep it that way. This kind of thing never bothered me before. Hell, it even thrilled me. But now, I barely recognize myself. The breakup did a major number on me. It took away my power, weakened me to my core. It's left me feeling . . . depleted.

"Mountain lion," the man says, his voice muffled by the neck gaiter. He tips his cowboy hat back and bends down to examine the poor creature. He runs his gloved hand over the protruding belly. "Female too. Ripe for breeding."

The mountain lion's eyes have taken on a glassy sheen. Only seconds ago, they were so alive. Now they're dead eyes. I picture the feline stalking her prey through the forest, not knowing that her life was about to end in one unlucky *flash* of accelerated metal.

"This girl would've popped out some fine cubs this spring." The man straightens up and aims his rifle at the still-twitching predator. "Shame. Not many of them left in these parts."

Bang.

I flinch at the sharp crack of gunfire as he shoots her cleanly through the head. The mountain lion shudders, then falls utterly still.

"Mercy killing," he says with a wink. "She wasn't gonna make it."

Without ceremony, he pulls out his hunting knife—the serrated kind—and slits the belly open he was caressing only a moment ago, from neck to genitals. Steaming guts spill out into the snow, instantly melting it and sinking.

My stomach churns harder, making me want to vomit, but I can't turn away.

The man makes quick work of disemboweling the mountain lion, tossing aside the gelatinous entrails into the snow off the side of the road, then straightens up and tips his cowboy hat at us. He wipes his bloody knife on his pants, leaving thick, dark smears.

"You girlie girls better be off now," he says, pointing to the sky, which is looking even more threatening. "Blizzard's a comin'. I'll clean this mess up. Heck, I should be thanking you. I don't have to bother the missus 'bout supper." He lets out a raspy chuckle.

"Uh . . . you're welcome," Hannah stammers, backing away from the crime scene.

She mimes a puking gesture as the man hooks the mountain lion under the front legs and starts dragging it away through the snow into the thick woods, leaving a trail of blood and gore. After they vanish through the trees, I can still smell the coppery tang of blood in the air.

"Tell me he was kidding about the supper part?" I say in a weak voice, swallowing back against the bile threatening to singe my throat. I can't shake the image of the shiny, fresh guts spilling out. Despite my revulsion, I can't stop staring at the grisly carnage.

That's exactly how Noah has made me feel.

Gutted, wrenched open, dying a slow death as my insides spill out.

"Mountain lion tastes like . . . chicken," Mia deadpans. "Or so I hear."

We all try to laugh at her bad joke, but it comes out strangled and weak. I can't take my eyes off the red-tinged puddles in the snow.

Hannah rechecks the front of her car, deeming it still drivable.

We all climb back in and fasten our seat belts as Hannah guns the accelerator. A few minutes later, the car lurches up the icy driveway, saved by traction control, and arrives at the Namaste Center, which materializes out of the dense forest.

Off the grid.

In the middle of *fucking* nowhere.

I know I'm supposed to be here for my great healing journey, or at the very least, to get my eyes off my phone and my ass off the sofa and my mind off . . .

I won't say his name again.

All I can think as our destination comes into stark focus ahead is:

I'm trapped here.

No phone.

No internet.

For an entire week.

Kill me now.

Hannah pilots her car into a parking spot, jamming it against the snowbank. It's an inelegant arrival, but I don't care. All I want is to get out of this car. I'm carsick from the twisty road and the mountain lion murderfest, not to mention lightheaded from the altitude. On the upside, I'm not thinking about my misery and heartbreak.

I've got that going for me.

I scramble out of the backseat, suck down the cold, fresh alpine air, and look around me.

A smattering of other cars are parked nearby—luxury models like Range Rovers and Mercedes. Probably from the other guests this week, though I only think of them as *victims*. I wonder if their friends also dragged them here against their will for this boring retreat.

That's the truth, though I haven't dared to tell Hannah and Mia. They wouldn't understand because yoga and meditation and sound baths are all the rage now, but I find them mind-numbingly boring, preferring a kickboxing class instead.

The kind where you can imagine punching someone who did you wrong—*hard*—until you can't feel anything anymore. I used to have a favorite target: my father. But now, I have a new one. However, I'm pretty sure that punching things is frowned upon here.

I scan the area, taking in the fancy resort. The sprawling campus is built into the mountains and surrounded by forest. The main lodge is sleek and modern, all raw redwood and big glass windows overlooking the majesty of the wilderness, bougie but rustic vibes.

I can see why it's so exclusive. This is definitely the kind of place that attracts the bored elites and celebrities seeking faux spiritual enlightenment.

"Think that creepy hunter was right?" Mia says, climbing out and shouldering her pink overnight bag. "And there's really a blizzard coming?"

"How should I know without my weather app?" I grumble, wishing Mia would take pity on me and give my phone back. "Not that it would make any difference up here," I go on darkly, remembering there is no cell service. "It's like living in the 1980s—"

"Or the future! Welcome, ladies!" A buoyant voice greets us, grabbing our attention. It belongs to a woman who sashays down the path leading from the main lodge.

I give her a quick once-over. She's clad in white, billowy, cuffed pants, matching white robes, and too many scarves to count. Over that, she wears a white, ankle-length, fur-lined coat. Probably vegan leather and faux fur, given her crunchy vibe. The finishing touch is a white turban wrapped around her head with blonde dreadlocks spilling out of it down her back. Various wooden beads and crystals adorn her neck and wrists, plus a septum ring.

She's definitely giving off major New Age, cult vibes, plus a hefty dose of cultural appropriation with her getup. I immediately start judging her. She looks a little older than us, thanks to the fine lines around her lips—thin, pale, and not plumped with filler—and also her eyes—not Botoxed or smoothed out. But I could be wrong. I'm not used to seeing someone from our generation who hasn't tried to forestall aging.

She arrives at our car, accompanied by the pungent odor of patchouli, Palo Santo, and sweat from ineffective—probably organic—deodorant. My nose crinkles in disgust.

"I'm Guru Shava, the director and spiritual guide of the Namaste Center," she says with a glassy-eyed, flaccid smile. "I'll be your main yoga and meditation instructor for the retreat. I'm also known to play a mean gong." She pauses awkwardly, and I realize she's waiting for us to laugh. That was her punchline. I force out a chuckle, while inwardly wincing at the cringey joke.

Guru Shava brings her hands into a prayer pose and tips her head toward us in a solemn bow. "You must be Hannah. I've been expecting you," she says in her dreamy voice. "And these must be your guests. Let me be first to honor you for taking this week away from your busy lives to uplift your chakras. Namaste," she chants with another head bow.

"Namaste," Hannah parrots, mimicking our new spiritual advisor.

Mia and I follow suit, though I feel silly for greeting this total stranger like this. Mia catches my eye and smirks.

Good old Mia.

She knows this is cringe.

"This way up the hill," Guru Shava says, finally coming up for air from her solemn bow, though her eyes remain glassy. "Let me take you to the main lodge for registration. Then I'll escort you to your accommodations for the week. You're in our Cliffside Cabin."

We follow after Guru Shava and her patchouli stink, trudging toward the lodge. I start breathing hard right away. The elevation here is no joke. I swig from my water bottle, trying to quench my thirst and wash away the sick taste from the bile still backing up my throat.

I can't shake the image of that mountain lion twitching in the snow.

"As you know, this retreat is a digital free zone," Guru Shava goes on. "If you brought any phones or tablets with you, that's totally fine. We just ask that you leave them in your cabin. Besides, they won't work up here. There's no cellular service or Wi-Fi. We don't even have landlines installed in the lodge."

"But . . . what if there's an emergency?" I ask, feeling unsettled.

My boots clomp over the freshly shoveled snow, and I'm thankful I'm not trudging through it up to my ankles. I picture all manner of horrible scenarios. I think about the mountain lion again. And that creepy hunter dragging the body away. Not to mention the incoming blizzard.

"Oh, don't worry," Guru Shava says quickly. "We have a CB radio installed in the main lodge, just in case. It's connected directly to the forest service. They're the only first responders up here."

"CB radio?" I say, not liking the sound of that. "No phone lines?"

"I know, it does sound a little old-fashioned," Guru Shava says. "But trust me, it's more reliable than landlines around these parts. They always go down with the first big snowfall anyway. No point in repairing them until spring. Plus, isn't that the whole reason to come here? To disconnect? Get a break from the toxicity of the digital world?"

Hannah shoots me a pointed look to stop grilling our new spiritual savior. "Yes, exactly!" she says, in an overly cheerful voice. "I couldn't agree more. We're all too hooked on our phones. It's like Steve Jobs put narcotics into those things."

"Disconnect to reconnect," Guru Shava says in a stern voice. "That's our slogan. We expect you to adhere to our strict no electronics policy. We've never had to expel someone, and I hope we can keep it that way with your help."

"Of course," Mia says, nudging me, not too subtly. "I can assure you that we plan to follow all the rules and stick to the program."

"Excellent," Guru Shava says, the edge leaving her voice. "Also, in case you still have concerns, we've never experienced a serious incident at the retreat. A few poison ivy cases, but that's only in the summer sessions. And sprained ankles that could happen anywhere. But nothing requiring serious medical attention. Mostly just major spiritual breakthroughs," she adds with a wink.

"That's why we're here," Hannah says, her eyebrows rising.

"Uh, exactly!" Mia adds. "We can't wait to break on through . . . to the other side."

Her awkward quip hangs in the air fogged with our breath. Mia and I fall back a few paces to gossip, while Hannah sucks up to the guru.

Mia whispers to me under her breath. "I'm not gonna mention Botox . . . or celebs."

I snort a laugh. "Be careful—or you could get us tossed out. I'm pretty sure Hannah would never forgive us."

"You can say that again. She's already brainwashed."

Hannah overhears us. "I prefer the term *open-minded.* You should try it. Guru Shava is right. Our modern world is toxic."

Then she turns back, a bit miffed.

Mia grabs my hand, pulling me after them. "You can't argue with toxic."

She's right. I can't. Noah is toxic. So why am I still in love with him?

Before I can ruminate further, Guru Shava pulls open the wooden doors to the lodge. Warm air billows out like a blanket. She holds it open as we each squeeze through the door and into the cozy, rustic lobby. Her eyes fix on me.

I can't tell if it's my imagination, but they look dilated and empty.

Like she drank the hippie-dippie Kool-Aid.

I hate her already.

CHAPTER FOUR

BEFORE

NOAH

It's been two days since Morgan walked into my life.

Well, more like crash-landed into it.

Thirty-eight hours, to be specific. *And fourteen minutes.*

Not that I'm counting. I float through my workday, sitting in my cubicle at my father's investment company that in a burst of creativity he named "Barron Ventures." How original.

But my father's like that. He enjoys putting his name on everything, letting everyone know that he owns it. If he could put his name on the whole world, I know he still wouldn't be satisfied.

The office is abuzz around me with bankers rushing around, late trades hitting desks, Excel spreadsheets loaded with endless streams of numbers. But I can barely focus on anything except . . .

Her.

A smile graces my lips remembering how she almost stepped into traffic, rather than wanting to go on a date with me. Her embarrassment when she realized I was her date. How cute she looked when the blood hit her cheeks, making her blush.

A total cringe moment.

But it was magical. I'm not used to that—girls trying to avoid me. I don't mean to sound conceited, it's just a side effect of being Noah Barron.

That's why I signed up for the One in the first place. It promised a blind dating experience, where I could find a match who didn't immediately know who I am. On other apps, even if I hide my name, it's easy to reverse image search my profile pictures. Let's just say, they pop up pretty fast and give me away.

Some girls try to act surprised and hide that they already know who I am. But I can sense it right away. The way they act too interested—too eager—practically begging for a second date before I even get to know them at all.

But not Morgan.

She wanted to take a trip to the ER rather than be forced to have a glass of wine with me. *That* caught my interest. However, it was more than that. She looks like a city girl, coiffed and styled, but something about her is . . . different.

I don't think she wants anyone to know. I have a talent for reading people. My father calls it the Barron family acumen, as if we're all possessed of some special gene mutation that gives us a leg up on the rest of the suckers out there.

And maybe it's true. All I know is that I've always been good at reading people. But Morgan . . . I couldn't do it. She didn't fall into any normal patterns of behavior. Exhibit one was her attempt to get out of our date. Exhibit two?

When she agreed to ditch the bar and cavort around Central Park in the rain, like I used to when I was a kid in galoshes escaping the stifling oppression of our penthouse growing up with a former supermodel mother dulled on anti-anxiety meds and a father always working to expand his family's empire.

I sound like a whiny, privileged jerk. However, the truth is that being a Barron isn't all it's cracked up to be. But Morgan makes me feel different. For starters, she has no idea who I really am—and I want to keep it that way for as long as I can.

I also don't want my father finding out and ruining it. My mood instantly darkens at that idea—and what happened last time. But I quash it right away. I can't dwell on my dark memories. Besides, I swear this time is going to be different. I've changed.

Plus, I can keep my father away from her—I think—even though I can't prevent her from finding out eventually. However, I'd like to circumvent that and get to know the real Morgan before she does.

Oh, and that kiss?

That was the stuff of fantasies and rom-coms. The way she melted into me, turning into molten lava in my arms, while the rain soaked us both.

"So . . . who's the girl?"

A voice jerks me out of my fantasy.

Blake, my cubicle mate across the way, shoots me a knowing look. His clipped hair and designer suit are evidence of our six-figure starting salaries. He's built square—his head, his shoulders, his boxy frame—but a suit like that can do wonders. Plus, he wears a Rolex.

"She's . . . none of your business," I shoot back, even though I blush.

"Did you bang her?" Roger cuts in, leaning around his cubicle. "The One . . . You got a match?"

"Of course he did," Blake adds. "Less than a week swiping—and he's already scored."

I try to hide inside my three fabric-covered walls. Not even a hint of natural light, just those buzzing fluorescents overhead. I could have a corner office, but I don't want that kind of treatment. I insisted on being dumped into a cubicle with the non-nepo babies. Although, truth be told, everyone who works back here is a bit of a nepo baby. But I'm the worst one.

Not letting it go, they follow me, crowding over the top of the barriers.

"Hey, I better get credit," Roger says. "Best man at the wedding? The One was my idea, remember? I'm working on their IPO. That thing is getting downloaded like crazy by Gen Z."

"Marriage, really?" Blake says, rolling his eyes at Roger. "So, who is she? Give us the details. I'm married, and I'm bored. I live for this shit."

"Like I said, she's *none of your business*," I say firmly and excuse myself, escaping to the bathroom. *Shit, I have to do better at keeping this secret*, I think. *If I want it to work out.*

I can't let what happened before destroy it this time. I finish up and check my appearance in the mirror. The same chiseled face stares back at me. The lazy black curls and piercing blue eyes. I hate how easy pretty privilege makes my life. And then, add in the old money and family name.

As much as I've tried to earn my own way, never asking my father for help, I never really started from nothing. I've had help every step of the way thanks to winning the genetic lottery.

Morgan.

I can't fuck this up. She's pristine and blissfully unaware of all of this, including my past. I can't let her know. They say secrets keep you sick. But I think the opposite is true—secrets keep you safe.

More importantly, they keep her safe.

"Good morning, Mr. Barron," Chelsea, the receptionist, says as I whisk through the ornate gold-and-marble lobby on my way back from the bathroom. Her red curls bounce around her pale, heart-shaped face and bright, amber eyes.

She's a recent college grad, hoping for a chance to work her way up in the company from the bottom level. I don't have the heart to tell her that my father would never allow it. She graduated from a state college, not the Ivy League. But it's also something unspoken that you won't find listed on her resume.

My dad can sniff it out like a police dog. I can almost hear his voice. *Son, she's not like us. She would never understand.*

"Everything okay, Mr. Barron?"

Her worried voice breaks through my fog. Shit, I was standing there spacing out again. All thanks to Morgan. I've been like this all day.

I flash my most disarming smile. "I told you already, call me Noah."

"Okay . . . Noah," she says, giggling, melting. I know she's flirting, and I know she'd let me do anything I want to her. But I'm bored of that.

I beg off and continue back to my cubicle. The Barron name follows me—stationery, conference room signage, executive assistants answering phones, "Barron Ventures" ringing out. My father owns this whole bank. And a good chunk of the city too, thanks to our real estate holdings that have been in my family for generations, dating back to the founding fathers. But I don't want to ride on that.

I want to make my own way. That's why I work so hard and bust my ass when I don't have to. But these last two days, I can't focus to save my life. And it's all because of *her.* That both thrills and terrifies me in equal measure.

Growing up, I vowed never to work for him. I wanted to go my own way and applied to a Midwest liberal arts school behind his back. He found out and pulled my application, forcing me to attend his alma mater, Dartmouth. I hated that he won, so I slogged through with barely passing grades, then limped back to the city, where he handed me this job.

I've hated myself since then. Hated that I failed in my mission to be different. Hated that I'm turning into nothing more than his shadow, darker and fading, hiding from the sunlight. As time passes, his worst qualities seem to manifest in me, creeping in around the edges, like this unavoidable fate.

Then came Morgan.

I joined the One after Roger mentioned it, hoping it would connect me to someone not like me and my family.

And it worked.

I couldn't believe my luck.

Our second date has to be something good. Spectacular. Better than the first date. That spontaneity will be hard to repeat—cavorting in the park and kissing in the rain—and harder to top. But I have to try. I can't lose this chance.

I also can't let her know how badly I need her in order to escape . . . myself.

I pull out my phone. Her name glimmers in my texts. I waited the appropriate amount of time to reach out again, not to seem too eager. That can be like kryptonite to girls. I need to play this one carefully, very carefully.

NOAH: *How do you feel about lions?*

I figure that should pique her interest—and it does. The typing ellipsis appears instantly, then another second passes that thumps my heart and turns my stomach before a text bubble appears.

MORGAN: *We talking* Lion King *or* Wizard of Oz . . . *or the kind that eat you?*

NOAH: *We both know you're willing to risk your life. You'll just have to find out.*

MORGAN: *Fine. I'll wear my finest safari gear and prepare for more near-death experiences. Just name the place and time.*

NOAH: *Tomorrow? 6 p.m.? I'll pick you up. How does that sound?*

MORGAN: *Roar! It's a date.*

I smile to myself and set my phone down, savoring the moment and letting it sink in, remembering her lips pressed into mine, how soft and sweet they tasted, how much I wanted to devour her whole. How hard it was to wait.

Patience, I tell myself. One of the most important lessons my father taught me, along with how to wield our power. Exactly what I'm about to do right now.

Working my connections and deploying my irresistible charm to grease the wheels, I make the necessary arrangements. I can't leave anything to chance, not when it comes to her. It's not just the date itself, but what it symbolizes that gets me excited. Lions are brave, steadfast, and majestic—the kings of the jungle. Kind of like me.

Except New York is my jungle, and these finance bros are my pride. I watch them pecking away at their computers, tracking the markets like they're bringing home prey to feed us all. I'm not letting Morgan get away. Even though everyone I love . . . disappears.

Before I can stop it, my sister's young face, the way I remember it, flashes in my memory. The way I used to follow her everywhere like her shadow. Her annoying little brother nipping at her heels.

Until she went missing.

Dark thoughts cascade through my head before I can fight back against them. The memories of Zoe struggle to surface, but I stuff them back down. This time is different, I remind myself. Morgan is different. I'm not letting myself get out of control again.

And most importantly—

I'm not letting her get away.

CHAPTER FIVE

AFTER

MORGAN

"Welcome to your rebirth," Guru Shava says after she checks each of us in and hands us our keys—the actual metal kind on hand-braided leather keychains.

I wait for the punchline.

But it doesn't come.

She's serious. Zero irony.

"Don't you have to, like, die first?" Mia says. "In order to be reborn?"

Guru Shava gives her a mysterious smile.

"All questions will be answered over the course of the week."

She pivots, her fur-lined coat and scarves swirling behind her, and leads us from the main lodge to our cabin, following the windy gravel paths. Thankfully, they've been freshly shoveled. A brisk wind whips down, swirling the snow around us. Hannah walks behind her, while Mia and I lag back a few feet. I shiver and zip up my puffy coat, paltry defense against the real winter that's currently pummeling these mountains.

"They weren't kidding about the no electronics policy," Mia whispers, dangling her hefty key in front of me. "Did you notice at check-in, they don't have a computer?"

I nod. "Just one of those old ledgers with our names written down. I didn't know anyone still used those."

"I know. This really is a time capsule," Mia says. "I've only seen something like this in old movies."

"Yeah, the scary kind," I say, miming getting stabbed. "I wonder if they make movies about nice hotels that aren't haunted with ghosts or harboring serial killers."

Mia snorts. "Who would want to watch that?"

We follow our guru deeper into the pine forest. The retreat center's extensive campus reminds me of a quaint village with wooden huts erected in the pristine mountain landscape far from the clutches of civilization. Thick woods encroach on it, threatening to reclaim the land that was cleared to build it.

Walking paths split off and cut through the woods, leading to more cabins. I'm guessing that's where other guests are staying for the week, though I haven't caught a glimpse of anyone else.

"The property was donated to our nonprofit foundation by an anonymous benefactor," Guru Shava continues, "for the sole purpose of creating a center to foster healing and rebirth. Our core mission is to facilitate a way for our clients to escape the toxic noise and pressures of our modern world. Put another way, at the Namaste Center we strive to disconnect to reconnect."

We keep hiking farther in the forest. I struggle to keep up with her brisk pace. I'm already huffing and puffing in the thin air. So are my friends. Guru Shava seems completely unbothered. The winds pick up from the mountains, promising more severe weather. A chill seizes ahold of me. I shiver and pull my scarf tighter around my neck.

"I wonder who the mysterious benefactor was?" Mia whispers into my ear. "Probably somebody famous."

"Like a Kardashian?" I whisper back, making her giggle.

Hannah hears us and glances back, making us shut up.

"Your spiritual awakening begins today." Guru Shava lifts her arms, gesturing around. "These ancient mountains will witness your rebirth from the primordial waters of creation, watching as you distill and discover the divine truth within."

I resist the urge to roll my eyes . . . *hard.* Hannah seems completely enraptured by her, while Mia is warming up, especially with the hope of encountering famous guests.

I realize they went to a lot of effort to make this retreat happen—and it's because they care. I have to admit I've been in tough shape since the breakup. Maybe a primordial rebirth is just what I need. At the very least, I got a week off work with vacation pay. That has to count for something.

Still, I'm already starting to feel boredom creep in. Bereft of my phone—and my only connection to Noah—being yanked away, I don't know what to do with myself. I feel twitchy, like I want to jump out of my skin.

"You may already be experiencing symptoms of your digital detox," Guru Shava says, tossing a look my way.

I feel a jolt. *How did she know?*

"Those symptoms can include depression, anxiety, emptiness, listlessness, apathy, even fear and suicidal ideation. If you're feeling that, please inform me or our staff immediately for care."

"Wow, it's like kicking hard drugs," Hannah says. "I had no idea."

Guru Shava smiles. "A lot of our modern culture is extremely toxic to spiritual health and enlightenment. The profit motive lies in creating addictions—to products, devices, unhealthy food, pharmaceutical drugs like antidepressants, you name it."

"I think you just described my job," I say with a shake of my head. "PR and marketing expert at your service."

Guru Shava smiles. "Ah, yes. So if they're the drugs and the companies are the dealers, then you're the pusher?"

"Guilty as charged," I admit. "I mean, you gotta make a living somehow."

"Indeed," Guru Shava says. "Or you could step outside the system and start to deconstruct everything you've been taught by school, the news, the government . . . even social media."

"*Especially* social media," I say. "Is that what the Namaste Center is for?"

Guru Shava nods. "That, and so much more. You'll see . . ."

We come to a halt by a steep cliffside. The snow has let up, and the sun is breaking through the clouds, giving us a glimpse of our surroundings. My breath catches in my throat. The views of the mountain range are astounding—and not one hint of civilization as far as the eye can see. A lone hawk circles the skies in hunt of prey only it can spot against the white blanket of the landscape.

Guru Shava turns and places her hand on Hannah's artificially smooth brow, then shuts her eyes like she's sensing something. My skepticism rears up, questioning this performance. But Hannah seems utterly enraptured, leaning into the experience.

"I can see you're already opening up your third eye," Guru Shava says in a soft voice. "You've been craving this, haven't you? Something deeper and more connected. I can feel it. This week will do wonders for you."

Hannah smiles like a student who just got an A+ without studying. "Thanks, Guru Shava."

Then she turns to Mia—and repeats the ritual. "You have an especially strong aura. Very headstrong and determined, but you can soften here and get in touch with your feminine energy. You don't have to keep your guard up."

Mia smiles. "You're right. I feel like I'm always fighting it. That's what I get for working at a start-up and trying to keep up with the tech bros."

"I give you permission to let go," Guru Shava says. "We will work on that this week in your individual sessions."

Then she turns to me. I notice her eyes are light gray, like the skies above. Her delicate features and white-blonde hair give her an almost angelic appearance. The white robes and turban add to the effect.

Gently, she places her hand on my brow. I flinch back from her ice-cold hands, a chill running through me.

She frowns. "You're resisting. It's okay, Morgan, you can let go."

But I don't want to let go. I want her to stop touching me. This feels invasive and not at all like what I signed up for.

She squints, scrutinizing me. Her voice comes out a soft whisper. "Morgan, what are you hiding? What *deep secrets* are you keeping?"

That shocks me. But I quickly act confused. "Uh, what do you mean?"

She gives me a sharp look.

What does she know? I think, suddenly afraid.

A long moment passes, her eyes boring into me, before she speaks again.

"This week is your chance to open up and show the world who you really are for once. Stop hiding your true self."

"Uh, right, okay. I will . . ." My voice comes out faltering.

Her gaze lingers on me for another excruciatingly long minute, making my heart pound faster. Finally, she turns away.

"Uh, what was that all about?" Mia whispers in my ear as Guru Shava continues down the path.

"How should I know?" I say, forcing a smile to hide my discomfort. But Hannah joins in.

"Did I hear her say something about secrets? What did she mean?"

My cheeks burn with heat even in this cold. My friends don't know the truth about my past—and I've kept it that way for a reason. Horrible memories flash through my head. The sharp *smack* of my father hitting me. The blood rising to my skin, the mark taking forever to fade away. I flinch, then work to clear my expression.

I don't want my friends to find out the truth of what I've been through. I have a hard enough time fitting in with them as it is. I don't need another thing separating us.

There's no way they would understand.

"Oh please, that little act?" I say, feigning a nonchalant tone. "Probably the same pseudo-spiritual speech she gives to everyone checking in."

"Ha, you're right," Mia says. "She is pretty convincing though."

"I think she's onto something," Hannah says. "Did you hear what she said about my third eye? I'm already acing this whole spiritual detox."

She doesn't know anything, I reassure myself. She's probably a total fraud. Still, I feel a little unsettled by her mention of secrets.

We continue after her, sticking to the path that winds through the woods. My gaze catches on something—fresh prints in the snow leading toward the trees.

My curiosity piques. I deviate slightly, tramping through the trees and poking my head through the prickly branches, then startle back.

A creepy face stares at me.

I yelp before I can stop myself. Footsteps rush up behind me.

"Oh, you've found our meditation garden," Guru Shava says, pulling back the branches to reveal a clearing. "Some find themselves drawn to its power."

Rocks are stacked into strange pyramids. In the center of the meadow is a stone fire pit filled with fresh sticks over a bed of blackened ash. A faint whiff of smoke fills the air.

"What is that *thing*?" I say, pointing to the creepy stick figure hanging from the tree branches. The rope curls around its neck, strangling it. It's not the only one.

There are more of the crude wooden dolls strung up in the trees, all hanging by their necks. I get a bad feeling about it.

Morgan, get a hold of yourself, I mentally chastise myself. I'm tired of feeling so jumpy and on edge lately.

"Right, this is one of our spiritual exercises," Guru Shava says. "We make dolls to symbolize our past selves, then we sacrifice them to the forest."

"Oh, and then you burn them?" Hannah says, catching on.

"Like Burning Man?" Mia adds.

"Precisely," Guru Shava says. "Though the ancient Pagan ritual predates that festival. Our guests find it quite cathartic. But we are getting ahead of ourselves."

"Sorry," I mumble. "Didn't mean to crash your mini-Burning Man."

"Oh, don't apologize," Guru Shava says. "Like I said, certain guests seem drawn to the meditation garden."

"I've been wanting to go to Burning Man for years," Mia pouts.

"You'd never survive the dust," Hannah says. "No shower? For a week? You'd be running back to the city."

Everyone laughs. Guru Shava leads us back to the main path, but something else catches my eye.

Tracks lead away from the pit into the woods. I see what look like specks of blood, too. But before I can look closer, two hands wrap around my arm.

I spin around, breathless.

Guru Shava stares back at me. Gently, she guides me the other way.

"Come along," she says, but her voice has a slight edge to it. "We don't want you to get lost out here. While I assure you our meditation center is perfectly safe, this is still the wilderness, and we must remain vigilant. It's best to stick together with a group, just in case."

"I'll be more careful in the future. I promise," I stammer.

We continue through the woods, and I make sure to stick close to the group.

Still, I have a bad feeling.

I want to go back and see if there really is blood. But I'm probably imagining things after what happened with the hunter and the mountain lion.

A few minutes later, a small cabin materializes at the end of the path. I'm guessing that's our destination.

"Your accommodations for the week," Guru Shava says, unlocking the door.

It swings inward with a groan.

We hurry inside, desperate for the warmth. Luckily, a fire is already stoked in the furnace with a pipe that vents outside, probably the source of the burning smell. I take in the space.

The cabin is rustic yet comfortable with three separate bedrooms branching off the living room. A small kitchenette is tucked in the corner with a sink, microwave, compact two-burner stove, and mini fridge. The boho chic decor modernizes the old-fashioned space. Each room has its own bathroom. The primary has the fanciest one with a claw-foot tub, which Hannah claims, seeing as she arranged the whole getaway. I choose the smaller room with a nice view of the cliffside and the mountain peaks beyond.

"Wonderful; I'll leave you to settle in," Guru Shava says with a gracious nod. "My staff will collect and deliver your luggage shortly."

"That would be great," Hannah says. "Save us from carrying them—that was quite a hike through the woods."

"Indeed, I recommend sticking to the walking trails and using the maps," Guru Shava says, smiling. "Also, we use the buddy system here. Don't go wandering off alone. Always bring someone with you. You'll get the lay of the land soon enough. While the main center is on private land, many surrounding areas are public and open to hunters. They need permits. We don't condone it, but it's a small price to pay for such remote beauty."

"Hunters?" I say, catching Hannah and Mia's eye. "That explains it."

"Right, I think we encountered one on the way up here," Hannah fills in. "Before we got to the main lodge."

"Yeah, he was . . . interesting," Mia provides. "Definitely seemed like a local."

"I'm sorry about that," Guru Shava goes on, sounding annoyed. I'm guessing vegans and hunters aren't a good mix. "But unfortunately, there's nothing we can do if it's on public land."

"We understand," Hannah says quickly, smoothing it over.

"Oh, one more thing," Guru Shava adds. "I should mention my staff have all taken a vow of silence. So don't be alarmed if they don't speak or verbally answer questions."

"Vow of silence?" I ask uneasily.

"Yes, that is part of their desire to apprentice here at the center," she replies. "This retreat isn't silent, but we do offer those from time to time. It's a sort of ancient meditation practice."

"I visited a Buddhist temple in Kyoto where we had a silent lunch when I was on an exchange program in high school," Hannah says.

"You're familiar with the practice then." Guru Shava hands us each a folder with a bunch of papers. "Your welcome packets include the schedule and information on the retreat. Tonight, a light dinner will be delivered to your cabin. We officially kick off the program tomorrow at seven a.m. with breakfast and orientation. By the end of the week, you won't even recognize yourselves."

Ugh, so early, I groan inwardly. But I keep it to myself, accepting the packet.

"The schedule is quite rigorous, but you will have free time to explore on your own. I will conduct individual sessions with each of you throughout the week."

Her gaze fixes on me and lingers for so long, I start to feel uncomfortable.

Finally, she breaks it.

"Remember, we ask that you honor our no electronics policy. Not that you'll find much use for them out here. The lack of reception makes it an easy rule to enforce."

With another bow of her turbaned head, she swirls around and drifts out the door. It shuts with a loud *thud*.

It feels like all the air is sucked out of the cabin.

The finality hits me hard. I realize there's no going back now. One week in the woods getting inducted into what increasingly seems like some kind of bougie pseudo-religious cult. And what is with the creepy dolls hanging in the clearing, dangling by their stick necks? I shrug.

What could possibly go wrong?

CHAPTER SIX

BEFORE

MORGAN

"Since you like to live dangerously," Noah says, leading me into the lion's den. Literally—we are literally in a lion's den. The zookeeper shadows us, but he lets us enter the exhibit first.

"What makes you say that?" I say, feeling heat creep up my neck.

"You were attempting to step into oncoming traffic when I met you."

"You caught me in a bad moment."

"Oh, right. I forgot. You thought dying would be better than going on a date with me," he teases.

"A *blind* date," I correct him. "I didn't know who you were yet. And I have a spotty dating history."

"You still don't know who I am."

That's both scary and thrilling, I think as he leads me closer to the lions. My heart thumps faster. He's right. I don't know his last name, and vice versa. We've stuck to the blind dating experiment. I tried googling him after finding out he was an investment banker, but in this city and with a common first name, that certainly doesn't narrow it down. My hits came up empty. He's still a blank canvas for my heart to explore.

We near the back of the enclosure. My pulse races even faster. I'm letting a virtual stranger—a man whose true identity I don't know—lead me into danger. I'm not sure what to expect. I've never had a behind-the-scenes view of an animal habitat before. Adrenaline zips through my blood, flushing my face and making me feel exhilarated and strangely alive.

A normal person would want to run from this, but Noah is right—I like it.

He does, too. I can sense his clipped breath, how his heart is probably skipping faster. I can smell him, too. An intoxicating aroma of masculinity—clean sweat, woodsy cologne, and leather.

He reaches for my hand and squeezes it as we proceed deeper.

"Amazing, I can't believe it!" I gasp when I see them, stepping closer.

Several lions roam through the enclosure at the Bronx Zoo. Some prefer lazing about by the rocks in the soft grass, waiting for their supper. A brisk waterfall cascades behind them, misting the air. It's late summer but not too hot or humid. I'm wearing a cute blue romper with a white collar that's chic yet playful, that could go from the office to our date.

Still, up close, I can't believe how majestic the lions are with their tawny fur and matching golden eyes. The lionesses watch us carefully. They're the hunters, not the males, like many people think.

He squeezes my hand tighter. "I'm glad you appreciate them." He sounds pleased. "I knew I had to be creative to top that first date."

Blood rushes to my face. "You mean running around Central Park like kids on a snow day?"

"That was quite serendipitous," he says, surprising me with his smooth diction. "But I must confess, I think it was your lips that did me in." He smiles in a sexy, casual way.

"Oh, that part." I play coy, not wanting to admit how crazy that drove me.

How as soon as I returned to my apartment, my roommates could almost smell it on me. They demanded "deets" on my date, but I waved them off and rushed into my bedroom. I had to release myself, reaching down into my pants and feeling the heat.

Thinking of his soft lips roaming over mine, prying them open, his tongue mingling with mine, the warmth of him, how he tasted like cinnamon and something so delicious, I couldn't get enough of him. When we finally parted, I was breathless and already hooked.

Then I waited for his text.

And waited.

He had to text first. The number one rule for hooking a man: Don't be too eager. Play hard to get. And finally, he did get me.

When he asked for a second date, my heart leapt and plummeted in a way that made me nauseous yet exhilarated. And now, here I was.

He breathes into my ear. "Morgan—whose last name I still don't know—you are irresistible and delectable. I can't wait until I get to devour you whole."

"Better do it before the lions beat you to it," I deflect as the smoldering intensity of his desire rockets through me. I can't help but shiver into him.

"Oh, I'm quite competitive," he says in a soft voice, flirting back. "A fun fact about me: I hate to lose. Those lions don't stand a chance."

"Really? How can you be so sure?"

"This is how."

He kisses me again, deeply and unreservedly, while the lions watch.

He releases me, leaving me weak-kneed and jittery at the same time. We stand back and watch the zookeepers feed the lions—a carnivorous smorgasbord of ground meat, cow legs still on the bone, and whole rabbits.

I pretend to be slightly repulsed watching their canines tear into the meat and wrenching it from sinew and bone. The redness of the rabbit in particular rivets me. But not for the reasons he would think.

My father taught me how to hunt and trap when I was a kid, and I was a fast learner. It was how I survived when there was nothing in the cupboards. I've skinned rabbits, blood coating my hands, even eaten their tiny hearts raw. But I squelch the memory down.

Noah cannot know the truth. I have to play my new role.

"Too much for you?" he asks.

I can sense he's testing me. Feeling me out and gauging my reaction to the lions ravenously feeding. I lean into him.

"Actually, I find it fascinating," I say, and that part is true. "Plus, I know we're virtually strangers, but I feel safe with you. I can't explain it. Maybe that's a mistake though."

"You don't seem like the kind of girl who makes mistakes." He raises his eyebrows and runs his fingers along my arm, drawing more prickles to my flesh.

"Oh, is that so? Touché." I bat my eyelashes, extensions in full effect.

He returns my gaze. "If it makes you feel any better, you might be my first big mistake—but I'm willing to risk it. I like trying to figure you out, Morgan. I will confess, you're keeping me on my toes. Keeping me guessing. I'm not used to that."

I give him a gentle push, unbalancing him, and he laughs.

"So, it's working then?" I tease. "My nefarious plan to seduce you?"

He shakes his head. "Who are you really? And where did you come from?"

"The One, remember?"

"Some mysterious algorithm that paired us together? On a blind date? Knowing nothing? Should we trust it?"

This time I kiss him. When I come up for air, it's my turn to take advantage of his momentary discombobulation.

"What do you think?"

"I think . . . I don't have a choice."

We haven't talked much about our lives outside spending time together—really our resumes—which isn't how I usually date. In the past I've relied on those details as if they were a safety net protecting my heart.

If only they went to the *right* schools (preferably in the Ivy League). Chose the *right* career paths (as in one that brings prestige and a salary to thrive in the city). Came from the *right* sort of family (the polar opposite of mine).

Then my heart would be safeguarded, only allowing me to fall for the *right* sort of man. But the reality is that those other relationships felt so stale, squeezed of life and spontaneity. They were always doomed to fail spectacularly. Sometimes it was instant fails in the form of bad first dates, or solid first dates that led to one or even two-night stands, then imploded.

Sometimes, they grew into whole situationships, the kind where they meet your friends, yet won't commit to exclusivity or a label (even *girlfriend* being too much pressure on them).

But as soon as you pressed them for more, even just a tiny inch of commitment, they dumped you, sometimes heartlessly via text. The subtle message being: In the city with those resumes, they have so many choices at their fingertips on their phones, dating apps awaiting a swipe.

Unlike women, their value only goes up with aging in tandem with their salaries. Their fertility doesn't wane on any ticking clock, and their looks? Even unattractive bald men can date young supermodels if they have enough social and material capital at their disposal.

But this feels . . . *different.*

I'm scared to admit it. The One promised a blind dating experiment, and so far, we've stuck to it. Not divulging much about ourselves in a real-world sense, but relishing these thrilling moments spent together. Like here, in the lion's den.

We take a few more steps toward the pride. They shift around, pivoting to study our movements like we're being stalked.

I feel a surge of adrenaline, driving my heart faster. Goose bumps prick my skin. The animals are majestic, but deadly. They could kill us in an instant. The zookeeper keeps close watch, but doesn't stop us. It's after hours, and the zoo is closed. Noah pulled some strings.

I'm realizing he's a *pulling strings* kind of guy. I also noticed he had a car and driver when he picked me up from work. I'm starting to wonder, who is this guy, really?

"So, what made you do it?" I ask, prodding him. "Join the One?"

He thinks it over. "I wanted the true experience of going in blind for once. Meeting somebody new. Even if they were trying to step into traffic."

"I could be dangerous." I shoot him a wicked smile. "Aren't you afraid?"

He returns it with one of his own.

"Don't you think it's more fun that way? Not knowing? Statistically speaking, you're the one who should be worried. The dangerous ones are usually men. We commit almost eighty percent of violent crimes each year."

"Are you speaking from experience?" I joke.

"Fine. You've got me. Confessed true crime podcast and documentary junkie."

I laugh in surprise. "Really? No way. In that case, I also have a confession. I can't get enough murder porn. That's what my roommates call it. Hannah and Mia love to tease me."

He stiffens slightly. *Shit, I made a mistake.* I've shared too much and been too open. It's not attractive for women to be into hardcore stuff like that. I should've said I like rom-coms, safe girlie things.

But he recovers quickly, glossing over it.

He raises his eyebrows. "Murder porn?"

"Let's just say, there's a high body count in my Netflix Recently Watched queue. They know all about it since we share the same Netflix account."

"I live alone, so at least my TV habits are private," he says, intriguing me further. Living alone in the city means one thing—money. I couldn't swing it. My roommates could, but they took pity on me after college, knowing I'd need roommates to be able to afford living in the city. Plus, we're besties.

"I don't know if I could have roommates," he goes on. "My therapist says I don't 'play nice with others.' But I think maybe we could share a Netflix account."

"Great, I've got that going for me," I flirt back. "Count me in for the binge fest. And so far, I have to say. You seem to be playing nice with me."

"That's because you haven't seen my naughty side yet."

He grips my hand tighter, almost painfully, but I don't pull away.

The hint of his darkness teases me. I have darkness inside me, too.

"You sure you want to continue this blind dating experiment?" I say, daring him. "You could regret it later."

"Unlikely," he says. "And very much, I do. It's refreshing and thrilling, and I don't want it to end. Are you ready for part two?"

"Part two?" I ask, surprised.

"Of our date. The lions aren't the only ones getting to eat tonight. That's if my Netflix queue didn't scare you off."

"No, the more murdery the better. What if you only liked rom-coms?" I shudder in reaction. "Then I'd have to sneak around to watch my shows. It would ruin your algorithm."

"Luckily, we don't have to worry about that," he says in a flirtatious voice.

The lions are finishing their supper, chewing on the last bones. My stomach gurgles, proving his point.

I am hungry. But more than that, I'm hungry for him and ready for part two.

"Okay, mystery man. We can keep the blind date experiment going," I say and kiss him deeply.

When he comes up for air he grins.

"I'll take that as a yes."

The lions and the zoo fade into the background. Everything does, but *Noah.*

Part two defies all expectation. Noah's driver takes us back into Manhattan to a high-rise. We take the elevator to the penthouse—a flawless, modern apartment, subtly decorated with rich, warm tones. What looks like real art adorns the walls. He coaxes me through it quickly toward the back of the apartment, opening the sliding doors onto a wraparound balcony stretching around half the building. The warm summer air gusts into me, almost lifting me from my feet.

I feel like Wendy when Tinker Bell sprinkles fairy dust on her so she can fly. Outside, there's a table set with candles burning in a hurricane glass. He ushers me over, pulling out my chair.

"Dinner? You must be hungry."

"Famished," I say, my stomach grumbling again.

I gaze over the whole city. This is a ten-million-dollar view, maybe even a billion-dollar view. A waiter in a tuxedo hurries over. He pops champagne, the expensive kind, and pours it into two crystal flutes.

I'm speechless. Beyond speechless. Flustered and flabbergasted.

"Where are we?" I manage.

"We're in Midtown."

I shake my head. "I mean, how?"

"You sure you want to know?"

He's tempting me to ask for more details. Renege on the blind dating experiment. Curiosity stabs at me like knives, but I put on a brave smile and force it back. I'm smart enough to know—he's testing me. Trying to see if I'll fall for his money instead of him. That's the reason he's flaunting it so blatantly. Two can play this game.

"I'm good," I say with a demure smile. "The view just took my breath away."

He winks at me and raises his glass. "Great, that's what I thought. I called in a favor to my favorite chef in the city to cook for us. He's Michelin trained. Do you have any dietary restrictions?"

I shake my head. "No, I'll even eat gluten."

"Good girl," he says, and I find myself basking in his praise.

"So, even the dinner is a mystery?"

"Indeed. It's a *blind* dinner." He leans closer. "Does that frighten you?"

I lean closer too.

"As long as it's not raw meat like the lions, I think I can handle it."

He nods and whispers to the waiter, who rushes off, leaving the champagne chilling on ice in a silver bucket. The bubbles hiss in my flute, as bright and effervescent as the stars erupting overhead in the expanse of the night sky.

I breathe it in; I breathe him in.

"To blind dates," he says, raising his glass.

We *clink* and that first sip rushes through my bloodstream like cold fire.

The dinner passes as fast and smoothly as the champagne in my glass. Soon, he's leading me away from the table, kissing me over the balcony, tipping my head back so blood rushes to it, danger so tantalizingly close. He easily could let me fall.

But he doesn't.

He keeps a firm hand on me as his lips press into mine, daring me to lean back farther and tempt gravity. Daring me to take it to the next level of danger.

When I do, he's pulling me back, scooping me up in his arms, and carrying me into the penthouse, laying me down on the silken bedspread. Everything is white on white on white. The color of pure luxury.

He presses into me. I can feel his desire throbbing with each kiss, him hardening against my thigh, restricted by his jeans. I want him more than I've ever wanted any man.

But I force myself to hold back.

"Not yet," I whisper, breathless. "I want it to mean something . . . special."

I never do this. Resist. But I'm determined to make this time different. It worked once when I wanted to change my life and leave my past behind. Basically, I made myself do the opposite of everything I grew up doing. Down to how I spoke, erasing my accent. That wasn't easy. I had to study lots of YouTube videos and mimic others' speech patterns. Think before I spoke. Pronounce the hard vowels. Force the drawl from my voice. I trained myself—and it worked.

Except for my heart. That was the messy stuff where I always devolved into my worst instincts no matter how hard I tried. I was so desperate for a man—any man—to love me that I gave myself away wholesale, unable to resist. Major daddy issues; that much was obvious.

Not this time.

Instead, I slide out from under him—it's not easy when gripped by desire—and make him an offer he can't refuse.

"How about I use this"—I pout my lips—"to make you happy?"

Before he can respond, I slide down his body, kissing him as I go. I lift his shirt, pleased to be greeted by the six-pack abs I'd been feeling underneath it, then move down to his pants. I hover there for a moment, waiting for his implicit consent, teasing him a little.

He doesn't stop me.

I unzip and retrieve him, savoring the moment I take him into my mouth. I lick the tip of his head, so soft and already dripping. I relish the clean taste of him, faintly salty with a hint of masculine soap lingering on his skin.

I make him feel my lips, then a little teeth. He jerks and shudders. I slide him in deeper and deeper, taking it all.

He throbs and moans with desire.

That's my signal to keep going, faster, harder, feeling his desire build to a crescendo and explode, then sucking down every last drop of him. I swallow everything like expensive champagne.

"Wow, that was . . ." he stammers.

I slip to the bathroom and rinse my mouth for his benefit.

"Mind-blowing?" I provide, sliding back into the bed and kissing him, slowly and sensually.

He nods, dazed. "That's the word I was searching for."

I let that linger for a long moment, before giving him a sexy smile and parting my lips.

"Imagine what the rest will be like."

CHAPTER SEVEN

AFTER

MORGAN

I reach into my pocket, grabbing for my phone, but come up empty.

Shit, it's still being held hostage.

My gaze returns to the floor-to-ceiling windows in my designated room in our cliffside cabin. The mountains stare back at me with their sharp, imposing peaks caked in fresh snow. I shudder deeply at the sense of isolation. I know I should feel free, released from the clutches of the busy city, but instead I feel trapped. Deprived of my biggest addiction after Noah—my phone.

I barely recognize myself. Instead of embracing the sense of adventure and danger—the wildness of pushing boundaries—that used to fuel me, I'm standing here shaking like a leaf at the sight of these steep mountains. I press my forehead to the glass, feeling the cold bite into my tender skin, peering down the sheer cliffside plunging away from our cabin. At the bottom, jagged rocks reach up as if waiting for a victim. It would be such an easy way to die. An intrusive thought rips through my neural synapses, daring me.

Do it. Throw yourself over.

I jerk back from the window, catching my thoughts tempting me to the dark abyss that has haunted me since our breakup. I back away from the edge, my breath hitching in my throat.

My room looks like something out of *Architectural Digest*, boho and tasteful with demure colors and a little cultural flavor, but nothing to take away from the real star of the show—the killer view. The clouds overhead look like they're thickening, preparing for another storm.

I remember the hunter's warning of a blizzard coming, but I shake it off. This place is built to withstand the weather, I reassure myself, remembering what Guru Shava said earlier. That's part of the charm. The remoteness and the steely beauty of winter's frigid bounty.

I turn away from the windows and run my hand over the high thread-count bedding encasing the king-sized bed. The private bathroom off my room is chic and high-end with warm wood paneling lining the ceiling and a clawfoot tub perched by those same floor-to-ceiling windows overlooking the cliffside and the snowy mountains.

I can hear Hannah and Mia settling into their rooms on the other side of the cabin.

"Bitch, you ready to *namaste*?"

"Slay!" Hannah says back.

Their snarky laughter and banter echoes through our cozy cabin. But I don't feel like joining them. For the millionth time, I wish I had my phone back and actual service.

How will I know if he tries to text me and beg for me to get back with him?

The same question echoes on repeat with the same terrible answer.

It's been three weeks. If he hasn't texted you back by now . . .

Jealousy ripples through me, bringing heat to my cheeks. He's probably already moved on. I know how Noah is, how insatiable he can be when he wants something. He's probably with *her.*

I picture them together as a couple, feeling nausea rising, the bile singeing my throat. I swallow hard against it.

My fingers twitch for my phone again on automatic reflex. I remember what Guru Shava said about how digital detoxing has real symptoms. She was right about that.

How many times do I normally check it a day? A hundred? A thousand? Probably more since the breakup.

A sign stares at me accusingly, posted on the wall in my room.

DISCONNECT TO RECONNECT

No cell phones or electronic devices
Please respect our tech-free zone
Violators will be banned from the premises immediately!
—The Namaste Center

My stomach drops.

I have a secret, one that could get me thrown out.

What my friends don't know is that I downloaded some of my favorite true crime podcasts on my phone and snuck in my AirPods, just in case, so, I can listen to them offline.

I don't know why, but stories about serial killers narrated in a soothing voice relax me. Maybe it's because they make me aware that other people have it way worse than me. You could be the victim of a heinous crime, or your husband could be a murderer with bodies buried in your cellar, while you live your life upstairs, totally unaware of the darkness that lurks beneath the very foundations of your seemingly perfect marriage.

How easy it is to slip from a normal—even mundane—life into one filled with murder and other atrocities, like Alice falling down the rabbit hole.

How quickly it can all slip away.

That thought chills me and threatens to shatter my facade.

I distract myself by flipping through the welcome packet, wincing at the schedule that's packed with yoga and meditation and, worse, more yoga and meditation—on repeat.

I've always detested yoga. I've tried, hopping from trendy studio to studio, faking my way through sun salutations and hyperventilating breaths of fire, trying not to watch the clock, waiting for the boring torture sessions to end and release me from my purgatory.

I need heart-pumping, sweaty cardio, which is why I do kickboxing. Something so intense and all-consuming that requires total concentration, so it blocks out all my thoughts, self-doubt, and especially . . .

My memories.

The ones I've worked so hard to erase—and the past I've tried to escape.

That's why I downloaded those podcasts in preparation for this retreat. If I get too bored, I can always slip the AirPods in and cover them with my hair, covertly listening to the podcasts while I go through the motions, contorting my body into various poses and chanting *Namaste.*

I have to get my phone from Mia's bag. I can't just ask for it back. That would trigger her suspicions, plus an endless deluge of questions.

Ones that I wouldn't want to answer. My eyes dart back to the sign again.

Violators will be banned from the premises immediately!

I swallow hard. Getting kicked out of here would ruin the week. Worse, Hannah's VIP client might even find out. It could hurt her at work. Frustration courses through me, but there's nothing I can do about it now.

I toss the welcome packet aside, which also includes a leather-bound journal—*ugh, boring*—and unpack, shoving my slew of trendy athleisure wear into the cedar drawers, inhaling the woodsy scent. It tickles my nose, making me sneeze fiercely. I reach the bottom of my bag, where plastic wrappers crinkle under my touch. It's a treasure trove of snacks I pillaged from the samples closet at work—just in case. Glorified candy bars marketed as "healthy" protein bars or chips from our clients' various wellness brands. Hannah mentioned the raw juice cleanse, so I panicked and decided I needed a backup plan to survive being deprived of solid food.

Ugh, kill me now.

I change into a loungewear set—creamy white organic cotton with a crop top—and observe myself in the mirror. The white helps, but I still look washed out with dark circles under my eyes. Thin, tiny blood capillaries remain ruptured from the weeks of crying my eyes out. My cheeks look gaunt, hollowed out. I should force something down, but I can't stomach it.

On the upside, the breakup diet has done its job. Under the crop top, my belly looks concave with my ribs poking out. People pay good money for this kind of weight loss, I remind myself. Still, I'd give anything to reverse it and go back.

But time only moves one way, and each tick of the second hand carries me farther and farther away from him.

By the time I'm unpacked, the sun is already sinking below the mountains, casting our cabin into blue-tinged shadows. I feel another shudder, crossing my arms against the coming darkness. A sharp whistle emerges from the living area, and I step out of my room.

"Want some detox tea?" Mia calls from the kitchenette. "Not sure what that means, but I'm hoping *weight loss*."

"Please, you don't have an extra ounce of body fat on you," Hannah says, coming out specifically to roll her eyes.

We both slide onto the sectional, sinking into the buttery leather.

"You even had someone else's fat *injected* into your ass because it was so bony," Hannah goes on, flipping through the thick welcome packet.

Mia saunters in and wiggles her butt. "Yeah, and it was painful. Three months of no sitting! I had to get a standing desk for work, but it was worth it."

"So, beauty is pain?" I quip, though I have to admit, her figure is perfect—part genetics, part cutting-edge science.

"And money," Mia says. "Don't forget that part. Why do you think I bust my ass at a tech start-up? Pun intended," she adds for good measure.

We all giggle as she goes back into the kitchenette to pour boiling water into three ceramic mugs with tea bags. The astringent, herbaceous aroma fills the air. She hands us each a steaming mug and continues her lecture.

"Hey, laugh at your own risk. You think I'm kidding? The city is full of girls—hotter and younger ones—just waiting to pounce on my man."

"Wait, this is *Grant* we're talking about?" Hannah raises her eyebrows. "Please, he's hopelessly in love with you. He has been since freshman year. Plus, he's not exactly a specimen of male physique with his emerging dad bod."

"Yeah, and he proposed to you," I point out. "That means he's committed."

Mia shakes her head. "Mark my words. None of us can afford to grow complacent in our relationships. Men's dating currency only goes up proportionate to their age and income, while we're basically the exact opposite. Trust me, I plotted it on a grid once for a case study in my sociology class."

"You're barely in your mid-twenties," Hannah points out, tossing her curls over her shoulder. "And with medical interventions, I'm pretty sure you're always gonna look that way."

"Age may be a number," Mia agrees, "but men always know they can trade up. Or in this case, trade *down*, to someone younger, fresh-faced, easier to impress, and with better-functioning ovaries."

Mia perches on the sofa next to us, delicately sipping her tea. Her crop top displays her flat, rock-hard abs.

"You really think it's that simple?" I say, frowning. "Grant *loves* you. That has to count for something, right?"

Mia snorts. "Love? That's only a tiny part of the relationship equation."

"Like Morgan said, he *freaking* proposed to you," Hannah says. "With a giant rock. Same as Tyler. Our guys aren't like that."

"Yeah, well that's why we have to lock them down now," Mia goes on, sipping her tea. "While we still can. Even this rock isn't a guarantee. Women outnumber men in New York City. That's not conjecture; it's pure math."

"So, you're saying the odds are stacked against us from birth?" Hannah says, accepting her mug and sipping from it. "Maybe even conception?"

Mia nods. "Exactly. And it's our job to keep up and compete. I'm not giving him any reasons to stray . . ." She catches herself.

The room grows tense. Hannah shoots her a look. "Sorry, Morgan."

"Oh, it's fine," I say, taking a hasty sip of the tea. It burns my tongue and tastes like lawn trimmings and dirt. But I can't help but feel the judgement wafting off them like heat.

The questions tumble through my head. If what Mia is saying is true, then was it my fault Noah strayed? Did I let myself go too much? Should I have paid for a surgeon to alter my physique like Mia? Or gone in for Botox and lip fillers?

The self-doubt assaults me. I try to hide it, but fresh tears prick my eyes.

I blink them back and pinch my arm to snap out of it. I hate feeling weak and vulnerable like this. Usually, I keep tight control of myself and my emotions. I used to consider it my superpower, but somehow he destroyed that.

Hannah clears her throat awkwardly.

"Anyway, remember the Bechdel test?" she says, trying to deflate the tension. "Enough boy talk already. This is supposed to be our retreat from all that."

"Speaking of," Mia says, looking to gossip and spill the tea, "what do you think of our guru? Those white robes and that turban? Not to mention, the dreadlocks?"

"You mean *Guru Shava*?" Hannah says. "I thought she had some great insight. And she sure fits the vibe of this place. I can see why so many people are drawn to come here."

"For real, all that talk about auras?" I chime in. "By the meditation garden? Welcome to your *rebirth*," I say in a faux serious voice, imitating the guru's tone.

We all laugh, even Hannah.

I perk up. "Oh wow, I think we did it. We passed the Bechdel test. We talked about a woman in a conversation with other women, without mentioning a man."

"You're right—we passed," Hannah says. "It only took us a whole day."

That provokes more laughter. We celebrate this small win for women everywhere. Our easy banter fills the air, and we joke around like old times. Some of the heaviness starts to lift off my shoulders. Finally, it starts to feel like the escape from real life that I was promised.

Suddenly, a sharp *howl* cuts through the air. The shrill, mournful sound penetrates the cabin, filling it with the dirge. We jerk our heads to the windows, peering at the purple dusk.

"What the hell was that?" I ask, feeling jumpy again.

"Sounds like a coyote," Hannah says. "You only hear one, but there's always more of them . . . lurking in wait."

"Do you think they're hunting us?" Mia asks in alarm.

The coyote howls again, bringing goose bumps to my skin. I remind myself that even if it is hunting, it's not hunting us. We're too big of prey for it, and we're safe inside this cabin.

"Did you see our wake-up time?" Hannah says, pointing to her welcome packet.

"Ugh, six a.m.," Mia groans, reading the schedule. "Juice cleanse at seven, then orientation after that. Forget about your beauty rest. At least meditation is like a glorified nap."

"You can say that again," I say, but still, my stomach sinks.

The list of activities doesn't reassure me. Plus, the dreaded *no phone* rule. How am I going to survive and not die of boredom?

"The whole point is to try something new," Hannah says. "And clear out all that old, stagnant energy. Right?"

"And be reborn," Mia adds. "Forget the past, and especially . . ."

Him.

Nobody says it out loud, but his name hangs over us like a ghost haunting me.

As Hannah and Mia talk excitedly about the Namaste Center's offerings, I can't break it to them that this retreat isn't working. The silence and off-the-grid experience means only that my demons are louder than ever.

And I can't seem to shake them.

As darkness envelops the mountains and our early wake-up looms, we retire to our rooms to sleep. But sleep won't come. I thrash around in the pricey sheets. I return to the window, pressing my face to the window, staring at the frost bursts on the glass and feeling the chill sear my flesh.

Outside, the wind picks up and howls to the darkness. I shiver, watching as the snow starts to drift down, then fall harder and harder, driven into a frenzy by the wind whipping down from the mountains. *The blizzard isn't coming*, I think with a shudder. *It's already here*.

I pace against the night, the insomnia, the twitching in my brain and limbs, the sleep that won't come. Finally, I lie back down and fall asleep to broken dreams. They splinter into terrible nightmares, amplified by the wind barreling past our cabin and blasting it with heavy snowfall. Noah invades them . . . with his new girlfriend. They start kissing passionately. His arms wrap around her. I can't believe it. I scream and want to throw up. *No, how could you cheat on me?*

He turns to me and grins wickedly.

You made me do it!

His face contorts into my father's visage, morphing and shifting. His flesh is bloated and purple. His bulbous, bloodshot eyes protrude out. He raises his hand to strike me.

I'm frozen, unable to move.

I try to count to ten like I did when I was little—*one, two, three*—waiting for the violence and screaming and glass shattering to stop. But he always finds me hiding in the closet. His hands wrap around my neck and squeeze tighter.

I claw at his hands. I can't breathe. Stars dance in my vision. I'm about to black out, but his enraged voice rips through my brain.

"Morgan, you DID this to me!"

CHAPTER EIGHT

BEFORE

NOAH

Morgan did this to me, I think, lying back against my silken pillows.

I marvel at how completely she took me over, leaving me breathless and spent. Didn't even spend the night. I played my hand. My best date, which always works—private chef, my father's building, my penthouse apartment, the whole city spilling out before us.

Like I own it.

It's always worked. They've never resisted; never left me without succumbing to my seductions.

And her last words . . .

Imagine what the rest will be like.

I groan, hardening again even though I recently spilled everything into her throat. The silk sheets slide under me, completely unsullied. Not only did she resist letting me inside her, but she left me . . . alone.

My head spins. She tried to avoid our first date altogether, even risking injury. On our second date, she refrained from asking me anything about myself. I know she noticed the private car and driver, the behind-the-scenes zoo experience that could only be the result of favors being called in and major donor money, and the penthouse. Not to mention, the private chef.

Yet she committed to the blind date experiment. Refrained from asking. She doesn't even know my last name, despite the fact it's emblazoned on the building—Barron Tower. Everybody in the city knows about my father.

I don't know her last name either. I've also refrained from asking her anything. I enjoy figuring her out, playing with her, toying even. I picked her up after work, but she made me meet her at a coffee shop on a busy street corner, rather than letting me learn what company she works for.

I know I could hire someone to track her down. I've certainly done it before.

But where's the fun in that?

I like the game. The nature of the hunt. Chasing her down, wrestling her wildness into submission, even if she won't let me claim her yet. I keep playing with her, using all the tricks I've deployed in past relationships that have never, not once, failed me.

But the more I do, the more she resists and—even more surprising—gives it right back. Like what happened tonight. I'm seducing her, but really she's seducing me.

I groan again, squeezing the sheets between my frustrated fists. I know most guys would be happy, thrilled even, with getting the best head of their lives, but not me. I want more.

I want everything.

And I hate being denied. I want to break her into submission, make her mine so fully she would never think to leave me, no matter what happens. Maybe I learned that from my father, who's never found something he doesn't want to own and put his name on.

Daddy issues.

I've been psychoanalyzed to pieces since I was a child. Diagnoses have been thrown out like confetti. *Antisocial personality disorder. Sociopath.* But they're just labels that mean one thing in this city: I'm successful.

Like my father.

I realized I was smarter than those doctors with fancy degrees on their walls. I could manipulate them back. Convince them I was . . . normal. Precocious even. Caring and empathetic. Make them doubt their initial findings. I always knew I was different. That the things that hold most people back don't affect me. But as I lie here in my bed, something else surprises me.

Morgan.

She's different too.

Maybe more like me than I realized. The One has an impressive algorithm. For once, I might have met my match. My rival even.

She doesn't come from New York City though. As much as she pretends to fit in, her outsider status sticks to her. Most people would miss that and fall for her act. It's pretty flawless, sociopathic even. Shedding who you really are? Morphing into somebody else? That takes a certain talent. Most people couldn't begin to pull it off. I'm sure those doctors could diagnose her with all kinds of colorful labels.

She's got secrets. I know because I have them too. Dark ones that I hide.

That turns me on.

I throb against the sheets. It's driving me so crazy, I have to relieve myself again until I explode, thinking of her lips and the way she took all of me. I think of the lions devouring their prey, tearing it apart with their sharp canines, the blood soaking their fur. How her hand tightened around mine in anticipation. She was getting off on it too. More than she wanted to admit.

Desire rushes through me again. A heady rush of blood that makes me dizzy. Despite my recent efforts, clearly I can't satiate myself on my own lust.

Ugh, I hate being out of control like this.

Breathless and flushed, I reach for my phone and tap out one message.

NOAH: *What did you do to me? xx*

Little texting dots appear below my message, but then they vanish. She left me on read. I can't believe it—she's still playing games. Toying with me. Making me wait. Fuck, I hate waiting.

But I love the game.

And I know I'll keep playing.

The next day, when she still hasn't texted me back, I'm unable to focus on anything at work.

My thoughts keep drifting back to her. Obsessively so.

That second date. I can't shake her. It might sound creepy, but I didn't even shower. I didn't want to erase her imprint on me, her smell from my skin.

Still, my phone refused to chime, my frustration edging and peaking. Was it out of range? Drained of batteries? No, it was because of her. Morgan was making me wait.

"Earth to Noah. Come in, Noah," Roger says, pulling me out of my downward spiral.

I grind my teeth. Force myself to set it aside and engage with the real world.

"Whoa, it's gotta be that girl that's got him so distracted, right?" Blake peeks into my cubicle, studying my face. "What else could it be?"

"Yeah, and he's been like this all day," Roger says, scooting his chair closer.

They crowd my cubicle. The morning hustle and bustle of the office has died down into the afternoon slump, when everyone raids the espresso machine and tries to power through until they're freed from the daily grind. My computer screen flashes as the markets tick up and down, forming a jagged line. But I can barely pay attention. Clearly, my coworkers have noticed.

Unlike them, I don't really face any repercussions for slacking off.

And I am today. Mightily.

"For real, can't a guy get some privacy around here?" I grumble, annoyed at their intrusive questions. Plus, I hate showing weakness—of any kind—and Morgan is making me feel exactly the thing I hate the most.

Being out of control.

"Is it the girl you matched with on the One?" Roger asks with a frown. "Or have you already conquered her and moved on? What are we calling her? We need details."

"Yeah, bro. I'm married with a newborn, which means devoid of a sex life," Blake chimes in. "I live vicariously through you and your philandering ways. Stop holding back."

"Yeah, spill it already," Roger says in a hushed voice. "I'm seeing that Brazilian esthetician who fucks like a goddamned tiger, and I still can't touch your dating exploits."

They know me too well.

"Fine, it's her." I let out a frustrated sigh. "And if you must know, her name is Morgan."

"Wait, she has an actual name?" Blake says in surprise. "That you're willing to tell us?"

"Yeah, not some nickname," Roger says. "Like European Model Girl. Uptown MILF Divorcee. Bisexual Hipster from Vassar. Didn't you have a threesome with her and her lesbian roommate?"

"Guess she wasn't that committed to being a lesbian," Blake says with a leering smile. "Let's see, my recent favorite has gotta be Sorority Girl with the Freckles. Why are freckles so damn hot? Or this classic from a few years back: *Wannabe Actress Destined for Michael Bay's Casting Couch.*"

I throw up my hands in exasperation. Hearing my sex life regurgitated back at me does sound pretty bad.

But Morgan is different.

And I'm gonna be different this time.

"Enough already!" I mutter. "Yes, this one has an *actual* name. Now, get out of my cubicle. I'm not giving you any more sordid details. You'll just have to use your overactive imaginations."

"Oh, come on, please," Blake begs. "Zero sex life. Take pity on me."

"No, stop being a total perv," I say with a sharp frown. "This girl is off-limits."

They exchange a look.

"No shit," Roger says in a shocked voice. "Sure you're feeling okay?"

"Yeah, like are you feverish?" Blake adds. "Coming down with something?"

"I'm fine!" I snap back. "It's not that serious yet. We've had two dates. That's normal. More than normal . . ."

"Not for you," Roger says. "After a second date, if it even gets that far, you're either bored out of your skull, or you've already conquered them, and you're ready for the next hunt."

That's when my phone goes off.

The screen shows—

"MORGAN."

I feel a jolt. I can't help myself. I click it open right away with sweaty hands.

MORGAN: *Still thinking about me?*

Frustration courses through me, because I hate that she's right. I am still thinking about her. Hell, she's the *only* thing I'm thinking about since she left me on that bed, sweaty and drained but still wanting more. It's like she took a part of me with her when she sauntered out of my apartment.

Most girls can't keep my interest, especially after they succumb to my charms. My friends aren't wrong about me and my philandering ways. But maybe it's also because I have options. This city is full of girls, young and more than willing.

Put simply, I don't want to fuck it up. And when things like money and power and my family get involved, it always ends badly. I push that thought away.

I'm not letting it happen again.

I compose myself, willing my heart rate to slow down and my brain to regain control before I write back. My fingers fly over the screen.

NOAH: *You already know the answer to that, don't you? The real question is . . . are you still thinking about me? Don't lie, Morgan.*

MORGAN: *Giving me orders already?*

NOAH: *Yes, and you like it. Admit it.*

MORGAN: *Hypothetically, let's say I do like it. What's my next command?*

NOAH: *Meet me tonight. Don't say no.*

MORGAN: *I'll agree to the first part. I can't promise the second part.*

NOAH: *Ugh, you're teasing me.*

MORGAN: *And you like it. Admit it.*

NOAH: *No, I don't. You should know me better. I hate not knowing the answers.*

MORGAN: *That's why it's good for you. You'll just have to wait and find out.*

NOAH: *Fine, it's a date.*

Blake and Roger spy on me, leaning over the cubicle divider. I try to hide my screen from them, but not before they glimpse the text exchange. I should've waited for them to leave before writing back, but I was too impatient, needing to read her message right away.

"Holy shit," Blake whispers. "He saved her name in his phone."

"Dude, and he has a heart emoji next to it," Roger adds. "A *red* one."

He picks up his headset in his cubicle and starts dialing the phone.

"What are you doing?" I ask suspiciously.

He mutes his headset and replies while waiting for someone to answer his call. "If the One paired you with someone you actually *like*, I need to tip off my contacts to double their IPO shares. This shit is a goldmine."

"You know, that's not technically legal," I say, just to tease him. Bankers like us don't play by the rules. Hell, the whole city basically runs on insider trading tips.

"My whole career was built on *technicalities*," Roger quips. "Plus, the government is in on it, too. They're not coming after us, or they'd bite the hand that feeds them. How do you think a senator making government cheese becomes worth hundreds of millions of dollars?"

"Grease enough wheels, they turn a blind eye," Blake says, then lowers his voice. "Can I get in on it? At this rate, that algorithm is gonna give us both an early retirement."

I roll my eyes. Hard. "I'm one user—not exactly a scientific case study."

"That's where you're wrong," Roger says. "Look, I knew there was something to this blind date concept. I just didn't realize how great it was."

"Yeah, keep us posted," Blake agrees. "If it goes past a third date, you're right. We're gonna be as rich as the guy with his name on the company."

They both laugh, then get to work on using back channels to secure the IPO shares.

I shake my head, but I can't deny it. They're right. While this isn't the first time a woman has caught my interest, it's been a long time. So long, I thought I might never find it again.

Memories swirl up. There was one girl in my past who hooked me this way. But I don't like to think about her anymore. Our breakup devastated me—took me down bad—and probably accounts for my recent string of conquests. As far as I'm concerned, she's dead and buried. It's not worth dredging up the past. Especially when it's painful.

But this time is different. I won't make the same mistakes again. At least, that's what I tell myself. Even though it's possible that I'm already going down the same dark path. The one that nearly destroyed me.

And I'm helpless to stop it.

CHAPTER NINE

AFTER

MORGAN

"No, you're dead! I saw you die!"

I wake from my nightmare, breathless and sweaty, the alarm by my bed blaring. I smack it off and try to untangle myself from the sheets. It's like I was fighting something in my sleep.

I hear footsteps, then Hannah pokes her head into my room.

"Uh, you okay? I heard you yelling."

I flinch, wondering how much she heard. My father's bloody face flashes in my memory. I blink to force it away and make myself relax.

"Just a bad dream," I say, stifling a yawn though my heart is still racing.

"The detox tea?" Mia calls out from across the cabin. "I had some crazy sex dream about one of the Skarsgårds."

"Which one?" Hannah calls back. "Alexander is swoon-worthy."

I smile. "Don't forget the younger one. He mostly plays villains, but there's something sexy about him. Did you see him in that new vampire movie? Full frontal. Totally naked."

"I wish. Bill is totally fuckable." Mia pads over and frowns. "No, I think it was the dad. Is that weird? I mean, he's the definition of a GILF."

"*Grandpa I'd Like to Fuck,*" Hannah translates for me.

We all burst out laughing.

"On the upside," I say in a self-deprecating voice, "guess I wasn't the only one having nightmares last night."

"Yeah, that's what I thought," Mia says. "More fodder for my therapist to untangle next week. Daddy issues! Like she hasn't heard that one before."

"Nah, that doesn't qualify as a nightmare," Hannah says with a wink. "If you ask me, Stellan's still got it."

That provokes more laughter.

"Time to rise and shine," Hannah says, thrusting back the heavy, blackout curtains. "I stepped outside already. Looks like a few more feet of snow fell overnight."

"Wow, the blizzard?" I say, glancing out the window. But it's still dark outside. It's *that* early. I stifle a yawn. "I think I heard it starting last night before I fell asleep."

"You can say that again," Mia agrees. "A few feet? That's like a major snow event. I bet the roads are impassable now. Good thing we made it in yesterday."

"How are we going to make it back to the main lodge?" I ask, secretly hoping for a literal snow day and a reprieve from cleansing and yoga and whatever boring stuff is happening today.

"Oh, no worries about that," Hannah says, dashing my hopes. "Looks like those silent apprentices were already up and shoveled the walkways. The path to the lodge is cleared."

"Guru Shava runs a tight ship," Mia says. "That's impressive."

"Right. That's great news," I force out, feeling my hopes of staying in bed and relaxing today deflate. I'm groggy and tired from my broken sleep. Not to mention, I feel a little bit unsettled at the prospect of being trapped here with blocked roads.

But then Hannah whips us into shape, clapping her hands. "You saw the schedule. Orientation starts at seven. We gotta get down there. I don't want to make a bad impression on Guru Shava."

"Ha, 'cause you're the teacher's pet already," Mia says. "Just like back at boarding school."

"Don't forget college," I add with a knowing look. "She was always at the professor's office hours to clinch her solid 4.0 GPA."

"I can't help it if my aura is purple," Hannah says. "Or emerald. Or whatever the hell she said yesterday."

With that, they both leave me alone. I run one hand through my matted hair, feeling slightly better. I wasn't the only one having nightmares last night, even if the verdict is still out about whether Mia's sex dream qualifies. Outside my window, it's still mostly dark out, but the skies foretell of its advent, lightening at the horizon.

I take a deep breath—the kind that seems yoga-approved—and force myself from bed. I tell myself nice things as I slide into a new matching set of yoga clothes. That today will be different. That it's the first day of the rest of my life. My post-Noah life. One where I'm a strong and independent woman again.

Like I was *pre* Noah. The person I'd worked hard to become, shedding my old skin like a snake. I thought I'd left the scared little girl behind, along with everything else from my past. But I was wrong.

So very wrong.

Noah resuscitated that little girl when I wasn't looking, wrenching her body out of the past, then destroying her when he cheated on me. But she's not dead; just hiding and lying in wait.

I won't let him win—I'm stronger than him. And I'm going to prove it.

"Uh, is that for me?"

A woman holds out a bamboo tray with a mason jar filled with a thick, greenish-brownish muck, a single glass straw sticking out from it. The woman, wearing a white turban and long flowing robes, smiles and nods.

But she doesn't speak.

"Vow of silence, remember?" Hannah says, sliding up behind me and startling me.

She's already clutching one of the smoothies. Mia hurries up, holding her mason jar. She grins, and her front teeth are stained the same greenish-brown color as the drink.

"It's our juice cleanse," Mia says, slurping hard at the liquid slop.

"Oh, right." I grab the mason jar, watching the apprentice retreat with a soft swishing of her white robes.

My stomach turns as I peer down at the unappetizing sludge in my glass. It's so thick, the straw basically stands up on its own.

Mia follows my gaze.

"The taste is . . . well . . . just force it down. Beauty is pain, remember? The diet here is no solid foods for a week."

"Is that healthy?" I ask apprehensively, feeling my stomach rebel.

"More than safe," Mia says, slurping more down. Her jar is half empty. "I've done a month-long cleanse before. I got a little lightheaded, but it was worth it."

"According to the welcome packet," Hannah adds, "their raw juice program was developed by a top nutritionist to optimize detoxing."

"You know, get all the toxins out," Mia says. "The world is super toxic now. Microplastics. Chemicals. Food dyes."

"Just pretend it's Jungle Juice," Hannah whispers, nudging me. "You know, like freshman year?"

Mia snorts a laugh.

"'Juice' was false advertising. That stuff was pure booze. You just had to hold your nose and force it down."

"Yeah, you looked so lost at the frat party," Hannah agrees with a wink. "We simply had to rescue you."

I remember the three of us having this exact conversation the first time we met, after I had made the mistake of accepting a red SOLO Cup from a fraternity brother, then gagging at my first sip. My eyes watered and burned from the gasoline-level fumes wafting up from the syrupy, pink contents. Barnard was an all-girls college, so the real parties took place across the street at Columbia. I'd thought that a frat party would be the key to manifesting some sort of social life and starting to establish my new identity.

But I was a fish out of water, awkward and clumsy.

It was our first week at Barnard, and we were all freshmen, but because I hadn't gone to the same private boarding schools as everyone else, I didn't know anyone.

This was my first frat party. Most the boys, including the pledges, had gone to their boarding school, too. Mia and Hannah scooted up to me.

"You're new here," Mia said matter-of-factly. "We don't know you."

"Yeah, where did *you* come from?" Hannah said suspiciously, as if not growing up in New York City (their version) meant you came from another planet. But Barnard was full of kids like them, heralding from wealthy families and propelled through elite boarding schools that fed into college admissions. Feeder schools, they were called.

I'd finagled my way in on a scholarship, lucky that my test scores spoke to my acceptability, though I'd had to doctor my high school transcript a bit. It helped that I came from a poor town. *Dirt* poor. *Trailer park* poor. Not the kind of place where Barnard admissions officers sent representatives or recruiters. That made it easy to slip past them.

Luckily, I was deemed a diversity case, not because of my sexual orientation, gender, or ethnicity—but because kids like me didn't apply to Barnard. The truth about most of the diversity cases was that they came from rich families, too. However, I was deemed *socioeconomically* disadvantaged, which made me the rarest type of charity case at college.

But that's the quiet part, that's never said out loud.

However, one look at Hannah and Mia told me I needed to be careful how much I revealed, lest I repulse them. But I was prepared for this very moment. I'd rehearsed it in front of the hall bathroom mirror late at night, when nobody else was listening, mouthing the words until they sounded authentic. Until I believed them, too. It's not a lie—if you believe it.

I had a cover story concocted—how my father was in the diplomatic service, so I grew up abroad, moving from European city to city, attending American schools. I tossed out a few names I'd Googled, enough to make it sound impressive and varied.

Then I forced my expression to cave in. "But they . . . died."

Mia and Hannah gave me the perfect O-shaped looks, their mouths puckering like exotic fish trapped in a tank.

"You poor thing," Hannah said.

"How did it happen?" Mia gasped, putting her hand to her chest.

They both peered at me with pity.

"It was a car crash," I said, wiping away tears. "In Germany. You know, the autobahn? There's no speed limit . . ." I trailed off, choking up.

I knew about lying. The less you said, the better. Keep it simple, including killing off my parents like that. They were both dead. That was true. I was just fudging the *how*.

"No parents?" Hannah looped her arm through mine, steering me away from the drink line. "Sounds like we need to adopt you. What do you think?"

"Sign me up," Mia said, taking ahold of my other arm. "I'm getting a little tired of your stories," she said to Hannah. "We could use some fresh blood around our dorm room."

I had to look forlorn—every bit the pitiful case they believed me to be—but inside I was beaming. Their expensive jewelry and designer clothes and shoes gave them away. They were exactly the kind of people I needed to befriend to pull off the switch to my new life.

And they were right. They hadn't seen me around before. But now that I had arrived, they weren't getting rid of me. I'd make sure of that.

As the party unfolded around us, we were attached at the hip. Everything got blurry, the Jungle Juice doing its job.

Mia refilled my cup, handing it back to me. "Drink enough of that—and you won't remember anything tomorrow."

She was right . . .

The jungle juice did a good job of wiping away my bad memories. Just not the ones they thought haunted me. Those lies about my parents were invented, made-up. The real memories were so much worse.

"Morgan . . . Earth to Morgan?"

I jerk out of my memory. My half-drunk smoothie stares back at me.

I don't know if I can force the rest down. I take another big slurp, trying to finish it off, but the thick liquid lodges in my throat, and I can't breathe.

I feel my dad's hands on my throat again.

Morgan, you DID this to me!

The words from my nightmare reverberate through my head again, bringing a healthy shot of adrenaline. I wince, then frown and rub my eyes. I try to snap back to the present.

"Sorry, I think I'm still half asleep."

I shake my head to clear the tangles, hoping to dislodge the nightmare.

"Yeah, I never sleep well my first night in a new place," Mia says. "No matter how comfy the bed is. That early wake-up call didn't help matters. Plus, the blizzard all night."

"You can say that again," I reply. "I tossed and turned all night."

"Did you hear the coyotes?" Hannah says. "They were howling and yipping all night."

Now that she mentions it, I do recall their mournful cries piercing my sleep. Goose bumps rise all over my skin at how isolated we are from civilization—and how close to predators we are.

Hannah looks at my half-drunk mason jar and frowns.

"Morgan, you didn't finish your smoothie! It's the key part of the center's detox cleanse."

"Yeah, and I don't think I can," I say, my stomach churning and rebelling against the liquid. I suppress the urge to gag. Since the breakup, my appetite has evaporated.

"Remember what Hannah said," Mia adds. "Just pretend it's Jungle Juice."

"Exactly," Hannah says, raising her ginger shot in a toast. "Bottoms up, ladies!"

I follow her lead, downing the rest of the horrid concoction. And it works. The sludge glides down my throat, bypassing my taste buds. They both down their ginger shots, then we share that same secret smile, the one that started at that first frat party freshman year and bonded us together.

Our little threesome.

Before their boyfriends came between us, fracturing us apart and leaving me as the fifth wheel. I thought those days were gone when I met Noah, but I was wrong.

Other guests filter into the reception area, a great hall that's all warm, paneled wood, including the ceiling, and floor-to-ceiling windows. There's not even much artwork, just tasteful boho accents like ceramic vases glazed in natural earthy tones, cream-colored handmade weavings strung up across the walls, and sea-bleached driftwood arrangements tangled together, even though we're far from any beaches.

The apprentices wander among us, trading glances and remaining silent.

It's a bit unnerving, the idea of giving up your voice for a spiritual leader.

It reminds me of *The Little Mermaid.* Only she didn't give up her voice willingly. She was coerced into giving up her voice by a sea witch after falling in insta-love with a mysterious prince from land who she basically sacrificed her whole life for.

I always thought the story was more tragedy than fairy tale, and not suited for young girls. A cautionary tale about how falling in love can lead you astray, making you give up everything for a dark, handsome stranger you barely know.

I thought I knew Noah. I thought I was safe. I thought I'd protected my heart from breaking. But how well can you really know a person?

A voice snaps me out of my morbid thoughts. Shit, I'm ruminating again.

I turn to my friends.

"Look, don't you recognize her?" Hannah says, hissing into my ear.

She points across the room at a middle-aged woman in yoga gear. We're all basically dressed in some version of the same thing. Some have more flowy pants, some tighter. But it's all designer athleisure wear, mass-produced in China, made from synthetic fibers, and marked up for the American consumer.

The woman stands with a friend. They must share the same plastic surgeons with their tasteful eye lifts and a healthy dose of Botox and filler. They look older, but their skin is unnaturally smoothed out like porcelain dolls.

I squint at her face. "Yeah, she looks vaguely familiar," I murmur, trying to place the woman. "But who is she?"

"She's that DA. Barbara Richmond," Hannah says. "Her face has been slapped all over the papers lately. She's the one prosecuting the former mayor. The one accused of money laundering through his charity."

"And sexual assault," Mia adds. "Don't forget, he likes to grope women."

"Oh right," I say, realizing I do recognize her. It's just disorienting seeing her out of context—and without her signature designer pantsuit.

"No wonder she needs a retreat," Hannah says. "Her job must be super stressful. I read she gets death threats."

"His voters are the worst," Mia agrees. "I can't believe they support a felon—and worse, a sexual assaulter."

"This retreat is probably just what she needs to regroup so she can focus on her case," I say, noticing the way her face looks haggard, despite the work she's clearly had done.

The silent apprentices are circulating around again, handing out shots of a bright orange concoction to the guests. But still no sign of Guru Shava.

"Wow, turmeric shots," Mia says after grabbing one from the tray and downing it. I follow suit, grateful these are much tastier than the sludge.

"Oh, and look over there," Hannah whispers and points to a younger woman standing next to the DA.

There are about fifteen of us assembled now in the Great Hall, but this girl can't be missed. She has a quirky vibe with her patchwork quilted pants that flare out at the ankles and a flouncy, bedazzled crop top that shows off her midriff.

"Oh wow, it's Dame Tremaine," I gasp, truly star-struck for once.

She's the newest pop star sensation on every radio station and playlist, catapulting up the charts with her queer love ballads and upbeat dance tracks. She's famous for emulating drag queens at her elaborate concerts and festivals, which has made her pretty controversial. She gets criticized for appropriating queer identity from one side and for indoctrinating youth from the other side, so she can't win.

I study her impossibly smooth pale skin, powdered to look even paler, but still detecting the dark circles under her eyes the makeup can't fully camouflage. Her stomach is hollowed out, and she bears faint scars on her wrists.

Cutting.

Mental health rumors have been swirling around since she canceled several high-profile tour dates, and her fans didn't get refunds. Celebrity gossip articles, along with their angry posts, invaded my social media feed even though I don't really follow her.

"Remember how she canceled all those big festival dates?" I whisper, dredging up the TMZ updates I breezed through in my social media feed.

"Totally, I read she was checking into a rehab center," Mia says. "Guess she wanted to try something different."

"Like namaste and slay?" I repeat our catchphrase while studying the star.

Dame Tremaine has two friends with her dressed in gender-ambiguous clothes. The first one is Black and short with curly hair that's bleached white, while the other is the opposite, white with pale, almost translucent, skin and hair dyed jet-black.

"Maybe you can give her one of your client's shirts," Mia suggests. "Product placement at its finest. Their brand would go viral overnight if Dame Tremaine got photographed in it."

"That's true," I say, even though it makes me cringe.

"No way! You can't do that," Hannah says. "They're here to be just like us."

"What does that mean?" Mia asks.

"Normal. Like a civilian. Not famous." Hannah rolls her eyes. "Plus, that would violate the Namaste Center's rules."

"What rule?" I say, sipping at another turmeric shot I snagged from a passing tray but trying to watch the pop star out of the corner of my eye.

I realize we're all doing the same thing. Trying to look uninterested, even feigning boredom, while scoping out the other notable guests at the retreat this week, our eyes slanted in their direction, while our heads tilt the other way. Looking but not looking.

"Privacy," Hannah whispers. "It's one of the big touchstones of how this place works. We're all anonymous here. We leave our last names, jobs, and pasts behind to be reborn."

"What happens at Namaste Center stays at Namaste Center?" I joke.

"Exactly, so don't fuck it up," Hannah says with a sharp look. "My client wasn't lying about how VIP this place is. I don't want to ruin my chances of getting invited back."

We circulate among the guests as the clock ticks closer to the golden hour when we're all supposed to be called into orientation. I stare at the heavy double doors with a large wooden beam across them, locking the room from the outside.

That's strange. Why would they need that? Although it does fit with the rustic atheist meets trendy, quasi-New Age cult themes of the place.

More guests filter in, bringing us up to about twenty people in all.

We take turns identifying the notable ones, even though it goes against the Namaste Center's rule. We can't help it, and even Hannah gets excited. We spot a rising star senator from Vermont rumored to be running for president next year on a populist far left platform that emphasizes socialism and women's rights, especially abortion. She's been holding massive rallies at college campuses.

"Velma Torres," Hannah whispers in my ear. "She went from being a college professor in Burlington to senator. They say she could be the youngest president in our country's history."

"Oh, right," I say, studying her light brown skin and long black hair pulled up into a tight, high ponytail. "I've seen her mentioned on my social media."

"Yeah, she's gorgeous, too," Mia says, nodding approvingly. "Looks like a model. And her skin? Flawless."

We also spot an aging soap opera star who got fired for accusing her boss at the studio of sexual assault, leading to hundreds of women accusing him. He's facing trial—and a hefty prison sentence—while she's taking him and the network to civil court for a big payout.

"Antonia St. John," Mia whispers in my ear. "My mom grew up watching *Emergency Room*."

"She's won like a gazillion daytime Emmy Awards," Hannah adds. "I hear she's started a movement in Hollywood to oust and destroy toxic masculinity."

"Hashtag *AllOfUs*," I say, familiar with the recent social media trend.

"Yeah, since *MeToo* failed. It's like a rebrand," Hannah quips. "Oh no!"

She clutches at her stomach. Then Mia doubles over. The detox drinks seem to hit them all at once.

"Guess the cleanse really works," I joke under my breath.

"You can say that again," Mia says, stalking off with clenched butt cheeks.

"Oh, we're cleansing alright," Hannah adds in a pained voice, following Mia to the bathroom. "You coming?"

"I'm okay . . . for now," I add ominously.

I didn't drink mine quite as fast, though my stomach gurgles, telling me that a major toilet session lies in my near future. However, I'd rather wait and tough it out. Plus, I have to spare them—and any other potential witnesses—from these dietary crimes against humanity.

I pull myself away from the crowd, drawn to the impressive windows. I peer out at the lonely, snow-laden mountains as the sun threatens to crest their peaks and spill glorious light into the valley. The view is stunning beyond any measure. No photograph could do it justice.

BANG!

Something smacks into the window, startling me.

I scream in alarm, drawing my hands to my lips to stifle it.

A raven slides down the window, leaving a thin trail of blood on the glass, before landing in the snowbank. The broken, twisted body sinks, then stains the snow dark red.

I back away in horror, turning around to realize everyone is staring at me.

All the conversation has dried up, making my heart race in mortification.

The silence in the hall is deafening. Everyone's eyes seem to have found me. This triggers my trauma, and I want nothing more than to run away. I wasn't ready for this.

One thought ricochets through my head like the bird from the window:

I have to get out of here.

CHAPTER TEN

BEFORE

MORGAN

Hannah smacks the mirror in front of my face, making it spin on its axis. The mirror is wedged in the corner of my small room over a makeshift vanity table I got off Facebook Marketplace.

"Time to confess already—who's the mystery man?"

I jerk the mirror back into place and steady it. I'm trying to apply mascara, but she grabs the mirror again, tilting it away and making me smudge mascara on my cheek. I grimace.

"He's the man I'm going on a date with, that's who," I hedge.

"Avoiding the question." She narrows her eyes. "What kind of date?"

"Uh, the *mystery* kind," I admit. "He likes to keep me in suspense. He hasn't told me yet. It's our third date."

"A third date?" Mia barges in. Our flat is big for three mid-twenty-somethings, but their parents subsidize it *heavily*. "The One must really be working!"

"I've never seen you this twisted over a guy," Hannah adds. "Third date. That means—time for us to meet him. That's the girlfriend rule."

"Exactly," Mia says. "He has to earn our stamp of approval."

"Yeah, what if we hate him?" Hannah agrees. "You'd better get the best friend meet and greet out of the way before you waste more dates on him."

I roll my eyes at them. "If I love him, then I'm sure you're gonna love him."

"Whoa, you just used the L-word." Mia blinks hard, looking concerned.

"Third date," Hannah says in a panicked voice. "That's way too soon."

"You missed the most important word—*if.* It's a dependent clause," I point out, cleaning the mascara smudge and going back in with the wand. "The girlfriend rule is to have my back."

"No matter what?" Mia says.

"Yeah, what if he's, like, a total psycho?" Hannah says. "You haven't even properly internet stalked him—"

"And I'm not going to," I cut her off. I sigh, turning to face them, mascara on only one eye. "That's the whole point of this experiment! And you should be happy—no, thrilled—that it's working. That I don't know who he is, and he doesn't know who I am."

Yet.

As much as I want to live in this fantasy forever, the real world lurks, just waiting to pop the thin, porous membrane of our protective bubble. However, I want to stave it off for as long as I can. The truth is that I'm not completely in denial; I know some things about the mystery man (that I'm not sharing with my roomies yet).

For starters, Noah is smart. Maybe even brilliant. And he's loaded. I'd have to be stupid not to notice the details that give it away. Plus, I've spent years honing my social status detectors. Part of why I let Mia and Hannah sign me up for the One is that they heard about it as a beta test that's not open to the public.

Just social elites, as Hannah put it. She heard about it from a client and scored the special invite code for me. I wouldn't have gotten in on my own.

But that also tempted me to try it. That meant the dating pool had to be of similar caliber—meaning a better shot at landing a decent guy. Also, what did I have to lose?

Nothing else was working. I'd tried all the other ways to date. Failed app matches. Friends setting me up. Going out to fancy bars and ordering a martini for myself, hoping to catch the eye of a worthy suitor.

I'm glad I tried the One. I've got a feeling that Noah is someone special. That's why I have to be careful. I know he's testing me. I'm willing to bet he can sniff it out like a drug dog. That's part of what drew him to the One, and really what drew him to me. The fact that I don't know who he really is. And that I'm not dying to find out and internet stalk him like Mia wants.

I have to hold to the experiment. Plus, the most worrying part is that I actually like him. Okay, maybe it's even more than like. But I can't say that.

Out loud.

My roomies are right about that part. I worry because it's always dangerous when my heart gets involved in anything. The stakes are much higher than if it's just my attraction or pride.

"So, I'm sticking to the *blind dating* experiment," I go on after I finish my other eye. "Because it's working."

"Fine," Hannah is forced to admit, seeing as this was all their idea.

"Keep your mystery man," Mia adds. "But when do we get to meet him?"

"Soon," I hedge, "if everything keeps going well. I don't want to jinx it . . ." I trail off.

They know my checkered dating history. How much the last ghosting incident hurt me, sending me into my room on a Netflix binge that took them weeks to pry me out of . . . and get me back to the gym and my kickboxing classes. They exchange a pointed look.

"Just be careful, okay?" Hannah says. "You never know who you're getting matched with these days."

"Yeah, could be a creep," Mia says. "Like in those podcasts you love so much."

"Well, the upside of my true crime addiction is that I know all the red flags to look for," I say, ticking them off on my fingers. "Poor family situation. Antisocial behavior. Oh, and intelligence. That's the one trait I can confirm he shares with the FBI profile. But I'll keep my eyes open."

"You spout out that list in such a calm voice," Mia shoots back. "Maybe you're the one we should be worried about, not him."

"Yeah, you seem to know a lot about this," Hannah teases me. "The FBI would have a field day with your Netflix Recently Watched. God only knows what's in your search history."

"Well, for some people, murder is calming," I say with a shrug as I put the finishing touches on my makeup. "It reminds me there are worse things out there than my problems."

"Like people getting hacked to pieces?"

Mia slashes her hand at me, making me jump back.

I grab her wrist. "Exactly."

"Fine, just find out his astrology sign at least," Mia says, yanking her hand back. "So, I can at least check your compatibility. Oh, and if he's a triple Gemini, then you gotta dump him."

"Triple Gemini?" I say, confused.

"That means his sun, rising, and moon are in one sign—the psychotic one. It's a fact that most serial killers are either Virgo or Gemini. Go figure."

"Uh, wow. That totally tracks," Hannah says. "And if they're triple?"

"*Triple* the issues," Mia says. "Just promise you'll find out for me?"

I shake my head in exasperation.

"As long as you both promise to back off. I don't want to mess this one up. I think . . . I think I really *like* him . . ." I hate being vulnerable like this, but it's the truth. They trade another look.

"It must be serious," Hannah says. "You're not kidding?"

Mia nods. "Usually you want to psychoanalyze them to death with us, picking them apart and convincing yourself why they're terrible for you. So that when they inevitably break up with you, then you don't actually get hurt."

"Even though it doesn't work," Hannah says. "And we have to pry your depressed ass out of your dark room."

"Fuck, you know me too well," I say, letting out a frustrated sigh. I can't deny it. "Am I that transparent?"

"Yup, like a window to your heart," Hannah confirms. "But this one seems different. Maybe he is the One."

"Don't worry," Mia says. "We've got your back. We both found our guys. It's your time now."

I soften, willing myself to believe their supportive words.

I check my watch, realizing it's almost seven o'clock. Date time!

Quickly, I double-check my reflection in the mirror. Hannah comes over to fluff my hair, separating my curls, while Mia adds an extra layer of her signature lip gloss.

I press my lips together, making them glisten in the late summer sunlight slanting through the windows. Soon, the sun will grow scarcer as the city turns colder, drifting into autumn and then winter's grasp.

But for now, there's warmth and light—and my heart is full of hope.

"There, *now* you're perfect," Hannah says as they stand back from me.

"Ready for your third date with the mystery man," Mia says.

I nod, summoning all my courage. My heart thumps in anticipation. A flash hits me—*his lips, his hardness, his desire*. That mixes with my curiosity and intrigue. I'm so ready for my date. Only, I don't know what we're doing—or more accurately, what Noah is planning to do to me tonight. That's when Noah's driver pulls up to our building, and my phone pings.

NOAH: *Your driver awaits.*

MORGAN: *You still haven't told me where we're going! Or what we're doing!*

NOAH: *That's why it's fun. I like keeping you in suspense this way.*

MORGAN: *Fun for you! I don't even know what to wear. Shoes, especially shoes. Come on, a hint? PRETTY PLEASE!*

NOAH: *I like it when you beg. Fine, a hint. The "mystery" is the whole point of the experience.*

MORGAN: *Riddles aren't answers. You're evading my questions.*

NOAH: *And you're stalling! The sooner you get here, the sooner all will be revealed.*

I groan out loud.

He's right. I hate it when he's right. I throw my phone in my bag and pivot, blowing air kisses at my roomies, then flying down the five flights of stairs like Cinderella with a ticking clock on my way to the ball with Prince Charming.

I just hope the fantasy doesn't end at midnight.

"This . . . is for me?"

I can't believe my eyes. The most exquisite golden dress is laid out on Noah's bed. I check the tags, then startle back. It's a major designer. Not off the rack. It's the kind of runway gown you need connections to even get a shot at buying. I've thrifted and bought secondhand enough to know the difference.

"Of course it's for you. For tonight, and the surprise."

That word again.

Surprise.

Mystery brims in my heart. I want to know. I want to claw the answer out of him. But then my heart pounds faster, reminding me that the surprise makes it more fun, more daring . . .

More everything.

Outside the sun is dimming the sky, while the city's million lights sparkle, awaiting the excitement of the night and its endless possibilities. It's Saturday, so I don't have to work tomorrow.

I gaze at Noah and feel a shudder of attraction. He opened his apartment door wearing a close-fitting tuxedo with a slim black tie. The combo set off his most attractive features, especially his eyes and cheekbones.

The first major hint of the surprise tonight. Some kind of black-tie affair. The dress being the second hint.

But I have to control myself—and control the build of our connection.

I can't fall too hard or too fast, or I risk pushing him away. The more he reveals, the more I realize he's everything I've ever wanted, ever dreamed about.

But I have to play it cool.

Noah makes a show of leaving me alone to put the dress on, vanishing into the kitchen. I hear the soft *pop* of a champagne cork. I make myself at home in his master suite, slipping into the golden dress, shocked at the fit.

The almost see-through, golden mesh fabric fits my figure like a glove. I unpin my curls and add another layer of eyeliner to darken and pop my makeup for evening. Then I turn to leave, stumbling upon a pair of gold stilettos with red bottoms nestled inside the designer's shoe box, clearly left for me.

I slide into them, rising several inches, again surprised at the perfect fit. I'm immediately suspicious.

How did he know my exact measurements and shoe size?

A soft rapping on the door draws my attention. "Come in," I murmur.

I'm standing in front of the mirrors in his bathroom. He comes up behind me, snaking his arm around me to hand me a crystal flute and kiss my neck, the delicate part that makes me shudder.

"You look like . . . *perfection*," he says, spinning me around.

The dress expands and swirls around me, then collapses and hugs my curves again. He admires me through the mirrors, getting the full 360-degree view. I can't help but marvel too. I've never looked this spectacular. The golden sheen draws the bronze out in my skin.

"Is this what you imagined it would look like on me?" I ask, unable to help it.

"Even better," he says softly. "You continue to surprise me at every turn."

I want to revel in his praise, however my natural cynicism creeps back in.

"How'd you know my measurements?" I ask him accusingly.

I'm worried he cheated on our experiment to get information. Not that I'd even know my own measurements. Everything I buy comes secondhand or from a thrift store, faking my social status, piece by piece. I've even taught myself how to clean the difficult, finicky fabrics and remove any odors from previous owners, restoring them to their original condition. But anyone with a good eye can tell. Shit, I'll bet Noah can tell . . .

The sudden insecurity grips me, but he comes over, running his hands over my body inch by inch, tracing my curves hugged tightly by the dress.

"This is how," he murmurs in my ear. "I'm a very good student when I have a subject that fascinates me. Which means I must want you, because I have an *excellent* memory."

At his touch, more chills run through me. Our recent encounter flashes in my memory. How I took him in my mouth and made him convulse with his final pleasure.

I remove his hands one by one—it's not easy—and turn to face him head-on. I give him a sexy, flirtatious smile.

"You studied me? Is that it?"

"Morgan, you are my favorite subject," he replies, matching my smile. "You should know that by now."

"Are we ready for the mystery date?" I say, gesturing to the outfits. "The formal attire. I admit, I'm curious."

"Not yet," he says, shaking his head. "We're still missing something. Wait here—and drink up. I'll get it."

I dutifully sip the champagne, watching as he leaves and enters his walk-in closet. This vintage has a slightly different, more sour taste. I frown, but take another sip, knowing it's likely to dissipate until I get used to the unusual flavor. I don't have a refined palate for vintage champagne, not like Noah does.

I quickly finish off the glass, but Noah is still riffling around in the closet. I grow fidgety, wanting more champagne, so I take a chance and enter the closet. He's in the back, digging through the top shelves, and doesn't notice me.

I take a moment to scan the room. It's a large walk-in closet with wooden floors and a leather ottoman in the center. His clothes are meticulously organized with whole sections of designer suits arranged by color and pattern.

Glassed-in shelves reveal several watches neatly arranged, almost like a store display. I recognize the designer names, but some look more exotic and expensive.

But that's not what catches my eye. Sitting on a shelf is a framed picture of him and a girl. My heart drops. I worry it's his ex, or worse, his current girlfriend. She's quite striking, exotic and gorgeous. I can't take my eyes off her. I stand there frozen. Who is she?

"Morgan, what are you doing?"

His voice sounds sharp, accusing almost. I spin around.

"Just, I'm out of bubbly . . ."

I hold up my empty flute, but his eyes are locked on the picture. His whole demeanor darkens.

"Zoe . . . my older sister."

Of course, I think, mentally cursing myself for jumping to conclusions.

It's just so hard to trust anyone. And the blind dating experiment has challenges. All the times I've been cheated on and lied to by men rush through my head.

I push them away. Noah hasn't given me any reason to doubt him.

"I'm sorry," I say, feeling bad. "I wasn't trying to snoop. She just caught my eye. She's so beautiful. You haven't mentioned a sister before."

He runs his hand through his dark curls and lets out a shaky exhale.

"Look, it's not that I didn't want to tell you about her. I just don't like to talk about it. She ran away on the day she turned eighteen. Never looked back."

"Why? What happened?"

"I don't know," he admits. "And that's the hardest part. We were close when we were kids, but as we got older, we grew apart. She's a few years older than me. I guess we didn't have the same interests anymore."

"Did you ever look for her?"

He shakes his head. "Dad wanted to hire someone, but I made him promise to let her go. It's what she wanted." Pain contorts his voice.

"I'm so sorry," I murmur back, running my hands along his back.

I hate seeing him in so much pain. It's the opposite of how he usually appears, so confident and calm. He takes me into his arms and hugs me tight against his chest.

"I just miss her so much sometimes."

"Did she leave a note?"

He shakes his head. "Nothing, she just disappeared like a ghost. She didn't even take anything with her."

My heart thumps faster at this private insight into his life. We're keeping to the blind date experiment, but little by little, pieces of us are falling into place like the tumblers in a lock slotting together. A subtle deepening of our connection. It feels more intense precisely because I don't know who he really is. I only know the parts he chooses to reveal to me.

I glance at his sister's face again. It's slightly blurry, as if she was already in the act of leaving when the picture was taken. She must have turned her head at the exact moment when the shudder snapped shut. Still, I can make out her features and clear resemblance to Noah despite his younger age in the picture.

They look similar, except where he's dark, she's lighter, with blonde hair spilling down her back. I catch the age difference now. In the picture, she looks almost eighteen. I wonder if the photo was taken right before she left.

I'm an only child, but I always wanted a sister. I used to pray for one before bed every night. That was before Momma died and Pop raged at her absence, drinking hard to fill the gaps. A full bottle of whiskey in the morning drained by nightfall.

That meant it would be a bad night.

I'd hide in the closet, steadying my breathing and trying not to make a sound. In the darkness, my face pressed to the bare floorboards,

I used to think a sister would make it more bearable. That we could hide in there together, comfort each other. But eventually, I realized something else, too. A younger sister would've become just another punching bag for his grief and rage. So, it was a blessing, I decided. And I stopped praying for a sister.

Instead, I started plotting how to escape. How to disappear completely.

How to change myself.

That's when . . . Morgan Steele was born.

I can't tell Noah any of that. Even when we finally end the experiment and come clean, my past has to stay there—dead and buried. For me, this is a double-blind experiment. A deft trick, a sleight of hand, lifting one disguise to distract from the other one that remains firmly in place, hiding my true identity.

He pulls back, glancing at his watch.

"Shit, we're running late."

"Did you find it?"

He nods, grabbing a dark mahogany box from the top shelf and lifting the lid.

I gasp when I see what it contains. Inside, nestled on purple velvet cushioning, are two masquerade masks. They're both bejeweled, studded with amber stones. The way the gems catch the light, I'm pretty sure they're real. The gold plating too.

"The final touches." He offers me the one that looks like a lioness.

I study it closer. The mask will only cover half of my face, leaving my lips exposed. He stands behind me as I place the mask over my face so he can tie the velvet straps, binding it over my features to conceal my identity. I remember what he texted me earlier.

The "mystery" is the whole point of the experience.

It all makes sense.

"A masquerade ball?" I say, adjusting the mask on my face.

"You'll see," he teases me. He hands me his mask. It's also a golden lion's face, but this one has a mane.

I tie the black velvet straps behind his head, then we turn to admire ourselves in the standing mirror in the corner. We look magnificent in our formal attire with the matching golden masks.

"The king and queen of the jungle," he murmurs in a soft voice. He looks at his watch and perks up. "Hurry, we're going to be late."

He rushes me toward the door, but I pull away, wanting to go back for my purse, but he waves me off.

"You won't need it where we're going. In fact, it's not allowed."

"Even my phone?"

"Especially your phone."

I frown as we arrive at the private elevator. Is it safe to leave it behind? Admittedly, my phone is my crutch—but also my lifeline if something goes awry on the date.

"Do you trust me?"

His eyes bore into me with intensity. My heart stutters and drops. I lick my lips and reach for his hand. He thumbs the button, pushing—

UP.

"There's a higher floor?" I ask with a questioning look. "I thought the penthouse was on the top level of the building."

He smirks. "It's the highest apartment. That's true."

The elevator arrives, and the doors whisk open. He corrals me inside. It rises another floor, spitting us onto a rooftop—with a helipad. A helicopter with a pilot awaits us. He pulls me toward it as the blades spin faster, making us duck down.

We clamber inside the cabin. I'm breathless and exhilarated, my entire body thumping with adrenaline. My mask stays firmly in place. The pilot doesn't seem surprised by our attire, and it occurs to me this isn't the first time he's witnessed this kind of odd behavior. This isn't Noah's first mysterious party.

"Hold on," Noah says, buckling me into the seat next to him. The harness grips me, but so does he, holding me tight as the blades spin faster.

I want to ask where we're going. I want more details. But I keep my mouth shut and stay in the moment as the helicopter lifts off in a rush of propulsion, making my stomach drop, and whisks us away into the night.

CHAPTER ELEVEN

AFTER

MORGAN

Everyone is staring at me, and my cheeks burn. I turn back around to peer down at the dead bird. Beady, glassy eyes. The oily black feathers slicked with blood.

I watch as it twitches, the life struggling to leave its broken body.

I can't tear my eyes away.

My heart beats faster and faster, watching . . . *death*. I don't know why I can never look away from it, why I'm so transfixed by the darkness. Suddenly, a familiar voice startles me.

"Guess he didn't want to fly south for the winter," Hannah quips.

"Ugh, gross," Mia adds, joining us to rubberneck. "I think I'm going vegan. Between this and the mountain lion . . ."

"Yeah, until a major post-period cheeseburger craving hits," Hannah says. "Or maybe . . . *fried chicken*?"

Mia winces. "Barf, stop it."

I can relate to that raven, even though I can't tell them that. This place makes me want to kamikaze too. At least, then I could escape it.

"All these close encounters with nature," Mia goes on in disgust. "I think I've had more than enough for one day."

"Well, it's us, *two*—nature, *zero*." Hannah nods toward the dead bird. "So technically, we're winning."

"Don't you mean *slaying*?" I mutter darkly, making them giggle.

Another voice reaches us.

"Such a shame," Guru Shava says, interrupting our unintentional wake. "They do that from time to time."

She floats over in a swishing of white robes and scarves. Her turban looks more ornate today, decorated with beads and shiny jewels that wrap around it, while her blonde dreadlocks spill down her back. I notice that she's barefoot and has the tiniest, daintiest feet.

She cranes her neck to spot the carnage below. "I feel bad for them since we erected this manmade monstrosity in the middle of their natural habitat. But then I remember how many lives we've saved here."

"Uh, right," I say in a weak voice. I can't shake that outsider feeling I get sometimes. Like I don't belong here. Imposter syndrome. Because I am just that.

An imposter.

Everyone turning to stare at me when I freaked out isn't helping either. However, now that the guru has joined us, they've returned to conversing, but really they're straining to overhear us.

"If it wasn't you, then someone else would build some monstrosity here," Hannah points out. "And they'd probably be much less conscious of the environment than the Namaste Center."

"Precisely," Guru Shava says with an approving smile. "You understand."

BONG.

A gong goes off. The deep noise reverberates through the Great Hall.

Guru Shava gives me a sharp look like she did on the tour, as if she can see right through me, then bows her head gracefully. Her hands come to prayer.

"That's my cue," she says, whipping around in a great fluttering of her robes. "Follow me into the meditation studio."

The wooden doors shut behind us with a bang, sealing us inside the meditation room. I hear the sound of the thick wooden slab clanking down on the other side of the door, locking us in from the outside. I flinch at the observation. It's not like any yoga studio I've ever been to and feels more like a sensory deprivation chamber.

I start to feel twitchy. Not only do I find yoga and meditation head-explodingly boring, but the idea of being trapped in a room like this totally freaks me out.

"Yeah, that's not creepy at all," I whisper to Mia, who's sitting next to me on her yoga mat. We've discarded our shoes in the cubby by the door and claimed purple mats and Mexican woven blankets that are now folded under our sit bones for cushioning.

Everyone is still staking out their spots on the wooden floors. I watch as Hannah drags her mat our way. Dim lighting stretches across the ceiling casting a TV-studio-like glow over us.

"And what's with the *Fight Club* vibes?" I add in a low voice.

Mia giggles. "I'd join just for Tyler Durden. It's peak Brad Pitt cinema."

We clam up as Hannah positions herself on my other side. This was her idea, and she's taking the whole thing a bit more seriously. Mia usually plays both sides, but I can tell she thinks the whole vibe is a bit on the crunchy, cringey side, like me.

Guru Shava takes her seat on the raised dais on the stage, looking down on us. All around her, the stage is draped in flowers, golden chimes, and the centerpiece—a giant, silver gong—hangs behind her. The metal is engraved with what looks like Sanskrit, but I can't be sure. More hangings line the walls with the faces of men in turbans watching us. I'm guessing they must be other gurus.

Total cultural appropriation, I think. But nobody seems to mind the obvious display. Guru Shava waits for everyone to settle in their spots with a blissful, almost snarky smile.

Like she's hiding a secret.

"That's right," she speaks into the microphone. "Grab a mat and a blanket and take a seat so we can begin."

I wonder what it's like to watch us obey her orders and splay our bodies out at her feet, ready to do her bidding.

She leans into the microphone again, amplifying her voice around the chamber. We all tense in anticipation. I notice Dame Tremaine whispering to her friend, while the prosecutor narrows her eyes in judgement, like she's waiting to be convinced of the guru's qualifications to spiritually heal us. The soap opera start looks positively giddy, clasping her hands in prayer.

"Buckle up," Hannah says. "I think she's the real deal."

"Let's hope so," I reply softly. Even though I've been vehemently against this whole thing, I do need help. I feel that in my heart.

I know the breakup has unhinged me, cracked me open and left me down bad. Shattered my armor and the tough exterior I'd constructed over many years, working so hard to remake myself.

And now, I'm falling apart.

All thanks to him.

Ugh, I hate how I sound like a broken record, skipping over the same sad emo track.

"Welcome to your rebirth," Guru Shava says, almost like she can hear my silent plea. "Today, everything changes."

What feels like an electrical surge of energy shoots through me. Everyone quiets down instantly and stops shifting, all eyes on her.

"This week will be life-changing for everyone," she goes on once she has our undivided attention. "Our program consists of morning yoga and meditation sessions, individual spiritual guidance meetings with me, and our signature detox cleanse—patent pending," she adds in an amused voice, casting her eyes over us.

We all chuckle right on cue. Her minions for the week.

"The diet is a liquid regimen," she continues, striking that delicate balance between seriousness and whimsy that all yoga teachers seem to deploy. "So, apologies in advance for depriving you of solid food."

More laughter breaks out.

I try to join in, but my stomach churns unhappily. If this morning was any example, I'm decidedly un-thrilled. I just hope it's enough calories to sustain us.

"However, I assure you it is nutritionally optimized to your individual needs," she adds, "based on the comprehensive form you submitted when you applied to our program."

"*What form?*" I whisper to Hannah.

She shoots me a guilty look.

"Oh, I sort of filled it out for you," she whispers back.

A flash of anger ignites in my chest. Just like she did with the One, when she and Mia signed me up for the dating app without my consent, filling out my profile with personal details that eventually led me to Noah.

But before I can dwell on it, Guru Shava is continuing the orientation. "We will also have some special nighttime rituals and ceremonies intended to facilitate your healing work, lift your consciousness, and elevate your chakras."

That sounds like a bunch of nonsensical New Age jargon. Still, I'm trying to give this program a chance, despite being here against my will.

"While the welcome packets detail a number of the activities, many remain a secret to maximize their impact."

Guru Shava runs her fingers over the metal chimes, releasing their sound.

Once the chimes die out, she leans into the microphone. Her breath rasps over it, creating a hushed sound.

"But first, you have to . . . *die*," she says with that mysterious smile, provoking gasps from her captive audience. "Don't worry, we're speaking metaphorically."

Awkward laughter ripples through our rows of neatly lined up mats. One of them is a bit askew, triggering my OCD. I look over in condemnation.

It's the soap star, Antonia.

She glances over, catching me staring at her. Her eyes are so crystal blue and startling. I avert my gaze, mentally chastising myself for getting busted spying on one of the VIPs.

Guru Shava continues her monologue. "But metaphors have deep power to unchain us from what has been, to unburden us from our pasts and our traumas, the people that hold us back.

"Death is the only way to be reborn. To shed the darkness, the things we'd rather avoid thinking about, let alone reliving. But today, we're going to do just that."

I don't like the sound of that, but I try to keep an open mind. I steady my breathing like I've learned in prior classes, keeping my abdominals firm. Sitting can feel surprisingly active.

"Let's begin in child's pose," Guru Shava says.

She instructs us to lean back, separate our feet, and take the pose.

The class moves in unison as we're led through a series of poses designed to open up our bodies and our chakras. My heart rate elevates a little, but it's nothing like a kickboxing class.

I can tell a lot of the other guests are experienced yoga practitioners, more than me. But on the upside, I can study them to emulate the correct poses. Dame Tremaine moves in a particularly graceful manner, revealing her dance training, while the DA moves in a power yoga style. Mia and Hannah hold their own, though Mia wobbles and exchanges a wink with me.

Unlike any other teachers I've taken classes from, Guru Shava doesn't do the routine along with us. She remains seated on her pedestal in a cross-legged position, speaking into the microphone to call out our movements. Finally, she returns us to a seated position with our ankles crossed, sliding our blankets back under our sit-bones, if desired. I definitely do desire it.

The longer we go, the harder holding the poses become. Even though I'm in decent shape thanks to my workouts, yoga uses different muscles. My arms and legs start to shake, while my core aches in ways I didn't know were possible. Right when I think I might collapse in a sweaty heap, she calls us back to child's pose, then sitting.

"Now, it's time for the Breath of Fire," she says, making me perk up. I haven't heard of this before. "Breath of Fire can help energize you by increasing your heart rate, body temperature, and blood flow. It can also help clear your nasal passages . . . better than Claritin."

More ripples of laughter.

A strange combination of seriousness and joking that is surprisingly charming.

"But it's also known to take you to a higher plane, if you let it," she goes on. "First, inhale through your nose, feeling your belly expand. Then, exhale forcefully through your nose while contracting your abdominal muscles at the same time." She demonstrates it.

We all follow suit, doing the inhale and exhale, pushing out our breaths.

It does feel cleansing. Like more than oxygen is leaving my body. Maybe there is something to this.

Before I can get comfortable with it, she continues speaking.

"Now, we're going to repeat the inhales and exhales in a rhythmic cycle at a rate of about one breath per second. We'll go for about thirty seconds."

One breath per second?

Yoga is usually all about slow breathing, controlling it. But this sounds unhinged, like the total opposite.

It sounds more like . . . hyperventilating.

Before I can question it further, she bangs the gong. The deep sound reverberates out through the room.

Everyone starts doing the Breath of Fire, rapidly pushing their diaphragms, creating the breathy sound. I force myself to do it. How hard can thirty seconds be? After about ten, I start to see stars dancing in my vision. Lightheadedness envelops me.

Still, we keep panting. Like women in a Lamaze class. Or getting ready to birth a baby.

I suppose that's the point. Some kind of primordial rebirth of our spirits. The whole thing is bizarre and cultish, but I can't deny that it does get me a little high. I start to feel like I'm floating.

As darkness threatens to snuff out my consciousness—

Bong.

She bangs the gong again, signaling for us to stop hyperventilating.

I'm relieved as I'm feeling slightly sick from the cleanse and breath work. I glance around the room, expecting more sympathy, but I'm surprised to see everyone looking glassy-eyed yet elated, like they all just got collectively high.

"We've reached the end of our practice this morning," Guru Shava says once we all come back down a bit. "It's time for Shavasana. Also known as the corpse pose, this yoga pose helps to relax the body and mind. *Shava* means corpse, while *asana* means pose."

I startle in recognition.

Guru . . . Shava.

Her name means *corpse.*

That's a bit creepy. Then I remember it's like some sacred yoga saying related to death and rebirth. So, I guess it does fit her whole vibe.

Before I can question it any further, she instructs us to lie down on our backs, eyes closed, with our legs straight and arms relaxed at our sides. I shut my eyes tight against the light. My head is still swimming a bit from the hyperventilation session, not to mention lack of proper sleep and no solid food.

I try to ignore the warning bells in my head telling me that's what cults do: deprive you of food and brainwash you.

Then I feel guilty. Hannah and Mia aren't complaining. I'm just looking for reasons to be a hater, like I always do.

"Relax and steady your breathing," Guru Shava goes on in a hypnotic voice. "Allow it to occur naturally. Let your body feel heavy on the ground and release any tension."

We're all splayed out like corpses scattered across the yoga studio. My body starts to feel heavy—impossibly heavy—as though I'm sinking into my rubber mat.

"That's right," Guru Shava says softly. "You have to assume the corpse pose—you have to die to be reborn. While we're in this relaxed state, it's time to invite our traumas to come out in the light and join us. By exposing them, we rob them of their power over us. In other words, that is the only way to finally defeat them."

I feel a shudder work its way through my body. That's the *last* thing I want to do. I hope we don't have to share anything publicly. I guess I can always lie, make something up that's safe.

Something that protects my secrets.

Hopefully it doesn't come to that.

Bong.

The gong goes off again, but I have my eyes shut tight. The sound brings gooseflesh rippling through my body.

Guru Shava's voice rings out.

"Now, I invite you to journey to the deepest, darkest places. Childhood abuse. Trauma. Let the gong release them. We're cleansing out the darkness."

As her soothing voice keeps chanting, I feel myself sinking deeper and deeper into the darkness, like drowning in quicksand. The thick mud flows down my throat, clogging my airway, making me choke on the damp earth.

Two arms clamp around me. It's my father again. His angry, bloated face invades my mind. *No, get off me!* I struggle, thrashing around and trying to fight him off, but he's too strong.

Slap.

He smacks me across the face. *Morgan, wake up! You're in danger!*

I struggle to reawaken and come out of the meditation, to reclaim my consciousness from the nightmares and trauma.

I jerk awake, sitting up on my mat. I must have fallen asleep. I glance around, but the whole class is still in corpse pose. But then I see it—

They're all covered in . . .

Blood.

Thick and viscous. Like lambs to the slaughter. Gaping wounds expose their innards, spilling blood and guts all over their mats.

A voice echoes out.

"You okay, Morgan?"

I jerk my head to the right. Mia stares at me with her eyes gouged out, and I gasp at the sight of the bloody eye sockets.

"Wh-what happened to you?" I stammer in horror, trying to back away.

Hannah grabs my arm. I turn around, only to see her head topple off.

It hits the ground and spins around to look at me.

Her lips move, trickling blood. She lets out a hysterical, shrill cackle.

"Did you become a corpse yet?"

CHAPTER TWELVE

BEFORE

NOAH

"Wow, this is incredible!"

Morgan gasps into her headset as the helicopter lifts off into the air, carrying us away. We removed our masks to don the headsets for the short helicopter flight. The lion and lioness stare back at us from our laps.

A rush of anticipation at what lies ahead hits me, an urge to take her right there in the air, but I work to calm my heart and stay focused. I can't get too excited . . . yet. The night is still young.

And she's not ready for that.

I follow her gaze through the window as my private helicopter carries us from the city's grasp, whisking us away into the night. The buildings grow smaller and smaller, the highways transform into narrow ribbons of light, and then it all falls away behind us.

"Your first helicopter flight?" I say, pulling her closer to feel her heart race.

I've flown so many times that the thrill wore off long ago. Getting to experience it all over again, witnessing it through her virgin eyes, excites me.

Her cheeks redden. "Is it that obvious?"

She sounds ashamed. She pretends to be more experienced than she really is.

I've held back researching her, preferring to study her in the wild instead, like a research subject. She's rough around the edges, which I like.

It makes her . . . *different.*

Darkness beckons to us the farther we fly. She's riveted by the flight, unable to take her eyes from the window.

"Now you're not a helicopter virgin anymore," I say softly, making her shudder against me, though it could be the helicopter. We bank to the right, and the world angles beneath us as we tilt sideways.

"Does that excite you?" she asks, speaking into her headset.

She gives me a look, trying to act tough and sexy, like she's in control. That's one of the things I am starting to love about her, that's drawing me in closer and making me want to wrestle it away from her bit by bit, until she's *mine.*

"What would you say if I admitted that it turns me on?" I say after a moment. My words hang between us.

I feel her tense even more.

The helicopter banks again before she can respond, thrusting her harder against me. We're flying into the wilderness, beyond the greedy reaches of the city, where nature hasn't been paved over and still lays claim to the lands. I pull her closer, feeling the pounding of her heart as we soar over the mountains.

Eventually, the wildness gives way to a massive country estate with tall stone walls. The crown jewel is the mansion lit up with golden lights.

The helipad lights in the middle of the thick forest flicker on, bathing the field in bright light. The circular target flashes, welcoming us down.

My chopper lands, settling down with a soft *thud.* The tree branches bend back from the force of the wind.

We remove our headsets and trade them for the golden masks. I make sure to tie hers firmly into place, tightening the velvet straps against her curls.

A long line of limos and town cars pulls around the circular driveway to drop guests off at the front entrance. The couples all emerge dressed in an array of animal masks paired with formal attire. Two burly doormen in tuxedos with silver moon masks stand guard at the doors, waiting to admit each couple.

As we start toward the entrance, sticking to the walking path, I lean in and whisper. "Tonight, there are important rules you have to follow . . . or there will be consequences."

"Rules?" She looks alarmed but tries to hide it. "Like what?"

"The first big rule is don't take your mask off. You can't reveal your identity to anyone here, no matter what. Or mine. But luckily, you don't know who I really am."

She play-punches my arm.

I have to give her credit. She's kept to the experiment. I worried the helicopter might tempt her to ask more questions. But she's held her tongue.

"Let's just say," I go on, "secrecy is important to protect the gathering."

"Okay, so let me get this straight," she replies, taking it all in. "This is basically a *blind* date to a *blind* party? You're really taking our experiment to the next level tonight, aren't you?"

I can't read the expression concealed behind her mask, but I can picture it based on her tone—snarky and challenging. That turns me on.

"Yes, that's right," I admit, trying to slow my racing heart. I have to maintain control—if I want to control her. I keep my voice low, whispering in her ear. "I can tell you the VIPs here all wish to remain anonymous. I promise you'll understand why when we get inside."

"That sounds like something from a movie. Like that Tom Cruise and Nicole Kidman one . . . Wait, is this a sex party?" Her voice hisses, sounding scandalized as the realization hits her.

She digs her heels in, grinding to a halt in her stilettos. I have to reach out to steady her. I drink in her reaction: the trepidation and moral objections. But also, the rampant curiosity.

This is a test. To see what she will accept. To see how far she's willing to push it.

"Well, that's one way to put it," I say, testing her even further. "The second rule is simple—you don't have to do anything you don't want to do. A lot of members prefer to just watch."

Those words hang in the air. It's still late summer, but the nights are growing colder, promising fall's vengeful return.

"Like, voyeurs? I don't know which is crazier," she says in a shocked voice. "Being a watcher or the watched."

"Both," I provide as we stand in the dark under the moonlight. Our masks shimmer even in the dim light. "Or maybe it's the hunter or the hunted."

"And we're the hunters?" she says, tipping her lion mask toward me.

I nod slowly. "Exactly."

Still, she hesitates, watching the parade of couples in various masks heading for the doors. I wait patiently, letting her consider all the options. I know the question on her lips. The one she's dying to ask me.

Who are you . . . really?

I love the way she doesn't really know, though she guesses that I must be somebody important. Someone with connections and power. Someone she wouldn't usually get the chance to date, except for the luck of an algorithm on a dating app.

"I meant what I said on our second date," she says finally. "About waiting."

"Ah, yes. How could I forget?"

It all flashes through my head. How nobody ever resisted me before, not after I rolled out all the stops on our first two dates like that. How much I wanted to conquer her . . . fully. But she held me back, then tamed me. Left me wanting more, sweaty and drained, but still hardening.

How nothing could satisfy me except seeing her again. And again. And again.

I am the hunter.

She is the hunted.

Does she realize it yet? I don't think so. She's still wrestling me for control, even now, asserting her own rules.

"I respect your rule," I agree. "As long as you respect mine tonight."

She nods and holds out her arm in acquiescence. I take it, escorting her toward the doormen. "Password?" the first one asks.

I lean into his ear and whisper.

"*Aeternus eternus.*"

He straightens right away—he knows who I am—and lets us through.

"Secret password?" she says softly. "That really is like the movie."

"You have no idea."

That's the last thing I say before the doormen swing the doors wide open, and we step into the debauchery inside.

The marble foyer opens to an array of other rooms, each offering distinct delights. One room is for feasting with a long marble table laden with caviar, lobster, sushi, and—most notably—oysters. All the aphrodisiacs. Waiters roam around in moon masks with silver trays filled with crystal champagne flutes filled to the brim. I watch her, waiting to see when she realizes . . .

They're all topless.

Some are men with chiseled chests, while some are women wearing silver pasties bejeweled with diamonds.

I wonder if this is the moment Morgan will back out. I brace myself for disappointment. It's happened before, but only once or twice. Of course, that was the last time I ever saw those dates.

But instead, Morgan reaches for two champagne flutes, handing me one.

"To new experiences," she says, toasting me. "And third dates."

Clink.

Relief surges through me as the delicate crystal reverberates. We both sip eagerly. The cold bubbles hit my throat, igniting my other senses. I want to drink it down before I drink her in. But I must be patient. I escort her around the party, taking in all the ornate masquerade masks, each different creatures—wolves, panthers, cheetahs. The whole jungle has turned out.

"Is that the theme?" she asks. "Are there other lions?"

I shake my head. "Only us."

I don't add *tonight.* Or mention who else wears the lion masks.

We continue to the next room—the fountain room. Rivers of heated water spill down from several waterfalls, filling the many pools. Couples in various stages of amorous acts occupy them, all beautiful bodies, shining and intertwined.

We stand there and watch. She clutches my hand tighter.

I wonder if it's hitting her yet—the little something I slipped into her champagne back at my place. I'm starting to feel the waves of pleasure undulating through me. The lights are shimmering and bending, reflecting back from the pools like tiny diamonds. All of my senses are heightened.

"Do you feel it yet?" I whisper.

"What?" She closes her eyes behind the mask and inhales deeply, feeling it. "Wait, did you—"

"Ecstasy," I whisper back. "High-grade MDMA, very safe, I promise. Just a small dose to elevate your experience."

"How could you?" she hisses. "You should have asked me first."

She tries to pull away, but I don't let her. I pull her in close and kiss her. Hard at first, then softer.

Tasting her, pushing my tongue into her mouth until she stops resisting and responds, kissing me back. The kiss elongates and endures, becoming a moment we both don't want to end. When I finally force myself to pull back, we're both panting and enraptured.

"That's how," I say breathlessly.

And now, she gets it. Some other partygoers watch us with interest. The heat emanating off us is apparent. I cup her face in my hands, bringing our intense gazes together.

We peer at each other through the eye slits.

"I wanted you to get the most out of tonight. Please don't be angry with me. It was a risk, bringing you here, but third dates are make or break it. Most times, it doesn't go past this . . ."

I trail off, waiting for the rebuke. I did drug her without consent, though it was a small dose of a very safe substance. I only procure the purest, safest chemicals from the top dealers.

"You're right. The crucial third date. This is usually when everything either sparks to life or dies out. Usually, the latter. So, you decided to drug me and take me to a sex party?"

I can't help it. A laugh slips out, but she doesn't seem very amused.

"Please forgive me if I overstepped." I shake my head, feeling stupid for even taking this risk. It was too soon. "It's a very low dose, I promise," I go on. "I only wanted to enhance your experience with me, open up your senses so we could be in the moment. Together."

"I haven't done anything like this since college." She seems to reminisce for a moment, pulled back into her past, then shakes it off and refocuses on me.

"You mean, a masquerade sex party?" I joke back. "Or ecstasy?"

She doesn't respond to that. Just turns her back to me, so I'm forced to take in the view from behind as she saunters off with a sexy gait.

"What are you waiting for? Clearly not my permission," she adds in a teasing voice, looking back at me. "What else do you have to show me tonight?"

I savor the moment before I respond.

"Only . . . everything."

I lead Morgan through the mansion, weaving between bodies and masked faces. The strangeness and anonymity only heightens the transgressive nature of the evening.

Once she stops worrying and gives in, she starts to enjoy the experience. I can feel the shift in her energy. Her body loses the tension, shifting into excitement. She looks around the rooms, dazzled by the chandeliers and sensory elements.

Or that could be from the ecstasy.

"Who are all these people?" She gasps in awe at the elaborate costumes.

"That's the one question I can't answer," I say, nuzzling her ear.

My lips taste the tender part of her flesh as we watch the gatherers.

They parade before us—deer, dogs, lizards, dolphins, even an elephant couple—all in pairs like Noah's Ark. There's a symbolic reason for this. This party represents life and procreation, unlike the other gathering. But I don't want to think about that right now. In comparison, our costumes are milder, but tastefully so. It's what I always wear to this gathering—and what my date does, too. However, the way that dress hugs Morgan in all the right places, making her sultry yet goddess-like, takes my breath away.

"This mansion is spectacular," she goes on as I lead her into yet another ornate room, this one decorated with furry animal rugs and animal-print furniture. She runs her hand over the tactile leopard-print sofa, caressing it. "It's like something out of *The Great Gatsby*."

I smile at her, hoping it doesn't come off predatory. The mask probably adds to the effect. "As many times as I've been here, it never ceases to amaze me."

She lies across the sofa, begging me to slide onto her. I oblige, fitting my body into hers like a puzzle piece, and she runs her hands through my hair.

I want to do more to her, but I hold myself back and honor her rules.

"How many times have you been to one of these parties?" she presses me.

I know what she really wants to know—how many women I've brought here. But she won't ask that directly and reveal her insecurity.

I push my finger to her lips.

"Ah, yet another secret I can't reveal. But you like my secrets, don't you?"

She glowers at me, but I can see the desire simmering in her eyes. The only part of her face I can glimpse through the golden lioness mask. It turns me on more than I care to admit.

More than I want her to know.

"The only thing that matters," I go on, running my hand down the length of her body, tracing every single curve, "is that I'm here with you tonight."

She shudders in response, her body supple and tempting.

"A mysterious night for our mystery experiment?"

"I had to do something big for date number three. Don't you think?"

She reaches down, emboldened, and grips my hardness, feeling it through the thin pants. Her hand strokes it, coaxing more blood to flood my member.

"That's not the only *big* thing."

Now, it's my turn to shudder.

We caress each other, and I give in to the heat and waves of pleasure, knowing the enhancements are doing their job. Undoubtedly, she's feeling it, too.

Just like I planned.

Down-tempo music pumps through the room, while the chandeliers flicker in soft rhythm overhead. Another couple, wearing dolphin masks, slides onto the fuzzy sofa next to us, after waiting for our nods of approval. The woman wears a silvery, flowing dress that she hikes up, straddling her date wearing a matching silver suit. They start grinding next to us in a sensual dance to the bass-thumping music.

We watch, entranced by their public display. The woman shrugs off the straps of her dress, revealing perky breasts dusted with silver glitter. The man buries his head in them.

"Well, they're not shy," Morgan whispers, not taking her eyes off them.

"The *watchers* and the *watched*," I whisper back. "Both are fun."

Morgan seems riveted, though probably blushing under her mask. I've brought enough dates over the years to know how to initiate newbies into it. So far, she's holding up beautifully, even managing to impress me with her verve.

After a few more minutes of voyeurism—which we both enjoy—I untangle myself from her, and pull her up from the sofa.

She adjusts her dress before we make sure our masks remain tied in place.

"Are you ready for more?" I ask, offering her my arm. "You can always back out now. It might make this level seem rather tame."

An elongated beat passes.

She thinks it over. I worry she's about to call the whole thing off and insist on leaving.

But then, she locks onto my arm.

"I want you to show me . . . *everything*," she murmurs in a sexy voice.

A wave of pleasure courses through me, tempting me further. I know this is pushing it for her first time—but I need to see how far she can be pushed. That's the whole point really. I have a hunch she's the one who can go all the way with me. Nobody has before.

I lead her downstairs to the dungeon rooms. We wind down a spiral stone staircase, twisting deeper underground and emerging into a darkened corridor with rooms branching off it, each offering different temptations.

The first one we pass is medical themed with a hospital gurney and rolling steel tables laden with various medical instruments. A shapely girl in a latex dress with a pig mask is tied down to a table with leather restraints, while an impossibly tall man, also in a pig mask and a white lab coat, bends down between her legs to examine her.

Morgan gasps at the display. "I didn't think stuff like this was real," she says, shocked but unable to look away. The man reaches for a speculum. "Like it only happened in movies."

I tighten my grip on her waist. "Those movies are inspired by us."

I let her take the lead. We move on and reach another room, this one a cave where two men in horse masks hang from the ceiling by leather harnesses with their hands tied behind their backs. They're being whipped by their dates, also in matching horse masks.

We remain clothed—*the watchers*—and I'm not surprised. This is usually how it goes the first time. I let my dates decide how far to push their boundaries. The gatherings happen twice a year. I've attended so many that I've lost count with various women on my arms. So many, I had become bored.

But not tonight.

It all feels fresh again—new. I feel like the virgin tonight, excited to feast on the range of sensual desires the night holds. Once we peruse the rest of the dungeons—the red velvet room, the office, the asylum, and the stables—I let her lead me back upstairs.

We wind up the spiral staircase, emerging onto the main floor.

We're both hot and breathless from the experience—and also the drugs coursing through our systems. We grab more flutes of golden liquid before plunging outside onto the balcony.

The fresh air hits us, and we breathe it in, then chase it with gulps of cold champagne. The extensive grounds are lit by perimeter lights that dissolve into the dark tangles of the forest. Over the soft music filtering out, a lone owl takes up a mournful cry.

"A penny for your thoughts?" I say, reaching around her waist to hold her.

She takes a moment to respond, drinking down the last of her champagne.

"Is this your kink? BDSM?"

I shrug. "Not exactly," I confess. "Though I am somewhat flexible. What turns me on is what turns you on. I will admit there's not much that I haven't tried, at least once. I guess I like to push experiences to the very limit."

"Or you get bored?"

"Exactly," I say, surprised. "You understand then. Most people live very safe lives. They never test the edges."

"Because they're afraid to fall."

"Fortunately, felines are exceptionally good at landing on their feet." I tap my mask, feeling the mane curving away. "Oh, and they have nine lives."

"How many have you spent already?"

I flinch as dark memories cloud my mind. I push them away, trying to cover it up. I don't want to answer that.

"Probably as many as you. I mean, you were trying to step into oncoming traffic when I met you. What secrets are you hiding in your past?"

It's her turn to flinch.

So, we're even then.

We're so similar, both hiding from the darkness yet drawn to it. The mirror she holds up to my face tells that much. I recognize myself in her.

"So then, what is it?" She turns to face me. "You didn't answer."

She peers at me through the golden holes in the mask, almost purring.

"My kink?"

She nods, waiting—no, *daring*—me to tell her. I study her in the statuesque dress that hugs each curve, encasing her body as if her figure is cast in gold. The soft curve of her breasts pushing out of the top, begging for me to free them.

I reach for them and squeeze. *Hard.* She gasps.

Then I whisper—

"You're my kink."

CHAPTER THIRTEEN

AFTER

MORGAN

Bong!

I startle awake to the sound of the gong.

I'm contorted on my mat like a homicide victim with my arms and legs splayed out and my heart racing. I can't shake the bloody vision. I snap up to sitting, too fast. Blood rushes to my head making everything spin. I jerk my head around toward my friends.

Everyone appears perfectly normal, if a little sleepy-looking. Hannah and Mia stretch languorously, slowly rolling to their sides before sitting up, the way you're supposed to. The total opposite of what I just did.

Guru Shava glosses over my yogic indiscretions, thankfully. She smiles, looking down from her podium.

"I hope you all got closer to releasing your inner demons today. Some of you more than others." She fixes her eyes on me.

My heart plummets. I wonder how much she noticed, if I wasn't so silent when I screamed in my nightmare. I flash back to her words on the trail earlier about me having *deep secrets*.

But then, she looks away and dismisses us with a benediction. "*Namaste*."

The class repeats the word as I stumble along, still feeling freaked out.

I hurry to roll up my yoga mat, collect the blanket, and return them to the proper bins, and retrieve my Ugg ankle boots from the cubby. I slide back into the sheep's wool lining, then join Mia and Hannah to depart the studio.

Clearly, I nodded off into another nightmare during the meditation. And no wonder, since I'm sleep-deprived, and food-deprived too.

I'm still jumpy and anxious as we're released back into the Great Hall. The apprentices lift the heavy wooden slab, opening the double doors and letting in a rush of cold, fresh air into the room.

Bright sunlight streams in through the floor-to-ceiling windows, obscuring my vision. The position of the sun indicates it's already midday. How long were we in that meditation? Where did the time go?

Everyone else appears a little dazed and confused, disoriented by the sudden emergence into reality. I watch the DA and the soap star flinch back and blink hard at the light, while Dame Tremaine dons oversized, sparkly pink sunglasses handed to her by her friend. They're bigger than her petite face. *Sunglasses indoors*, I think. Total celeb move.

"Hey, are you okay?" Hannah asks as we move into the reception area.

"Yeah, you seemed a little uncomfortable coming out of that Shavasana," Mia says with a frown.

"Uh, totally! I guess that meditation was just intense." I force a smile. "Really got me thinking about dying."

They both laugh. "It's not called corpse pose for nothing," Mia quips.

We break for our next "meal" before another meditation session, although I'm not sure you can call it a meal when it's liquid slop, no solids. As I force down the brownish, greenish liquid, I think what I wouldn't give for a fucking cheeseburger dripping with saturated fat and grease.

Before long, Hannah and Mia and everyone else are glowing with *Zen energy*—or so Guru Shava calls it—as we whisk from juice cleanse refuel to meditation class to more yoga then back again in the same vicious loop. True to her word, Guru Shava perches on the podium and leads all the sessions.

By late afternoon, my brain is screaming with boredom at the same level of intensity that my stomach is screaming for solid food. I'm miserable. I'm hungry. I'm bored out of my mind.

And I miss my *fucking* iPhone.

My fingers twitch at the possibility.

But there's more. What happened in the morning meditation continues to haunt me. Those terrible memories from my past that resurfaced and threatened to pull me back into the trauma I thought I escaped. The vision of the dead bodies, bloodied and sprawled out on their yoga mats. Mia's eyes gouged out. Hannah's neck slit and head toppling off.

I shudder, flashing back to it. I know it's some kind of complex PTSD. I don't need a therapist—or a yoga guru—to tell me that. But I can't risk it happening again. I have to block out those mind games Guru Shava is playing here. If I want to survive . . .

And not spill my deep secrets.

After all, it was her prompt about childhood demons that caused my horrific visions. I have to find a way to block her out—along with her pseudo-spiritual nonsense.

We file back into the meditation studio and grab our mats. I settle down, still feeling jumpy. I glance around at everyone on their mats. They all look . . . elated. Like they took some drug that elevated their moods, and I'm the only one having a bad trip.

Regardless, one thing is clear. I can't let Guru Shava coax me into a relaxed state like that ever again. I need something to distract myself and stay grounded. And I know just the thing.

When the next juice refuel comes up—a green concoction with the exact appearance and consistency of snot, served in hand-carved wooden bowls—I beg off to our cabin, clutching at my stomach. "Sorry, TMI, but I'm majorly detoxing. I have to go to the cabin."

I start to back away toward the door, almost running right into Guru Shava.

"Leaving us so soon?" she says with a frown.

"Uh, I'm just detoxing." I clutch at my stomach for effect. "I'll be back."

"Namaste," Guru Shava says. She tips her head in my direction, giving me one of her creepy, blank-eyed smiles. This retreat is better than Botox, judging by how relaxed her facial muscles appear.

"Namaste," Hannah says, bowing and imitating Guru Shava's affectations.

They wait for me to do it, but I can't say it back. I want to, but my lips rebel and my brain screams at me. Instead, I return their sentiments with a tight-lipped smile, hoping they don't notice my fingers twitching, the telltale sign of phone withdrawal.

On the upside, we're definitely passing the Bechdel test. No more boy talk—just detoxing, bowel movements, and New Age cultish jargon. At least we've got that going for us.

I know this weekend was supposed to help me get over Noah. But now, I miss him more than ever. I can almost hear his deep voice, flecked with subtle sarcasm, making fun of Guru Shava and her patchouli stink with me. He'd have snuck in a flask and spiked our snot shots with the smoky whiskey he loves so much. He'd approve of me breaking the most sacred rule of this place. The one that's posted on every fucking wall and door, including the one I'm itching to escape through.

Finally, Guru Shava wafts away on a patchouli cloud, and I can make a run for it. I grab my puffy coat, force the doors open, and barge into the cold.

I have one goal—

Get my *fucking* phone back.

Back in our cabin, I raid Mia's purse, a bohemian black hole of girlie detritus: stretched-out hairbands, errant bobby pins, power bar crumbs, drugstore lipstick, sugar-free gum, designer wallet, fraying tampons.

I paw through it all, my fingers finally alighting on the cold glass of my phone. I snatch it quickly, like there might be cameras watching our room.

My heart races, hoping that despite the warnings, I can find some bars. I toggle a few settings and wave it around. But no luck.

Dead zone.

Not even a roaming signal. I double check just in case, making sure the setting is on. My paranoia spikes. I wonder if they block cellular signals out here on purpose just to isolate us. But of course, that's silly.

Once I glance outside the window at the snowcapped mountains reminds me that we're in the middle of nowhere. No need to block signals that never reach a spot in the first place.

Still, I feel a pang of anxiety. There is no way to find out if Noah texted me back. Or even the possibility of finding out until after we leave here in a week. That's practically a lifetime in our relationship. What if I miss something important from him?

I know it's super pathetic to be pining after my cheating ex like this. Or, at least my brain knows that. But my heart seems to have missed the memo. Falling for him that fast and that hard was dangerous, but I liked the thrill.

Usually, I keep my heart locked up, but somehow he got inside. Broke down all my barriers and scaled my castle walls. I wasn't supposed to actually fall for him. And now I'm paying the price. That dark thought tanks my mood—more than it already was.

Part of me wishes I could get kicked out early and end this misery. But guilt chews at me, reminding me of all the effort Hannah and Mia went to help me since the incident, including footing the bill for the week. They would never forgive me. I already lost Noah.

I can't lose them too.

So, I have to be extra careful. I toggle to the podcast app and click on it. I'm rewarded as a slew of pre-downloaded entertainment floods the screen. I zero in on the first one that catches my interest. My heart races faster in anticipation. While I flip through my entertainment options, I reach in my bag and stuff a protein bar into my mouth, forcing myself to chew and swallow. I'm hoping it will counteract the raw juice cleanse currently rumbling in my stomach.

Unsolved Terrors: JonBenét Ramsey

That poor little girl whose parents probably murdered her, but it remains an unsolved mystery. All those pictures of her in those creepy child beauty pageants flash through my head. I wonder what new evidence the podcast dug up on the case. It'll be the perfect distraction to keep me from falling into another nightmare trance and keep my past buried.

I slip my phone into my pants, then check my reflection in the mirror. The hard outline of my phone tucked into the wide waistband of my yoga pants is concealed by my longer tunic. There's still no reception, but it doesn't matter. I feel less restless already with my electronic pacifier cued up with the podcast. I fish a pair of wireless earbuds out of my bag, slipping them discreetly into my ears. The earbuds chime as they synch up with my phone. I feel a thrill, knowing I'm breaking the rules. I just have to be extra careful.

I've got a feeling that Guru Shava could morph from Zen to angry schoolmaster in two seconds flat if she caught me with my phone. Not to mention her creepy "silent" apprentices. They even made us sign a waiver when we checked in stating that we agreed to their unjust no electronics policy. Oh, and that they were released from any liability for medical issues suffered as a result of their medically unsanctioned raw juice cleanse.

Basically, we all signed our lives away coming here. But at least I have a solution to survive my week of misery.

I reach down, feeling the hard outline of my phone hidden under my clothes.

This better work.

Or I'm fucked.

CHAPTER FOURTEEN

BEFORE

MORGAN

"You're my kink," he whispers into my ear after I gasp from his firm touch.

I don't know if it's the thrill of the helicopter ride, the surprise of the masquerade party, or the drugs coursing through my veins making me release my inhibitions and pushing the pleasure to the next level, but this hits me *hard.*

"How can you be sure?" I whisper back, my breath coming out jagged.

He leans into me.

I can feel how hard he is through his pants, how much he desires me. His member straining makes me go weak.

"That's how," he hisses, pressing against me and making me feel it.

Ugh, I want him so bad.

But I can't give in yet. I have to stick to my rules, just as he sticks to his rules.

Somehow I manage to pull away and turn my back to keep him chasing after me.

I like it when he chases me.

I know he's testing my limits tonight. He wants to see how I react to the subversions he throws at me. And I have to throw them right back. I confess I've never been to anything like this, but I'm tougher than he realizes.

I lead him back into the thick of the party. A DJ has taken up in the main room, playing sexy, low electronic beats. I know I should be afraid, even repulsed by all of it. Noah drugged me without consent and took me to this party.

But I'm not—I'm secretly thrilled.

The masks add an extra layer of anonymity and safety. Who are all these people? You can practically feel the power emanating from them. The way they prance around, totally uninhibited and unafraid, grasping for the edges of experience, pushing it to the limit.

Like Noah.

He seems to enjoy my enjoyment. Maybe that's his kink. My newness—*my virginity*—to these experiences that must feel so well-worn to him. But not to me. It's a world I always dreamed of but never knew existed.

I pull him onto the dance floor, writhing alongside the other bodies, some half-dressed, some still fully clothed like us, all of us enraptured. The lights are dimmed, while a mirror ball spins, casting diamonds of light over us.

I whirl around, moving my body to the sexy music and dancing up against him. He reciprocates in appreciation, moving with me in rhythm to the beat. I spin around, getting into it, and come face-to-face with another couple.

Their raven masks stare back at me, making my stomach drop. They're wearing elaborate black costumes, stitched with black feathers. Their beaked faces peer back at us, and they cock their heads.

The woman starts to dance into me, pulling me so close that I can smell her perfume and sweat. Her lips are rounded and glistening. Suddenly, I want to kiss them, and so . . .

I do.

She tastes soft and sweet, almost like caramel, nothing like any man. I'm not gay, not even bisexual really, but I've had some experiences in college, both with ecstasy and women, experimenting, wanting to try it all.

Noah looks surprised but then pleased. He pushes up behind me, finding my neck to softly kiss me, while I continue to dance against the raven-masked woman.

"Stop it—or you're going to drive me mad," he growls in a low voice.

That's when her partner grows mildly possessive. With a sultry glance back at me, she lets him pull her away.

The writhing crowd closes the gaps around us. All those bodies and exotic masks. Beautiful bodies. It should freak me out, but it's beyond intoxicating. Noah pushes against me, molding my body to his fit frame.

I start to get hot and feel like I can't breathe. "Fresh air," I say into his ear. "Please, get me out of here."

He reacts right away, protecting my body as he carves a path from the dance floor. I know it's the ecstasy—it can cause overheating and dehydration—but I want to let him play the hero and rescue me. He snags bottles of water for us on our way outside.

We plunge onto the balcony, and I gulp the water thirstily, along with the crisp air.

"My hero," I say, nuzzling into him, playing up the damsel in distress act.

He studies me through his mask. "Something tells me you're not somebody who needs rescuing."

I shrug. "Everybody is strong until something breaks them. One of my favorite writers once said, 'The world breaks everyone . . .'" I trail off.

But he picks up the quote. "'And afterward, many are strong at the broken places.'" I give him a surprised look, so he adds, "Hemingway is also one of my favorite authors, especially *A Farewell to Arms*."

I get that rush again and wonder if this is what it feels like to fall in love. I'm not sure I've ever truly fallen for another person. I've had plenty of flings, even hints they could grow into something more serious, but they never did. That commitment always eluded me. I'd grown to think maybe I wasn't capable of love. That my childhood had broken me, and afterward, I was strong at the broken places. However, that also led to my heart hardening into an impenetrable shield that repelled all the princely suitors trying to pierce me.

But not Noah. This feels different, both exhilaratingly and terrifyingly so. Usually, I work hard to maintain control so they can't break me.

The look on his face tells me he's thinking something similar. He leans in and kisses me again, deeply and thoroughly. I know there are other partygoers scattered around us, but they blur into the background. The longer we kiss, the more it's only us—him and me—locked together.

He grabs my ass and lifts me up, setting me on the railing of the balcony. The drop is precipitous—probably twenty feet down to the stone terrace. I'm teetering on the edge of death again, perched high above a fall to my death. One small move, or if I tilt my weight back just a little, and gravity would do the rest.

The rush of adrenaline hits me. I see it lighting up his eyes under his mask.

"Since you like danger," he says, daring me to protest and resist.

"Touché," I reply in a soft voice. His arms hold me firmly in place.

"I won't let you fall," he promises.

I lean down and kiss him while his pelvis grinds into me.

He rubs against me, hard and ready. I can feel him straining through the thin fabric of his pants, and I think I might give in no matter what promises I made to myself to wait for commitment this time.

His fingers reach up through my gown and slip inside my panties, feeling the soaking wetness. I shudder against him, dying for his touch, begging for him to stroke me.

All around us, other couples are similarly engaged, some too focused on their partners, some with roving eyes.

Noah watches me watching them. He reaches for the straps of my dress, waits for my nod of permission, then unties them, letting the top of my dress fall away, revealing my naked breasts to the moonlit sky.

I shiver with lust, but also from the rush of adrenaline. From being exposed to the others watching us. He dips his head, teasing my nipple with his mouth, making it stand even more alert. He drags his teeth over it, and I moan softly into the tangles of his hair.

I've always been a sexual experimenter, but never to this level. Never with so many other like-minded couples all participating.

I always thought it would feel strange and even repulsive, but it's the total opposite. I don't know if it's the masks offering a layer of protection, or the formalwear and upscale nature of the party, but it doesn't feel seedy at all.

And I'm shocked to find that I love it. It turns me on, both the watching and being watched.

Noah strokes me again, making me pulse with pleasure. I'm going to give in. I can't resist him . . .

I reach for his zipper and tease it down an inch, making him groan and bite into my shoulder, gnashing my skin gently.

"Your rule?" he says.

"Screw the rules," I hiss back.

He moans again, softly. I tease the zipper down another inch when something catches my eye in the distance.

Someone is staring at us through the window from inside the mansion. It's a man wearing a tuxedo and a lion mask, the twin of Noah's. But earlier, he said nobody else would be wearing lion masks tonight.

So who is that?

"Noah." I subtly nod my head in the direction of the house. Noah turns and looks.

"Fuck," he says, before placing his body between me and the man, blocking the view. Is it to protect me from the man? Or the other way around—to hide me from him?

"What's wrong?"

"This is bad. Shit, he was supposed to be out of town."

"Who?" I ask, feeling the blood drain from my face.

Noah turns back to face me, but I'm still watching the man in the window. Another figure, in a gown, steps behind the man, wearing a sleek lioness mask.

Noah utters two words that come out like a curse.

"My father."

CHAPTER FIFTEEN

AFTER

MORGAN

Stay calm—and don't let them catch you, I think as I reappear in the Great Hall in time for our next yoga class. I hurry into the meditation studio right before the apprentices shut the doors. They remain silent but shoot me disapproving looks.

I know I just broke a major rule. *Don't be late.* It's printed in the schedule.

I force myself to remain calm, despite the contraband phone and earbuds.

There's no way they know. Still, the way they look at me freaks me out.

"*Namaste,*" I whisper, rushing past them, then kicking off my boots and grabbing a yoga mat.

I pick out Hannah and Mia in the middle of the floor. They've saved me a spot in between them.

I feel relief at my friends, then immediately guilty that I'm breaking the rules that could get me kicked out and force them to leave too. But I didn't sign up for this retreat, I remind myself. I was forced to come against my will, and this is the only way I can get through this week.

"All detoxed," I proclaim to Hannah and Mia, unfurling my mat. I crawl into lotus pose and exhale deeply, trying to project an aura of relaxed centeredness. "Wow, I feel like a whole new person."

"Right? I knew you'd love it here," Hannah says. They both reek of patchouli now. When did that happen?

"I feel like I just lost a whole human in the bathroom," I quip. "It was probably all the toxins."

"I think it's those raw juice shots," Hannah whispers in my ear, looking mildly pained. She glances at Guru Shava, making sure she doesn't overhear us. "Goes right through you."

"You can say that again." Mia winces. "But it'll be worth it. I bet I lose those stubborn last five pounds."

"Not to mention, your chakras will be thankful," I say, trying to affect the same mumbo-jumbo New Age jargon to fit in. "Namaste," I add for good measure, but they both give me weird looks.

I don't think I'm using it right.

Damn the cultural appropriation. I should have paid more attention in the handful of yoga classes I've been dragged to over the years despite my best attempts to avoid them. Pilates, too. I distrust anything that involves chanting or strange contraptions that resemble medieval torture devices.

I glance at the stage where Guru Shava is getting set up. A few apprentices are arranging a set of white crystal bowls in different sizes descending from largest to smallest, almost like Russian nesting dolls. Guru Shava clutches what looks like a crystal wand.

The large gong hangs behind her on a stand along with some silver wind chimes and a few handheld drums.

"Is it Harry Potter time?" I whisper, nodding to the wand in her hand. "But seriously, what are those bowls for?"

Hannah follows my gaze. "That's for the sound bath after yoga."

"Sound bath?"

"You've never done one?" Hannah says. "They're all the rage."

"This class isn't flow-based, but more Zen," Mia says. "You know, holding poses and opening up your body to prepare for the sound bath."

"Oh, I can't wait," I say, but inside I cringe. That sounds boring AF. But I smile beatifically, trying to hide my discomfort. Besides, I won't have to listen to any of it.

My true crime podcast is waiting to be played.

The tiny Bluetooth buds in my ears give me reassurance. I'm so glad I have them today. I can't let Guru Shava put me into an overly relaxed state again and risk having another bloody vision or letting one of my secrets slip.

As we wait restlessly on our mats for the class to begin, I glance around the room. The other guests are in various poses and stretches to prep for the class. The DA is limbering up, while the soap opera star is in lotus pose with her arms splayed forward in a V-shape.

Something out of the corner of my eye grabs my attention. It's the pop star. I bend into a stretch so I can watch more closely but not be obvious about it. Her friend, the one with pale skin and jet-black hair, is talking to her frantically, pointing to Guru Shava. She looks pretty upset, but Dame Tremaine waves her off.

Is anyone else seeing this? I wonder. I look around and all the guests seem focused on their own journeys. How freaking noble of them. But the apprentices are watching the exchange from the doors.

I glance back at Dame Tremaine and her friend. They're still bickering over something. Finally, Dame Tremaine throws up her hands. The friend stalks away, leaving the studio. The other friend—the one with the short bleached hair—whispers to Dame Tremaine heatedly, then tries to comfort her.

Dame Tremaine looks pretty upset, too.

I wonder what that was all about. A lover's quarrel? Or something else? And why was she pointing to Guru Shava?

Before I can worry or ask Mia and Hannah if they noticed it, Guru Shava calls us to order. *Let the torture session begin.* Surreptitiously, I reach into my waistband and hit Play.

The female host's soothing voice starts up, piped into my ears via the earbuds hidden carefully under my hair.

"Welcome to *Unsolved Terrors: JonBenét Ramsey,*" she narrates over the dramatic intro music as it builds to a climax. "Have you ever wondered what really happened? Are her parents innocent victims like they claim? What if their secrets are far darker and more sinister?" the host goes on. "What if we discovered that the *perfect* family wasn't so perfect after all?"

That's it—I'm hooked from the jump. I listen as the host recounts the sordid tale of how their beautiful little girl was found murdered in their house.

I love how the narrator's voice is so calming as she recounts each grisly detail, every gore-filled beat. Best of all? I'm not thinking about Noah at all. Or bored out of my mind, feeling like I'm trapped here.

I follow along with the class easily enough. Guru Shava sits on the stage. I see her lips moving as she speaks into the microphone. This one isn't as intensive, like Mia said. Plus, I learned enough in this morning's torture sessions.

The funniest part is how the podcast contrasts sharply with the yoga class, giving my dark side a little jolt. My own little protest against the center's insane rules. I've always enjoyed breaking rules. And just like that—in this moment of subversion—I feel a little spark of my old self flare up again.

Immense relief floods through me. Noah maybe have snuffed it out for a while, but he didn't put my fire out altogether. And maybe, just maybe, this week of no cellular signal and podcast binging will help me reignite my own inferno.

The class comes to an end with us descending into corpse pose. We're all dead bodies lying on our mats as Guru Shava begins playing the quartz bowls, rubbing the mallet around the tops. She also intersperses some chimes, drums, and her ever-present gong.

Dimly, I hear the trippy sounds emanating throughout the room. I start to feel a little twitchy as my episode comes to an end. I crack my eyes open to see if everyone is meditating to the sound bath. They're all deeply relaxed, splayed out on their mats with their eyes shut.

I shudder, realizing I'm the only one not drinking the Kool-Aid.

I look at Guru Shava and am startled to see she's looking right at me. I quickly shut my eyes. My heart races, hoping she's not suspicious. But then episode two kicks in, whisking me away. I relax to the horrific tale, feeling the best I have in weeks.

The rest of the day passes with ease, thanks to my secret. The podcast is beyond addictive, and the last classes give me a chance to binge the first episodes. They go down easily. I'm on the edge of my seat waiting to find out what they dug up about the case and who really killed that little girl.

By the time we have our dinner—more liquid sludge that turns my stomach—and trudge back to the cabin, we're all exhausted from the long day.

"Wasn't that amazing?" Hannah says as we tramp through the snow.

She slots the big key into the front door. It swings inward with a deep groan. Outside, the sun has already set, and darkness has fallen over the mountains.

They ask if I want tea, but I quickly beg off to my room for the night. I can't tell them the truth, that I need to charge my phone so I can finish this podcast.

One day down, only six more to go, I think as I slip into my room. But on the upside, I downloaded a few seasons of this podcast and a bunch of other true crime shows. With any luck, I've got enough content to keep me in murder-land through the end of the week. That cheers me up as I enter my bathroom, lock the door—as a precaution—and crank up the shower.

I plug my phone into the charger as the bathroom steams up. I climb under the water, feeling my sore muscles unclench. I still prefer my kickboxing and martial arts cardio classes, but I take back what I said about yoga not being a workout. It may not be intensive cardio, but it definitely works your muscles.

After showering, I peek my head into the main room, but it's dark and quiet. Hannah and Mia went to bed. It looks like Mia's light is still on, but Hannah's is out. She's probably asleep, and Mia will probably pass out soon too.

The coast is clear.

I climb back into bed and clutch my secret under the covers. A nearly full moon shines in through the window as I slip in my earbuds, also freshly charged, and hit Play, drifting back into the podcast.

I listen far into the night, riveted. Each episode ends on a cliffhanger to hook you into the next one. First, I think the parents really did do it, but then suspicion shifts to a handyman drifter who did some work on the house. Then away from him to a stalker known to frequent the kiddie beauty pageants. Theory after theory. Red herring after red herring. Suspect after suspect.

The point is, you keep listening, on the edge of your seat, to find out what happened. At some point, I have to pee. And my earbuds are dying. But I can't risk listening without them, so I know it's time to give it a rest. Plus, the early wake-up call will come sooner than I want.

Reluctantly, I hit Pause. I struggle out of the fluffy duvet, flinging my feet to the cold hardwood floors. I trudge to the bathroom to plug my phone into the charger. I return the earbuds to their case and also plug that in. Finally, I empty my bladder.

I shut the bathroom door behind me, figuring I can risk leaving them on the chargers in there. I made sure to cover them with a towel just in case.

Outside, clouds pass over the moon, casting the snow-covered landscape in darkness then light. A coyote howls, giving me the creeps.

As I pass by the windows, I pause, scanning for a glimpse of the nocturnal hunters.

But instead of coyotes, I see the dark silhouette of a man standing in the trees. I press my face to the frosted glass, then startle back.

It's dark, but I could swear he looks like the hunter. The one we encountered on the drive up to the center—the one who put that poor mountain lion we hit out of its misery.

I flinch, remembering the sharp crack of his gun ripping through the head. My heart beats faster as I watch him trudge by our cabin. He's dragging something behind him through the snow. Something big and heavy, based on the way the hunter struggles through the trees.

Not an animal, based on the shape and size. My heart is pounding now.

I blink my eyes closed, trying to make sure I'm not hallucinating, then reopen them.

He jerks his head my way and I instinctively crouch down. Can he see me? No, that's impossible.

The moonlight appears through the clouds, illuminating the scene. I press my face to the glass again, and my blood runs as cold as the ice frosting the window. I freeze in shock, unable to look away from the danger.

It looks like he's dragging a dead body wrapped in a tarp.

But this one doesn't look animal-shaped, like the mountain lion or even a deer.

This one looks . . . human.

CHAPTER SIXTEEN

BEFORE

NOAH

No, this can't be happening, I think in shock. I blink hard, but he's still there.

I lock eyes with my father then turn away quickly. Morgan's top remains untied, revealing the beauty of her full bosom curving against her spine.

"Shit, this is bad," I say, tensing.

Concern explodes in Morgan's eyes. She struggles to pull her dress up. She thinks she did something wrong and offended me, when it's the opposite. This is all my fault. I shouldn't have brought her here. She wasn't ready for this.

Or maybe I'm not ready. I want her to stay my little secret, hidden away from the realities of my world and the burden that comes with knowing my last name—and who my family really is. My father was supposed to be out of town on business. Closing that new deal. I double-checked his schedule with his secretary right before we left, just to be sure. He never cancels business trips. What is he doing back?

He watches me for another long moment. His gaze pivots to Morgan pointedly before he turns away, leading his date—who is not my mother—away from the windows. However, I know this isn't the end of it. The wheels are turning already with him trying to figure out who I brought tonight. It's been a really long time since I've come with a date to the gathering. He knows I would only bring someone I felt strongly about.

Shit, I think again in dismay.

"What's wrong, Noah?" Morgan whispers into my ear. The party continues around us, unaware of my family drama. The sultry music and couples writhing around us suddenly feel wrong and seedy, shameful even.

I want to jump out of my skin and run. Get Morgan far away from here.

"Shhh! Don't use my name," I chastise before I can stop myself.

More hurt flashes in her eyes. She flinches back. I hate hurting her.

I wish I could take it all back. Just rewind and erase it—tonight, maybe even the app and meeting Morgan—so my father doesn't know about her.

I want to protect her, but I've failed.

"Sorry . . ." she stammers, looking ashamed. "But what's going on? Why would your father be here? And who is he with? Is that your mother?"

She scans the party through her mask, trying to make sense of what's happening. The attendees are engaged in fertility rituals—on the balcony, inside scattered around the wading pool, slung over the velvet sofas in various carnal poses straight out of the *Kama Sutra*. Some are clothed in sheer lingerie with convenient holes, some only in body paint and decorative jewelry, and some naked as the day they were born.

We're the most restrained. Partially, because I know she's not ready for, well, this, even though she's intrigued, turned on even, by the display.

Then there's my father and his mistress. One of them, anyway. My parents have an arrangement. They've always had an arrangement. The model is one of many who rotate through his life, ferreted around on his private jets, provided with luxury apartments and expense accounts, signed to strict NDAs. My mom is probably home in bed asleep.

I don't want to be like him. That's why I signed up for the One. That's why I can't let him find out about Morgan and destroy this for me. Not when I'm actually starting to care about her and see a possible future for us. That means we have to get out of here—*now*.

He's probably on his way out to the balcony right now, locked on us like a predator that sniffs blood in the air.

I know running away won't stop the interrogation, but it will delay it until I can figure out an explanation or some other way to appease him, and thus get him off the trail and off my back.

I try to cover my shock and kick into action, grabbing her hand and pulling her the other way around the balcony.

"I'm sorry, but we have to leave," I say stiffly.

I try to be gentle, but my fingers dig into her arm as I steer her around the balcony toward the front entrance that's our only escape route. I reach in my pocket and quickly text the pilot. The helicopter should be ready and waiting to get us the fuck out of here.

"Wait, you didn't answer my questions," she hisses as I rush her away. "Forget the experiment—what's going on? Why do we have to leave?"

"Look, I've already told you too much," I say, shaking my head. My curls dip into my eyes. "The less you know, the better. You have to trust me—"

But she digs her heels in. Refuses to budge. Every second, my father will close the distance. Head us off before we can make a hasty, inelegant exit.

"No, you can't lie to me," she says, stubbornly. "We're honest with each other. That's why this experiment is working. What's really going on?"

Our masks remain in place, but her eyes are fiery. She looks every bit the fearsome lioness.

"Fine." I grit my teeth. "That is my father—but the woman isn't my mother. And I don't want him to see us together."

"What's your father doing at a party like this?"

I see the cascade of other questions on the tip of her tongue. *Is he divorced? Is that his girlfriend? Your family goes to sex parties . . . together?* Things we probably would have already covered in a normal dating situation where we asked normal life questions about each other, including our families.

And I might have already divulged the complexities—slowly, not all at once so as not to shock her. About my father and my mother and their long-standing arrangements. About how when I hit the age of consent in New York—seventeen years old—my father brought me to my very first gathering, and I was initiated into the family tradition.

That scares most women away, which is why I don't really date. I more hook up with girls then dismiss them. Or if they come to the gathering, I know they won't last much longer. Or they pretend to be into it, but really they're just after the money and status. The lack of authenticity bores me, and then I'm the one running the other way.

But that ship has sailed. Morgan and I launched our experiment. I'm the one who messed up bringing her here. And now, I'm stuck in the middle of this nightmare situation.

"Right, it's complicated—and a much longer story," I say tightly. "As you've probably gathered, my family is a bit different. I don't want him to ruin what we have . . ." My voice cracks. "Look, I made a mistake bringing you tonight. I just wanted to impress you. And maybe I was testing you a little."

She purses her lips. "To see how much I could take of your crazy life?"

"I guess," I say glumly. "The problem is—I actually like you. Uh, like, really, really like you," I confess, knowing how lame that sounds. "I can't stand the thought of losing you. So, I'd rather you run if you can't handle my life before it gets harder for me and the worst possible thing happens."

She stands there stiffly, still not budging. "What's the worst possible thing that could happen?"

I take a deep breath, then blurt it out. "I actually fall in love with you."

There, I said it. The thing you're not supposed to say out loud. It feels like all the air is sucked out of me the moment I utter those words.

"Look, I know it's too soon," I say quickly before I overthink it. "But it's the truth. And you asked for the truth. No, you didn't just ask for it, you demanded it. Everything tonight was perfect—*so fucking perfect.* The dance floor, the balcony . . . until my father crashed the party and ruined it."

Out of the corner of my eye, I spot him winding his way through the house toward the front door. Our chance to make a clean escape is about to vanish.

"I was trying so hard to impress you for our big third date," I say miserably. "And now I'm afraid I've gone and messed everything up."

My heart feels like it's trying to rip out of my chest. If she thinks this is too much—if she dumps me right here, which wouldn't be surprising—I think it just might do that and kill me. But instead she steps closer. Her breath whispers over my face, smelling like vanilla and cinnamon and some other alluring chemical I can't place but probably is what's driving me mad for her in this primal, pheromonal way.

"You don't have to impress me," she says softly. "I'm already yours."

I'm stunned. Beyond stunned.

"And my family?" I stammer, knowing time is ticking away fast.

He's coming to intercept us. To shatter the illusion I've so carefully crafted to keep her safe.

"Listen, keep your dark family secrets for now," she says quickly. "My family . . . let's just say, I don't talk about them for a reason. I think that's why this experiment is working. It's just us—you and me. Nobody else."

My heart beats faster.

"You promise?"

"Yes, no matter what."

She steps toward me and kisses me—swiftly and hard—then jerks back and reaches for my hand. "Now get me the hell out of here," she says, snapping back into action.

I don't need to be told twice.

I seize her hand, clammy, but it instantly warms at my touch. I pull her across the balcony that wraps all the way around the house, dodging couples in various throes of passion. I track my father inside—he's shifted around to watch us—but he's not coming after us. He knows I'm fleeing. I'll have to deal with the fallout later. But for now, I have Morgan, and that's all I care about.

He can't have her.

I shoot him a look through my mask like I'm the lion challenging another predator vying for my targeted meal. We reach the other side of the balcony, slipping back into the entryway. The doormen open the doors, and we slip outside. I look back for a minute. I watch him with his date in their golden lion masks before the doors slide shut. Then we're racing across the driveway and down the footpath.

My helicopter alights on the landing pad with blades whipping the air and surrounding trees into a frenzy. The pilot gets out to open the door for us.

We reach it and I help her up first, then climb inside. He shuts the door. Instantly, the air feels like it is sucked out of the small space. My heart is racing. And then I'm all over her.

Kissing her neck, feeling her body warming and curving against mine. Safely protected by the tinted windows, I slide her mask off her face and behold her beauty. She slides mine off too. Our eyes lock together.

"Don't be afraid," she says. "I won't let your father come between us."

"It's complicated—" I start, but she raises her hand to silence me.

"But our blind date experiment isn't. We're eliminating the variables that usually get in the way and sabotage our relationships. It's just you and me. Nothing else matters anymore."

"Yes. It's just us," I say, trying to reassure myself as much as her.

We're about to take off, so we fasten our harnesses, but even they can't restrain us. The thrilling rush of propulsion flips my stomach. Her face lights up with wildness and ecstasy.

I'm all over her again until the helicopter spits us out on my rooftop even though the night has grown cooler. I can't keep my hands off her as we board the elevator.

Encased in glass above the cityscape, it does feel like a universe of our own making, shielding us from the outside world's problems. Her arms and legs wrap around me as I lift her up so she can straddle me.

Dark thoughts still haunt me, but she's right; it is just us. He doesn't have to know who she really is. This time, I'll convince him to stay out of it. *I can hold him off,* I tell myself. But another voice pipes up—

But for how long?

We reach my penthouse. I carry her through the doorway and into my bedroom, throwing her across the silk duvet. She has the lioness mask in her hand and toys with it before binding it over her face again with its luminous golden sheen.

She lies back suggestively and beckons for me. I can hardly resist.

"Are you going to conquer me?" she says in a sexy voice. "Like I'm your prey?"

She lies there, tempting me, daring me to pounce. I want nothing more.

My heart throbs, making the rest of my body fill with a rush of heat and blood, and my dick strains against my pants.

Ding!

The sound of my phone startles us both.

Shit, I think, cursing myself for not turning it off before we got home.

My dad's face flashes across the screen—dignified, chin cleft, a full head of white hair slicked back, a million-dollar smile, because it probably cost that much for the veneers—like my older, lighter shadow.

I look just like him, and now since my sister left, I'm also the one who will inherit everything. But there's more—the one who will carry on his secret legacy. I miss Zoe, but I understand why she did it. Why she ran away and erased herself.

That's why I stepped up to work at his company after she vanished, destined to become the CEO one day and inherit his vast fortune. A heavy crown to bear, but one that I've claimed, if reluctantly so. I'm still holding him off, insisting on my cubicle at the office where I can have semi-real friends. They know who I am destined to become, so while they bro around with me, it's all tempered and filtered through that lens.

Still, I cling to that normalcy for as long as I can, fending him off. Just as I cling to Morgan. She doesn't know who I really am—and I want to keep it that way. She guesses, but unlike every other girl I've dated, she's refrained from asking any details. Her curiosity has remained at bay, shockingly so. Even tonight when I took her to the gathering, she played along with my games and didn't question it.

And now, she's lying on my bed, but we haven't escaped *him*.

I slump down on the bed to study my phone instead of pouncing on her. A message from my father appears on my home screen. *We'll discuss this tomorrow, son.*

I wince, unable to hide my distress. At least he's not asking about her . . . yet. Maybe I can play it off as the fling of the moment like everyone expects from me. But now I realize I made a critical mistake by fleeing from the party.

Like she mattered.

Like I wanted to protect her.

Like she wasn't a mere fling.

Yeah, I fucked up bad this time. She can see it written all over my face. The way I crumple in this moment. The way I deflate. But she scoops me up, pulling me onto the bed next to her and holding me close until I fall asleep in her arms, knowing I'll do anything to keep her safe. That I can keep her a secret.

That's when I say it—and it's crazy because we haven't even fully consummated our union yet. I haven't pushed inside her, making her feel every inch of me and claiming her as mine.

But I say it anyway. Because my heart beats insistently—*thump, thump, thump*—and forces the words from my lips. I can't help it.

"I love you, Morgan."

I feel her tense, freezing. That's it—I messed up. I know it with every fiber of my being. She waits, maybe to see if it's a mistake, if I try to backpedal and take it back. But I don't. Instead, I pull her closer, tighter, breathing into her hair.

"I love you," I whisper again.

And this time, she softens and breathes back—

"I love you, Noah."

I let her words wrap around me like a blanket, but worries rise up anyway, assaulting me.

"Even though you don't know my last name? Or who I really am?"

"*Especially* because I don't know your last name."

I relax into her. She reaches around to stroke my hair, threading her fingers through my thick curls. "But you're wrong about that," she adds. "I do know who you are—the real you that you hide from the world. Maybe I'm the only one who really knows you."

"You're right," I admit with a deep sigh. "I don't like to let anyone in . . . People always leave me."

I think of my sister. How she was the first one to really abandon me. How growing up, she was the only one who really understood what we went through with our family. And then she simply . . .

Vanished.

Didn't even leave me a note.

"We're the same," Morgan goes on, biting her lower lip in a way that drives me crazy. "My roomies would call us *twin flames.* You know, soul mates. Wait, you're not a triple Gemini, are you?"

I laugh. "I don't even know what that means. But I don't think so. Why?"

"Okay, good. I guess most serial killers are triple Gemini or something. Just some crazy stuff they said."

"Right. I'll make sure to check for you." She play-punches me. I wince, pulling her closer. "What about you? Should I be concerned?"

"About what?"

"Maybe that you're a crazy triple Gemini serial killer?" I joke back.

Her face contorts—just for a split second—then hides it. "I can't help you on the *crazy* part. Since this whole situation with you is . . . well, it's a little bit crazy. Maybe even certifiable."

I play innocent. "Oh, how so?"

"The blind date experiment?" she says, ticking the reasons off. "The masquerade sex party tonight? But as for being a serial killer? Well, if I say no, you can't trust that."

"What makes you say that?"

She smirks. "Because that's *exactly* what a serial killer would say. So, how can you be sure?"

"I guess I'll just have to take my chances," I say. "And you love me? You're sure? I know it's soon, and maybe you just said it because I did. You can feel free to take it back—"

"Noah, I *love* you. There, I said it again. Pinky swear," she says, holding out her finger. "No take backs, okay?"

I smile. "No take backs."

We pinky shake, then I drift into the deepest, most peaceful slumber, not realizing how easily that peace could be shattered into a million tiny pieces.

CHAPTER SEVENTEEN

AFTER

MORGAN

I slap my hand over my mouth to stifle the scream building in my chest. It comes out more like a muffled sob. I can't have Hannah and Mia rushing into my room right now. They might barge into my bathroom and see my banned electronics charging.

The hunter vanishes into the trees, leaving a trail of footprints behind our cabin. He looked right at me. Even though I'm pretty sure he couldn't actually see me, it still freaked me out.

Was it the same hunter we encountered on the road? Guru Shava said the land was open to hunters. Still, my mind races with paranoid thoughts. It sure looked like him. Although all hunters look kind of the same: camouflage clothes and guns. Why was he hunting at night though? Some animals are nocturnal, so you'd have to hunt at night. While it seems a little unusual, there could easily be a logical reason.

Another scary thought hits me. Could he be stalking us? I didn't get a good feeling from him. The way he leered at us, almost hungrily. How he called us girlie girls.

Major ick.

I wait a few moments longer, scanning the moonlit landscape, but all is quiet. Nothing disrupts the trees. A distant owl takes up a gentle nighttime lullaby.

Still, my heart races. I sink down onto my bed, pulling the comforter around me, wrestling with my thoughts as they ping between paranoia and fear and logic and reason—until I finally fall into a restless sleep filled with broken dreams that shatter into more nightmares.

"What secrets are you hiding, Morgan?" Guru Shava whispers.

Her blue eyes narrow at me.

Bong!

I wake up with a start, the nightmare still fresh in my memory. I'm breathing hard, and the sheets are soaked with sweat. The alarm clock is blaring. It's not even light outside.

The face reads six a.m.

I don't want to, but I force myself from bed. My feet hit the freezing cold floors, and I stumble into the bathroom. I barely got any sleep last night. I shouldn't have stayed up so late binging the podcast.

Suddenly, I remember the hunter. For some reason, the vision had blended into my nightmares, mixing together. I frown, trying to untangle what was real from what I imagined in my sleep. Was it only a hallucination?

No, I definitely saw him. I rush back to the window, scanning for fresh footprints in the snow, but it's too dark to make anything out.

I return to the bathroom, checking my phone. Fully charged—but still no service. I thumb back to the text message to Noah that he left on read.

It's possible he's been texting, trying to reach me, but I've gone MIA.

And I have six more days here. Kill me now. At least I have the podcasts. They worked like a charm getting me through the boring yoga and meditation sessions yesterday afternoon. It's surprisingly easy to tune out most of what Guru Shava says and just follow along with the visual cues from the class.

Plus, at this rate, I'm gonna binge every one of these podcasts before the week is over. I'm almost done with season one. Noah would understand why I was binging murder porn podcasts at a peaceful yoga retreat.

That brings a smile to my face. He'd think that was funny, too.

Damn it, and just like that, I miss him all over again, like a knife to the heart. All those inside jokes and little memories we shared. The thousand tiny, invisible moments that build the foundation of every relationship.

Tears prick my eyes, but I blink them back and force myself to get ready. I repeat my method from yesterday, tucking the AirPods under my hair and the phone in my waist. I'll probably need a midday charging session, but I can fake another detox bathroom trip. That should buy me enough time. Hell, I may not even need to fake it, I think with a wince, remembering all the horrid concoctions I was forced to drink.

My stomach churns unhappily. I step into the living room to find Mia slumped on the sofa. Hannah pokes around the kitchen, making tea.

"Your hair looks different today," Mia says with a frown, making me freeze.

"Uh, what do you mean?" I reply. I fidget with the low, loose ponytail that's hiding the AirPods.

Did she notice them?

"You usually wear it in a top bun," Mia says, locked on now. "I've never seen you do it that way."

"Oh, you don't like it?"

She smiles. "No, actually it looks way better. Don't go back to that ugly top bun. Those went out of style ages ago."

"Sure. You got it."

If only she knew the truth, I think as we leave the cabin and head toward the main lodge.

I want to tell them about what I saw last night, but I'm afraid they won't believe me without proof. Hell, I don't even fully believe me. It's possible the murder podcast wound me up. I was half asleep after all, and my head was filled with that stuff.

I'll check for the footprints when I sneak off for a recharge session.

About five minutes later, we stumble into the Great Hall. We shrug off our coats, hanging them on the wooden hooks by the door. A fresh fire blazes in the stone hearth, but the now familiar stink of Palo Santo and patchouli hits me.

The silent assistants are circulating with their trays of sludge smoothies and raw juice shots. The other guests are grabbing for them eagerly and downing them. Watching them, I feel a wave of nausea and revulsion sweep through me. It feels like being the sober person in a room full of drunks. That's the best way I can describe it.

We wait to be summoned in for meditation, when I see something.

Dame Tremaine stands by the fireplace, sipping a sludge smoothie. But today, she only has one friend with her. I scan the room to double-check, but I don't see the other friend anywhere.

Dame Tremaine also seems kind of upset. I study her closer from the corner of my eyes, trying to be subtle about it. Her eyes look red, as though she's been crying. I flash back, remembering the heated conversation they had before the sound bath. How her friend had stormed away.

I nudge Hannah. "Do you see that?" I nod to the pop star. "Remember how she had two friends with her yesterday?"

"Lower your voice," Hannah snaps, glancing around to make sure nobody heard me gossiping. "You sound like a total stalker. Remember the rules about privacy?"

I lower my voice and lean into her ear. "Fine—but one of her friends is missing today. And well, I saw something in the woods last night."

"Wait, what did you see?" Mia says, barging into our huddled conversation. "And why are we all whispering?"

"It's about Dame Tremaine," Hannah says. "Morgan says one of her friends is missing today. And she saw something in the woods last night."

"Really? No way. What did you see?" Mia says. "Okay, I need all the tea."

They both peer at me expectantly. Quickly—and in a low voice—I fill them in on the hunter dragging the dead body through the woods outside my window last night. When I get to the end of my story, they look skeptical.

"Are you sure?" Hannah says. "It must have been pretty dark."

"It was probably an animal," Mia agrees. "How can you be sure?"

"The missing friend is how!" I hiss, jerking my head toward the pop star. "I wasn't sure before either, but now someone is missing from our retreat."

"That's not exactly proof," Hannah says in exasperation. "Maybe she left early. Or she's not feeling well and stayed back in their cabin. Or maybe she got caught violating the rules. Guru Shava wasn't messing around."

"Yeah, the one about the no electronics," Mia says.

That jolts me. I can feel my phone pressing into my skin at the waistband of my pants and the AirPods in my ears. But I can't let it go.

"No, I think something happened to her," I insist in a low voice, feeling more suspicious. "Also, the blizzard dumped at least a foot or two of snow. How would she leave if the roads are blocked? I bet it'll take them at least a week to dig out, especially this far up in the mountains."

"So now you're an expert on snowplowing?" Hannah says with a scowl.

"You don't care what happened to her?" I say, feeling hurt.

"The point is that it's *none of our business,*" Hannah replies with a frown. "You're supposed to be focused on yourself—not snooping on other guests. Especially the celebs."

"Who is missing again?" Mia says, scanning the group.

"I told you already," I say, growing frustrated but trying to keep my voice even. "Yesterday, Dame Tremaine had two friends. Don't you remember the other friend? The one with the black hair?"

They both shake their heads. *Damn it, why am I the only one who remembers her?*

"Are you sure?" Mia says. "I just remember her having one friend."

"Yeah, that one"—she points to the woman standing with Dame Tremaine—"with the blonde hair," Hannah says in a soft voice.

Tears prick my eyes. Frustrated tears. I can't believe they don't remember. "Please, you have to believe me. I know what I saw yesterday. And I know what happened last night, too."

They exchange a worried look.

"I love you, Morgan," Hannah says carefully, "but you do have bad nightmares sometimes, remember? You've been so upset since your breakup. You're not thinking straight."

She places a sympathetic hand on my shoulder. They're right. I can't deny it.

"Guru Shava says sometimes we can hallucinate when we're purging," Mia says. "Remember in class yesterday?"

"Uh, of course," I stammer, even though I don't remember that at all. I was probably zoned out with my podcast. But I can't let them know that.

"Right, are you sure?" Hannah says. "What else did she say yesterday?"

"Uh, namaste?" I try to lighten the mood. But Hannah looks upset.

"You weren't paying attention, were you? You have to surrender to the process if you expect it to work and heal you."

"We talked last night," Mia says. "We're worried you're self-sabotaging. Guru Shava said the program will only work if you let it."

"Fine. But why do I need it to work?" I spit back, crossing my arms. "I didn't ask to be here. You forced me."

They both look hurt. I wasn't supposed to say that out loud.

An awkward moment passes. I feel guilty, but they ganged up on me. I had to defend myself.

"Well, how else are you gonna get over him?" Hannah says. "You certainly weren't improving back home."

"I wasn't that bad. You didn't need to kidnap me and bring me to the middle of *freaking* nowhere. You're exaggerating—" I start, but Mia cuts me off.

"The Morgan-shaped groove in our sofa begs to differ," Mia says. "And the Netflix Recently Watched queue. All that murder porn."

I deflate a little, but I'm stubborn.

"Just let me show you where I saw him after class, okay? If there's nothing there, then we can give it a rest."

They exchange another look but nod reluctantly. It's official—they think I'm crazy. But at least, they agree to take the field trip.

Bong.

The gong summons us to class. As I shuffle into the studio with everyone else, I can't shake the feeling that something wrong is going on here. The wooden beam slides into place, trapping us inside, and Guru Shava begins. She sits cross-legged in front of the microphone on a meditation pillow. She looks the same as yesterday in her white robes and turban. The wooden bead and crystal necklaces layered around her neck and covering her chest complete her crunchy but holy vibe.

"Welcome to the second day of your death and rebirth at the Namaste Center . . ." I click Play, mercifully drowning her and her cult-like monologue out.

After class, Hannah and Morgan don't look happy when I bring it up, but they keep their promise to accompany me to our cabin. They follow me around to the back, where my window looks out at the thick woods on one side and the sheer cliff on the other side.

"The hunter came out of the trees over here," I say, leading them toward the woods. I feel my heart start to race, remembering the scene from last night.

I expect to find large footprints in the snow, or signs of a body being dragged. Maybe even a few blood spatters for good measure. In my true crime podcasts, they always talk about that—spatter patterns. I feel like a virtual expert.

But then, I start to deflate.

There's nothing here. No footprints. No crushed down snow from a dead body. No blood.

"Are you satisfied yet?" Hannah says in annoyance. "Hurry, it's freezing. Let's get back to the lodge already."

Mia's eyes are sympathetic. "Look, Morgan, we gave you the benefit of the doubt. But look around—there's nothing here."

I poke around some more anyway, sticking my head through the trees. A branch smacks my face, while briars dig into my legs, piercing my tight yoga pants. I feel something warm on my cheek. It drips down, spattering onto the snow. My own blood.

"I don't understand it," I say, giving up. "It must be the fresh dusting of snow that covered up his tracks. Or maybe the hunter covered them up . . ."

I trail off. They don't respond to that. I tell them I'll meet them at the lodge, so I can sneak into our cabin and do a quick charge on my devices.

I force the door open, stamping my boots to shake off the snow. I'm shivering. I check my face in the mirror. Sure enough, I cut my cheek on the tree branch. Tiny droplets of blood on my cheek under a razor-thin cut. They're already drying up and flaking off.

That's not all I see. Pale skin. Dark circles under my eyes. I look worse than when I got here—and that's saying a lot. I'm not glowing from the detox like the rest of our group. I look jumpy, worn out, strung out.

Maybe my friends are right. Maybe I am being paranoid. But I can't shake the uneasy feeling the rest of the day.

My podcasts help distract me at first, but then I'm down the rabbit hole again, spinning through what I saw last night and why one of Dame Tremaine's friends is gone, searching for clues to explain it. As we once again take Shavasana—corpse pose—lying on our purple yoga mats, I keep circling back to one especially chilling thought.

Who's going to disappear next?

CHAPTER EIGHTEEN

BEFORE

MORGAN

The weeks pass so fast, and fall arrives before I barely notice the significant chill in the air, almost like time itself dissolves. Being with Noah is like hitting fast-forward on life. It makes sense, since we've been dating in fast-forward.

Or maybe it's more like rewind.

Doing everything backward. Saying *I love you* before we even know each other's last names, or before we've done the obligatory friends and family introductions, let alone post about each other on social media. I don't even know if he has social media.

How crazy is that?

I cut through Central Park after work and a quick stop home to freshen my makeup and grab a heavier coat before heading to meet him for drinks. The leaves crunch under my fur-lined boots with my designer jeans tucked into them. I clutch my overcoat tighter.

The park is teeming with other professionals getting off work like me, along with some of the mom-and-stroller or dudes-with-dogs crowd who work from home so they don't have to put on pants with zippers. Or maybe they're wealthy nepo babies who don't have to work, or they live in a walk-up with six other roommates while they pursue acting or modeling or fashion. In the city, you never know.

As I walk briskly to keep up with the relentless pace of the pedestrians, I ponder Noah's social media situation. He seems like the type that wouldn't want to put his life on display for the masses like that, I decide, instead clinging to his privacy, almost like he heralds from a bygone age.

I haven't internet stalked him, much to Hannah and Mia's dismay. They've threatened to do it for me. But I've made them swear on our friendship to refrain from letting their curiosity run rampant and ruin everything for me.

Plus, they don't really have a choice. They don't know what he looks like. His picture wasn't on his dating app profile, thanks to the One, so reverse image searching is completely out of the question. They also don't know his last name. Hell, I don't either. *Noah* is a surprisingly common name these days.

He's still my mystery suitor. And for now, I aim to keep it that way.

It's also thrilling. Unlike any dating scenario I've ever experienced. He is also unlike any man I've ever met, let alone dated.

I suppose my friends could hire a private investigator to tail me. Or even stalk me themselves. But so far, they've shown enough restraint. For now. But I know the day is coming, sooner rather than later, when I will finally have to parade him around and introduce him to our little friend group that mostly matriculated from Barnard and stayed in the city, combined with a smattering of their wealthy prep school friends.

We meet for drinks on a semi-regular basis, though I've been skipping it more often than not since I met Noah. They don't approve of that either.

"You know, it's a major red flag if you cut off your friends when you start dating someone," Hannah said just before I left.

"Yeah, it's like he's isolating you," Mia added, looking up from filing her nails. They were in the living room on our overstuffed sofa with a reality show streaming on the TV.

I was in a hurry to leave and didn't want to stop for a pointed interrogation.

"Just because I'm missing drinks tonight?" I shot back. "Look, I'll make it up to you guys next week. I promise."

"Is that when we get to meet him?" Hannah said in a whiny voice, needling me for the hundredth time this week. "You can bring him."

"I can't commit to next week," I hedge, pulling on my overcoat. A piece of my hair gets stuck in my mouth, and I yank it out with a grossed-out face.

"Oh, and why not?" Hannah asks.

"You already know the reason," I reply. "We're still sticking to our blind date experiment. Plus, you signed me up for the One, remember? This was all your idea. You should be happy for me."

"We are. But it's still majorly sus," Mia said. "Like he's hiding something dark."

That hung in the air. She was right—I was keeping things from them. I still hadn't told them about the masquerade sex party. Even if I sugarcoated it and removed the *sex* part of it, they'd still get majorly judgmental.

They wouldn't understand that I actually enjoyed the experience—how exciting and exhilarating it was. If I told them about how he slipped ecstasy in my drink, they'd probably call the NYPD right then and there. I couldn't have them overreacting and ruining it.

That's how I rationalized it. But the little secrets kept building up to bigger secrets, things that made sense in the context of our special bond, but that outsiders would judge and label. The more secrets you kept, the more secrets you had to keep in the future.

I also didn't tell them about his father catching us, and how upset Noah got. They would definitely file that under *major red flags*, a mental accordion file they seemed to be keeping on him. The less they knew, the better.

For now.

Until we were ready to make our situation official, which would be after he committed—not just said the L-word, but something more substantial, I'd decided. And, of course, when we finally consummated the relationship.

Hannah shot me a look.

"Yeah, maybe he has another girlfriend," she suggested, sipping her prebiotic soda. "Or more than one! Guys in the city like to play the field."

"Oh, yeah, he's juggling *three* other girlfriends." I tried to ignore their disapproving looks as I slid on my boots to go meet him. "While spending all of his free time with me."

"Fine, but the clock is ticking," Hannah said. "We have to meet him."

"Or we really will hire a PI," Mia threatened, narrowing her eyes. "I've done it before, you know."

"On Grant?" I said, surprised. "He's borderline obsessed with you. He dotes on you. He'd never cheat."

She shrugged. "That's what the PI said. It turned out all the pictures he got were of us together. Or him playing video games with his friends."

I snorted a laugh. "See, you were just being paranoid. Like you are with me."

That was the last thing I said before I bolted from our apartment and down the steps. But my thoughts still feel a bit unsettled, making me worry that I'm making a mistake. My heart lurches—with love and affection—but my brain screams to slow down and be careful.

Maybe it's time to take the next step and confess our true identities. But the way we're doing it makes me feel young and free again like I was in college.

Okay, strike that.

I was never exactly young and free. My childhood prevented me from having a typical upbringing. So, maybe this is my early life crisis when I finally get the chance to rediscover and reclaim what was taken from me by my father.

I think back to the masquerade party, feeling a shudder work its way through my body, how he almost pushed me over the edge that night. If his father hadn't caught us . . . Noah brushed it off the next day, assuring me he had just overreacted and it would be fine.

I'm not so sure it's that simple. I get the feeling he's protecting me. It's obvious his family is wealthy—old money. The stink of ostentatious wealth follows him around everywhere. That penthouse alone . . .

I know what something like that must cost. Even if you have the money, it doesn't mean you'll be permitted to purchase an apartment in it. Buildings like that have co-op boards that exist solely to keep the wrong sort of buyer out of the building.

But as much as I hoped something like this would happen, it's more than that with Noah. He's reached a part of me I thought was gone forever, penetrated the shield I'd erected long ago to protect my heart. And that's what's so dangerous about him.

I'm actually falling for him.

I love you.

I wasn't just saying those words performatively after our third date. I meant them. That's why I'm in trouble with him. But if I'm drowning, he's drowning too. It's just like *Titanic*.

Does that mean only one of us will survive?

And if so—
Which one?

A few minutes later, I arrive at Noah's building where we planned to meet. I'm so lost in thought that I don't notice the dark figure hovering in the alleyway, waiting for me. A hand grabs my shoulder.

"Hey, get off me!" I yell, jerking away and whipping my head around. My eyes fall on the perpetrator.

It's Noah.

"Sorry, I didn't mean to startle you," he says, apologetically.

His hands are shoved deep into the front pockets of his slim navy, pinstriped suit. The material looks expensive, tailored perfectly to his tall frame. He looks as dashing as always. But something grabs my attention. He seems a little jumpy, nervous even.

"Is everything okay?" I study him for some clue to why he seems rattled.

"Of course," he says, dodging the question and bending around to kiss my cheek. A quick brush of his soft lips.

"Is your car coming?"

I peer around for the familiar town car with driver that I've come to expect.

"Not today," he says, gesturing to the park. "It's such a beautiful day, I thought we could walk to dinner."

"Oh, being romantic?" I tease him.

He holds out his elbow for me to loop my arm through, and we begin our stroll, retracing the path I took.

He's right. It's a perfect, idyllic fall day. A light breeze brings a chill, tossing the freshly fallen leaves around. Our shoes crunch over them. I've come to love this time of year—the last gasps before the hard, wet winter descends.

I probably wouldn't mind the cold rain and wet snow as much if I didn't have to brave the elements and public transportation—if I had a driver and car at my beck and call like Noah. But maybe that's my future?

I glance over at him. He still seems nervous.

"Is it your father?"

Worry explodes in my heart. It's been a few weeks since the incident at the party, and the truth is Noah has seemed a little withdrawn since then. We've had fun dates and plenty of make-out sessions at his penthouse—still no sex though. But it's felt like something important has been on his mind.

"Morgan, I told you not to worry," he says with a sigh. "I'm sorry that I overreacted. I've just had some bad experiences in the past when he tried to interfere in my relationships too much. But I stood up to him this time."

"Wait, you did?" I say, surprised. "You didn't tell me that."

"Like I said, I didn't want to worry you. He tried to corner me the next morning, but I told him it was none of his business. That when there was something *official*, I'd inform him, and we could do it the proper way."

"You mean not at a masquerade sex party?" I joke under my breath.

"Ha, exactly." He shakes his head. "I'm impressed you stuck around after that. I figured you'd break up with me."

I give him a penetrating look. "Should I have?"

He laughs. "I think most girls would have run for the hills—or at least suggested I seek professional help for massive childhood trauma."

It's my turn to laugh. "Hey, who doesn't have a touch of childhood trauma? It keeps it interesting. I haven't told you about my family yet either."

I keep my tone light. But darkness creeps into the edges of my voice.

I have my fake story ready to deploy at the right moment about their tragic deaths in a car crash right before I left for college, orphaning me. That part is true. I am an orphan; they're both dead, just not the way I say.

"I can't wait to find out all about your miserable childhood," he teases me, snapping me out of my morbid thoughts. "But I'm sticking to the rules."

"Ah yes, our experiment." I mull that over as we pass other couples also walking arm-in-arm. Central Park has a storybook, fairy-tale vibe sometimes. "How long should we stick to it?"

"Ugh, forever?" he groans. "Is that possible? I want you all to myself. I hate the idea of sharing you with anyone."

He leans over and kisses me sideways. I love his possessiveness.

"Sounds like a dream," I say, then turn more serious. "But eventually, you have to wake up. My friends have been asking me nonstop.

No, more like interrogating me. They're mad I skipped drinks with our friend group tonight."

"Mine too. My coworkers won't leave me alone. Roger and Blake. They wanted to go out for drinks tonight."

I act shocked. "I got first names this time? Wow, things are moving fast."

"I figure you can't find out much from that. They're pretty generic names."

"Valid. You need friends with highly unique names, so I can internet stalk."

"Sorry to disappoint."

We both laugh.

"But seriously, how long do we have to wait?" I say, pressing him. "You really think we can keep this going?"

"If it was up to me, we'd do this forever." A wistful expression crosses his face. "Maybe we could run away together. Leave this all behind."

He gestures to the park and the expansive city beyond the trees.

"Start over somewhere where nobody knows who we are . . ." He trails off. "Where none of that matters."

"Wait, are you being serious?" I ask, feeling my heart drop.

I've fought so hard to arrive here that running away when everything feels like it's right at my fingertips hurts. I feel my stomach drop. I know I love Noah not only for his wealth or status, but they're intrinsically intertwined.

If he were a poor nobody, would I have let myself fall so hard and so fast? Would I have even given him a chance? A second date? I want to be naive and claim that stuff doesn't matter, but deep down, I know that would be a lie.

And he knows it too.

He may have withheld his last name, but he's used everything else in his arsenal to seduce and conquer me. The penthouse. Private chef. Helicopter. Masquerade party. Even the drinks and dinners at all the top restaurants.

"You mean, run away like your sister Zoe?" I say, feeling bad for digging at this deep pain. My words hang in the air. The moment elongates. A dark look flits over his face. But then he smiles sheepishly and shakes his head.

"An impossible dream," he murmurs. "Like you said, eventually we have to wake up. But let's stay in the dream for as long as we can. Okay?"

I nod my agreement, grateful the moment passed and he wasn't serious.

We reach Gapstow Bridge, the iconic stone bridge covered in vines that arcs over the pond. Ducks swim in the water below even though winter approaches. To the south you can see the dramatic skyline of the city.

This is one of my favorite spots in the city. I know it's cliché, but that doesn't make it any less true. When I first arrived in New York as a transplant, walking through Central Park was one of those touchstone experiences that told me I'd really made it. That's why I still walk through the park when I could take the subway or the bus sometimes.

"Recognize this bridge?" he says, coming to a halt with me on his arm.

"Everyone does," I say, turning to face him. "You know it's one of my favorite spots. I took you here on our first date. Remember?"

"How could I forget. After I talked you down from stepping into traffic."

I give him a playful shove.

"In my defense, I was having a bad day. After a slew of bad first dates."

That's when he pulls something out of his pocket. A velvet jewelry box.

My heart skips. This must be why he was acting so jumpy earlier.

"Morgan, I've had the most amazing last few weeks with you," he starts. "And I just don't want it to end. Every time I see you I'm counting down the days until the next time I can see you."

I stand there speechless. The box looks too big to hold an engagement ring, but I recognize the logo of the pricey jeweler.

"Please accept this gift as a promise of more to come. So, I guess I want to make us official." He flicks the box open. "Will you be my girlfriend?"

Inside the box is a beautiful platinum and diamond necklace sitting on a soft velvet backing. The diamond pendant forms a shape that resembles a tiny map. I run my fingers over the studs.

"What does it mean?"

"They're the geo coordinates for this spot, where we had our first date."

With that, my heart melts. I can't take it. This is like something out of a movie. Something I thought I'd never have.

A fairy tale.

I can't stop the tears that pool in my eyes and threaten to spill down my cheeks. I blink them back hastily.

"Is that a yes?" he asks.

I'm so struck that I forgot to answer. "Yes, of course I'll be your girlfriend."

He kisses me then, passionately, so long that I forget where I am for a minute. When we finally come up for air, he pulls the necklace from the box and fastens it around my neck. I flip it over to read the back. Etched into the metal it says:

Morgan + Noah

It's stamped over the date we met. Then another message underneath that reads *Endless as the stars.*

The cold metal settles around my collarbone, instantly warming on my skin. I can't believe this is happening. That he hasn't bolted or ghosted me like all the guys before who ran if I dared ask for any kind of commitment, let alone the actual girlfriend title.

"What does it mean exactly?" I say, running my hands over the charm.

Real diamonds.

"It's a promise of more. That we are committed to growing our relationship into something real. Morgan, I want to give you everything, every bit of me, every last drop."

That last part he whispers, and I shudder with desire.

"For now, you're my girlfriend. *Officially*. One day to be my wife."

I can't believe it. "Really?"

He gives me a sincere look. "I've never meant anything more. You're not like anyone I've ever met. I'd be a fool to let you slip through my fingers."

"And now it's my turn—to keep my promise. Remember my one rule?"

"No sex until commitment?"

My lips curl up as I finger the promise necklace. "I think this counts."

He leans into me. I feel his desire simmering and then exploding in the way he kisses me. When he finally pulls away, he whispers, "Morgan, you're mine."

And with that, we ditch our plans and rush back to his penthouse, my heart pounding in anticipation.

He's going to claim me tonight—and I know I'll be helpless to resist him.

CHAPTER NINETEEN

AFTER

MORGAN

My fingers drift to the promise necklace around my neck. It's become a habit, like a fidget spinner.

I darken, remembering how much I loved him—and how much I lost with his one indiscretion.

I jerk my hand away. A murderous urge rises up in me again.

That girl.

The one who took everything from me. Maybe she was the real problem—and problems can be eliminated. More dark thoughts crowd into my head, like they used to when I was younger.

But then, I calm my mind, taking a few deep breaths. Count to ten—*one, two, three, four* . . . I've trained myself to wrestle the darkness and force it back down into the shadows where it belongs. The problem is that it seethes and lies in wait for an opening to burst from the depths back into the light.

Gradually, they retreat. *Guru Shava would be proud of me,* I think darkly.

I force myself out of bed and walk into the bathroom, the light catching on the necklace. I know I should get rid of it. Throw it into the ocean like that old lady in *Titanic,* even though it's probably worth a fortune.

I know I'm showing my weakness, but I can't bring myself to shed one of the last vestiges of our relationship. I pull on my yoga pants, then add a crop top paired with a fresh, long-sleeved shirt with a higher neck that hides the necklace. If Mia and Hannah knew I still wore it, they'd probably rip it off my neck.

But the nearly indestructible stones, formed under intense seismic pressure that crushed and purified them, are still tucked underneath and nestled against the tender flesh of my collarbone.

His chokehold on me.

It's day three of this torture session, and I feel anything but rested and relaxed. In fact, I feel jumpier and more anxious than ever. I had another night filled with vivid, horrible nightmares.

I pad into the living area. It's still dark outside, and I feel an overwhelming desire to stay in bed for the rest of the day. No, scratch that, more like the rest of the retreat.

"What do you think is in those smoothies?" I ask Hannah casually, finding her in the kitchen brewing some kind of strong medicinal smelling tea.

She lifts an eyebrow. "Raw stuff that's healthy and detoxifying."

I lower my voice. "You don't think she might be drugging us, do you?"

"Like with shrooms or something?" Mia says, joining us for tea. "I wish! That's my one complaint about this retreat. A little booze would liven it up. I would kill for some *actual* drugs."

Hannah rolls her eyes. "Be serious—you're probably just detoxing."

I wince. "Yeah, probably."

"Detoxing can have major side effects," Hannah says. "Headaches, body aches, chills, and of course, the TMI bathroom issues. The more toxins in your body, the worse it is. Not to mention, emotional baggage . . ." She trails off delicately, not directly mentioning my toxic breakup.

They both look at me in a way that says—*You're pretty fucked up.*

"Don't worry. It'll get better as your body adjusts to the program." Hannah smiles in that glassy-eyed way. "I feel the best I have maybe ever. I'm sleeping better. My skin is clearing up, including that stubborn hormonal zit that pops up on my chin like clockwork every single month. I feel amazing!"

"Same here," Mia says, also smiling in that creepy way that reminds me of a cult. "Not to TMI you, but I've had some GI issues. All my bloat is gone, along with those extra pounds!"

I scrutinize their appearances. They look basically the same to me. Maybe Mia's stomach is slightly flatter, but she was always skinny no matter how much she complains about those invisible five pounds—a figment of her imagination, if you ask me. But it's a secret part of girl code. No matter how stunning and gorgeous you are, you have to find something you *hate* about your appearance and want to change—and complain about it loudly to your girlfriends, even if it's completely made-up.

But I can't tell them I don't see any differences and ruin the hype.

"Oh totally! You both look amazing." I turn to Mia. "Now that you mention it, I think you are skinnier."

"Right?" Mia says, patting her flat stomach and beaming at me.

"And look at your skin," Hannah says. "When we get back, nobody's gonna believe we didn't have plastic surgery. That's how good it is."

I slide into my Ugg boots, getting ready to tramp up to the lodge for our morning torture session. I've got my phone and AirPods charged and ready to go, but they give me weird looks.

Hannah frowns. "Where are you going?"

I freeze. "Morning meditation?"

They shake their heads.

"Weren't you paying attention yesterday?"

"What do you mean?" I swallow hard. I had my earbuds in and my podcast on the whole time so I clearly missed something. What fresh horrors could today's schedule bring?

Hannah digs through the welcome packet, producing the schedule. "Today, we have our private sessions with Guru Shava. I can't wait."

Sure enough, my appointment stares back at me from the schedule. I force a smile. "Uh, great. Mine is at ten."

What I don't say is that I'm completely dreading this.

Worse, my podcast can't save me.

"Let's dig right in, shall we?"

Guru Shava stares at me in a way that makes me squirm in my chair. She's dressed in her usual uniform of white robes and a white turban with her blonde dreads spilling out of the back. When I arrived at the lodge, I was escorted by a silent apprentice into a little waiting room, then into her office.

It has the same vibe as the rest of the center—boho, with leather and wood furniture, an imposing desk that looks hand-carved and polished from a thick slice of tree trunk, light wood finishes, soft lighting, a crackling fireplace, and floor-to-ceiling windows that look out onto the mountains. Oh, and that same patchouli stink that follows her everywhere and itches my nose.

She kicks back in her chair, flipping open a file in her lap. I swallow hard.

"Uh, sure," I saw awkwardly, trying to stifle the sneeze tickling my nose.

"According to your application, you recently had a toxic relationship that culminated in a tough breakup. Care to tell me more about what happened?"

My cheeks burn. That's the *last* thing I want to do. My eyes flick to the file. Hannah and Mia completed it for me. The same way they signed me up for the One without telling me.

Mortification.

"Uh, right," I stammer. "I guess you could say that. Though I don't think the relationship was toxic, exactly. Just, it didn't end well . . ." I trail off.

The pain stabs me, still fresh.

She raises one eyebrow. "According to this, it was *toxic.* Why are you changing the narrative now? Rewriting history to make it more palatable and exonerate him?"

So, my friends think the whole relationship was toxic. That's news to me. I press my lips together, feeling my anger building as I try to process this.

"I'm not justifying what he did," I say, trying to find the words to explain something that's going to sound bad no matter how I phrase it. "I know he cheated on me. Worse, he slept with my friend. Well, not my friend exactly, but someone from our friend group."

Guru Shava nods, then scribbles. "Not to press you, but you seem to be dancing around the *friend* label to make it sound better. Typically, if someone is a friend of your friends . . ."

"That makes them your friend," I finish for her. "But that's where you're wrong. This girl was the toxic one! I never liked her. She went to this fancy boarding school with my friends."

Guru Shava nods. "Go on."

"So she wasn't really my friend. I was just trying to be nice. We all kind of hung out together. But I felt like she had bad intentions from the beginning. She was obsessed with my boyfriend—"

"Your *ex*-boyfriend," she corrects me.

"Right. My ex-boyfriend. I just hate thinking of him that way." My thoughts spiral from the simple correction. Just a slight change to the semantics.

My ex-boyfriend. Even if it's true, it sounds so definitive. I don't want to modify the title. I'm not ready to accept that it's real yet. Like Mia and her imaginary extra five pounds, I guess I have an imaginary boyfriend.

She gives me a sympathetic look. "Morgan, I'm not a therapist. I'm a spiritual advisor. But I can offer insight and healing. I've worked with hundreds of women just like you."

"I know," I manage. I hate how weak I feel right now. I've always hated therapy, but usually I can keep a wall up and manipulate the situation.

However, my breakup rendered me vulnerable. He pierced the armor I'd wrapped around my heart and kept strong for years. Of all the things Noah did, that's the worst by far.

"The only way to release the past and become unburdened is to shine a light on your experience." She leans forward, placing her hand over mine. "Listen, we've all been there."

That comment surprises me. "You? But you seem so . . ."

She smirks. "Put together? Strong? Enlightened?" She snorts derisively. "I wasn't always like this. Believe it or not, I've had experience with abuse too. Finding a spiritual purpose and calling saved my life. And now, I do that for other women."

A realization dawns on me. I can see through the faux spiritual exterior that there's a real woman under there who hasn't always been sequestered in the mountains, but who has lived a real life full of real pain—and who might, if I give her a chance, be able to help me get over Noah.

"That's why I care so much," Guru Shava goes on. "My concern here is that if you don't shut the door completely and cut him off, he can come back into your life . . ."

A haunted look crosses her face, like she's remembering her own traumatic past.

She clears her throat, and it's gone.

"I know. You're right," I admit. "And my friends are right. They say the same thing. I have to cut him out completely. Not give him any opening. Cheating narcissists have a way of coming back. They like to have control over you."

She nods sympathetically. "Exactly. This retreat is designed around the themes of death and rebirth. Only by letting something die—*by killing it*—can we be freed and therefore reborn. Death and rebirth are part of the same cycle."

"That makes sense," I say, finally grasping some of what she's been saying. "But what if I'm not ready?" I can feel the necklace hanging heavily around my neck like a chain.

She nods, picking up her pen to write in my file. "Well, let's start at the beginning. Sometimes, you have to go backward in order to move forward."

"Right. What do you want to know?"

"How you met. How you started dating. But let's start with his name. You've been avoiding saying it."

I flinch before I can stop myself—she's right. I have been avoiding saying it out loud because it hurts too much. But I start to relax, feeling the sisterhood. She's not all superior and high and mighty, judging us mere mortals like I thought at first. More than that, she's right. Toxic masculinity is *everywhere*. Our relationships. Our workplaces. Our fathers. Even out here in the woods. I shudder, thinking of that hunter lurking outside my window.

No wonder women in the woods would prefer to encounter a bear over a man.

But here at the Namaste Center, Guru Shava is creating a safe space for women to heal. It isn't easy, but I decide to give it a shot and open up.

"His name is . . . Noah." My lips tremble saying it out loud.

"That's great, Morgan. I'm proud of you." She looks down at the papers on her desk. "It says on your application that you met him on a dating app. Can you elaborate on that?"

I laugh. "Yeah, that was their idea. Hannah and Mia. They're my best friends from college. Clearly they lack healthy boundaries. They're always trying to fix me."

"Let me guess." she replies. "This retreat was their idea too?"

"Ha, yes. How'd you guess?"

We share a lighter moment, but she turns more serious.

"Tell me more about Noah and your first date."

"The app is called the One. It's a blind dating app," I start, forcing myself to go back to the beginning and recount everything.

Just like that, the flood gates open and the memories come bubbling up and spilling from my mouth. I keep talking, losing track of time, recounting all the good things that brought us together. Finally, she gently interrupts me as we near the end of our hour-long session.

"I want to hear more," Guru Shava says. "But unfortunately, we're at the end of our time. Actually, we're a little bit over time."

"Sorry," I say, feeling self-conscious. *How long was I talking?*

"No apologies in here please," she corrects me with a kind smile. "That was great how you opened up. We can pick it up at our next private session. How does that sound?"

"That sounds great. Thanks." I'm shocked that I mean those words.

As I stand up, I realize how exhausting that session was. I'm feeling all talked out. But also, I've let my guard down. Started to trust Guru Shava. Maybe I was wrong about her and too quick to judge. Before she can show me out, I summon the courage to ask her something else that's been bothering me.

"I wanted to ask," I start, not sure how to broach the question without sounding paranoid. "Has anybody left the retreat early?"

She freezes. Her eyes narrow. "What do you mean?"

"The first day, I noticed that Dame Tremaine had two friends with her. But yesterday, one of them was missing."

An awkward beat passes.

"Morgan, here at the Namaste Center, we have very strict privacy rules. I'm sure you can understand since you seem to have recognized one of our—shall we say—more notable guests."

"Of course," I say quickly, feeling like a glorified stalker.

Shit, I made a mistake using the pop star's name.

"If a guest decides to leave," Guru Shava goes on, "or in the unfortunate event they're asked to leave for violating our rules, that also remains confidential as well."

Her usual Zen energy becomes hard and unyielding.

"Of course, I'm sorry I brought it up," I quickly backpedal, worried I just broke the privacy rules and put myself in danger of following the same trajectory as Dame Tremaine's friend, who nobody seems to acknowledge but me.

"Great, thank you for your understanding," Guru Shava says, but there's still an edge to her voice. She looks back down and scribbles in my chart. I swallow hard, imagining what she might be writing down.

I shouldn't care what some faux spiritual advisor thinks of me—she's not even a real therapist—but the annoying thing is, I do.

"Is there anything else?" I ask in a tight voice.

She looks up and shakes her head. Her face gives nothing away. "You may show the next guest in."

When I get outside her office, I recognize the DA sitting on the leather sofa. The one with that big case against the corrupt politician. She doesn't notice me at first. She's holding a notebook, scribbling rapidly and totally absorbed.

"Guru Shava is ready for you," I say with a stiff smile, aiming to project a friendly tone. She jumps and slams the journal shut. Her face looks pale with dark circles under her bloodshot eyes, but it could be from the detox cleanse.

"Thanks," she says, shoving the journal into her bag and hurrying inside. Just before she closes the door, she looks back at me in a paranoid way. I watch her with an uneasy feeling. I wonder what that was all about?

As I walk back to our cabin after my session, I feel worse than when I went in. I follow the icy trail that cuts through the thick woods, noticing a stirring in the trees. A raven takes off with a startled caw.

I jump back, then recover. The oily black feathers vanish into the trees. The remoteness of our situation hits me anew, how easy it would be to take a wrong step and get lost, never to be found again. The wind whips up harder, rustling the trees, coaxing the snow down. I shiver from the sharp chill biting the air.

Silence creeps back in as the wind settles. My mind is anything but silent. Dredging up Noah in my therapy session stirred up all my painful memories. I can't stem the torrent. My thoughts drift back to the night he claimed my body and dug his way deeper into my heart and mind so completely that I could no longer resist him.

His sexy voice echoes through my head—

CHAPTER TWENTY

BEFORE

NOAH

"You're *mine* tonight."

I lead Morgan to my bedroom. I already set everything into motion. I *knew* this would be the night, so I've prepared. Bloodred rose petals are scattered across the black silk sheets. I light several candles placed strategically around the room, giving off a soft, seductive glow.

The promise necklace sparkles around her delicate neck, chaining her to me in a way that's deeply arousing. I've laid out a gift for her, wrapped with a bow, which she fingers then unravels, opening the box to reveal a black silk lingerie set I special ordered from France for her. It leaves precious little to the imagination, including the thong with a V-shaped opening at the bottom.

She lifts the lace number out of the box.

"Oh my . . ." she gasps, bringing her fingers to her lips. "It's incredible."

"Indeed, but not as *incredible* as you," I reply, savoring the moment. "Now be a good girl, and go change for me." I nod toward my bathroom door. It's not a question.

She lifts her eyebrows at my forcefulness, but I cut her off before she can defy me or say something snarky.

"I said *now.*" My voice is deep and gravelly. She agreed to promise herself to me. Now, she must obey and submit to my desire.

She knows it—and I know it.

"Your wish is my command," she says with a flirty glance.

She scoops up the lingerie and disappears into my expansive en suite bathroom with its black marble finishes.

The door shuts with a soft thud.

Even that turns me on. The idea of what she's doing in there. Priming herself for me. Donning the lingerie, tightening the straps to fit her form. Pushing her breasts into the mesh. Freshening up and fluffing her hair as her anticipation grows for me.

We've done just about everything else you can do, except the final act.

The consummation.

I abided by her rules, even though we also transgressed at the gathering. Dark thoughts shoot through my mind, softening my desire for a split second.

My father's face flashes in my memory, hidden under that mask. Anger shudders through me, igniting a firestorm in my blood. I simmer over the way he cornered me at work the next day, demanding to know who the girl was.

I couldn't tell him the truth.

That I didn't know.

That I met her on a blind dating app and that we've held fast to the experiment because, for once, I wanted to know that she was into me for *me*.

Not for my family.

Not for my last name.

Not for my wealth and power.

I managed to put him off and not give him any information on Morgan. But he also gave me a ticking clock. Break up with her. Cut her off. I'm supposed to marry a certain kind of girl. One with his stamp of approval who comes from a family of a certain status that benefits our dynasty, and more importantly, who understands and accepts our unconventional lifestyle.

Instead, I'm doing the exact opposite. Running away was my sister Zoe's act of rebellion. I'm doing my own version of that. I'm going against my father's explicit wishes. He thinks I'm having fun sowing my "wild oats," as he called it. But he's made it clear that I need to end things with Morgan before they get serious. "Sooner rather than later" being his exact words.

Instead, I've continued to pursue Morgan, deploying all my charms to solidify my claim on her. I had the promise necklace crafted by my private jeweler to my exact specifications. I also meticulously planned today as my secret act of rebellion against him.

An arbitrary marker from her perspective—a seemingly random weekday in the depths of fall—but make no mistake. It was chosen to defy my father. It's the anniversary of the day my sister ran away all those years ago. Morgan doesn't know about that, or my father's strong disapproval of her. I've tried to shield her from the more unsavory aspects of my family's history and the fallout from my mistake of bringing her to the masquerade party.

After tonight, when it will be too late to take it back, we can begin to break from the experiment and introduce ourselves to the larger world. Slowly at first, starting with her friends. I can put my father off a few more weeks, until we can't be undone.

I also believe that my father is wrong about her. I think Morgan is actually the perfect partner to complement me. She's behaving perfectly today, obeying my commands.

I hear shuffling noises in the bathroom as she prepares herself for me. It shouldn't be much longer. I can initiate her into our lifestyle, I think. In fact, I've already started.

There's something special about her. *Different.*

I can't put my finger on it exactly. She's like a wild animal that's been caged but never truly tamed, only waiting for her chance to break free. She possesses a toughness and tenacity of the mind. A willingness to transgress.

The gathering proved that.

I remember how she wrapped her legs around me on the balcony, soaking my hand and begging me to break her one big rule and take her right there. My father ruined it, but maybe it's for the best. He forced my hand, making me act faster and pushing my plans forward.

Morgan may not be from a family like mine with generational wealth and power, but she's a chameleon who can shift and disguise herself among us. That much I've gathered from her few slips. The accent that escapes in unguarded moments. It's faint, and I still can't quite place it. In the thralls of passion, I've managed to coax it out of her mouth a few times.

I have restrained myself from digging deeper into her past, but she has dark secrets. I can sense it . . .

Because I have them too.

What happened back at boarding school taunts me, but I repress it. That's over and done with. This time, it's different, I reassure myself.

Morgan and I are different. Together we could be magnificent. We could take over one day, push my father and family out for good.

My uncle—my father's silent partner—is also a powerful force to be reckoned with. He's more behind-the-scenes, while Dad is the public face of Barron Enterprises. But I could take over and put them both out, if I had someone on my side who could help me do it.

Click.

The bathroom door handle turns, releasing the lock. My desire for her returns. I immediately snap out of my spinning thoughts and refocus on her. On this moment.

"Ready?" Her voice teases me.

"Always," I murmur in a growl, feeling my predatory instincts flare.

The door swings open. She steps out in the lingerie. The lace cups her breasts. Her nipples harden, pushing through the sheer fabric, while the lines cut down her torso to her lower regions. The black color of the lingerie gives her an almost dangerous look.

I immediately harden watching her parade past me and crawl onto my bed, crushing the delicate rose petals, her hair tousled, giving me a glimpse of her backside with the thong running through her. The diamond-encrusted necklace shimmers around her neck, nestled against her delicate collar bone.

I have the urge to grip her throat and squeeze—choking the air from her. Making her fight me a little bit. I wonder how far I can take her.

I run my hand through the knot in my tie and unsling it, pulling it from my neck. I wrap it around my hand and approach the bed.

She flops back on the bed and gives me an irresistible look as she fingers the necklace. "Well, what are you waiting for? Permission?"

"You already gave it to me."

She nods. "You have lived up to my requirements with your promise."

She rises to her knees on the edge of the bed, then reaches up and unbuttons my shirt down to my navel, button by button, revealing my abs.

She smiles in appreciation, running her fingers over each indentation. I work hard in the gym before work to attain this physique.

But I push her back, snapping her arms behind her back. Her eyes widen, but she doesn't resist as I bind her wrists behind her back with my crimson tie.

I reach for her delicate throat that I could choke in an instant. But I hold back, knowing I can't push her that far yet. Instead, I reach into her hair and pluck an errant leaf out of her curls.

"A souvenir from the park?" I say, showing it to her cradled in my palm. I snap my fist shut, crushing the dry leaf.

Still, I don't pounce on her . . .

Yet.

I elongate the moment, savoring the taste of her desire begging me to conquer her. While she's bound, I lean over and press my lips into hers, tasting her, flicking my tongue deeper inside.

She moans softly. I trace my finger down the length of her body, over the soft curve of her firm breasts, feeling the gooseflesh of her nipple, then down her torso and around the curve of her belly. I flick my fingers through the V-shaped opening, the slick that greets my touch.

She's ready for me.

More than ready.

I watch her reaction as I unbuckle my belt and unzip, offering myself to her. I untie her hands, then press her onto her back, where she crushes the rose petals.

Now freed, she pulls me onto her, ravishing me with her lips and roving hands, reminding me of a wild animal. My lips lock onto her as I push myself against her, dying to force my way inside her. But I tease her, gently.

"Do it. Take me . . ." she breathes, trying to pull me into her.

But I hold back. I'm stronger.

I look deeply into her eyes. I tease her again, making her shudder. "If I do it, it can't be undone."

"I know."

"Are you sure?" I ask, teasing her again. "There's still time to back out. You still don't know my last name." I feel the darkness stir inside me.

"I'm warning you now," I add in a halting voice, "there are dark secrets."

We both freeze for a moment. I'm so hard and engorged, I fear I won't last.

Her lips part— "Just watch me when you do it. I want to see the look in your eyes."

That breaks every last bit of resistance left inside me. I can't hold back any longer. I thrust hard, penetrating her in one swift motion.

She grimaces, then moans. She takes every last inch of thickness inside her. I ease into our connection with some slow, deep strokes, but I can't hold back. "I need everything," she hisses into my ear as I thrust harder, faster.

She drives me to the brink, then pulls me over the edge, clenching around me.

I explode inside her, emptying myself and giving her all of me.

She shudders in pleasure, taking it in.

I hold myself above her, gasping hard, then slowly rolling to the side. I gather her into my arms and hold her close. Our sweat percolates and mixes together. I stroke back her hair, damp with sweat. I whisper into her ear. "Morgan, I love you."

"I love you too, Noah."

I brush my hand over the smooth flesh of her stomach, knowing my seed lives inside her. I gave her everything, spilled it inside of her. It both thrills me and terrifies me. One thing is certain.

There's no going back now.

CHAPTER TWENTY-ONE

AFTER

MORGAN

"Nooo, get off me!"

I wake up with hands choking my neck. Only a strangled scream comes out. I jerk my hands to my neck, but it's only the promise necklace tangled into knots that are digging into my flesh. The predawn light reflects amethyst light off the snow. This retreat was supposed to help me get over my breakup—and whatever ghosts from my past are currently haunting me. But if anything, it's only making it worse, my nightmares more intense.

I wonder if it's the boredom with nothing but my thoughts to keep me company. But could it be more? My head feels fuzzy, making me wonder what's in those smoothies and raw juice shots. I wonder again if Guru Shava is secretly drugging us.

Low-dose psychedelic and ketamine therapies have become trendy. I even have a client with a mail-order subscription program that promises to cure depression with such concoctions. Happy Dose is the name of the company. They're skirting several federal laws, and we have to be extra careful in the ad copy.

My questions only beget more questions. I only have to survive a little while longer and I'll be back in the city. I count it off on my fingers.

Four days down—three more to go. Just over halfway. For the thousandth time, I regret agreeing to this retreat, or more like kidnapping.

I relax slightly, sinking back into my pillow. At least the bed is comfortable. My hand drifts down to my stomach. Still concave, not showing anything yet.

But I know what's taken root deep inside me, even if I can't feel it yet.

I'm pregnant.

I took the pregnancy test the day before we left for the retreat. My period wasn't late yet, but I had to know for sure. It was one of those early detection tests bought at the shady corner store around the block. I peed on the stick and waited, my heart thumping hard.

The lines struggled to materialize. First, the test line came in strong. I felt blood drain from my body. But then another line appeared. Faint, barely there. Then darkening over the next sixty seconds until it was stark and unmistakable. Standing right next to the control line like a sentry.

My shock hit me next.

The proof was in my hands.

I was pregnant.

A rush of thoughts entered my head next. What do I do? Do I keep the baby? Get an abortion? It was too early for a doctor's appointment still, and my state has liberal laws that give me plenty of time to decide. One thought was louder than the rest. Whatever I did, I didn't dare tell Noah. Not until I figured out a plan. He was too powerful. I was still too in love with him. I couldn't think straight, and I worried he would manipulate me into doing something I didn't want to do.

I didn't even tell Hannah and Mia, for the same reason. I felt too vulnerable and confused.

I reach into my overnight bag and raid the stash of snacks, grabbing a protein bar. I tear off the wrapper, stuffing it in the bathroom trash can under some tissues to hide the evidence. I don't want to get caught cheating on the retreat's strict diet—but more than that, I don't want my friends to guess at what's really going on with me. They're like private detectives. They can sniff out secrets like coroner dogs on the trail of a dead body.

I'm famished and devour it quickly. I raided the samples closet at work to pack extra snacks for this retreat, worrying that a raw cleanse might be harmful in early pregnancy. I also stashed some prenatal vitamins that I've been taking every morning, though they're not helping with the nausea or lack of appetite. At first, I thought it was the shock of the breakup causing my unpleasant symptoms. Everyone knows you lose weight on the breakup diet, not to mention you feel tired and depressed and generally like crap. That's part of why I didn't test sooner.

Turns out, those complaints mirror early pregnancy symptoms exactly. I worry that I didn't start the vitamins early enough, or that I unwittingly did damage to my baby by having some drinks. But I also know plenty of women get pregnant on liquor-soaked honeymoons and have perfectly healthy babies. Besides, I haven't made up my mind about what to do.

I turn to my side, imagining what it will feel like when my breasts start to ache and my belly bulges into a cute little baby bump. The truth is that I've always wanted to be a mother, to have someone to love and care for—the opposite of what my parents did.

But I didn't think it would happen like this, after a toxic breakup.

I shudder at the reminder of my shitty situation. I knew I was taking a risk with Noah, but I was so caught up in him, so in the thrall of our whirlwind courtship, that I fell for the fairy tale. I thought something like this would nudge him along toward a proposal and cement my place by his side, so that nobody could come between us.

Not even his father.

I was wrong. So very wrong.

I had been clinging to the hope that Noah would text me back finally. That the pregnancy would be an excuse to test the waters again and see if there was anything left to salvage. That's why I've been so frantic over my phone.

My heart lurches at the thought. The baby is my last tether to him. That's the ugly truth. The dirty, dark, anti-feminist desire. Part of why I don't want to go through with an abortion is because it would mean destroying the last remnants of our relationship.

Am I ready to do that?

My heart sinks, telling me there's no easy answer. And worse, I have no idea what the right answer is. Either choice, either way I go, I'm losing something I can never get back.

Something outside my window draws me out of my thoughts. It's the *crunch, crunch, crunch* of boots on snow. I stagger up from bed, shedding the warm down comforter. The cold chill hits my skin. My hand is still resting on my stomach.

I look outside.

The hunter is out there again. Staring at me.

His face remains covered by the neck warmer, but he looks the same as the day we met him on the road. The sun is starting to rise, so unlike the other night, I can see him more clearly. It's definitely him.

He's holding a crossbow.

He raises it and mimes shooting me. That's when I scream.

A second later, a flustered Hannah comes rushing into my room. "Morgan, what's wrong?"

I look over at her. "The hunter . . . He's out there. He's stalking us!"

"The hunter?"

She comes over, but when I look back at the window, he's gone. Hannah follows my gaze, scanning the landscape, then frowns.

"Morgan, there's nobody out here," she says in a concerned voice.

Mia comes through my door, slower and groggier. "What's the ruckus?"

Hannah shakes her head slowly. "Morgan thought she saw someone outside, but it's nothing. Probably just the wind rattling the trees and casting strange shadows across the snow."

"No, I swear he was out there!" I insist, heat flushing my cheeks. "I saw him! The hunter from the road. He had a crossbow. He aimed it at me."

"A crossbow?" Mia says, still muddled with sleep. "You mean like something from *Game of Thrones*?"

I realize how insane I sound. I deflate, my righteous indignation fading away like the last gasps of nightfall.

Hannah pats my shoulder sympathetically. "Just try to get some more rest before class. Being out of the city in the wilderness can be scary."

I scan the crowd gathered in the Great Hall, mentally counting. *Wait, that can't be right.* I double check, sweeping my gaze over the group for a second time.

Now, I'm certain—

The DA is gone.

I grab Hannah's and Mia's attention, pulling them away from their smoothies.

"We're missing someone else today," I whisper, glancing around to make sure Guru Shava and her creepy apprentices aren't watching us. "The DA is gone."

I don't mention the hunter to them again, but I saw him out there this morning. I'm sure of it. Now, I'm starting to think that he is stalking us.

"She had that big case, remember?" Hannah says. "I bet she got called away for work. That happens all the time."

"The one piece of good advice my dad gave me: Don't go to law school," Mia says. "I make twice as much in tech and didn't need a graduate degree."

"And you don't have to prosecute creepers," Hannah says. "I bet that gets to you after a while, seeps into your life and gets super depressing."

"I may not have to prosecute creepers, but I do have to work with them," Mia quips darkly. "Tech bros are the worst."

Hannah laughs. "Valid."

They seem completely unbothered. But I can't let it go that easily.

"She's the *second* person that's vanished from the retreat. First, it was Dame Tremaine's other friend."

"The one that nobody remembers seeing besides you?" Hannah says.

Her accusatory tone makes me flinch. They think I'm seeing things, being paranoid.

"There were a lot of new faces that first day." Mia nods to the pop star and her friend with the blonde hair. "Maybe you just got confused and saw the same person twice?"

I search my memory. "No, she had pale skin and jet-black hair. Kind of the opposite of the other friend. She got upset with Dame Tremaine and argued with her, then stormed out of the meditation studio. I remember her . . ." I trail off.

They shrug. "You're the only one who does," Hannah says.

Frustration surges through me. I lower my voice and lean in closer.

"Fine, but you remember the DA, right?" I insist, not letting it go.

"Sure, but there are a million perfectly acceptable reasons why she might have left the retreat early," Hannah points out. "Work demands, family emergency, or maybe she just couldn't hack it here."

"But why didn't Guru Shava say anything to the group about it?" I sound desperate, but I can't help it.

Hannah frowns like it's obvious. "Rule number one of the Namaste Center is *privacy*. Remember?"

"Maybe she broke one of the rules," Mia says. "You've seen all the signs. Maybe she got caught trying to use her phone."

The implication hits me hard. I'm the one breaking the rules—and I could get kicked out. I have my earbuds in, carefully tucked under my hair, while my phone is stuffed into my waistband. It digs into my skin, making me squirm.

Hannah pats my arm. "Morgan, you just need to relax. Stop worrying about everyone else. Ever since the breakup, it's like you don't trust anyone."

"Yeah, it sounds like major PTSD," Mia agrees. "You know, not everyone is a cheating, lying, creep like your ex. Maybe Guru Shava can work with you on that in your next private session?"

"Yeah, okay," I say, dropping it for now. It's an argument I can't win.

Bong.

Instantly, everyone falls silent, like somebody flipped a switch. The effect is kind of eerie. They march over to the doors like robots. Even Hannah and Mia immediately turn away from me and head to the studio. I follow along, but I'm a little weirded out by how much everyone acts the same now.

I catch one of the apprentices watching me closely. She gestures to another one, who also scrutinizes me.

I try to fall in line and mimic everyone else, getting with the program. I don't want to draw their attention or risk being kicked out, especially since I'm breaking the rules with my phone.

After a minute, they finally look away. We enter the meditation studio, marching in an orderly line. The doors shut behind us with a dull thud followed by the wooden bar sliding into place, sealing us inside. The gong goes off again. I jerk my head to the stage. Guru Shava stands holding the mallet. The large, bronze gong vibrates behind her with a low, droll sound.

We lay out our mats and blankets and stand at the top of them with our feet parallel and hands in prayer in mountain pose.

She hits the gong again. Everyone starts moving through a sun salutation automatically. She's not even speaking instructions into the microphone. Instead, she uses her mallet and gong to conduct us, like an orchestra.

At the start of class, I discreetly hit play, so I'm listening to my podcast, but I can tell her lips remain still. I do my best to keep up and follow along.

Still, my paranoia spikes at the strange progression and how everyone is moving like automatons. But I reassure myself—we're just getting the hang of it now. A few days of intensive yoga sessions will do that. You learn the poses and anticipate the transitions. Even I've gotten better.

But the whole time, my mind keeps drifting back to the missing DA. Hannah and Mia have to be right. The DA probably did just leave early for any number of plausible reasons. But I can't stop worrying. It reminds me of the mysteries in my true crime podcasts.

Two people are missing. And more, I'm sure I saw that hunter outside our cabin—twice.

I can't shake the image of him dragging something heavy, resembling a dead body, through the snow.

I catch myself, quickly blocking out that thought. I jerk back to the present, realizing I'm out of step with the group. I lose my balance and stumble, almost falling over.

Guru Shava locks onto me and frowns in disapproval. *Shit.*

I catch her apprentices watching me from their spots by the doors too.

Everyone is jumping down to plank, but I'm still standing in prayer. I quickly catch up, cursing myself for losing focus and getting distracted like that. I can't let that happen again. I focus harder, while my podcast drones on. Uncertainty rises up inside me. Maybe I am seeing things that aren't there. Maybe it is my past haunting me.

But one thing is certain. The DA is still missing. She's the second guest to disappear from our retreat without any explanation. I need to find out where she went. But I have to be careful.

Or I risk getting kicked out too.

CHAPTER TWENTY-TWO

BEFORE

MORGAN

I spent the night. Broke every rule.

The promise necklace dangles around my neck. I savor running my fingers over it, tracing the diamond constellation embedded in the platinum setting. Noah snores lightly next to me. His sleeping face looks so angelic, like it was carved out of marble with his soft lips and sharp cheekbones. I shudder remembering everything he did to me.

Everything.

I slip out of bed and walk to the floor-to-ceiling windows and stand there, bathed in the moonlight, as the city offers itself to me on a platter. It's still predawn, though the sunrise looms. My milky skin reflects the luminous light. I'm naked except for the necklace.

I feel powerful.

A fresh dusting of snow blankets the streets and the park. It's the first early winter storm though the calendar still says fall.

My mind starts to wander. I imagine living here as Mrs. Noah . . . whatever his last name is. While I've kept to the blind date experiment, I wonder if he has too. Or whether he's looked into me, tried to dig up my past.

When the incident happened with his father at the masquerade party, I worried that might spell the end of us. I'm not stupid; I know Noah's family possesses money, but more importantly, power and influence. I don't need to internet stalk him or hire a PI to know that. I just need my eyes and ears—my sharp senses.

Under closer scrutiny, even with my Barnard degree and cover story, I wouldn't measure up. To my surprise, Noah continued to pursue me, and then yesterday he made that promise. All the pieces fell into place just like I planned.

But I made a critical mistake that haunts me. I swore I'd keep my heart safe from him. That I'd play the part and get him hooked and make him fall deeply for me. But that I'd have all the power because my heart would remain safe from his clutches. The problem?

I couldn't help it. I actually fell for him too. At first, I was playing a game, but then I broke my biggest rule. I got greedy, I guess. I wanted it all—the social climbing and the love story. The kind of thing you see in movies. The kind of love that's always eluded me. Until Noah. But it leaves me vulnerable. He could shatter me into a million tiny pieces.

I finger the necklace again to reassure myself, but doubt creeps into my mind anyway, planting treacherous seeds. Clearly, he could have any woman. I glance back at him, still sleeping soundly. He's attractive and charming. Educated.

Oh, and this fucking penthouse.

But I have something going for me that other girls don't. The experiment. He wanted something different. He wanted to rebel and defy his father. My thoughts slip to his sister, Zoe. He said she ran away. Clearly, that was her act of defiance. And therefore, I am his.

Buoyed by that thought, I tiptoe into the bathroom, careful not to wake him. The black marble and gold accents have a distinctly masculine flare. But once we make things more serious, once he really proposes and I move in, I could remodel it and feminize the space.

I know it's dangerous to let my mind wander to future possibilities when the present remains undetermined. But confidence blooms in my chest. I feel a fluttering in my stomach but work hard to calm my nerves and focus on getting myself together.

I freshen my makeup stealthily so I can pretend I just "woke up this way," freshly tussled, not sullied, always ready to sink my lips onto him again, pleasing him and swallowing, promising a future of eager pleasure.

And not the bed death my friends have in their long-term relationships where their sex life falls over a cliff, or stops altogether. Most LTRs dry up like that, the fire going out with nothing left to burn, arid as the desert. But I know we're different—that won't happen to us.

I'll keep him pleasured and satisfied, so he'll never grow bored and stray. I have plenty of tricks to play in that department. All the casual hookups through college helped me hone my skills.

I slide back into bed as dawn cracks the sky. Like I never left his arms. I will myself to fake sleep until he stirs and mumbles, pulling me closer. His warm breath kisses my ear.

"Morgan, you're mine now."

He takes me again without any foreplay. I'm still slick from the night before, ready for him to slip inside. This time, it's more frantic and desperate. We crash together in another tempest. He moans, filling me up again, then lies back onto the soft, silken pillows.

I curve my back into him, so he can wrap his arms around me and pull me closer. We fit together like two jagged puzzle pieces who have searched their whole lives for the perfect fit. His hand drifts down to the tender flesh of my stomach, gently caressing it. His fresh seed swims deeper into me, joining with last night's remnants. Double the chances, double the risk.

I stroke his strong hand. We didn't discuss birth control. I'm not on the pill. Everyone in my generation knows those chemical pills are terrible for you. An IUD just seemed so invasive and painful, especially when I wasn't in a relationship. He never brought it up, and neither did I. I suppose the transgression was too delicious and enticing to dispel. We're both tempting fate, but I wanted to take the risk.

We both did.

Wordlessly, with only our actions, we recklessly bound ourselves together.

I wanted to push everything to the limit with him. I've been doing that since our very first *fated* date. And there's more. This is an insurance policy in case his father proves too meddlesome. I planned it, carefully.

It could be my imagination and I know it's not possible to know yet, but I swear I feel something stir deep inside me as the cold morning light spills over the bed, and the fresh snow continues piling up outside our high-rise fortress of glass and metal. This is the moment life takes hold . . . and doesn't let go.

There's no going back now.

He belongs to me.

* * *

"You sure you have to go to work today?" I say, flopping onto the bed and pouting my lips. "We could play hooky. Look outside—it's a snow day. You could do some *work* on the bed."

He gives me a look. "Tempting, but alas, I have to work. And so do you."

He finishes dressing in front of the mirror, tightening the knot on his icy blue tie. His Italian gray pinstriped suit is perfectly tailored to his long, lean physique that I've explored so slowly. I slip behind him and give him a helping hand, even though he doesn't need it, my fingers flitting along his throat. I can tell he enjoys my careful ministrations, the way our bodies and now our lives filled with their tiny, daily routines begin bleeding together.

We crossed a big line in our relationship. Exclusivity. I got the girlfriend title I'd been dreaming about.

"Come on. We could still play hooky. Have a repeat of last night."

I reach for his crotch, but he pushes my hand away. Desire percolates in his eyes, while heat flushes his cheeks. He leans over to whisper.

"You have no idea how *tempting* that is, Morgan." He gives me a probing look. "But we can't do that in a city that never sleeps . . . or takes days off."

It's true. Even one inch of ice or snow where I grew up would shut everything down. But not in New York City. The underground subway runs whether it's sweltering and humid or there's a blizzard raging.

I glance over at the clock.

It's seven thirty a.m. I'm still in yesterday's clothes. I have to get home and change then commute to work.

I gather my things to leave, but he stops me. "Wait, I'm taking you home."

I pause, struck by that.

"You don't have to be my escort," I point out. "I'm a big girl. I've gotten home on my own plenty of times."

He shakes his head. "For starters, I don't want to let you out of my sight. Last night changes everything," he says in a possessive way that thrills me. "Secondly, you've seen where I live. But I still don't know where you live. It's only fair."

That's true enough. I've kept him away on purpose for one reason: my nosy roommates.

He grabs his wool overcoat, pulling it around his tall frame. But still, I hesitate.

"You do realize there's a high chance of a close encounter with my roomies?"

He nods. "I'm well aware."

"Are you sure?" I say hesitantly. "They're pretty unfiltered. And prone to prying. Plus, I've been keeping them away these last few weeks, so they're dying to meet you. I can't promise they won't ambush you."

"I can take a little friendly fire." He flashes a sexy smile. "If it's for you."

Are we ready for this? That's the question that plagues me. The magic of our relationship lies in the mystery.

"You know we're already running on borrowed time," he admits, turning to face me. "Our experiment always had to come to an end."

"I know. You're right," I agree with a deep breath. "I can't put my friends off much longer. They've already threatened to hire a PI. In fact, it's a minor miracle they haven't."

He nods. "My father isn't far behind them. Or my coworkers. That said, I'm just taking you home. There's a good chance I'll remain your anonymous suitor, right? Even if they meet me, that doesn't mean they'll know who I am."

"That's true. Damn it, why is everyone so nosy?" I say, feeling annoyed at the intrusiveness. I love our little bubble where it's just the two of us. But to get what I truly want, I have to take steps to solidify my place in his life, and vice versa.

"We live in the Information Age," he says with a grimace. "Everything is online. Our entire lives put on vulgar display for the world to rifle through and judge."

I smirk at him. "Let me guess: You don't use social media."

"Does following the Nasdaq count?" he shoots back. "Or cryptocurrency?"

I shake my head. "Nice try. I already know you're a finance nerd. But that doesn't count as social media."

"Then I guess I'm an anomaly in this digital era," he says with a shrug. "But I did use the One. My coworkers talked me into it. And it led me to you. But I don't know if I would've given it a shot without the blind dating experiment."

"Mr. Mysterious," I tease him. "You need to uphold your secrets."

"I don't like the world prying into my daily activities," he replies.

"Then you are an anomaly," I say, planting a soft kiss on his full lips. "But you're my anomaly."

We take the elevator downstairs. The lower we descend, the faster my heart races. It's all becoming so real.

"What's the plan?" I ask him. "Want to walk me in? Meet my roomies?"

"You sure? That's a big step."

I gesture to the promise necklace. "Now that you've made it *official*, they might actually follow through on their threats to hire a PI if we don't bite the bullet."

"Bite the bullet, huh? You know, it could end the experiment. Is it time?"

I shake my head, not wanting the fantasy to end. "A few more weeks? You said it before. Meeting them doesn't blow your cover. It just might make them calm down and chill out."

"Fine, then I can walk you in," he agrees. "I'll be my most charming self."

I smirk. "Aren't you always?"

"Well, you haven't seen me when I'm not. It exists, you know—a dark side."

I remember the look on his face when his father busted us at the party. The haunted look that flashed in his eyes, hinting at the deeper, darker shadows.

"And you haven't seen mine."

He leans over, hovering over me. His warm breath kisses my face. "So, when will we reveal the darkness?"

That question lingers before it's interrupted by a *ding* as the elevator reaches the lobby. The answer is—sooner than I know. However, as I finger the necklace, I'm still caught up in the love-swept dreams that carry us into the snow.

"This is it?" Noah says after his town car deposits us on the sidewalk in front of my building. The car idles on the street, awaiting his return so it can whisk him to work.

"My humble abode," I say, taking in the red brick facade studded with barred windows. "Complete with *five* flights of stairs and *two* very nosy, best friend roomies."

I laugh in a self-deprecating way and glance at the top floor, half expecting Hannah and Mia to be spying on us.

He grins at me. "Yes, so I've been warned. And you don't give it credit. I think it's quaint and quite charming."

To my relief, he doesn't seem put off by the contrast between where he resides and . . . *this*. Not that it's a cheap apartment by any means. Nothing in the city is cheap. Our monthly rent dwarfs most mortgage payments elsewhere.

But it's a world apart from his metal and marble fortress in the clouds.

"Right, it's not too late," I say nervously. "You can still back out . . ."

Noah shakes his head.

"I promised I'd walk you in, and that's what I'm intending to do."

True to his word, he escorts me into the building on his arm. No doorman or fancy entrance. We hike up the five flights, and he doesn't complain once. I feel jittery—nervous even—but I'm confident his true identity remains safe.

I slide my key into the lock and twist. The deadbolt turns. I listen carefully, but there's no sound of footsteps. I breathe a sigh of relief, thinking they already left for work. I crack the door open. That's when I hear it—pounding feet.

Hannah and Mia come running into the living room and skid to a halt when they see Noah and me standing in the doorway.

Confusion contorts their faces.

"Wait, is this a joke?" Hannah gasps.

"Noah Barron?" Mia adds in shock. "You're dating *Noah Barron*?"

He steps inside behind me and thrusts his arm around me protectively. He raises his steely gaze to meet theirs with a sheepish smile.

"Well, hello there, Hannah and Mia." He shakes his head incredulously. "Isn't this a small world?"

I glance from him to my friends. I never told him their names.

"Wait, what do you mean? You know each other? How is that possible?"

I'm shocked. Blown apart. I can't believe how wrong I was. This is the exact moment when the bubble bursts.

Our fantasy is over.

CHAPTER TWENTY-THREE

AFTER

MORGAN

The front door is locked, so I scale around to the back porch and get lucky.

The sliding door isn't locked.

My heart pounds as I double check to make sure nobody is watching, but the thick trees encroach on the wooden building, shielding it. Unlike our cliffside cabin, this one is deep in the woods off a dead-end trail.

I peer through the glass, making sure the coast is clear, then slip through the sliding door and into the living area. This was the DA's cabin. It wasn't hard to find out. I snuck a look at the ledger by the reception desk. The low-tech aspect made it much easier to find this information.

I shouldn't be here. I'm risking everything, breaking even more rules. But I figured there might be some clue about what happened to her. I'm not sure what I'm expecting, something like the grisly crime scenes in my podcasts, maybe.

The interior of the cabin mirrors our accommodations, except it's a single with only one bedroom instead of three. It hasn't been cleaned either. Another stroke of luck. Maybe I can find evidence. There are some mugs and dirty dishes sitting in the sink. I walk into the bedroom. This one has a peaceful view of the pine trees instead of the mountains.

Crumpled sheets and towels are strewn across the floor. The closet doors are flung open with hangers scattered all over. It's in disarray, giving the impression that she left in a hurry. I move into the bathroom.

Everything again looks messy. Toothpaste mars the sink, while wet wash cloths decorate the counter.

I find nothing incriminating, aside from the fact she left in a rush. But that could point to a work or family emergency, nothing sinister.

I deflate slightly and return to the bedroom. I sink down on the bed, trying to put myself in her shoes like the investigators do in my podcasts, so I can see through her eyes. I feel around the bed, under the blanket, then the pillows.

I freeze as my fingers hit something hard stuffed underneath them.

Feeling a rush of adrenaline, I pull it out. I'm clutching a leather-bound journal. We each got one with our welcome packets. I flip it open. The front cover reads *This journal belongs to* with a line underneath to write your name. Sure enough, she's scrawled it down in the proper place.

Barbara Richmond

That's the DA's name. I remember Hannah and Mia talking about her the first day. She's been in the papers a lot for her high-profile cases. She's one of the top prosecutors in Manhattan.

I pause, listening, to make sure nobody is coming. We're on a juice cleanse break, but I used my detox excuse to sneak out again, saying I was heading back to our cabin. I can't stay gone too long—but I have a little time.

Feeling exhilarated, like it's my own true crime investigation, I flip open the journal, then frown in dismay.

All the pages are torn out. Jagged edges peek out of the binding. Except for the last page. Jagged, frantic handwriting slants across the page. Erratic and unhinged. Not like the neat, sloping cursive of her name.

Get out NOW! They're coming . . . in danger . . . can't trust anyone . . .

I can't believe what I'm reading. And what was on the torn-out pages?

A noise sounds from outside and sets my heart into overdrive. I slam the journal shut, shoving it into the pocket of my puffy coat. Then I retrace my steps, slipping through the sliding door and back onto the porch.

A hard wind whips down from the mountains, hitting the trees behind the cabin. The branches rattle and shift again, parting slightly. I see a flash of movement and camouflage.

A glint of metal.

I freeze in terror, ducking down behind the railing. When I look outside again, the wind has died down. I scan the tree line, but there's nothing there. I'm sure I saw something though. I feel jittery and paranoid. But the thought can't be dislodged.

Was it the hunter watching me?

I wait until we're back at our cabin to shower before I show the journal to Hannah and Mia. Tonight, we have some kind of bonfire ceremony, which I'm completely dreading.

Not only is it freezing with the temperature dropping precipitously, but also the idea of the woods at night freaks me out, especially after what I saw that afternoon snooping around the DA's cabin. That hunter is stalking me.

I'm sure of it.

The problem is nobody believes me, not even my friends. They all think I'm being paranoid. It's true, I haven't been myself since the breakup. The true crime podcasts probably aren't helping either. But now I have proof that something is wrong. I rap on Hannah's door. She's wrapped in her robe, towel drying her hair. Mia is draped over her bed, also in a robe with wet hair. "What do you wear to a bonfire ceremony?"

"I dunno," Hannah says, sticking her head out. "Witchy, hippie stuff?"

"I think I forgot to pack that," Mia says with a snort. "No, wait, I don't have any because I have actual fashion."

They both laugh, then turn to see me standing in the doorway, clutching the journal. Hannah smiles in approval.

"Oh, good," she says. "You're journaling? That's a great idea. It should help you process everything."

But I shake my head, lowering my voice. "This isn't my journal."

Mia sits up straighter. "Okay, weird. Why do you have someone else's?"

"Did you take it?"

I shift uncomfortably, averting my eyes. "Sort of . . ."

Quickly as I can, I cough up the whole story of sneaking into the DA's cabin and finding it in disarray, then discovering the journal shoved under her pillows. Before they can chastise me, I hold up my hands to stop their tirade.

"I know what you're going to say—that I'm being paranoid again. And worse, breaking the rules. But please, hear me out. That's all I ask. Then you can render judgement. Okay?"

They blink at me, then reluctantly agree. "First of all, she clearly left in a hurry. And look at this. All the pages are ripped out except the last one."

I flip it open for them and point to the unsettling final journal entry with its creepy warning. They study the erratic print on the last page, then examine the first page with her name in elegant cursive.

"See, you were right," I say, pointing to the name. "Barbara Richmond. She is that prosecutor. The one from the news. And I think something happened to her."

Mia looks worried, but Hannah flips it shut and stares me down.

"Exactly! Like you said, she's a prosecutor. That means, she goes after major criminals. Corrupt politicians. Organized crime. In her line of work, she goes after a lot of bad guys."

"What's your point?" I say, biting my lower lip. My eyes dart to the journal.

"Think about it," Mia said. "She's after that big politician for rape. He's rumored to be running for president on a populist platform. He has ties to a lot of organized crime too."

"You see?" Hannah says. "Anybody could be after her! In her career, you make a lot of enemies. Powerful ones. Dangerous ones. That's probably why she had to leave early."

"Fine, you're right," I'm forced to agree. "But what if something happened to her at the retreat? Her cabin looked like it had been ransacked. Also, why would those pages be ripped out from her journal? Why did she hide it under her pillow?"

Hannah looks exasperated. "Rooms always look messy when you check out. Trust me, our cabin will be a shitshow on the last day. I dunno, maybe she was journaling in bed and shoved it there and fell asleep. Then when she checked out early, she forgot about it."

"There's a million possible explanations that make perfect rational sense," Mia chimes in. "None of this means something bad happened to her. Right?"

They both stare at me. I resist the urge to fidget with the promise necklace hidden under my shirt. I don't want them to know that I'm still holding on to it and chastise me.

"Okay, but I also saw the hunter outside my window this morning, remember? And he was dragging something that looked an awful lot like a dead body."

Hannah throws her hands in the air. "Again, it was probably a deer or whatever mammal he killed for dinner. That's what hunters do; they hunt."

"Fine, but I still think something happened. The DA, Barbara, is the second person to go missing."

Hannah sighs. "Morgan, for the hundredth time. Nobody remembers the other woman with Dame Tremaine. She does not exist."

"I asked Guru Shava about her," I insist, feeling my cheeks burning.

"Oh, and what did she say?" Hannah says, trading a worried look with Mia.

I deflate a little. "Just that I was violating the privacy policy," I admit. "But don't you think it's a little sus that she wouldn't say anything to us? It's like she's hiding something . . ."

They both look fed up now. Hannah shakes her head, handing the journal back. "Morgan, people leave trips early sometimes. Life happens. Guru Shava is right. It's none of your business."

"But what if something happened to them? And she's covering it up?"

"Enough already!" Hannah shouts. "I don't know to put this delicately anymore, but since the breakup, you're losing your shit. Get it together!"

I flinch back, feeling like she slapped me. Tears brim in my eyes. The worst part? I know she's completely right. I do sound paranoid and unhinged. Ever since I caught Noah cheating, it's like I don't even recognize myself anymore.

What was I thinking sneaking into that cabin? Taking a stranger's private journal? And the podcasts too. I've been risking everything, fighting the program. It's almost like I'm afraid to heal, because healing also means letting go of . . .

Him.

The dark truth—the secret that I keep buried in my heart—is that I'm not ready to do that yet. My hand slips to my stomach again, where life blooms.

Life I might keep.

Or stomp out.

I still can't decide. And I can't let on either. Secrets upon secrets that I'm not ready to grapple with.

I have to snap out of it. I fix on my friends, who aren't my enemies, even though that's how I've been acting lately. They're only trying to help me, and I keep fighting them at every turn. I have to stop. Or I risk losing them, too.

"I'm sorry." I backpedal. "I promise—I won't bring it up again."

Hannah puts her arm around me, then Mia piles onto the group hug.

"We just want what's best for you. That's the whole point of this retreat, right?" Hannah says. "Maybe stop resisting and give the program a try. Maybe it will help you heal. I mean, at this point, what do you have to lose?"

"Tonight we're supposed to bring something from our past that we want to release," Mia says, nodding to my throat. "I know it's hard, but it might be time to let that go . . ."

My hand darts to my neck as my cheeks color. I had tried to keep it from them that I was still wearing the necklace. The necklace that symbolizes every single promise he broke.

"I know."

"Tonight, in honor of the full moon, we celebrate death and rebirth," Guru Shava says, standing in front of the fire.

The firelight refracts off her eyes and dances behind her white robes. She raises her arms toward the sky as if channeling the fire energy higher. The apprentices stoke the flames, piling more wood onto the blaze. I'm shivering and miserable. In short, I wish I was back in my cabin, tucked into bed with my podcast playing. Far away from this madness.

Hannah catches the scowl on my face. She nudges me, not subtly, then whispers, "Stop fighting it."

Was I that obvious?

I clear my face, trying to embrace the experience. If nothing, it makes for a good story. That time I got kidnapped to a bougie retreat that's more like a cult.

Above, the stars push through the dark sky, while the moon rises, cresting over the snow-covered peaks. We're standing in our coats and boots around the circle of stones in the meditation garden. The creepy stick dolls hang from nooses in the trees.

I shudder watching their silhouettes dancing in the wind whipped up by the intense heat wafting off the bonfire.

"You must die first in order to be reborn," Guru Shava chants. She uses prongs to catch some embers and place them into a large stone bowl. She sprinkles herbs over the embers, letting them spark. "The Native Americans on whose sacred land we stand practiced this cleaning ritual," she continues in a solemn voice. "We honor their legacy tonight."

She paces around our circle, making a show of holding the smoking bowl under our noses and wafting the smoke over us in a cleansing ritual.

I want to roll my eyes and comment on the blatant cultural appropriation, but I do my best to clear my face. Finally, she reaches me and sticks the bowl under my nose, making it itch.

"Inhale deeply," she coaxes me. "Birth and death, two sides of the same coin."

For once at this retreat, I do as I'm told. I breathe in deeply. The sickly sweet taste of the smoke hits me, and I cough hard, my eyes watering.

"Some of us need to cleanse a little more," she jokes in her way.

The whole circle laughs. My cheeks heat in embarrassment, while my eyes are still burning and nose itching, but I stifle the urge to sneeze.

Thankfully, she moves on to Mia. I focus on the fire, and suddenly a woozy feeling sweeps through me. The tension in my body starts to release and I find myself drifting off. The flames change colors, shifting from red to dark blue.

What was in that smoke?

Before I have a chance to worry about that, I drift away even more. Everything after that becomes fluid and unhinged from reality. We're each given stick figures that represent what we want to cleanse from our lives, then led to the bonfire to toss them in the flames.

"*Noah*," I whisper to my doll.

The prickly figure made of sticks bound with twine stares back at me. My heart thumps harder, wrenched with pain.

I open my fist and watch it plummet into the fire, then spark and ignite. The flames dance from blue to purple. I watch as the doll dissolves into nothing more than ash, wishing it was really him burning alive in fire and flames.

For what he did to me.

A cruel smile twists my lips. I think of my father suddenly. How easy life can be snuffed out like a dying fire.

"*Time to burn*." I hear his gravelly voice. *"Little darlin', burn it all down."*

I snap out of that hallucination, but the message remains clear. I reach up to my neck and unclasp the necklace.

The chokehold releases from my throat. I grasp the diamond strand in my hand. How many times have I run my hand over it, soothing myself with the tether to Noah?

I clench up at his name. My stomach curdles. "*Little darlin', burn it down*."

With that command whispered under my breath, I fling my wrist and throw the promise necklace into the bonfire. I watch as it's consumed.

Hannah and Mia witness this ritual cleansing. They cheer for me. And then, we're all dancing around the fire in a circle of women, primal and released.

I notice Dame Tremaine especially gets into it with her friend. They get feral, twisting their bodies and baring their teeth.

I don't know where the red paint comes from, but we're painting our cheeks with it, streaking them. The paint smells coppery, almost like blood.

I hear drums permeating the darkness. *Thump. Thump. Thump.*

The apprentices emerge from the woods, beating drums covered in animal hides, while the stick figures dance in the tree branches and the fire burns and Guru Shava weaves her arms through the air like she's conducting a great symphony of burning.

I watch everything burn.

That's the last thing I remember before it all goes black.

CHAPTER TWENTY-FOUR

BEFORE

NOAH

You're dating Noah Barron?

I cringe hearing my full name like that. The cadence tells me they're in awe. That the high profile I carried even back in school isn't lost on them. We're standing in the doorway to Morgan's apartment. Her face contorts with confusion, making it even worse. She turns to me with a questioning look.

"I can't believe you know them," she marvels, shaking her head in shock.

She's not the only one in total shock right now. I'm stunned to be standing face-to-face with Hannah and Mia—and that they're Morgan's roommates and two best friends from college.

How is this possible?

"We all went to that same boarding school," Hannah says, filling in the gaps. "He's a Woodbury alum. And then we met you at Barnard."

"Don't you mean Woodbury brat?" Mia says. "With how much money his family donates to the school, I'm surprised it's not named *Barron* Prep."

I wish I could curl up into a ball and disappear, or erase my last name and family. I never should have offered to bite the bullet and walk her up. Last night solidified our relationship, and it was only the proper thing to do. Plus, I meant it when I said I didn't want to let her out of sight. She's *mine* now.

I think back but realize our experiment kept me blind to this possibility. My boarding school is a feeder for Barnard and other liberal arts colleges, especially those located in the city. However, I didn't even know what college she attended. Also, she never told me their names. She always referred to them simply as her roommates or best friends from college.

"Of course," Morgan says. "That makes sense. What are the odds?"

"Basically, Manhattan is like the *biggest* small town," I provide helplessly as the pieces slot together in my mind.

Hannah smirks. "It is like super incestuous. But don't get too creeped out. He's a few years older. We didn't overlap at Woodbury."

"But the *Legend of Noah Barron* endured long after he graduated and went to Dartmouth," Mia says.

"Wait, what do you mean?" Morgan asks, blushing.

She looks at me, but my head starts pounding.

I'm helpless to stop what's coming. My history always rises up and bites me. This is why I signed up for the One. Why I hoped our experiment would save us from, well, this.

"Everybody at school had a crush on him," Mia says, appraising me with her eyes. "And many have tried to land him, but he never *officially* dated anyone, except that one girl. What was her name?"

"Yeah," Hannah jumps in. "What ever happened to her?"

I cut her off before they can dig deeper. "I hate to break the news to you and all my supposed Woodbury admirers, but I am officially off the market."

Hannah and Mia both gape at us in astonishment, while Morgan smiles bashfully. She fingers the diamond cluster necklace at her throat.

"What is he saying?" Hannah says.

"Hurry up and spit it out already," Mia gushes. "We need all the tea."

"This is a promise necklace," Morgan says.

I reach over and hold her hand, giving it a hard squeeze. "Yesterday, I asked Morgan to officially be my girlfriend."

"And I said yes," Morgan adds.

Hannah and Mia freeze, too flabbergasted to respond for a long moment. Then they start jumping with glee and hug their friend, inspecting the diamond necklace closer.

"Oh my, that is big news," Hannah says. "Noah Barron is off the market."

Mia nods. "Wow, all our friends will be so jealous when they find out."

"Yeah, it's the craziest thing," Morgan says. "Since we matched, it's been such a whirlwind. I actually didn't know who he really was until right now."

I smile sheepishly. "Right, the blind date experiment. But now that we made it official, we felt like it was time that I meet her friends—"

"Beyond time," Hannah cuts in. She gives me a hard look. "Candidly, it was starting to get a little creepy. But now that we know the truth, it kind of makes sense."

"We were, like, dying for deets," Mia adds, then turns to Morgan and whispers loudly enough for me to hear. "But you realize this changes everything. You landed Noah Barron. His last name is on buildings, for Christ's sake."

I wince at my name again and worry about what they'll tell Morgan after I depart. However, the cat is out of the bag now. No use trying to put it back in. I just hope the worst gossip has already been spilled—the proverbial tea—as Mia kindly put it.

Still, my mind races. I am a few years older than them. We didn't overlap at all. That means my secret should be safe.

"Sorry, I have to get to work," I beg off. "I wish I had more time, but my team has an important investor meeting this morning."

Morgan also jumps to attention.

"Ugh, me too."

I give her a firm kiss—the kind that shows both our comfort level and deep connection—plus a little bit extra just to make her friends jealous. I know how girls work. It will give Morgan extra social cred, and in Manhattan, that's everything.

I pivot and make my way back down the stairs to my waiting car, but their voices echo, making my head pound. This is so cringe.

"Wow, you landed Noah Barron. Nobody will believe it!"

I wince, wondering if this is a good thing—or a bad thing.

Nothing I can do about it now. I'm in deep with Morgan. *Too deep.* My heart flips just thinking about her. I played all my best cards. Even defied my father and his wishes.

She is truly the One.

I hurry into work—late—rushing past the conference room where my father and his top execs are huddled in a meeting with clients. I pray he won't see me, but he jerks his head up. His steely blue eyes lock onto me and narrow. I grimace, knowing I'm late. But it's more than that.

Hopefully, he's busy today, and I can continue to avoid him. His warning to break up with Morgan before it becomes too serious is still fresh in my mind—and also how I did the exact opposite and instead made Morgan my official girlfriend.

I slide into my cubicle and fire up my computer. After the shock of this morning, I'd like to keep my head down and lose myself in work. It's not long before my phone chimes with incoming texts.

The first one is from my father.

I dread reading the message, but I don't really have a choice. I click it open.

DAD: *Did you do it?*

He adds a clock emoji. As in, the clock is ticking. Before I can figure out how to respond, another incoming text alert crowds the screen.

MORGAN: *Guess it's only fair I should tell you my name *deep breath**

NOAH: *Remember, it doesn't change anything. It's still just us.*

I type those words out, but they feel hollow. I glance over my cubicle at the conference room where my father remains with his white hair and high cheekbones, the spitting image of me. Just older and more distinguished.

The dots reappear indicating Morgan is typing out her response. Two words appear in the text bubble.

MORGAN: *Morgan Steele.*

It's a simple addition to her first name that changes everything.

She knows who I am. I know who she is. Not that it has exactly the same impact. Her name doesn't come attached to anything that rings a bell. Aside from her college best friends, I'm guessing we've never crossed paths.

Though, it's possible she was sitting at the bar nursing a martini while I dined at the best table in the back. But we would have been like two ships passing in the Manhattan night, unaware we were on a collision course.

NOAH: *Morgan Steele. Has a nice ring to it. But don't get too attached.*

MORGAN: *Oh, what do you mean?*

NOAH: *The necklace is only the start. You're mine now, and I mean to claim you. That includes your last name.*

I hit send, then turn my phone over, wondering if those words made her heart pound the way they did mine. I savor the moment, envisioning the future I'm already planning for us, despite my meddling father. But then curiosity rears its ugly head. His doubt mingles with my uncertainty, curdling it. Turning everything rotten and sour. Dark thoughts flood into my mind.

My fingers twitch at my keyboard. I can't resist. I glance around to make sure my dad is still caught up in his meeting and also that I'm not being watched. Thankfully, the coast is clear.

I hide in my cubicle and open a private encrypted browser on my computer, typing her name into the search engine. *Morgan Steele.* I'm still getting used to how it looks and sounds.

I get too many hits. Turns out that's a common name. I narrow down the search with more terms, adding "Barnard. New York City."

Instantly, search results flood the screen. My stomach drops as I scan them, fearing the worst and worrying that my dad will be proven right.

I'm relieved when I don't immediately find anything nefarious. A well-curated social media page with typical posts. Her and her friends at various trendy bars and restaurants around the city. Central Park. The bridge—our bridge, as I now think of it.

I click through the pages and try some other search terms. I'm rewarded with more biographical details. Barnard checks out. I breathe a sigh of relief. I track back in time, but the older hits with her name aren't her. Frustrated, I realize I can't dig up much on her before college.

I contemplate that, but it's not unusual. A lot of kids don't have social media before eighteen. Or at least not that you can find by searching their name. Once it became clear that colleges and employers might use dumb teenage shit against you, we all wizened up.

I avoid it altogether. Again, I have my reasons. The notoriety of my family's name being top of the list. All I told Morgan was that I like to protect my privacy. It's not a lie. But it does sidestep the real reason.

I'll bet she's searching my name now. The history of my family is well-documented in the public domain. We pop up in the news on a regular basis, mostly for our high society charity endeavors and our expansive business empire. But she won't find anything personal. I'm always in the background, standing behind my parents and uncle, trying to blend in.

I don't want to be noticed.

I hate the attention because nobody knows who I truly am on the inside. They just see the polished exterior and make their own assumptions. But Morgan changed all that by falling in love with me without knowing my true identity, though I'm sure she guessed that I had money and influence.

That's different than realizing I'm Noah *Barron.*

Fuck, she's probably already found the embarrassing piece that ran in *New York Magazine* last year branding me the city's "Most Eligible Bachelor." I cringe, imagining her reading it. The fluff piece even mentioned how mysterious I was, always avoiding the spotlight as much as possible and hiding in my family's long shadow, but they concluded that it only made me more attractive. My family's publicist gave them a curt "No comment" when they reached out. That only fanned the flames. It got picked up by the tabloids and a lot of influencers.

Morgan didn't know any of this before today. I have to cling to that now since it's all I have left.

"Why are you hiding in your cubicle?" Roger butts in, draping himself over the divider. "Is this about Morgan?" He uses her name, elongating it and giving it extra emphasis.

I quickly shut the window, the screen reverting to the Nasdaq exchange. Blake scoots his chair over, cornering me inside the three-and-a-half padded walls of my cubicle.

"It's gotta be. Look how jumpy he is. Oh no, did it end?"

"Even if it did, it's his longest relationship by a long shot," Roger says. "At least, since we've known him. That shows major growth. Just like that IPO for the One that's gonna let us both retire early."

They high five, then turn back to me and force sad faces. "Oh yeah, sorry about the breakup," Blake says.

"But it was distracting you," Roger points out. "You haven't done any real work in weeks. Our team has been covering for you so your father wouldn't notice. But we can't keep it up forever. So, it's probably for the better."

"Yeah, and no drinks with the boys," Blake says. "Or fun sex escapades to entertain me and make me forget about my total lack of libido."

Roger claps him on the back sympathetically.

"My condolences," he says. "You wifed up too young."

They both turn to me, trying to look forlorn, but I can't ignore their glee over the prospect that I'm single once again and back to my old ways.

I clear my throat. "First of all, her name is Morgan Steele. And we didn't break up." I let that sink in, before I add the next part tactfully. "Second of all, she's my girlfriend now."

Their eyes pop wide open. "Whoa, the *official* girlfriend title?" Roger says in disbelief. "That's, like, never happened in the entire history of Noah Barron."

Blake nods. "And she has a last name? Call the *Times*—that's front-page news! When's the wedding? Is it gonna be at Barron Plaza? Or maybe a destination extravaganza in Italy?"

I roll my eyes and smile sheepishly.

"Don't get ahead of yourselves. And keep it between us for now."

I look pointedly at the conference room. They catch my drift right away. I don't say much about my father to them directly—I have to be careful—but they work here, so they know that my father runs everything—even his son's life.

I lower my voice and give them a hard look. "I'm trying to figure out next steps."

They get it right away.

"Of course," Rogers says quickly. "We've got your back. You know that."

"Congrats," Blake adds, clapping me on the shoulder. "We'll keep it extra hush-hush."

"Like it's a confidential upcoming merger," Roger says. "Don't worry—your little secret is safe with us."

Relief washes over me.

"Just don't leave us off the guest list," Blake adds with a shit-eating grin. "I've always wanted to go to the Amalfi Coast. Your wedding will be the *perfect* excuse. Even the wifey can't say no."

I roll my eyes again, but they've already returned to their desks.

Still, I feel a thrill at his words. Despite me putting them off and saying to slow down, I want to do the opposite. I remember claiming her body last night and then again early this morning. I don't care what my father thinks.

I just have to figure out the best way to break it to him and contain the fallout. I've managed billion-dollar mergers and major IPOs. I can handle finally debuting my relationship.

Morgan Steele.

She won't be that much longer.

Morgan Barron.

I'll claim her name too. For one reason: She belongs to me now. Even if she doesn't fully know it yet.

Still, something nags at me. Her next text only makes it worse.

At first, I'm excited and grateful that it's not my father.

MORGAN: *Now you can't get out of it. Our friend group has monthly drinks. Bunch of Barnard and Woodbury alum. Thursday happy hour.*

NOAH: *Oh jeez. Sounds thrilling.*

MORGAN: *Sorry, but Hannah and Mia won't take no for an answer.*

NOAH: *When is the torture session . . . err, I mean, drinks.*

MORGAN: *Haha. Very funny.*

NOAH: *I was being serious.*

MORGAN: 🙄 *Tomorrow night. 7 p.m. happy hour at Luna Lounge.*

That's tomorrow. I frown in frustration.

I want Morgan all to myself. I'm not ready to share her with everyone—and especially not with a bunch of entitled Woodbury alumni. I should know because I'm one of them.

But I don't have a choice. Morgan is right. Our experiment is blown wide open for the outside world to peer in and judge. I'm a few years older than her friends, so I'm probably safe. I don't know them that well, and vice versa.

That's all ancient history anyway. We covered my tracks. Kept it quiet. Even my school file has been wiped clean—and the girl's file has been purged altogether. My father made sure of it.

But something about how Hannah looked at me gives me cause for concern. How much does she know about what happened back then?

And will she tell Morgan?

CHAPTER TWENTY-FIVE

AFTER

MORGAN

I wake from a terrible nightmare in a panic. Noah's furious voice echoes through my head.

You destroyed us!

I try to scream, but only a soft gasp comes out. I'm breathing hard and sweaty, tangled in the comforter.

Where am I? What's happening?

It's dark in my room.

My room. That's where I am. I grasp for the strands of reality filtering back in. I'm safe and back in my cabin at the Namaste Center. But how did I get here?

The last thing I remember is the bonfire ritual. That weird smoke, then how everything got blurry and trippy. I reach for my neck on reflex, but my hand comes up empty.

My promise necklace.

It's gone.

My heart drops like a cold stone. What happened to it? I comb through my memories, then get a sickening feeling. A blurry image flashes through my head. I tossed the doll into the flames after naming it Noah.

Then I threw the necklace in, while Hannah and Mia cheered for me.

Regret hits me full force. I'm not ready to let go of him . . . of us. That promise necklace represents everything.

I have to get it back.

I fling off the sweaty, twisted comforter and leap out of bed. I still feel dizzy and off-balance. Now I feel certain that Guru Shava drugged us with that smoke. I wasn't in my right mind when I cast off the necklace. But another thought occurs to me. Diamonds and platinum don't burn. I can still find it and get it back.

I yank on my clothes, then struggle into my boots and coat. I thrust open the front door. It's dark outside, but the edges of the sky are tinged with pale light. Sunrise will come soon.

I pull out my phone and turn on the flashlight. I find the path and follow it as it curves around. I have to find the meditation garden. I stay alert and vigilant, knowing that wild predators lurk in the woods.

There's also the hunter. I pray he's not out tonight.

While not as dangerous, I also can't get caught with my phone. Not to mention, I'm alone and not using the "buddy system." I'm guessing that I'm breaking at least a few rules with my little adventure.

The cold penetrates my body despite the layers. I tramp through the snow, starting to breathe hard. My exhales fog the air, dancing in front of the flashlight beam.

I continue deeper into the woods while regret pools in my heart. I have so many regrets. How far back into my past can I follow them?

I trace it back to the moment the second Hannah and Mia learned the truth about who I was dating. That's when everything started to unravel and fray, only I didn't know it yet. I should have kept him hidden. My little secret. Until it was too late.

My hand drifts to my stomach, slipping under my coat. The life that grows there. Will it survive this? I feel lost and adrift, clinging to anything that offers certainty. And right now—

I have to get that necklace back. That thought drives me forward. But I get lost, losing the path. The forest is a labyrinth; each turn looks the same. I keep going, trying to find the path again, only to trip over a tree branch.

I fly headfirst into the snow and taste the ice in my mouth. My face burns from the cold.

I hear something in the trees. It's faint, like the whistling of the wind.

"Who's out there?" I call out, struggling back to my feet.

I whip around, scanning the darkness.

Behind me, I hear a branch snap.

I freeze in my tracks and strain my ears to hear. The wind dies down. Everything falls silent.

I relax. I'm just hearing things. I start forward again, forcing my frozen limbs to obey me, when suddenly a voice rings out.

"Come out, girlie girl!"

The hunter.

Shit, he's found me. What was I thinking trekking out here in the dark all alone? *Snap.* Another branch.

I zero in on the sound.

He's somewhere to my left.

I flick off my phone's flashlight, then take off running in the other direction. Branches slap my face, stinging me. My breath pants in and out in a staccato rhythm. I am lost.

Right when I'm about to completely panic, I burst through the trees and stumble into a wide clearing. The air still smells like charred wood. I look down. The snow is packed with our boot prints.

The meditation garden, I think with relief. I strain my ears, but I don't hear anything in the trees. I must have lost the hunter . . . if he was even there.

I remember hallucinating last night and realize I don't know what to believe anymore. I fall forward on my knees and start digging through the fire pit, searching for my necklace, but my fingers only sift through ash. I shine my flashlight on the pit, hoping it'll catch on the diamonds. But nothing. The sun rises and illuminates the clearing, but still I find . . . *nothing.*

It's gone.

But that's impossible—platinum doesn't burn, and diamonds only burn at super high temperatures. It should have survived the flames. Did somebody take it? I jerk my head, startling as the stick figures stare down at me from the trees. Immediately, I think of the silent apprentices.

I back away from the fire pit, searching the ground for any clues.

A set of footprints leads away from the fire pit, into the forest. I follow them as the sun rises higher, bursting through the trees and lighting the way.

I keep following the tracks, desperate now to find my necklace.

I take a step forward, and the ground gives way beneath me, sucking me down into a large pit.

Something hard jabs my back. I feel around with my hands, struggling to make sense of it. The pit is filled with what feels like sticks and rocks, but then I pick up one of them and gasp in fear. I'm holding a bone.

I'm trapped in a large pit filled with skeletons. Too many to count. Bones piled upon bones. I scramble to get out but lose traction and slip back down, landing flat on my stomach.

A skull stares back at me with empty eye sockets.

That's when I scream.

CHAPTER TWENTY-SIX

BEFORE

MORGAN

"Tell me if I'm being too clingy," Noah says, handing me a crisp glass of Chardonnay. Before Noah, I drank whiskey on the rocks. But he's been nudging me away from that, gently, over the course of our last few dates.

I take the hint, flash my best smile, and sip the icy-cold wine. It tastes sour and bitter on my tongue. But I don't dare speak up to order something different. This is all part of my training.

I am slightly jealous of the scotch on the rocks in his glass. But it's manly and more appropriate for him, I guess.

I justify it by reminding myself there are so many subtle ways we change ourselves when we pair up in relationships. Mia and Grant, for instance. They're standing across the room, bodies tilted inward toward each other to stake out their claim. How she'd never be caught dead listening to country music before him, but now she cranks up Zach Bryan and Kacey Musgraves instead of the pop music she truly loves. They weirdly seem to dress alike. I wonder if that's pre-planned or just happens naturally.

Hannah and Tyler move toward the bar in lockstep. I think of how she swapped her pastel crop tops and matching sets for demure sheath dresses and preppy sweaters once she paired up with Tyler. And how Hannah and Mia slowly stopped going to frat parties, instead preferring upscale cocktail bars.

Like this one tonight—wood-paneled with sexy, low lighting and a well-curated list of speakeasy craft cocktails named after 1920s movie starlets. We take it over for happy hour one Thursday every month for our little gathering.

I drag my eyes off them, turning back to Noah. "You could never be too clingy," I reply with a sexy smile. I lower my voice and whisper in his ear. "Besides, I like when you cling to me. Maybe later, after this horrid event, you can cling to me harder."

He blushes and whispers back. "I'd love nothing more." He tightens his grip on my waist, communicating the extent of his desire for me. "Do we have a secret hand signal or code word for when we can safely abandon ship?"

"I'll just do this," I say, stepping closer and kissing him deeply. Then I drag my teeth over his lower lip and back away out of his reach.

"Ugh, Morgan," he gasps. "You're killing me. How much longer?"

I raise my eyebrow. "We have to do a few more rounds, so we can sear into everybody's brains that we're together."

"Right, boyfriend duty," he agrees. "I suppose I've been shirking that since we met, keeping you all to myself. But it's time I stake my claim."

His eyes drift to the diamond promise necklace. I savor his attention, almost unable to believe how smoothly the transition to real life is going. I'd harbored some fears that once we announced our true identities and tried to drag our whirlwind courtship into the outside world, everything would implode, draining all the passion.

So far, it's been the opposite. It's kind of hot and audacious to be parading around this room with him, knowing everyone is talking about us.

"Shall we mingle?" I suggest.

"Your wish is my command," he says, snapping off a salute.

I lean in again, my breath raspy. "I promise, I'll make it up to you later."

Then I saunter off so he can appreciate the view from behind of my ass in the little black dress I selected that accentuates the diamond necklace perfectly.

As he follows after me, he groans. "Fuck, Morgan. You're killing me."

True to his word, he sticks by my side all night long, almost possessively. The trendy bar is full of our friend group, mostly Barnard alums and their partners, along with a few Woodbury brats. I enjoy their eyes roving over him, landing on me, then how they whisper conspiratorially, wondering how the hell I hooked him.

Hannah and Mia have their plus ones draped over them, but I take pleasure in noticing that my date is both hotter and richer.

"I still can't believe you're dating Noah Barron," Hannah said for the hundredth time while we were getting ready for drinks. No, maybe *thousandth.*

"Seriously, pinch me now," Mia added, swiping on more mascara. "Crazy that we all went to Woodbury."

They both sounded positively ecstatic about the surprising turn of events. They hadn't been able to stop talking about it, begging for more details and dissecting every aspect.

Hannah draped her arm around me while I primped in the mirror.

"Look, I know you didn't go to boarding school with us, and you don't come from our world," she said delicately, "but you're acting way too nonchalant about *who* you're dating."

"Most girls would die to date him—or even just fuck him," Mia adds, brushing on an extra layer of lip gloss. "Let alone be his *official* girlfriend."

They both stare at me like Noah and I dating is some kind of strange equation they can't quite figure out, making me feel like a total outsider again.

Hannah is right. I don't come from their world. The one filled with trust funds and elite boarding schools. I've done my best to social climb, but that has its limits. You can't buy the silver spoon—you have to be born with it.

Then another thought hits me. *Maybe you can marry into it.*

The thought sends my heart jumping in my chest, but I will it to slow down, and not get ahead of itself. I don't want it to get broken.

Mia frowns. "I'm still shocked you got him to commit. What are the odds?"

"What do you mean?" I asked, trying not to let my insecurity show.

"Just that, I thought he'd end up with someone else." Mia shrugged. "It's not what I pictured back in school."

They're jealous, I realized, *that I landed him.* They couldn't understand why he picked me over someone like them.

"Maybe that's precisely why he fell for me," I pointed out, giving them a smirk. "He wanted someone a little bit different. That's the reason he signed up for the One in the first place."

Hannah cleared her throat. "I guess that makes sense. So, how serious is it?"

"I don't want to jinx it," I said in the proper self-deprecating tone, "but he made it exclusive, of course, and he's already talking about more."

They shrieked in unison.

Hannah gasped. "Wait, seriously? What kind of *more*? Like, proposing to you?"

The accusation lay in the nuance. I blushed again but held firm. I'd worked hard to get to this position. I wasn't handed it like my friends. That was also why they couldn't understand any of it. I batted my freshly made-up eyes.

"Yes. To little ole me."

The happy hour drags into the evening with everyone enjoying the craft cocktails and blowing off steam after work. I'm enjoying every second of it. Noah does a masterful job charming the girls and participating in all the boring financial conversations with the guys, since practically all of them also work in banking and finance.

But something keeps bothering me. I pull Hannah aside.

"Who's that girl?" I ask, nodding to a blonde in a red dress sulking by the bar. She came alone, as far as I can tell, and I don't recognize her from our other get-togethers. She's been fixating on Noah all night. She won't stop staring at him. But then, when she spots me standing next to him, she starts scowling.

Hannah rolls her eyes. "Oh, that's Sophia. She was in our class at Woodbury. I thought she moved to London for some fancy consulting job."

"Well, looks like she's back," I say casually, not wanting to sound desperate and clingy.

"Maybe she's back home for a visit." Hannah shrugs and sips her drink. "Or maybe she decided to move back. Her family owns a big real estate firm in Manhattan. Why do you ask?"

"Oh, nothing really. She just seems a little too interested in my boyfriend."

Hannah smirks. "You'd better get used to it. Sophia might be a little more obvious about it, but everyone in this bar is *interested* in your boyfriend."

"Right, I know," I say, blushing.

"Listen, I'll put it this way." She scans the room and appraises the social hierarchy then lowers her voice. "All the guys wanna be him—and the girls wanna fuck him. Probably some of the guys, too."

"Ha, that's one way to put it," I whisper back, so he doesn't hear us.

Noah is deep into a boring stock market convo with Tyler next to us and oblivious. I try to keep my tone light and joking, but the truth is that my insecurity is getting the best of me.

Hannah spots it and shoots me a sympathetic look.

"Don't worry," she says, patting my arm. "I'll get some intel on Sophia. And whether she really moved back to town—or she's just a tourist."

"Thanks, I appreciate it," I say, relieved to have a friend who always has my back. But still, I inch closer to Noah. His arm snakes around my body in a gesture of possession.

Stand back. We're together. She's mine, it says.

I'd be lying if it didn't give me a secret thrill. He's the handsomest guy here, easily surpassing Grant and Tyler, who are both cuties, plus his family practically built this city. There's a reason he was dubbed "The Most Eligible Bachelor" in New York City.

I searched his name as soon as I found out his true identity. It's not like I was snooping. I didn't even have to look that hard. He's sort of famous. The second I typed his name into the search engine, I was rewarded with a slew of hits. Articles and images filled the page. I scanned them, growing more and more excited. Noah is everything I've always dreamed about, and I'm not letting anyone come between us—especially Sophia.

"How am I doing?" Noah asks, hugging me to his side.

I sip my sour wine, wishing it was the caramel sweetness of whiskey, and lean into him to nuzzle his neck.

"Perfect," I praise him. "I think you might even be boyfriend material."

He smiles back at me. "Boyfriend? Is that all? Wow, I was hoping for—"

The chime of his phone interrupts him. He pulls it out. I spot "Father" on the home screen. He tilts the screen away, swiping up to scan the text message.

A dark look passes over his face, but he quickly covers it.

"Morgan, I'm so sorry. I know I promised to be Velcro tonight and chat up all your friends, but there's an emergency at work."

I pout a bit in disappointment. I can't help it. It's my big night with him, showing him off. But I quickly force my selfishness away. He has an important job. The kind that demands attention even on the evenings. The kind that will provide the caliber of lifestyle I've always wanted.

"I promise I'll make it up to you later," he adds, whispering in my ear in a raspy voice. "We can *cling* together all you want."

I put on a supportive smile. "You'd better, or you're missing out."

"Fuck, I know."

Desire burnishes his eyes. I kiss him, drawing it out, then hide my disappointment as he bounds out of the bar and disappears down the rainy, dark streets. A chill envelops me as the door wafts cold air my way. The cold white wine isn't helping. I immediately ditch it and lean into the bartender.

"Whiskey on the rocks. Jameson."

As I wait, someone leans in next to me.

"I'll have the same," a woman's voice echoes out.

I whip around. It's Sophia in her slutty red dress. Immediately, I realize she's drunk. Swaying on her feet lightly, standing a little too close. She narrows her eyes.

"So, you're the one who landed Noah Barron."

Her astringent breath wafts out. I'm taken aback by her directness.

"I'm sorry, have we met before? "I say in a bitchy, dismissive tone.

She doesn't take the hint.

"Oh, I'm just another Woodbury brat."

She waves her arm around the bar, but it's a floppy, disjointed gesture. Our drinks arrive, and she slurps eagerly, spilling more than a few drops down the front of her dress.

"Oops, how clumsy of me." She giggles, reaching for the stack of square bar napkins to mop up the mess.

I take the distraction as an opportunity to study her closer. She's curvy in a way that makes it clear Pilates isn't on her morning agenda. Her blonde hair is thick and curly yet frizzy, while her upturned nose gives her face an unevenness. However, her designer clothes testify to the money and privilege bestowed upon her by her family.

"My two best friends are Woodbury brats. Hannah and Mia, do you know them?"

She smirks. "The inseparable duo. It appears they've adopted a"—she looks me up and down—"stray. Where did you say you come from again?"

There's an edge to her voice. A challenge that I don't belong here.

"I didn't," I spit back, matching her tone.

Then I catch myself and soften. I have to be careful.

I spill my fake story. Growing up an ex-pat in Germany. The tragedy of my parents dying in a car crash. My acceptance to Barnard being my ticket to start a new life. How lucky I was to meet Hannah and Mia freshman year. How they accepted me and took me under their wings.

"Germany, you say?" She purses her lips in distaste. "You don't have an accent."

I flash a tight smile, dying to get away from her. Her pointed interrogation makes me uneasy. I sense there's a deeper reason for it, something to do with Noah.

"An unfortunate side effect of living here for years, I suppose," I say lightly, sipping my drink, not wanting to give away my years of practice and study to erase my origins. "I'm sorry," I add with a frown. "I don't think we were officially introduced. I'm Morgan."

I don't want her to know I already asked Hannah about her. I can't let on that she has any kind of power over me. I keep my voice stiff.

"Oh, sorry. Where are my manners? I'm Sophia," she says with a giggle. More of her drink sloshes onto her dress. I frown at the crude display.

"Funny, my friends never mentioned you." I give her a snarky look, then prepare to make my escape. "Well, it was great meeting you."

I start to leave, but she cuts me off.

"You know, you look a lot like his ex-fiancée. The one he met at Woodbury."

That stops me dead in my tracks.

"Noah had . . . a fiancée?"

Shock emanates through me, turning my blood to ice. This is news to me. She catches the alarmed look on my face and flashes a satisfied smile.

So, that was planned. She cornered me at the bar, making it seem casual, acting tipsy to appear harmless. All of a sudden she seems stone-cold sober.

"Oh, you didn't know?" she goes on, sipping her drink. "I thought everybody knew." She pauses, savoring my discomfort. "There was even an article in the school paper about it."

I blush harder. "No, I had no idea. I didn't go to Woodbury."

"Oh, right. You're from Germany," she says with obvious distaste. "Still, I'm surprised Hannah and Mia didn't mention it since he's your boyfriend now. The girl was a year behind us, though Noah had graduated a few years before. In fact, he was already out of college."

"You said he was dating someone younger?"

She arches her eyebrow. "At first, it was a bit of a scandal. The age gap, him coming around campus after he'd already graduated. But everyone understood. They'd all have killed for the chance to date him."

"Right, I've heard that before," I reply, but my voice is tight. My heart picks up speed as questions rush through my head. "Wait, you said she looked like me?"

She nods. "You two could be sisters. But there's something else about you that reminds me of her. Can't put my finger on it exactly. Maybe it's just a coincidence. And who knows? She could look totally different now. This was like eight years ago."

"What happened to her?" I ask, hating how badly I *need* to know.

She frowns as if she's dredging up the old forgotten memories. "She was a scholarship kid. Didn't come from much. Midwest or something? Anyway, she didn't really fit in at our school."

I pick up the insinuation.

Something else reminds me of you. She was a scholarship case too.

"But you said they were engaged? Obviously, they didn't get married." I laugh nervously, taking a big swig of whiskey to hide my insecurity.

"That's the scandalous part," Sophia says, leaning in and whispering. "I mentioned the age gap. Well, the dean got wind of it. I heard Noah proposed to make it okay, that they intended to marry. She was only a few weeks away from her seventeenth birthday, too."

"Is that the age of consent?"

She nods sloppily. "She *claimed* she was saving herself for marriage. So, Noah wasn't breaking any laws . . . technically. That's what she told the dean anyway, and I guess he bought it and agreed to leave them alone. But we all knew it was a big fat lie. Then Mia dropped that article in the school newspaper. She didn't name any names, but everyone knew who it was really about."

"Is that why they broke up?"

She nods, clearly enjoying sharing the malicious details. "Anyway," she goes on with a smirk, "the crazy part is that shortly after that, the girl is the one who broke up with him."

"She did? Why?"

"She said he was too clingy."

I flash back to what Noah said when we arrived tonight. *Just tell me if I'm being too clingy.*

I don't want to listen to this girl, but I can't stop.

"At least, that was the story she told everyone. But between us, I heard something else."

My heart speeds up. "What's that?"

"The way I heard it, Noah's father got wind of the relationship and tried to put a stop to it. But Noah refused to break it off."

"What do you mean?"

"She wasn't the *right* kind of girl for *the* Noah Barron."

My heart pounds fiercely. All I can think is . . . *she sounds a lot like me.*

"His father intervened and made the girl end things," Sophia continues in a low voice. "Her parents got involved, too. His father threatened to sabotage her father's business and poach his clients if she didn't."

"Are you sure?" I say, my mouth dry. "That sounds pretty extreme."

Sophia shrugs. "It was a bit of a scandal with her age and background. And it wasn't good for his family's reputation." She gives me a look. "You do know about his family?"

"Yes," I gulp in a strained voice. "They're old money. They control a lot."

"Not a lot," she corrects me. "They control *everything.*"

Her words hang in the air ominously. But I can't break this conversation off until I know every salacious detail. My relationship depends on it. I force myself to focus and stay calm.

"What happened? I feel like there's something else you're not telling me."

She leans in and lowers her voice. "Noah got obsessive—even borderline stalker-ish—after she ended it. Reports of him lurking around campus, until finally she dropped out of school abruptly and vanished."

"Vanished? Where?"

"The rumor was she moved back home to finish school. That it all became too much for her between the whirlwind affair, the engagement, and the breakup. Her grades plummeted."

"That makes sense."

She shakes her head, finishing her drink in one long swallow. "There was another rumor."

My stomach sinks. "Oh, what's that?"

She's whispering again. "That she got pregnant. That's why she dropped out. She didn't want to tell him because he would never let her leave. So, she fled home to have the kid in secret and raise it herself."

"You're kidding," I gasp. Her words circle through my head like a bad pop song.

"I know, so crazy. But it's probably not true. Like I said, it was just a rumor. Anyway, since all that stuff went down, he's been single and ready to mingle. Kind of a player. Wouldn't settle down. Went through a string of girls. Guess you changed him." She raises her eyebrow and flips her hair. "Well, congrats again on landing the most eligible bachelor this side of the pond. Glad I decided to move back. I missed it here."

"Oh, welcome back home," I say, unable to hide my revulsion.

She smirks, then turns to leave, but I stop her.

"Wait, what was her name?"

She turns back. "Who? The girl?"

"Yeah, Noah's fiancée." I have to force the words out—they feel unnatural on my tongue. My heart keeps racing, making me dizzy.

"Emma Albright. That was her name. Although Emma *Barron* has a better ring to it. Poor girl never got that far. Maybe you'll do better."

I ignore her snide comment, but she's not quite done with me yet.

"Good luck," Sophia adds with a knowing smirk. "You'll need it."

She winks, then saunters away. I watch as she collects her coat and exits the bar with her mission accomplished. The doors swish shut behind her.

I scoff at her obvious desperation and jealousy that Noah chose me. But the doubt is planted. She expertly dug the hole in my heart and buried the seed. The old me I thought I left behind flares up in a white-hot streak of rage.

My vision blurs.

I want to chase her down the street and punch her. Or throw my drink in her face and tell her to *back the fuck off my man* like a white trash girl.

But I don't.

I count to ten. I breathe. I plaster a smile on my face. Most of all, I behave.

Hannah comes over, sidling next to me. Mia flanks my other side.

"What was that all about?" Hannah's eyes track Sophia as she stalks past the windows in a blaze of red.

"Oh, nothing," I brush it off. "She's just jealous. You're right, everyone is."

"Scoreboard," Mia chants like we used to at college volleyball games.

"He was on your arm all night. Didn't leave your side. Have you seen the way he looks at you? He is all in." Hannah narrows her eyes. "Are you sure that's all it was?"

They're both scrutinizing me, and I can't help but blurt it out.

"Emma Albright. His girlfriend at Woodbury. Something about him being obsessed and her breaking it off?"

They exchange a concerned look.

"Oh, don't worry about that," Hannah says. "That's ancient history."

Mia nods, a little too emphatically. "Yeah, that was a really long time ago. Practically another lifetime."

But their faces betray them, and I know they're keeping something from me.

Just like that, my doubt starts to grow.

CHAPTER TWENTY-SEVEN

AFTER

MORGAN

"She's over here!"

I come to at the sound of rustling and pounding feet. Mia and Hannah appear above me, and strong arms clamp around me and pull me out of the pit of bones. They gently lay me on my back. The snow molds around my body. I blink hard. Did I pass out? What happened?

"Say something!" Mia demands, sounding freaked out. They both stare down at me with worry etched onto their faces.

I cough weakly. Force my voice out. "*Something.*"

"Hey, that's not funny," Hannah says, but she sounds relieved. "We woke up and you were gone. We organized a search party."

"Then we heard you scream," Mia jumps in. "You can't go wandering off like that in the woods by yourself."

"What if you got lost?" Hannah says. "Hypothermia can set in fast."

"You're just lucky we heard you," Mia says. "You could have—" She doesn't finish her sentence; she doesn't have to.

"Sorry," I say, feeling guilty.

That's when Guru Shava materializes in a swirl of robes. She has a white wool cashmere poncho wrapped around her shoulders with a hood covering her head. Her breath fogs the air, dancing around her face.

"Morgan, what happened?" Guru Shava asks. "This is why we discourage solo hiking. At the Namaste Center, we use the buddy system for a reason."

"Right, I know. I'm sorry. I lost my necklace at the ceremony," I stammer, searching my memory. "When I woke up, I realized it was missing. I thought I dropped it in the meditation garden, so I went to look for it."

Hannah hardens. "You didn't lose it—you cast it into the fire."

"It was about time to get rid of that reminder," Mia adds. "You're holding on to it, but you have to let it go! He cheated on you. You broke up with him. That necklace was his *promise* to you. The promise he broke."

"You can't keep wearing it," Hannah agrees. "It's almost like you want to get back together, the way you're still pining over him, waiting for his text."

They both stare at me. Tears prick my eyes. I can't deny it. I know they're right, I just didn't realize they knew.

"I just wish I could forget what he did. Go back to *before*. He said it was an accident, he was drunk." My excuses sound hollow and weak, even to my ears.

Guru Shava places her hand gently on my forehead. "Last night was about cleansing and death. Only by killing off the past can we be reborn and reach our full potential. If you gave the necklace to the flames, then it was time to let it go, and to let him go."

A sob bubbles up in my chest. "I know, but why does it hurt so much?"

The floodgates open, and I cry. And cry some more. Guru Shava holds space for me, letting me get it all out. I know they're right, but what if I don't want to do what's "right"? What if I want Noah back?

Finally, I get a hold of myself and sit up. I turn to Guru Shava urgently as more comes flooding back to me.

"When I was looking for the necklace, I thought I heard the hunter in the woods. I think he's stalking us. And then I fell into that pit. It's filled with bones."

They all look at me like I'm crazy. Guru Shava looks especially worried.

"I can assure you the only people allowed on the property are a couple hunters," she says sharply. "But they're harmless."

"Then how do you explain those remains?" I stagger to my feet, pointing down to the pit. "Clearly, someone has been killing people out here. It could be a serial killer, and he's after us."

She follows my gaze, looking down into the pit.

"Morgan, those are animal bones," Guru Shava says gently. "This land is an old Native American hunting ground, remember? That's probably the explanation for this old gravesite."

"You mean, they're not human?" God, I'm embarrassed.

I realize she's right. Not that I know a lot about animal skeletons. The femur bones look surprisingly human, but now I notice the elongated skulls and large ribcages that make it clear they're animal remains. Upon closer inspection, I'm guessing they're deer skeletons.

"Remember the ceremony last night?" Hannah says. "Look at them. They're not fresh."

"A serial killer?" Mia rolls her eyes. "I told you to stop watching all those true crime shows. They're bad for you!"

"Right, I guess my imagination ran a little wild," I admit.

"Thanks for finding it," Guru Shava says. "We'll inform the local tribes to see if they want to dispose of the bones. But first, we should honor the souls of the creatures who gave their lives so we could live. The cycle of death and rebirth."

Guru Shava approaches the mass gravesite, bows her head over, and says a prayer over the remains. Hannah and Mia follow suit. I try to join them, but my blood still thrums with adrenaline. I study the bones piled into the pit and realize they are old remains.

Still, I know I heard the hunter in the woods. And the footprints that led me here were fresh. While they finish praying to the grave, I try to find the boot prints again, but they've been trampled over and erased.

A voice jerks my attention away.

"Morgan, where'd you go?"

Hannah appears behind me, making me jump. "Oh, sorry," I say quickly.

"We have to get back," Hannah says, grabbing my arm and pulling me the other way. "Hurry, we have morning sessions. If you feel up to it."

"Never been better," I say, forcing a smile. "And I promise not to wander off in the woods alone again."

Satisfied, she clutches my arm and leads me back toward the group. As I turn my head, I swear I glimpse fresh blood splatters melted into the snow. But Hannah is pulling me along, and we pass out of sight before I can see for sure.

I want to go back, but I know it will look bad. Especially if there's nothing there. I give in and don't fight it.

Some of the apprentices have gathered by the pit. They're listening to Guru Shava and gesturing to the gravesite of old animal bones. She's probably telling them to contact the tribes and get it cleaned up. I'm guessing a mass animal cemetery isn't the vibe the Namaste Center wants to project with its vegan raw juice cleanses and upscale clientele.

Two more days, I think. I'd give anything to leave now, but I can survive a couple more days.

They can't pass quickly enough.

Despite my little field trip, we reach the Great Hall in time for the morning sessions. The apprentices wander around, passing the trays of juice. Everyone drinks heartily, but my stomach protests and rebels. I grab one for show, pretending to sip it while planning to ditch it in a bathroom trip or discard it quietly.

But Hannah and Mia are treating me differently, not letting me out of their sight. Something feels off about them. I can't place it. I'm mostly unharmed, just a few scratches to show for my adventures. However, something is still nagging at me.

"Seriously, no more wandering," Hannah says, swigging a shot then depositing the empty cup on a passing tray and grabbing seconds. "Remember the mountain lion we hit? Not to mention all the coyotes we keep hearing at night. You can't be too careful."

"And that creepy hunter. If he's even real," Mia mutters under her breath.

The conversation grinds to an awkward halt.

"He is real," I shoot back in a frosty voice. "We saw him on the way up to the center, remember?"

"That's true," Hannah allows. "And he was helpful! He killed that poor mountain lion. Put her out of her misery."

"That doesn't mean he's been back around the property," Mia says with a pointed look.

"I saw him," I insist stubbornly. "Outside our cabin, watching me."

They exchange another look like I'm crazy.

"Is that why you really went out last night?" Hannah says. "Were you out there looking for him? You can tell us."

"No, it was the missing necklace," I say, feeling attacked. "But I did hear him in the woods. He was following me."

"Your necklace isn't missing—you threw it into the bonfire."

"Yeah, and good riddance," Mia says, toasting her smoothie with Hannah's juice shot. "About time."

"How do you explain that it's missing from the fire pit? Diamond necklaces don't burn." I lower my voice, glancing around. "I think the apprentices took it."

"You think they stole it? Seriously, let it go already," Hannah mutters in an exasperated voice. "That was a big part of your healing process. Why do you keep going backward?"

"The apprentices probably cleaned up after the ceremony," Mia says. "Even if they did take it, it doesn't matter. That's in your past now. The point is that you shouldn't be holding on to it anymore. It's too big a reminder of—"

She stops, unwilling to say his name. My blood starts to boil.

"*Noah*," I hiss. "You can say his name already. Pretending like he doesn't exist doesn't erase him! I still love him. I can't help it. I know what he did was wrong—my brain does anyway." I fall silent, then force the last part out. "But tell that to my heart."

An awkward silence falls. They exchange a look. A look of *pity*. Embarrassment flames my cheeks.

"We only want what's best for you," Hannah tries. "You know, he cheated on his fiancée? The one from Woodbury?"

Mia nods sharply. "With another classmate of ours. Once a cheater, always a cheater."

"That was the rumor," Hannah agrees. "Though we never found who he cheated with. But now after what he did to you, I'm certain the rumors were true."

Her words hang in the air. Confusion sweeps through me. I'm stunned and don't know what to say, or why they didn't tell me all this before, the moment they learned I was dating Noah Barron.

The gong goes off, summoning us into the meditation studio. Instantly, Hannah and Mia turn away and head for the doors, everyone else falling in line. I stagger up last. Somehow, I'm always a half-step behind them.

A fluttering of white catches my eye, and I turn.

Guru Shava approaches one of her apprentices standing by the doors. She doesn't see me, so I take the opportunity to eavesdrop. She leans over and whispers to them. "I fear we may need to move the timeline up on the final ceremony. Can you let them know?"

The apprentice nods, then hurries off. I watch her vanish from the hall, feeling even more paranoid. What did she mean? Before I can worry about it, we're herded into the studio. I grab my yoga mat and blanket. I have my earbuds in and a podcast loaded up, ready to go. Frankly, I could use a major distraction right now, especially after that argument with my friends.

I can still feel their judgement over the necklace and Noah. The fact that I went back to the bonfire looking for it only cements their concern that I want him to take me back.

They don't know about my other big secret. The one hidden just below my skin still tying me to him, even without the promise necklace. I can't tell anyone about that yet.

Guru Shava takes the stage and grabs her mallet. I reach down and hit Play on my podcast. The host begins narrating another grisly crime—this one where the wife caught the husband cheating and took her revenge, slowly.

Even that podcast can't quell the mutiny in my brain today. Dark thoughts keep circulating. I try to focus on Guru Shava's serene face as she conducts our practice, and we move under her command. I wonder what that stuff I overheard was all about.

It's probably just something to do with the schedule logistics and doesn't concern me. She's running a whole retreat, after all. Lots of moving parts.

Still, I can't shake the feeling that it had to do with my little adventure in the woods this morning—and worse—that something terrible is about to happen.

Feeling like the host in my podcast, I run through what I know. That hunter has been lurking in the woods. Those footprints I saw were fresh. Two people suddenly went missing. I don't care if nobody else remembers them, I know they were here. The DA's last journal entry flashes through my head again, filled with urgency.

**Get out NOW! They're coming . . . in danger . . .
can't trust anyone . . .**

Maybe all these aren't connected. Maybe the two guests did leave early for unconnected reasons. Maybe I am seeing things in the woods—things that aren't really there, spiked by my paranoia, the podcasts, and whatever drugs they're putting in our drinks.

Since my breakup, I haven't been thinking clearly, consumed with my thoughts of Noah and our baby. I've come unhinged, unable to trust anyone. I argue with myself, back and forth, without coming to any conclusion.

All I can think as we move through the practice is: Who's next?

CHAPTER TWENTY-EIGHT

BEFORE

NOAH

"Cheer up!" Roger says, shoving another drink in my face. "This is supposed to be fun! We nailed that earnings target. Plus, it's Friday! We have to celebrate, right?"

"The old ball-and-chain really has you whipped already," Blake adds, shaking his head. "Welcome to the club, bro! Unlike you, I'm happy to get out of the house."

"Right, thanks," I say in a glum voice, trying to get through it.

The dark wood bar is teeming with Barron Ventures employees, all celebrating. I feel bad I had to leave Morgan's happy hour early last night, and even worse I had to cancel on her again tonight. But my team insisted I come and wouldn't take no for an answer.

They're right. We've worked hard all year and surpassed expectations. You'd think that would make my father happy, but nothing does. He tried to confront me again last night about Morgan, but I put him off, saying we could talk this weekend.

That's why I left early. I didn't want her to hear the fight and witness my distress. I don't want her to worry. I want to protect her from him at all costs. I can't forget what he did to Emma. I won't let that happen again. How he threatened her family and drove her away, forced her to break up with me.

But Morgan is tougher. She's not from a family he can strong-arm. She's an orphan, after all. That's part of her appeal (even though I can't tell her that).

I've been planning my little speech, what I'm going to tell him. I'll explain why she's perfect for me—and that I'm planning to propose before the new year. I'm already ring shopping. I snuck out to the jeweler during lunch and have my eye on a sizable vintage yellow diamond on a rose gold band that would look stunning on her finger.

I'll stand up to him, once and for all. It's time I became my own man.

And if I have to go out on my own and start my own venture, break away from the Barron name and all the privilege that comes with it, that's just what I'll do. I'm sure Morgan would support me becoming more entrepreneurial and going out on my own, even if I had to give up my penthouse and lavish lifestyle while I built my business independently. Buoyed by that thought, I down the rest of my whiskey and lean into the bar. "I'll take another," I say to the bartender. "Make it a double please."

A woman leans in close to me. Her arm brushes mine. "I'll have the same."

While the bartender is busy pouring, she pivots to me. "Oh, funny to bump into you here. Remember me?"

I whip my head around, trying to place her. On first glance, she's sexy as hell. Long, blonde hair in a perfect blow-out. Manicured nails. Gold dress that's skintight and hugs every single curve.

I feel a strong pulse of attraction, but I quickly quell the thrum of blood. I'm not like that anymore, I remind myself. That's the old me. I'm in love with Morgan. Meaningless sex and hookups don't do anything for me anymore. The problem is—my past always comes back to haunt me.

"What, you don't remember me?" She acts insulted, then leans in closer. "And what we did that night? I guess my hair was shorter. Oh, and I probably didn't have these yet." She caresses her clearly surgically enhanced breasts.

I frown. "What do you mean?"

She bats her fake eyelashes.

"I'm a Woodbury alum too. A year ahead of your ex-fiancée. You were having some problems with her. You crashed our party and got drunk."

The memories come flooding back in blurry flashes. A younger, slimmer version of the woman, with shorter hair, feeding me disgustingly sweet drinks from the punch bowl. Listening to me vent about my father and my fiancée. Luring me back to her dorm room, seducing me . . .

No, I don't want to remember that!

I flinch, pushing it down into the shadows. "I was faithful to Emma—I loved her!" I say in a low voice. "I would never cheat on her! I'm sorry, but you must be mistaken." My fists curl up into tight balls.

She smiles at the reaction she provoked.

"Of course you were," she says softly. "Such a good boy. The time wasn't right for us back then. But now, everything is different. You like them younger, don't you? Just like your ex-fiancée? That was quite an age gap." Her voice is husky, barely a whisper. "Wasn't your precious Emma underage when you met? When you fucked her and stole her virginity?"

I immediately reel back in disgust.

"Don't you dare mention her!" I hiss back. "Keep her name out of your mouth."

She smirks, clearly enjoying my temper. "You like other things in my mouth, don't you? Does that jog your memory? We can do that again tonight . . . and more."

I work to control my temper since she's clearly enjoying my reaction.

I turn my voice cold as ice. "Sorry, I have a girlfriend. I'm not interested, so you can move along—"

She cuts me off. "Oh, I know. Morgan *Steele*." The drinks arrive, and she grabs hers and sips it delicately. "I know all about her. She's not right for you."

"How dare you?" I say, feeling outraged. "Who the *fuck* are you? And how the fuck did you get in here? Barron Ventures reserved the whole bar."

"I got a special invitation." Off my confused look, she adds, "You really don't remember me? Wow, I knew you were drunk, but I didn't realize you blacked out."

Sweat breaks out on my brow. I study her and search my memory, but it remains painfully blank. I need to figure out who she is . . . and get rid of her fast. Before there's any collateral damage. I work to compose my features into a cold mask and slow my racing heart.

"I'm going to ask you one more time before I get security. Who are you?"

"Maybe this will jog your memory." She does a shimmy, showing off in her dress. "Sophia Warner, remember? Aren't I more your type? Oh wait, I forgot you like charity cases."

My calm facade evaporates as my words stutter out.

"Why would you say that?"

"Emma was a scholarship kid too," she says with a sneer. "She didn't belong at Woodbury. And you know it. Just like your new girlfriend, Morgan Steele. She doesn't belong here either. She's a complete imposter trying to trap you."

My heart stops. "What do you mean?"

"Just that your girlfriend isn't who you think she is. Your father thinks I'm a much better fit for you."

My father.

My cheeks burn hot. "That's outrageous. How can you say that?"

"Let's see, my family owns Walden Capital. Merging our families together would also merge our business empires." She runs her hand seductively down my shirt. "Plus, there's that little indiscretion we had back at school. Let's just say, we have major chemistry."

Now, my heart is thumping, but I'm frozen and unable to pull myself away.

"You've got the wrong guy. That never happened. Although, you do sound just like my father," I fume. "What you're proposing isn't love—it's a callous business arrangement."

She smirks. "*Love* can come later. I have some naughty tricks in the bedroom to keep you satisfied. I promise." She reaches for my crotch, but I swat her hand away.

"I *love* Morgan. Not that it's any of your business. She accepts me for who I am—the real me. I plan to marry her. I'm going to propose. I already started shopping for a ring." At this point, I don't care if this gets back to my father.

She flinches, then glares at me. "And what about your family's ways?" she threatens in a low voice. "Think she'll be accepting of that?"

I freeze. "What do you mean?"

"Oh, don't play dumb with me, Noah. Our fathers are involved in the same, shall we say, hobbies. I've grown up knowing all about it. My mom taught me how to turn a blind eye."

"That's sick," I say with less conviction this time. "I'm not like my father. I'm committing to Morgan, and that's it."

"You say that now, but what about when everything gets dull and routine? When the sex becomes boring? What about when she starts refusing to participate in the annual gatherings? What then?"

"How do you know about that?" I say, caught off guard. "Besides, you're wrong about her. She had a delightful time at the last one."

"Sure," Sophia says with a smirk. "But she's trying to impress you, get you to commit, pretend to be the exciting, thrill-seeking girlfriend. Once she has her claws in you, that'll change."

I flinch back. "How do you know that? Have you been spying on us?"

"Don't be ridiculous. I have better things to do than stalk you and your pathetic girlfriend. Simple—it's what I would do if I were your girlfriend. All fun and games until she lands you, then all that will change. Trust me."

"No, she's different," I insist. "I'd never get bored with her . . ." But I trail off. I hate how she's getting in my head, stirring up my emotions and confusing me.

"Look, I know you," she whispers, dragging her nails over my arm and raising goose bumps. "You need stimulation. You need variety. You need something more. Urges that no woman can satisfy. You have bloodlust running in your veins—"

"No, I don't," I say, shrugging her hand off me. "You're wrong."

But there's that doubt again.

"I'd be okay with that arrangement. And with the other *hobbies* our families like to indulge in. You know the oaths they swore, that you will swear."

"No, I'm not doing that," I hiss back. "I already told my father—"

She leans in and tries to kiss me.

I push her away.

"Leave me alone!" I snap. "You're wrong about me. I'm different, and so is Morgan. It's time for things to change. This sick legacy can't continue. I'm going to prove you and him wrong."

She crosses her arms, glaring back.

"Maybe your father can change your mind. Talk some sense into you."

"What do you mean?"

She smiles and sips her drink. "He's in the back room—waiting for you. I think you'll be quite interested to learn what he dug up on your girlfriend."

Now I know for certain. My father arranged this whole thing and put her up to it.

"What did he find out?" I grab her shoulders and squeeze hard. "Damn it, what do you know?" I squeeze harder.

Her eyes blaze with fire. She likes the pain I'm inflicting, leans into it even.

"Just that your precious little girlfriend isn't who you think she is."

I leave the bar and storm into the back room. My father sits at the table with a glass of scotch, probably very expensive. Two glasses sit in front of him, untouched. He was expecting me.

He wears a simple gray suit, slim-cut, and a red-and-gold striped tie. His usual uniform. He looks like any businessman in the city. Generic, almost unnoticeable. You'd never know the power he wields.

His eyes bore into me. "Son, have a seat."

I want to tell him off and storm out right away, but my eyes land on something sitting right in front of him—a thick manila envelope. A name is printed on it.

Morgan Steele

That freezes my heart. I do as I'm told and slide into the seat across from him at the long wooden table. The room is clearly meant for a private tasting dinner with the chef.

"I'll get right to it."

He doesn't reach to pour the scotch or offer me anything to drink. Instead, he leans forward and steeples his hands under his chin. Another long moment passes. I want to scream.

"You've been avoiding me and defying my wishes," he says with a disapproving frown. "So, I had to take matters into my own hands. Everything you need to know is in here." He slides the manila envelope toward me and taps it. "I'm confident that once you read it, you'll see things my way and do the right thing. I had my associates look into your girlfriend."

"How did you know her name?" I stammer, my head spinning. "I didn't even know her last name until recently."

I can't believe this is happening.

"That's right," he goes on in a businesslike voice devoid of any emotion. "You withheld it from me on purpose. But you made a critical mistake. You searched her name on your work computer. Our security firm monitors everything closely."

I lean forward, glaring at him. "You've been spying on me this whole time?"

"Again, son, it's for your own good—to protect you and our family." He nudges the file. "I think once you read the report, you'll understand. I have your best interests in mind."

Another word jumps out at me. Scrawled next to her name in brackets.

[ALIAS]

What?

My father follows my gaze and nods.

"Break up with her," he demands. "If you don't end the relationship, I'll be forced to cut you out of the family business and disown you. Or worse."

"No, I can't. I love her." I hate how weak I sound, but I can't help it.

"Don't forget what happened last time. This is your last chance."

He rises to leave then says one last thing. "Don't worry. You'll recover eventually. You did last time. Besides, I've already found a more suitable partner for you . . . and our family."

Sophia.

Ugh, how disgusting. My heart drops, while my head pounds fiercely.

My dad leaves me in the private room at the back of the restaurant with the file staring back at me. My hands are numb, my mind spins. I tear open the envelope.

The first piece of paper is a news article stating that *Morgan Steele* died in car crash at age seventeen in Atlanta, Georgia. The newspaper photos show a horrific scene of twisted metal; nobody could have survived that.

I flip to the next photo of Morgan Steele's driver's license—only the girl in the photo is not my Morgan. She has curly red hair, a constellation of freckles, and a roundish baby face.

That's followed by the coroner's report showing she died from internal injuries sustained in the grisly crash.

Morgan Steele is dead.

My mouth drops open in shock. A torrent of questions races through my head, but what horrifies me the most—

Who am I dating?

My mouth is dry and my hands shake, but I force myself to keep reading. There's a map of southern Louisiana with a spot circled in red by the bayou. Another newspaper clipping from a local paper, this one about a man who drowned in the swamp behind his trailer. The lead photo shows a run-down shack that could barely be called a house. There's another smaller photograph of the banks of the swamp behind his cabin, littered with a litany of liquor bottles. According to the police report, the man's body was never found.

How is this related?

I scan it again, just as confused. But then, I get to the last part. It's on the second page of the article, clipped in a jagged jigsaw shape from deeper in the newspaper. The article states the local man was reported missing by his eighteen-year-old daughter, who told the police he probably fell into the swamp when he was drinking out back.

I don't want to look at the accompanying picture, but I force myself anyway. I don't have a choice.

Ragged clothes fraying at the knees. Matted, greasy hair. Grime smeared on her cheeks. The photo is grainy but it's clear who she is.

That's Morgan.

Only it's not her name. I read the caption printed below it.

Tammy Lou Hinkley

The shock hits me with the force of a freight train. It can't possibly get any worse. But it does.

A square, yellow Post-it note in unfamiliar handwriting is stuck to the second page under her photograph.

DID SHE KILL HIM?

Looking into it, but haven't turned anything up yet.

My heart drops. That's impossible, right? There's no way Morgan killed her father.

I flip through the article again. The pieces are all there. The backwater cabin that looks more like sticks hammered together than an actual house. The muddy bank by the bayou littered with empty whiskey bottles. The stagnant waters of the swamp that can quickly claim a body, especially if they're blackout drunk. Alligators live in the bayou. It's easy to picture exactly what happened.

The story adds up perfectly. Maybe a little *too* perfectly.

I jerk back to her eighteen-year-old picture. She looks so scrawny and pathetic, it's hard to imagine. Tears streak her grimy cheeks, but it's her eyes I focus on. Hard and unfeeling. Like the eyes of a cold-blooded killer.

My brain can't compute this. Everything in my body freezes. I don't even breathe. The only thing I know for sure is—Morgan's been lying to me this whole time, our relationship a facade.

I feel like a fool. This is cheating. No, it's beyond cheating.

I defied my father and risked everything for her. His threat to disown me rushes through my head again, making me feel sicker. And for what?

Anger chases that thought as I stare at the gritty black-and-white image. A lowlife, social-climbing con artist who's been manipulating me this whole time. Probably to scam me out of my fortune.

The whole point of signing up for the One was to find someone who loved me for me—not my money and family. Someone I could really trust loved the real me. That was the whole point of the blind date experiment. But even when she came clean and told me her name, she was still lying to me.

Anger surges in my veins, fiery and hot. She betrayed me. That bitch.

My fist clenches, crumpling up the picture of *Tammy Lou Hinkley.*

Dark thoughts swirl through my head like a violent tempest, threatening to consume me. This rage is familiar.

When my girlfriend from Woodbury betrayed me and broke up with me—well, Emma paid the price dearly. You don't cross me like that . . . ever.

I shred the file into pieces in a fit of rage, but it's not enough. I seize the full bottle of scotch, not caring how much it costs, and drink it down. Once it's empty, I wipe my mouth. But wrath still simmers in my heart, so I storm back out of the room to the main bar.

Roger spots me. He signals to Blake, grabbing his arm, and they hurry over.

"You okay?" he asks, glancing at the entrance. "Your father just took off."

"And he looked pissed," Blake adds in a low voice.

"Everything is *fine*," I say in a slurred, slightly deranged voice. But I don't care. "In fact, more than fine. I've never felt better! Just some family business. You know how families are."

That's code for *back the fuck off.*

They get the message and leave me to stew in my own misery. I order another double whiskey and down it right away, then have the bartender refill it. He looks worried, but obeys.

I'm Noah Barron, after all.

I keep drinking. Everything turns blurry and uncertain. At some point, Sophia materializes next to me. I don't remember her climbing onto the barstool, or draping her arm over my shoulders. But she keeps feeding me drinks. And she's in that dress. She whispers in a sultry voice.

"I'll do anything you want, things your uptight girlfriend would never do."

I don't remember much after that. More drinks. Laughing too loud with Sophia. Staggering out of the bar late. Almost stumbling into a puddle. Her righting me. Gripping my arm hard. Guiding me into my waiting town car.

And then, she's all over me, lips and hands. I try to push her off, but I'm too dizzy and drunk. That's when it hits me—I feel drugged, even. My father. The bottle of scotch he left.

Now I realize, he never drank a sip of it.

This was all a setup.

The file. The spiked drink. It was in the bottle of scotch he left behind.

And most of all, the temptation.

Sophia.

I struggle to remain conscious, to resist her lips and more.

"No, please, I love her," I mumble weakly. But I can't push her away.

I'm woozy. My vision doubles.

My phone chimes.

I manage to slide it out of my pocket—an incoming text from Morgan crowds the screen.

Sophia takes my phone away, sliding it in her purse. She unbuttons my pants, leans over, and takes me inside her mouth. The warmth is comforting while the world spins wildly around me. Everything is spinning out of control.

Just like the last time.

CHAPTER TWENTY-NINE

AFTER

MORGAN

After a break for our juice cleanse, Guru Shava herds us back into the studio for our afternoon session. We spread out around the spacious room. My toes sink into the sticky malleable foam of my mat.

I exhale a deep breath, following along as the class begins.

"Namaste," I say, bowing my head.

I slip my hand into my waistband and click Play as the lights dim for the class. The soft drone of the podcast I'm binging starts up. It's a true crime story about a convicted killer who murdered his girlfriend, but he might be innocent. As the reporter digs deeper into the case, the reasonable doubt grows. I'm hooked. I don't know how they can make murder feel cozy, but they do.

The lights dim even lower. The soft, meditative music picks up. Guru Shava leans into her microphone from her perch. I watch her mouth move but am blissfully unaware of what she says, thanks to Steve Jobs. My own personal lord and savior. Deliver me from yoga. I imagine him in his black turtleneck and wire-framed glasses. He smiles at me and bows his head in solemn prayer. "Namaste," he says.

As we lie in corpse pose—the same ending to every yoga class in the known universe—Guru Shava turns to her gong, striking it with her mallet.

It overwhelms my podcast; I can feel the vibrations cut through my body.

Then she starts chanting, as usual. I can't hear the words, but I see my classmates repeat the chants back with robotic precision. I move my lips in imitation, still hooked on my podcast. I feel a glint of satisfaction at my small act of rebellion. It's surprisingly easy to fake it and mimic what everyone is doing.

Guru Shava bangs the gong again, making me vibrate. I notice that she's donned a red robe instead of her usual white. So have the apprentices standing around the room, watching us. That's odd. More of her weird theatrics.

The crimsons robes billow around her ankles as she moves around the studio touching our foreheads, marking them with some kind of oil. It stinks, forcing me to stifle a sneeze.

The oil feels cold and viscous on my skin. A buried memory from my childhood surfaces. My father polishing his rifle. Military-issued from the Vietnam war. A relic he smuggled back and maintained. The metallic reek of the gun oil. That's what it smells like.

I resist the urge to wipe it off.

If it weren't for my podcast, I'd be squirming out of my skin at this point. I peel my eyes open and risk a glance around our group. Everyone lies stock still on their sticky mats in the perfect iteration of corpse pose—on their backs with their legs splayed and their arms at their sides. They all truly look dead.

Guru Shava finishes going around our group with the oil. She returns to the stage and bangs the gong again.

I'm jolted out of my reverie as the emergency exit door at the back of the studio bursts open, ushering in a bitter wind flecked with snow. In a synchronized motion, the women from our group all stand up and assume mountain pose with their hands in prayer and feet parallel on their mats.

I stumble along, not prepared for this sudden shift that's different from the end of our other classes. I glance over at Hannah, then Mia. They both stare straight ahead, not even blinking.

I must have missed something, I realize guiltily. I try to relax my facial muscles and stop any urge to blink or move. I keep my hands pressed into prayer and my feet perfectly parallel with my mat, doing the best I can to fake it.

With the help of her apprentices, Guru Shava herds all the women toward the emergency exit, barefoot and underdressed. *What the heck?* The cold bite in the air outside can be felt inside the studio now. A big storm seems to be kicking up.

No way I'm tramping barefoot into the snow. On impulse, I take a risk.

When they're not looking my way, I slip into my fur-lined boots that I kicked off. I'm always last anyway, so they don't pay me any particular mind.

Mia and Hannah move swiftly toward the door, like it's beckoning them. *Maybe this is part of the detoxing program?* I think as I follow our group. *Freezing our asses off in the snow?*

But I'm afraid to click my podcast off so I can hear. Guru Shava might catch me, and then I'd be in real trouble.

Our group files outside and into the frigid cold. They walk in perfect synch together. I don't know why I'm following along, but I do. Something about wanting to fit in and not wanting to get caught for breaking the rules. I try to catch Mia's eye and whisper into her ear.

"Where the fuck are they taking us?"

Hannah is a true believer. The retreat was her idea. But Mia usually shares my skepticism. However, her eyes are glassy. *Dead eyes.* Hannah has them too. All the women do. Fear rises up inside me as the cold bites into my body like knives, and I know something horrible is about to happen.

They filter out of the woods like scarlet ghosts. Men in red robes with peaked hoods. They stare out at us. They're not wearing masks, so I can see their faces. But even without that, I'd know they're men because of their height, broad shoulders, and something subtle about the way they move that I've internalized over the years. Dominant, unafraid, like they own the world.

Men. So many men.

Twenty. Maybe thirty.

Men with rifles and crossbows and hunting knives.

Panic shoots through me, spiking my blood with adrenaline. I scan their faces, startled to recognize one of them.

The hunter.

He's their leader, standing front and center in the group. The more I look, the more men I recognize. Senators. CEOs. Supreme Court justices. Tech billionaires. I've seen them on cable news shows, posed in photographs on the front pages of newspapers and magazine covers.

All white men.

All powerful beyond belief.

Why aren't they trying to hide their identities? Why aren't they wearing masks?

Another dark thought hits me. They don't need to wear masks because we're not getting out of here alive.

I wait for general shock and panic to set into our group, but the women don't move. They stand there in a circle with glassy eyes. No reaction to these hooded men in red robes armed to the teeth, materializing from the woods.

Panic gnaws at my pounding heart, my extremities, my brain. I force myself to remain still as I struggle to understand what's happening. My brain feels foggy and sluggish. I don't dare break rank. One wrong move, and they could shoot me on the spot. They watch us like hawks.

Like we're their prey.

That's when it dawns on me. Guru Shava wasn't drugging us through the juices, she was hypnotizing us.

In the yoga class with the gong. That's the only explanation. I land on it, even though it sounds insane. It reminds me of a trending true crime podcast from last year about a Kundalini yoga cult. The dim lighting, the lack of solid food, Guru Shava and her soft voice and chanting. I'm the only one who didn't get hypnotized because I'm the only one who wasn't listening to her. I was listening to my podcasts instead.

The earbuds are still in my ears.

Before I can process anything else, Guru Shava bangs the gong again. Her apprentices have wheeled it out into the snow, leaving deep track marks in its wake. The sound reverberates through the still forest, pebbled with fresh snowfall. This world is windswept. This world is as unruly as the gale-force wind whipping down the mountain.

Bong! Guru Shava chants. My podcast has hit a break, allowing me to hear.

"We bleed every month, and therefore we cannot be trusted."

Everyone from our group repeats that in unison, like they've been programmed. *"We bleed every month, and therefore we cannot be trusted."*

I stumble to keep up with them, to blend in. I can't blow my cover.

They think I'm hypnotized too. That's the only reason they haven't shot me through the temples yet. I stare at the hunter. I knew I had seen him outside my window, even though my friends tried to convince me I was crazy. And now I'm certain he was dragging a dead body.

Dame Tremaine's friend, and then the DA. My mind whirls at a million miles an hour. I'll bet anything they got suspicious and had to be eliminated. Maybe Dame Tremaine's friend saw something she wasn't supposed to. And the DA?

Her job is to ask questions and poke holes. What if she caught onto the truth? So, they had to eliminate her early?

Then, this morning, when I heard Guru Shava say they had to move up the final ceremony. That was about me. I was getting suspicious. I found that gravesite, and they told me it was animal bones. I believed them. It made sense, but now I'd bet anything that animals weren't the only remains.

I keep my eyes fixed straight ahead, trying to render them glassy and dead.

Out of my periphery, I can still make out the red robes and cadre of weapons.

"Namaste," Guru Shava says and bangs the gong. The women unfreeze, like they're waking up. "Run, little ladies," the hunter says, holding a crossbow. "Such a nice group of girls. You'll be good targets."

The serrated knife is holstered at his waist, the one he used to slash open the mountain lion's guts. And who knows what other weapons he's got stashed inside his robes. The men crowd around him, readying their weapons. One man cocks his rifle.

"There's a reason you're all here," the hunter goes on, pacing in front of us. "All of you have defied the natural order and have been selected to be culled. It's a great honor—an ancient practice that even predates the founding of this country."

He stops in front of me, staring. I work hard to keep my face from giving away my fear, that my brain hasn't been hijacked.

"We're giving you a fighting chance," he goes on. "A head start is only fair, isn't it? Girlie girls, run like the wind."

Guru Shava bangs the gong. It's like a starter pistol goes off.

Mia and Hannah break for the woods. All the retreat women run for it, fanning through the trees but still half-zombified from the hypnosis.

I'm a half second behind them, but I sprint, trying to close the gap, branches slapping my face, filling my mouth with pine needles and icy snow.

We're being hunted.

That's the thought that shoots through my head. I chase after Hannah and Mia. They're only a few paces ahead. Our feet churn the snow, leaving deep tracks that make us easy prey. They mark our route through the trees.

I try to get my friends' attention, but they're still out of it from the hypnosis and won't respond to me. They've been programmed to do one thing—

Run.

I give up trying to get their attention and focus on keeping up with them. I can't believe they're barefoot in the snow, but they don't seem to notice.

About sixty seconds later, the gong sounds again. *Bong. Bong. Bong. Bong.*

They sound like a heartbeat. I know what it means—

They're coming for us.

CHAPTER THIRTY

BEFORE

MORGAN

I hold off until the next day after work, when I go home to stew. It's Friday night, and I'm alone. Noah canceled our dinner plans on me, after ditching happy hour last night. He promised to make it up to me. Though he left out any mention of his father, I could read between the lines of his cowardly cancellation message.

I'm sitting in front of my laptop with the blue light bathing my face and a stiff drink clutched in my hand. The search bar is open with the cursor blinking.

Don't do it. Don't use your Google superpowers!

I try to resist, but I can't get what happened with Noah's girlfriend—no, his fiancée—at Woodbury out of my head. The cascade of events that led me here tonight crashes through my head.

I flash back to last night when Noah's phone chimed with that text from Daddy. The panicky look that flashed over his face, how he rushed out of there. I'd tried to act the part of the supportive girlfriend; I had no choice. But inside, I was pouting and livid that he'd ditched me on the night that was our official debut as a couple. He had abandoned me, even though I had to keep up appearances and hide it.

I'd already envisioned the rest of the night after drinks: going back to his place, plotting the hot seduction that would lead to hotter sex. But that was quickly ruined. It only got worse when Sophia cornered me at the bar.

Her words rush through my head again now, making me doubt everything.

I hate that I'm turning into the paranoid girlfriend, but I can't help it. Hannah and Mia are out on a double date with Tyler and Grant, which is pretty adorable, but it makes me feel sick that I'm stuck home alone.

That feeling rises up again.

Abandoned.

They'd invited me, but I didn't want to be the fifth wheel. It would feel like going backward. When I met Noah, I thought that was over and that I'd finally have somebody on my arm too.

I was wrong.

And now I'm twitching. I down the rest of the astringent amber liquid in my glass and get up to pour myself another stiff drink. Whiskey. Not the expensive kind Noah drinks, but the Wild Turkey I keep secretly stashed in my bathroom in a mouthwash bottle, just in case.

The kind my daddy used to drink. The kind that turned his insides to rotgut and rendered him spittin' mean.

I seize the mouthwash bottle, feeling the flimsy plastic, and pour a second drink. I down it and move on to a third.

I check my phone again.

Crickets.

I half expected Noah would leave the drinks early and "make it up to me" tonight. No such luck. I get twitchier.

I know I'm being irrational. He's just out with coworkers. I shouldn't be worried, hovering over my phone. I try to keep my mind from racing, but it defies me and goes to dark places. Are there women on his team? I've heard about Roger and Blake, his cubicle mates. Noah insists on paying his dues like everyone else, even though he could have a fancy title and the corner office. It had impressed me, at first. But later, I'd simmered a bit.

He had no idea how lucky he was to be handed so much on a silver platter that he could afford to act humble, like it didn't matter, when I've had to claw my way out of the swamp—literally. Plus, that humility clearly doesn't extend to the perks of his penthouse, private town car with dedicated driver, and a helicopter.

The rage and anger I usually try to keep buried deep flares up again.

Abandoned.

A third drink appears in my hand. Things are a little fuzzy around the edges now. I'm on my computer already deep-diving.

First, I look up myself, hoping the past I buried remains buried.

I'm not the only Morgan Steele in existence. However, the others don't match my trajectory to New York City.

New name. New backstory. Like I was invented out of thin air.

Because I was.

The *real* Morgan Steele, whose identity I appropriated, is dead, killed in a car crash. I borrowed that too as a fake backstory for my parents. She was gone, so it's not like she could object, right?

It's surprisingly easy to get new identification and lift social security numbers from the deceased. I had to stash cash first by working at the local strip joint off the highway. Underage, but they didn't care enough to check ID. The underage factor basically got me hired.

It was disgusting, straddling leering truck drivers with beer guts and big, metal belt buckles that cut into my thighs, leaving welts sometimes, smelling their breath rancid with cigarettes, alcohol, or worse, minty chew. I still shudder at the stench whenever it wafts my way, like on the subway.

Once I got enough cash, I paid off a friend of a friend in Atlanta for the ID—social security card and driver's license—then another one for the fake high school transcript that would get me into Barnard, along with a personal essay that read like a talk show sob story.

The last obstacle:

Daddy.

There was only one solution. Dead men can't talk. I couldn't leave him alive.

I had to wait until I turned eighteen, plotting and saving up, so the state would leave me alone. Daddy was the only one who knew about the real me and could identify me later. I couldn't have my past coming back to bite me.

Plus, he deserved his fate.

I simply gave back the years of pain he inflicted on me in one deadly blow. The shovel walloped him so hard, he didn't even have time to blink. He was drunk as a skunk, making him easy prey. All I had to do was drag his body out to the bayou behind our cabin, which proved to be the hardest part.

We lived off the grid. No running water. No power. I didn't even have a birth certificate. Born on the dirt floor. I still don't know what my mother died from. I was too young, and it's not like we went to the doctor. One day she was hacking up a lung, and the next she was gone. No funeral or explanation.

His body was heavier than I expected. I had to drag him a few feet, then stop to rest. It took a few hours and nearly killed me. But finally, I floated him out deep enough that the swamp took him the rest of the way.

I scattered a bunch of the Wild Turkey bottles around the banks to make a good show for the cops. I also tossed the shovel into the ravenous waters, knowing they'd swallow it whole and not spit it back. I waited another day, then walked to town. Made myself look extra pathetic.

I walked into the sheriff's office and reported my father missing. I led them to the muddy banks of the swamp behind our cabin, where he liked to look for alligators and drink himself silly in a tattered lawn chair.

His body was never found. But I didn't count on the local paper showing up and snapping pictures. I'd figured that dirt poor swamp trash wouldn't warrant media attention.

I didn't notice them until the flash bulb went off, blinding me. And then, I couldn't run them off. I had to play the part of the grieving daughter. I even managed to produce a few tears for the reporters, but it wasn't easy.

Noah can't ever find out about any of this. Nor can my friends.

Nobody can.

I search my real name just to be safe, but thankfully, it's an internet dead end. The local paper archives aren't digitized for the search engines. I double-check *The Gator Gazette* website just in case, but I'm safe. It takes money to do that, and they're on the brink of dying out.

Most local papers are. I got lucky that way. There's nothing online about the old me.

I can't be sure there's nothing in the physical archives back home. And there's that contact who sold me the fake ID. But nobody is going down there looking, are they?

I breathe a sigh of relief. I check my phone, but there's just a text from Hannah making sure I don't want to meet them after dinner for drinks. She's taking pity on me, as always. The poor stray she adopted in college. I decline.

I'm having my own little party. I pour another drink. I've lost count, but I don't care. Still nothing from Noah.

Before I know what I'm doing, my fingers fly over the keyboard, internet stalking the Woodbury fiancée. The one Sophia casually mentioned—on purpose—to trigger me.

Emma Albright.

What gets to me the most is that she had a higher status than me. She got the ring and marriage proposal. My fingers jerk to the platinum and diamonds clustered in my collarbone.

All I got was a *promise* necklace. Whatever that is. Not that I was expecting an engagement ring already. That would have been too fast. But the comparison still stabs my heart.

I can't help it. I can't help feeling jealous and envious of this girl who came before me.

Too many results flood the screen, so I narrow it down by adding "Woodbury Prep" next to her name.

Bingo.

Pictures, social media links, and some school newspaper articles pop up. Greedily, I dig in. I find her social media profile with her smiling face and arms slung around three brats. I mean, kiddos. The story checks out. She's alive and doing very well, judging by the size of that house on Lake Michigan where they spend their summers.

I comb through her page, finding the husband.

Sure enough, she landed a handsome, age-appropriate, wholesome guy, the kind that looks like a Midwestern dude stock photo with a trim beard and ample collection of flannel shirts and work boots, but they don't disguise his blue blood roots and family money.

This doesn't match at all what Sophia said, insinuating that Noah's father had done something sinister to Emma. These posts are proof that she's fine.

So what if they taper off and her profile goes dark a few years ago. Probably being a busy mother of three saps all her time—and youth and energy. I've vowed not to let that happen to me, and luckily with Noah's vast wealth and resources, I'll have all the help I'll need to get adequate sleep and surgically repair my postpartum body.

My hand drifts to my stomach, searching for any signs of life taking root. I can't be pregnant already. It's too early to test. I haven't even missed my cycle yet. I also haven't been careful, drinking up a storm lately. But how many girls get knocked up on Vegas benders and go on to have perfectly healthy kids?

At least, that's what I tell myself. We didn't take precautions, but it's also unlikely that he already knocked me up.

A secret smile creeps over my lips. It's the perfect way to get him to commit, like he did with Emma.

And propose—sooner rather than later.

I flick through Emma's profile again, relaxing even more. Hannah and Mia were right—it's ancient news. She looks so midwestern homey now, having put on more than a few pounds. I find a few photos where the angles aren't as good and the pudge of her belly creeps out.

I zoom in on her stomach to reassure myself even more, knowing my abs are rock hard from kickboxing. She's not a threat at all. I was just being paranoid, twisted up thanks to Sophia. It's all her fault, this rabbit hole I went down.

Once I get the ring, I'll work on edging Sophia out of our friend group. She said she's moving back from London, but the engagement will give me enough social capital to flaunt it and drive her away—permanently. But then, something catches my eye as I'm zooming back out of Emma's profile. In her profile picture, there's a boy, her oldest.

I squint at him. Dark, curly hair, sharp cheekbones, but it's the blue eyes that get me.

He looks like . . .

Noah.

He stands out from his two siblings with their straw-straight honey-brown hair and brown eyes. He also doesn't look like his mother. I search for his age, landing on a birthday party picture. Then I do the math, adding up years, guessing he's about eight. Noah and Sophia broke up about eight years ago.

I remember what Sophia said about the rumor about why Emma dropped out of Woodbury suddenly and vanished.

Noah got her pregnant.

Could that be true? I stare closer, unable to convince myself otherwise. Does Noah have a bastard child with his ex-fiancée? A son he doesn't know about?

This changes everything. My conclusion that his ex isn't a threat evaporates, if he did have a child with her.

I reach for my stomach again, realizing that if I'm pregnant, this could be the second time this has happened with him. And I don't like being *second* in anything. I also don't want to feel like I'm a recycled pattern—a cheap replacement for the one true love that got away.

I clench my fists as murderous rage surges through me. I've kept this feeling suppressed for years. But now it forces its way to the surface, like a bloated, waterlogged corpse bobbing up in the bayou, like it does in my nightmares.

I snap out of it when my phone chimes.

NOAH: *Babe, I'm sorry. Drinks went late. Wanna come over? I miss you. I'll tell the doorman to let you up. Pretty please?*

At first, I'm thrilled he wants to see me tonight. But something gives me pause. *Babe*. He's never called me that before.

I study the out-of-place moniker but quickly shake it off. Clearly, he's just growing more comfortable in our relationship. That's all. I'm so relieved he misses me, I could cry. I need to get ahold of myself and do better.

Otherwise, I'll fuck it up.

This is why it's dangerous that I let myself actually fall for him, instead of sticking to my carefully laid plans. I take a few deep breaths to quell my anger.

I can't believe I let my paranoia go this far. I look at my laptop, where I'm still zoomed in on Emma's kid's face, like a psycho. Suddenly, he doesn't look as much like Noah as I first thought. Sure, he stands out from the younger siblings a little, but genetics are strange that way.

I see the half-drained mouthwash bottle sitting on the bedside table. How much did I drink tonight? And how long have I been sitting here in the dark internet stalking? Spinning out over conspiracy theories?

Regret hits me hard. I fucked up tonight. I close out the browser and clear my search history. I block his ex preemptively on my social media to try to avoid doing it again.

I grab my phone and tap out my response quickly.

MORGAN: *Anything for you. You better be ready for me. On my way!*

I dump the rest of the rot gut whiskey down the drain and toss the bottle, then brush my teeth hard to get the stink out of my mouth. I pull on the lacy lingerie he gifted me, pairing it with knee-high, black leather boots. The finishing touch, a simple black trench coat. An eloquent exterior to hide my slutty interior. He won't be able to resist me. I call an Uber and vanish into the backseat, working to clear my head as it whisks me toward his penthouse.

CHAPTER THIRTY-ONE

AFTER

MORGAN

The gong still reverberates through the forest. They come for us in their robes. They come for us with their rifles. They hunt us like animals. They hunt us like dogs. We flee through the woods. I make it as far as the ridge, then dart into the thick trees off the path.

Hannah and Mia are just ahead of me. That's when I see a flash of red robes coming from behind the tree line. But it's not one of the hunters. She's too small and timid to be one of them.

It's a silent apprentice.

She spies on us from behind a large pine tree. She could run off and alert the hunters. I don't think; I'm acting on instinct now. Something primal deep inside me that I buried in the swamp comes back to life. I remember hunting with my father, creeping through the woods, setting snares and traps for rabbits, skinning and roasting them on the fire.

If they're going to treat me like an animal, I may as well act like a feral beast.

I spring at the silent apprentice crouched behind the trees and tackle her, knocking away the walkie talkie in her hand. She flails, trying to resist. I wrap my hands around her throat and squeeze.

"*Speak!*" I order her, breathlessly. "Tell me what's going on! Why are they hunting us? How do we escape?"

She defies me, only uttering a choking sound. I shake her harder.

"I'll kill you if you don't talk!"

She only starts laughing, but no sound comes out. Her body shakes with it. She cracks her mouth open, and the horror dawns on me.

Her tongue has been cut out.

Permanent silence. That was the vow they took.

Sickness sweeps through me. I release her and back away, then turn and start running again. I have to find my friends. I have to save them. Snap them out of the hypnosis somehow.

They run in a straight line, unable to think for themselves, making them easy prey.

I catch up to them.

"Hannah, Mia, wake up!" I scream at them. But their eyes are still glassy.

They don't turn to look at me or answer me. Then I hear branches being trampled behind us.

A voice rings out.

"Come out, girlie girls," the mountain lion man clucks as he tracks us through the woods and snow. The way he says *girlie girls* makes it sound like a strange birdcall.

"All sluts must die," he clucks again. His voice sounds closer now. Just behind us, tangled in the trees. "Come out, come out wherever you are, girlie girls."

I hear the sharp *thwack* of gunfire piercing their air. Startled screams as the women go down, one by one.

I veer past a body, face up in the snow, and slow down slightly.

Dame Tremaine.

Her chest is blown open, leaking blood into the snow.

Her feet are shredded, frostbitten, torn to bloody bits. More gunfire pops in the forest like firecrackers followed by more mournful caterwauling as the women cry out as they perish.

There can't be many of us left. Hannah and Mia sprint just ahead of me. I leave Dame Tremaine's body and run ahead, catching up to them.

We run through the trees, but what we need to do is hide. But they won't wake up. I can't get their attention.

One second, Hannah is running next to me in lockstep, and the next her head explodes, her blood and brains flecking my face, warm and viscous. Mia keeps pace with me a second longer, then *thwack.*

She goes down in a heap, an arrow protruding from one eye, the other glassy and unseeing.

I keep running, tears streaming down my face. If I stop, I'm dead too.

I hear struggling behind me. I risk a quick glance over my shoulder.

The hunter catches up to Mia and slashes at her with his serrated hunting knife. A scream catches in my throat. But there's nothing I can do. I wrench my eyes forward and run for my life.

I hear her muffled grunts behind me, then something wet splashes against the snow.

Her blood . . . or worse.

A horrible image flashes through my head.

The hunter slitting her belly just like he did that mountain lion.

Bile backs up my throat and into my mouth, but I can't stop to puke my guts out. I swallow it down, tears streaming down my face from the acid burn, and focus on one thing—

Surviving.

I bolt through the forest, running in pure panic with tree branches slapping my face and blinding me, then skid to a halt on the ridge, nearly plunging over the precipice. Pebbles and snow skitter over the edge, cascading down the cliffside.

Shit, the retreat lands are wedged up against a cliffside—a natural barrier that traps us on the private property. Nowhere to run, nowhere to hide. *Think,* I order myself. I have to change course and evade them. I bolt back the other way, avoiding the path and disappearing into the thick trees, where it's harder to spot me. I try to render my body invisible in the tangles of forest.

I hear more gunshots.

More women dying.

I keep running hard, pushing every last ounce of power from my throbbing muscles, but they're fatigued and tiring fast. Thank god I grabbed my boots at the last second, or I wouldn't make it much farther.

I guess it's true what they say. In this moment, running for my life, everything flashes before my eyes. My life seems like it was lived by somebody else.

Maybe because it was.

I'm a fraud. A fake. An imposter. But one thing was real. My love for Noah. That was pure and sacred. I wasn't supposed to open my heart like that. I was supposed to keep it protected by steel bars, locked up and unreachable. I was scheming and social climbing, playing him like I thought he was playing me. But I broke my own rule, against my better judgement. I gave him my whole heart. I fell deep and hard, surrendering to him as he claimed me.

It turns out we were both playing dangerous games, gambling with our hearts. The risks were breathtaking and heart-shattering and so very tempting. I wanted to experience it all with him. I wasn't supposed to bet my heart like that, but I foolishly thought I could have it all. The social status I'd always dreamed about, and the real love stuff. I thought I could finally satisfy that gaping hole in my heart I'd been trying to fill since childhood.

I'd give anything to get that back. That's when I resolve two things. If I get out of here alive, if I somehow survive, I'm going to beg for him to take me back. The pregnancy. That's my key. I can overlook his indiscretion for the sake of our child growing inside me.

I just hope it's not too late.

That pushes me harder. I can't die out here in the snow like an animal.

I have something to live for.

Suddenly, the hunter's voice echoes through the forest.

"Girlie girl, come out, come out, wherever you are!"

I run faster, pushing my body to the limit, when my boot hooks on a hidden root. My momentum sends me sailing forward.

I plunge headfirst into the meditation garden. The stick figures dance in the branches as if taunting me.

Before I can get up, I hear the snapping of branches, then the hunter enters the clearing. He looks exhilarated, alive, radiant from the heat of slaughter.

Severed hands dangle from his belt by leather straps, each a trophy claimed.

Lacquered nails. French-manicured nails. Plain, stub-bitten nails.

"Girlie girl, you can run, but you can't hide," he says, raising his hunting knife, slick with fresh bloodletting.

I struggle to get up, but I'm stuck, my boot caught under that branch.

His shadow falls over me and his face splits into a cruel grin. His crimson robes billow out like curtains caught in the blustery wind.

"Come to papa, girlie girl," he calls. "Like the good little slut you are."

He squats down and pats his knee then cackles at my distress.

"Stop, let me go!"

I struggle harder, but the root won't release my foot.

I expect him to kill me like my friends, but instead he gives me a look.

"My nephew told me all about you. You've got quite a reputation in our family. We're honored you joined our hunt this year."

Before I can process what he's saying, another robed figure emerges into the clearing. I can't believe my eyes. I stare at him in shock. He's dressed in the robes and peaked hood, but unlike the other hunters, he's wearing a golden lion mask.

He slides the mask up, revealing his piercing blue eyes and all-too-familiar visage. The one that came up in my internet searches.

"You're Noah's father," I gasp.

Is he behind everything? Would he go so far as to murder me?

"Indeed," he says in appraisal. "You attended the first gathering. Our sacred fertility ritual. My son shouldn't have brought you. He defied my will, unfortunately . . . for you. So, now you're at our second gathering."

He fixes on me, still trapped, shaking his head in admonishment.

"Today we celebrate *death*."

Everything starts to fall into place, like a terrible puzzle. What Guru Shava kept saying about death and rebirth. I flash back to the secret masquerade party. The orgy taking place at the remote estate with everyone copulating like some ancient pagan ritual.

I struggle to process everything in those split seconds. *My nephew,* the hunter said.

That's Noah's uncle.

The resemblance to Noah and to Noah's father is uncanny. The signature sharp cheekbones and the bright, icy blue of his eyes.

He's Noah's father's business partner. The brothers rule over the Barron Ventures empire together.

This trap was planned ahead. He has been stalking me this whole time.

Noah's father holds a rifle. I risk a glance at his belt and notice one of the hands is wearing shiny pink polish with glitter. I recognize that hand. He's the one who shot Hannah. Noah's uncle clutches his hunting knife. Blood slicks the blade. *Mia's blood,* I think darkly.

They both lock their sights on me. He dad leers down at me. His lips pulling back from his canines, giving him a wolfish appearance.

"Time to die, girlie girl."

Another robed figure bursts from the trees then staggers to a halt. A golden lion mask adorns his face as well, but he slides it off immediately. His face is unmistakable. The lips I once kissed. The eyes I delighted in. The smooth cheeks I used to adore. He stands with his father and uncle, his hunting rifle aimed right at my head.

Noah.

Shock, betrayal, and heartbreak crash over me in one terrible torrent.

No, no, it can't be. I had held out some hope that he wasn't involved.

I can't believe what's happening. My words come out in a shocked whisper.

"Noah, what are you doing here?"

CHAPTER THIRTY-TWO

BEFORE

NOAH

Morgan broke up with me.

How could she? She didn't even let me explain. It was all a setup. It wasn't my fault. I was drunk, not in my right mind. Sopha took advantage of me.

I ran after Morgan, tried to explain, but the way she looked at me . . .

Cold, unyielding.

Judgement burned in her eyes. She left me there on the floor, groveling.

I can't let myself be weak like that ever again. I made a mistake thinking Morgan was different. This starts to feel like the last time. *She* paid the price, and now Morgan will have to learn. I'm not the only one with dark secrets. I remember the file my father gave me.

Fresh anger surges in my veins. Why did she have to lie to me? We could have been different. If only she'd overlooked my slip, then I could have overlooked her dark past.

I check my phone again. The text message is seared onto the screen.

TO: NOAH
FROM: MORGAN

It's over.
I hate you.
You fucked my friend.
You destroyed everything.
Never speak to me again.

Each time I read it, it hurts worse than the last time. I know she will be able to see that I opened it and didn't respond. I want her to know, to torment her, invading her dreams and turning them into nightmares. That's what she's done to me. And now, she'll get her wish. I'll bet she has no idea what true destruction looks like.

Well, she's about to find out.

I return to my bed, where Sophia awaits me, wet and ready. I channel my anger, pinning her to my bed and thrusting into her without mercy.

My stamina is stronger the second time. She moans and writhes under me. But I don't let up, even when tears burst into her eyes. I grip her throat and squeeze.

Imagining that it's Morgan's throat, Morgan's delicate veins popping out.

Right before she loses consciousness, when she's on the edge of blacking out, I release her and plunge one final time, emptying myself into her.

I roll over, wishing that would stem the flood of dark thoughts. She tries to snuggle against me, but I shove her away.

"Leave."

One word—my command. Sophia doesn't fight it. She's been trained. Groomed by her family. Her father is like mine, and so she obeys me.

She leaves me in the darkness. The city lights spread out beyond my box of glass in the sky. My sweat dries, and my body shivers, but still I lie there.

Stewing, seething . . .

Plotting.

I hate that my father won. But I can't deny that he was right any longer.

I pull out the file and flip through it again. Page after page of lies spilling out, only stoking the flames in my heart, building them into a giant inferno.

I form my hands into the shape of a gun and aim it at her face in a picture. In this one, she's leaving her apartment dressed for work, unaware of the man in the bushes spying on her for my dad.

Bang.

I imagine her brains splattering the sidewalk, turning her head inside out. That's the only thing that settles me and calms the black fire in my heart.

I've resisted my family for too long, I realize in that moment.

You can only resist for so long, but you can't run away from yourself, I think darkly. *Deep down, you're still a Barron. You always will be.*

I flip to the old newspaper article about Morgan's—or should I say Tammy Lou's—father going missing.

"You killed him, didn't you?" I whisper to the picture. Tears streak her face, but the sorrow doesn't reach her eyes. I study them closer, trying to uncover the truth hidden there.

They're cold, plotting.

The worst part? She really is like me. I know it deep down. This picture makes it clear. That's why I fell in love with her. That's why I actually felt something when I made love to her.

Not like Sophia.

That was an animal act, primal and instinctual, devoid of any connection.

A business transaction. Nothing more. Just like all the other women. Hundreds of them. I lost count long ago. When you're attractive and rich, the world really is yours for the taking. It's not hard to seduce women and conquer them.

Morgan was different.

She kept me on my toes, always guessing, until it all came crashing down tonight. With her dark past, she should have known better and at least given me a chance to explain it.

Or even, permission.

An arrangement of sorts. We could have had a lot of fun together. I saw her wild side at the masquerade party. I was grooming her to see if she could make it. And she responded beautifully.

If only my father hadn't cut his business trip short and caught us.

Too many *what ifs.*

They haunt me. Just like they did with Emma back then. But one thing I've learned—the past can't be undone. It can only be endured, or better yet shoved down and buried.

Just like Emma.

Her body twisted, bloodied. Tossed into the mass grave. The one hidden behind the retreat center. My father showed me a picture after it was done . . .

No, I don't want to remember.

I push myself out of bed and pace, my mind racing, the darkness consuming me until I can't fight it any longer. My phone dings.

A message from my father.

He's summoning me. I don't have a choice. The final day of the selection is tonight. The truth settles over me like a lead blanket. I push my revulsion down.

There's only one slot left.

He's saved it for me.

For Morgan.

My town car pulls up to a nondescript warehouse on the outskirts of the city. Only a small sign is posted on the side—*Barron Industries.*

I slide open the metal door, the wheels screeching, and storm into the building, all the way to the back, passing industrial equipment. This is part of our shipping empire. Better yet, it's a great front for other activities.

A doorman stands by the leather-bound doors, an extra layer of security.

He nods but doesn't speak. He can't speak, of course. He has no tongue.

A small sacrifice to pay to be in our service, even just in a security role. My driver is the same. Nobody ever seems to notice when they remain silent.

The help gets overlooked.

He opens the door for me with a bow. I enter the private clubhouse, scanning the familiar area. The lighting is low, simmering. The room is filled with masculine touches. Leather chairs placed elegantly around glass tables.

A bar in the back, all leather-bound, staffed by our silent bartenders. They pour drinks. Mostly scotch, neat. The expensive kind.

Men are gathered in red robes, sipping drinks and conversing. The mounted heads of big game adorn the walls—elephants, lions, even a giraffe that has to peek out from the floor.

I walk to the door at the back of the room. That's where my father is waiting for me. I don't bother getting a drink. I'm not even fully sober yet. The sexual escapades burned some of it off, but it still taints my blood.

"Father," I say, stepping into his domain. He sits there in his robes.

"You know what you have to do, son," he says, waving me inside. "It's time you took your place at my side."

I scan the bulletin board with the faces pinned to it, along with their litany of crimes. Each target has been carefully selected and curated. The next hunt is already being planned, meticulously. The retreat center is the perfect trap.

I have Morgan's picture in my hands. From the file my father gave me exposing her for who she really is.

Morgan Steele is a lie. A fake identity she used to manipulate me.

She never really loved me.

That's what I tell myself, even though my heart refuses to let her go.

There's only one way forward. One way to purge her from my life.

I have to kill her.

My father doesn't look surprised that I'm here. I'm a mess from crying and drinking, sweaty and un-showered.

I walk up to the board, grab a pin, and add her picture to the last slot on the board, next to that pop star. I grab the red pen and paint a target over her face with a bullseye on her forehead.

"The roommates?" my father says. "They'll have to be eliminated too."

I press my lips together. I can't back out now. "I know."

"You'll have to take your oath finally. Are you sure you're ready, son?"

I've been avoiding it, thinking I could stay on the periphery, not directly get involved. Leave the dirty work to them. Let them build the empire. But he'd been pressuring me.

And then, I met Morgan.

Hope had blossomed in my heart again. I thought I could escape my fate and run away like my sister. But then tonight, everything came crashing down.

My uncle joins us in the room. He hands me a red robe, crimson like blood.

I pull it on, then the hood. He hands me the lion mask. Lastly, a hunting rifle. I've been trained, of course. I grew up taking hunting trips to the Berkshires, tracking deer and eventually bigger game. We've taken trips to Africa and all over the world to prepare for the real hunt. Eventually, you tire of beasts, even the big game that are illegal to poach. You crave more and push the boundaries. The most dangerous game.

I cock the rifle.

This will be my first *real* hunt. After my initiation—after I kill her and drink fresh blood from her heart, smearing it on my face, and claiming her body in death—I become one of them.

Forever.

CHAPTER THIRTY-THREE

AFTER

MORGAN

"Noah, please, what's going on?" I stammer through my cracked, dry lips.

Shock emanates through me, pinning me as much as that stubborn root.

Noah stares down at me like a predator.

Snow starts to drift down, slowly, beautifully peppering the meditation garden in total contrast to the current situation. I wait for the punchline to the joke. For him to tell me this is all just an elaborate gesture, some kind of sick joke, so he can beg me to take him back. That all those women—my friends—aren't really dead. That it's all just a masquerade. A performance. But he doesn't break. Their weapons remain aimed at me. I'm still trapped.

Regret contorts his features. He whispers softly to me, so his father and uncle can't hear.

"Look, I didn't want to do this. It didn't have to be this way. I thought this time, it would be different. I thought you were different. I'm sorry, Morgan, but you left me no choice."

He wrenches one hand through his hair, pushing his hood back. He looks tormented, angry, almost demented.

"How could you?" he shouts now. "You don't break up with me! Ever!"

I flinch back like he slapped me.

His voice is full of rage.

"You broke my heart!" I say, a sob catching in my throat. "It's your fault—not mine. How could you cheat on me?"

Now it's his turn to flinch. But he recovers quickly, his anger flaring back up.

"It was one tiny indiscretion! Why couldn't you overlook it? Or at least, give me a chance to explain. I was drunk, it wasn't my fault! Why did you have to listen to your friends? Don't you see what they did? They poisoned you against me!"

His father places a supportive hand on his shoulder, while his uncle flanks him, closing ranks—the Barron family men.

"Son, you're doing the right thing," his father says. "You know she can't be allowed to continue, right? Remember what happened the last time?"

That seems to calm Noah down. He refocuses on me. The snow picks up, falling harder. Chunky flakes accumulate in his hair and pile up on his shoulders.

"I'm sorry, but these are our ways," he goes on, pacing around. "My family has followed the old rituals for more than a thousand years. I thought we could escape it—together. Because of you, I wanted to do things differently. But Morgan, don't you see? When you abandoned me, you left me no choice."

I'm reeling with a hundred questions. I have to keep him talking. It's my only hope of getting out of this alive.

"Then what are you?" I gesture at them. "The red robes, the guns, hunting women in the woods? Some kind of secret murderous cult of rich and powerful men?"

"We're called *Sanctum Victus*. We're older than the Illuminati."

"What does that mean?" I ask.

"It's Latin for *Sacred Hunters*," he replies.

"So, this whole retreat was an elaborate trap? To lure us here off the grid—"

I'm interrupted by another figure dressed in red robes emerging into the meditation garden.

Guru Shava gives me a piteous look, then walks up to the Barron men.

"Hello, Daddy," she says, standing on her tiptoes to kiss her father's cheek.

Noah moves to embrace her. They stand side by side, the resemblance unmistakable. My head fills with a buzzing sound. I can't believe it. Guru Shava is Zoe, Noah's long-lost sister.

How didn't I recognize her sooner?

The only picture I saw of her was the one in Noah's closet, but it was blurry, and she was a lot younger back then. Plus, the dreadlocks, turban, and scarves obscured her appearance.

I stare at them in shock.

"So, you are behind this," I say in a cold voice. "I thought you ran away, had disappeared completely." I shoot a look at Noah.

Zoe appears torn for a second, but her expression soon levels out. "When I was younger, I didn't understand my family. I made mistakes. I was tormented, borderline suicidal, addicted to drugs and men. I did run away, but then I found my spiritual calling, and it saved my life."

"Why are you doing this?" I demand. "They're killing women!"

She looks pained. "I went to my father for help. I had a true spiritual calling to help other women. It was the only way I could get funding for my retreat center. We made a deal."

"You made a deal with the devil," I say to her. "Don't you see that?"

"One week a year, I permit the gathering in exchange for helping hundreds of other women. Sacrificing a few for the good of the many. It's the only way. You have to understand . . . this is my only family."

She gestures to Noah, her father, and her uncle. "We've been living this way for thousands of years," she goes on. "It's an ancient ritual that restores the balance. Don't you see that? Some women need to be cleansed. It's our duty to cull them from society—"

"By killing them!" I cut her off. "Call it what it is—coldblooded murder."

"People die all the time," Zoe says. "That's part of my teachings. Death and rebirth. These women give their lives for a greater purpose. It's been going on for millennia. The old ways aren't live and let live—they're far darker and more powerful. Just read the history books."

"The gravesite?" I ask, remembering the bones. "It's not all animals, is it?"

"Not all of them," Zoe admits with a frown. "I have to give you credit. You proved harder to manipulate than the other targets. You kept breaking the rules, snooping around. Asking too many questions. Then you found the graves."

"That's why you moved the hunt up," I say. "It was supposed to be the last day. But you had to do it sooner."

Zoe nods. "Like I said, you were becoming problematic. I had no choice."

"Because I didn't fall for your fake act. You're nothing but a fraud!"

She shakes her head. "I do have one question though. How'd you do it? How did you escape the hypnosis? I trained for years under the top practitioners. Using the yoga and meditation to relax you into a suggestive state. It's never failed on another person before you."

I reach up and pull out my ear buds. I hold them up for her to see. "Simple. I hate yoga and meditation—I think it's boring. So I broke your rules and was listening to podcasts during your classes."

"Ah, that explains it," she says, glancing at her brother. "I see why Noah fell for you. In another life, we could have been friends, sisters even. You aren't to be underestimated. I guess we learned that the hard way. Too bad."

"Now that I know how sick your family is, I can't believe I ever wanted that." I turn to Noah accusingly. "Let me guess: All you had to do was slip the idea to Hannah?"

"That's right," Noah says. "It was pretty easy. You were taking the breakup hard, weren't you? Hannah and Mia couldn't resist something so exclusive, filled with notable guests. I had a contact reach out to her to donate money to her family's foundation and mention the retreat."

I frown. "But why do it at all? Why go to this trouble? It's a pretty elaborate setup." I'm stalling now, keeping him talking. But also, I need to know the truth. Understand why this is happening.

"Power, plain and simple," his father cuts in. His tone is cold and businesslike. "The targets are all selected for a reason. They deserve to be punished. There aren't any victims here. They get what they deserve. How else are we going to get them all together in the woods and pry their phones away? The best part? They come willingly, like lambs to the slaughter."

"But how do you make them disappear?" I say. "Surely somebody will miss them."

"There are so many ways to die," his father says with a cruel smile. "We'll plant different stories over the next few weeks. The media is more than willing to play ball. Private planes go down. Strokes that make them drown when they're swimming laps in the pool. You get the idea. They all deserve to be targeted," he reiterates. "They defy the natural order with their sins."

"Of course, you picked them for a reason. The soap opera star and her sexual harassment movement," I stay, ticking through the roster. "The DA prosecuting the politician. The pop star and her feminist songs. They're all women who bucked the patriarchy, and you don't like that."

"That's right, girlie girl," Noah's uncle says. "Their sins are like a virus, spreading corruption and vile ideas. They didn't understand their place. Just like you."

"But that's sick!" I spit back, still shocked. "How could you kill them?"

Noah is struggling now, I can see it on his face. His father gives him a look. "Son, this is the only way. *Sanctum Victus.* Our family—we are the sacred hunters. It's our duty to step in."

Fall in line—or else.

"What about Emma?" I prod him, knowing it's a sore spot. "Your ex-fiancée? You loved her, didn't you? Did she deserve to die, too? I found her social media profile, but then she stopped posting. I thought she just got busy with her kids. What really happened?"

He flinches—I hit a nerve. He grinds his teeth.

"She had to be eliminated." He glances at his father. "She hid something from me, so she had to pay the price."

I meet his gaze and hold it.

"She hid your son." The boy in Emma's profile picture. It really is Noah's son. "She dropped out of school and ran away, but she was pregnant, wasn't she?"

Pain flashes over his face.

"She had no right to do that! She got away with it for years. Raising him in secret, not knowing his real father!"

"Where is your son now?" I ask.

"He's being cared for away from her toxic influence," he replies. "Don't worry. We're not total monsters. We have rules. We don't hunt children."

I give him a cold look. My hand drifts to my stomach, but I force it away. I can't let him know that I'm pregnant—that I did the same thing. Broke up with him and took his child.

They'll kill me on the spot.

The only thing I have going for me is his slight hesitation. That little part of him that still loves me. I've got to find a way to distract him and escape.

I'm wriggling my ankle, hoping to work it free from that stubborn root, but I'm still stuck.

"Look, I know you're going to kill me," I say, raising my hands in surrender. "I'm trapped here and outnumbered. Besides, I'm lost in the woods. There's no way I can escape."

His uncle narrows his eyes. "It's good you accept your fate."

"All I ask is that you give me closure," I stammer. "Just let me talk to Noah, one last time, before . . ."

His father starts to object, but Noah interjects.

"Yes, I think we can honor her last wishes. Just a few minutes?"

A tense moment passes—a family standoff. I hold my breath. I worry they'll overrule his wishes. But then, his father gives a small nod, almost imperceptible, and they back down.

Reluctantly, his family files away, leaving us alone in the clearing. The snow falls even harder, piling up around us and creating a strange, insulated sound buffer from the world.

"Noah, I know you love me," I say in a pleading voice.

"Not anymore." His words are cold as the snow dusting his beautiful cheeks.

"What happened? Why did you cheat on me?"

His eyes flame with anger. "You lied to me! About everything! Didn't you, *Tammy Lou*?"

His words hit me hard. My secret is exposed.

How does he know? I took care to cover my tracks. Obviously, not well enough.

"Don't ever call me that!" I snap, unable to contain the fury that surges through me. "I hate that name. And you're wrong! That girl is dead. She died a long time ago."

Noah takes a step closer. He kneels down beside me in the snow.

I can smell him. The familiar aroma of his expensive aftershave mixed with sweat; it's almost irresistible.

He sneers at me. "Did I touch a nerve? You've been lying to me the whole time, haven't you? Manipulating me, making me fall in love with you."

"How did you find out the truth?" I say.

He looks pained. "My father."

"What do you mean?"

"Tell me what really happened in the bayou, Tammy Lou," he says softly, reaching over to stroke my hair.

I shudder, wanting to swat his hand away, but I force myself to allow it. His handsome face stares back at me.

"Did you do it?" he whispers.

A long moment passes in the freezing cold. Everything has changed—for both of us.

"You can't prove it," I say. I'm not giving him the satisfaction of a confession, not now.

He smiles darkly.

"So, we're two killers?" he marvels with a wicked grin. "Who happened to meet on a dating app and fell in love. I told you we were the same when I met you, didn't I?"

I knew it, too. From that very first moment, standing on the curb, daring myself to step into oncoming traffic. I knew then our dark secrets would crash together—and the odds of us having a happy ending were slim to none.

He shakes his head sadly. "It could have all been okay, if only you didn't end things like that. You're more like me than you know. We could've been happy together. It was a simple slip. Just a moment of weakness. Not breakup-worthy. Don't you see that now?"

For a second, I find myself falling for his logic, getting swept up in him again. He is a skilled manipulator, just like me.

I snap out of it.

"You're insane—and you're a killer. And you're wrong about me. We're different. My father deserved to die. He was an abusive drunk. Unlike all these innocent women!"

My father used to hit my mother, and after she died, he turned his violence onto me, night after night. I would hide in the closet and pray, and when my prayers weren't answered, I turned to something else—plotting.

Noah cackles. He stands up and starts pacing around. "Oh, do enlighten me about how killing your father was a noble act. Denying him a proper burial? What about that poor, innocent girl who died in the car crash whose identity you stole?"

"And what about Hannah and Mia?" I hiss. "Did they deserve to die too? Those were my friends. They didn't do anything wrong!"

His eyes flare with anger. He reaches into his pocket of his robes, pulling something out. It sparkles, catching the light. The clasp is snapped, and it looks a bit tarnished.

"The promise necklace!" I exclaim. "Where did you get that?"

I was right—it did survive the bonfire.

And someone took it. Only it wasn't who I thought.

"I was watching you that night, Morgan," he says in a dark voice. "I heard you when you said my name and burned that doll. I saw when you broke the necklace and threw it into the flames. Your friends encouraged you. How could you do that?" he spits at me.

"You were stalking me?" I gasp. "Hannah and Mia were only trying to support me after you cheated—"

"They were bad influences!" he cuts me off. He stomps toward me. "They convinced you to break up with me, didn't they? I know them too, remember? I know what they did!"

"How can you be so sure of that?"

"Because they did the same thing with Emma." He pauses, letting that sink in. "Oh, you didn't know about that? Your friends lied to you, didn't they? Before you came along, Hannah and Mia had another third wheel they took pity on and adopted—my ex-fiancée."

I stare at him in confusion. They never said anything about that.

"Wh-what do you mean?"

"They love charity cases. Only they didn't like it when she got a boyfriend—especially one like me—and got a life. They were always whispering in her ear, feeding her lies about me, telling her I was too old for her, that she should dump me."

"That's not what I heard," I stammer, searching my memory. "Sophia said it was your father who intervened and threatened her family if she didn't end things."

He shrugs. "That's true. But then I proposed to Emma, proving I didn't care what my father thought. When she didn't end things with me—and instead became my fiancée—Hannah and Mia were livid, jealous. They took matters into their own hands."

"That article in the school newspaper," I remember now. "She alleged a student was dating a much older alum . . ."

"That meddling bitch!" he hisses. "It created a scandal. The dean had to get involved. He had no choice at that point. My father doubled down due to the bad publicity. Her parents intervened and flew out. It was all too much for Emma."

I take that in, thinking it over. But really, I'm still working to free myself.

My foot slips out another inch.

"So, she dropped out of school and moved back home," I go on. "Hid her pregnancy. Got married quickly, had a bunch of kids. Only, you found out that one of them was really yours."

Daggers shoot from his eyes. "Yes, and if it wasn't for your little friends, none of that would have happened. Emma and I would have been happy together—"

"You're delusional!" I cut him off. "Do you really think your father would've allowed that? Emma was an outsider too. You think she would be okay with these gatherings?"

He glares at me accusingly. "I never got the chance to find out, did I? So you see, it was all their fault. After that, I cut off my Woodbury friends. I also put my father off. I worked for him, but refused an office and a title. I wouldn't join the hunts. And I swore off any relationships. I knew nobody I dated would be safe."

"Until I came along?"

He nods. "How unlucky, for both of us. I thought with you, it could be different. I told you, New York is the biggest small town. You can imagine my shock when I met your roommates and realized my past would come back to bite me."

"Why didn't you break it off then?"

He shakes his head. "Don't you understand? I was already in *love* with you! I thought it was a sign, a chance to make it work this time. But it all came crashing down."

Now, it's my turn to simmer.

"Why Sophia? Of all people?"

"My father picked her," he admits. "He summoned her back from London. Her father has a business interest. My dad wants a merger of the families, but also of our business empires."

"You sound just like your father."

He flinches. "You didn't give me any choice. He confronted me with that file his PI dug up about who you really were. You were lying to me! The whole time!"

A brief moment of shame washes over me, but I remember how far I've come. What I've had to do to finally become someone. "You should be proud of me and how I changed my life. I pulled myself out of the swamp—"

"All filthy lies!" He looks disgusted. "Your name. That sob story about your parents dying in a car crash. I fell in love with you. But it turns out, you weren't even real—you're nothing but a ghost!"

He raises his rifle. Aims it at my head. His lips set into a menacing smile.

His next words chill me.

"That's why you deserve to die. And the sad part? Nobody will even miss you. Your friends are dead. Your mother. Your father, by your own hand. And now, you can join them."

He looks so different, nothing like the man I fell in love with, that finally in this moment, I snap out of it. All the pining and wishing that I could take him back evaporates and is replaced by cold, hard rage. Now, I have one motivation—to survive this nightmare.

So, I can kill him myself.

I only have seconds.

There's a noise in the brush. Noah's head whips around to see what it is, taking his eyes off me for a split second. I don't wait. I make one final jerk, ripping my foot out from the root. I grab a large rock and scramble to my feet.

When he turns back my way, I'm ready. I make one roundhouse kick to disarm him. All those years of kickboxing classes have honed my skills, not to mention my reflexes under pressure from my childhood spent hunting and trapping in the woods, when it was kill or be killed.

The kick is perfectly planted. His rifle goes skittering away behind him. Surprise animates his features. I take the rock and chuck it at his beautiful but deadly face.

It hits him square on the forehead.

"What the fuck," he screams in anguish, wheeling around.

He's blinded, disoriented. Blood trickles into his eyes. I follow with two quick jabs to his jaw, then a kick to sweep his legs out from under him. Yet another kickboxing sequence.

He goes down hard, the wind knocked out of him.

I don't have a second to lose.

I have to get out of here. He's not alone.

I make a run for it, skidding and slip-sliding down the steep hillside. Branches and rocks slice at my hands. I burst into a clearing, but I'm lost and turned around. *Which way do I go?*

A gunshot rips through the air.

Noah is coming, I think in a panic. I know it in my bones and the hammering of my heart. I disabled him and slowed him down, but he has no doubt recovered and resumed hunting me.

Worse, he's probably enraged now.

My ankle hurts, making me limp slightly. The snow is deep and harder to wade through the farther I get from any paths. But I force myself to run harder anyway. My hands are numb, my cheeks raw and burning. The cold air puffs in my lungs, then out in a burst of steam.

I push through another thicket of trees, branches scraping my cheeks, and barrel forward. "Oh no—" I gasp when I breach the line, propelled toward the cliffside.

But it's too late. My momentum sends me flying over the edge. I dig my feet in to slow my descent, grabbing at anything I can. Luckily, I'm saved by hitting a small shelf of rocks.

I almost plunge over it—where I'd fall hundreds of feet to my death.

But I manage to hold on to a branch sticking out from the cliff. It tears from the ground, but the roots catch at the last second and hold. I press myself into the sheer rock, hoping it'll hide me enough until dark when I can crawl back up to escape.

I hear shuffling feet overhead. A voice sends ice through my veins.

"That traitorous *bitch* can't escape," Noah seethes, his voice full of venom. "She needs to learn her place! I hope she's still alive, so I can have the honor of killing her myself."

More shuffling noises on the ground above the cliff.

I'm sure they're looking for any sign of my broken body at the bottom of the ravine. But I keep myself pressed into the rocks, tasting grit and dirt on my tongue. I hold my breath tight.

"The girlie girl must have jumped. Look, her prints lead right to this cliff."

Noah's uncle.

"Son, we have to find her body," his father replies in a dark voice. "Make sure she's dead. We can't allow any mistakes this time. Not like before. This hunt isn't over yet."

More noises before his father says one last thing.

"It's only the beginning."

As they tramp away, I wait, still clinging to the cliffside. I'm trapped in the wilderness. The hunters are out there, combing the woods for any women who escaped to pick them off, leaving nobody alive. Night will fall soon and bring subzero temperatures, while overhead, heavy-looking clouds threaten to bring a blizzard to the mountain.

Luckily I don't have to wait long for the sun to dip and darkness to fall. Without a coat or proper winter clothes, I'm freezing. I haul myself up the cliff, painful foot by painful foot, finally flipping over the edge and landing in a broken heap in the snow. More of it falls down, piling up and hiding all evidence of the hunt.

I force myself to my feet and take off running into the dark woods, ignoring the pain in my ankle. My heart thumps, pumping hot blood into my veins, telling me I'm still alive.

I can't give in now. I can't let him win. There's only one thing to do: I have to kill him. Otherwise, he'll never let me go. I know that with certainty now.

And it's not just me. Our child grows inside me.

We both have to survive.

Or die trying.

ACKNOWLEDGMENTS

This book began as a story I wasn't supposed to be writing.

I'd been awarded a winter residency at the Banff Center in the Canadian Rockies, where I was supposed to be working on a novel project. It was in a yoga class, while I lay in corpse pose, that I had a vision of women being hypnotized and marched into the snow to be hunted by a group of powerful men in red robes. The core of the story came from that murderous imagining.

In many ways, the Namaste Center was modeled after that idyllic campus in the snow, at the height of winter. I cheated on my novel and wrote a short story called *Namaste Bitches.*

That story went on to publish in an anthology, but it also caught the attention of people I respected, including some in Hollywood. I always thought the story deserved to be expanded, painted onto a larger canvas. Thanks to Stephanie Beard, who has long been a champion of my work starting with my debut trilogy, *The 13th Continuum*, I got that chance.

Brainstorming together, I hatched the idea of building out the short story, but also adding a second time frame—*BEFORE*—so we could see the unfolding of Morgan and Noah's courtship. In the original short story, just like this novel, we pick up in the aftermath of the breakup. But I wanted to know how it all went down between them, all the way to the bitter end. The further expansion added his POV, so that we could see Noah's voice on the page.

That had a neat (intended) effect. I want you to be seduced and fall for Noah, just like Morgan, even though you knew you shouldn't, because you know he will cheat on her.

Forbidden love is always the most alluring.

I also wrote this book a bit differently than my other works. Anyone who has seen me on panels knows that I usually outline in a pretty rigorous fashion, especially these days while trying to juggle so many looming deadlines. But this time, I "pantsed" it more, writing the story without a solid outline. I needed to let the characters—Noah and Morgan—lead the way. They came out far darker and more complex and layered than I had planned at first. Especially Morgan, who, in this iteration, has her own twisted secrets.

This book is the first in a duet—or duology—and book two will be packed with surprises.

I hope you'll keep reading to find out.

Special thanks to Stephanie Beard, Erin McClary, and my whole team at Podium Entertainment for bringing this series to the world. Also, thanks as always to Deborah Schneider, my longtime book agent, and the whole Gelfman Schneider team, and my manager, David Server at Venture Entertainment. They say it takes a village, and that is especially true the longer you keep writing. Until next time, when Morgan and Noah's story continues.

Buckle up, slay queens—book two is coming.

Jennifer Brody
Joshua Tree, CA
March, 2025

ABOUT THE AUTHOR

Jennifer Brody, also known as Vera Strange, is the award-winning author of the Disney Chills series, the Continuum Trilogy, and Stoker finalist *Spectre Deep 6*, which prompted *Forbes* to call her "a star in the graphic novel world." She is the coauthor of *All Is Found: A Frozen Anthology* and *Star Wars: Stories of Jedi and Sith*, in which she penned the Darth Vader story. A graduate of Harvard University, Brody is also a film/TV producer and writer and a creative writing instructor. She began her career in Hollywood working for A-list directors and movie studios on many films, including the Lord of the Rings trilogy, *The Texas Chainsaw Massacre*, and *The Golden Compass*. Brody lives and writes in Joshua Tree, California.

Podium

FOR A GOOD TIME

follow us on our socials

 podiumentertainment.com

 @podiumentertainment

 /podiumentertainment

 @podium_ent

 @podiumentertainment